Return Policy

HAILEY DICKERT

Copyright © 2023 by Hailey Rose Dickert

First released June 2023.

ISBN: 978-1960497024

Developmental Editing: Alli Morgan and Anonymous

Copy Editing: Anonymous

Proofreading: Alli Morgan

Discreet Cover: Books N Moods

Non-Discreet Cover: Maldo Designs

Published by Hailey Dickert

www.haileydickert.com

❋ Created with Vellum

CRYSTAL BAY
UNIVERSITY

BOOK ONE

Author's Note

Return Policy is a spinoff of Dickert's first novel, *The Sister Between Us.* Although it can be read as a standalone, there will be a greater emotional impact if *The Sister Between Us* is read first, as the main plot twist is frequently discussed in this novel.

There are multiple sexually explicit scenes in this novel, for those of you who'd like to find (or avoid) the smut quickly, please see the 'Dicktionary' on page 430.

This book contains serious topics that could be difficult for some readers. For a complete list, please see the 'Content Warnings' on page 431.

Should you be having a mental health crisis, please reach out to 9-8-8, The National Suicide and Crisis Lifeline. Your mental health is important. Your life is important.

Should you need to speak to someone regarding sexual assault, please reach out to 800-656-HOPE (4673), The National Sexual Assault Hotline. Your voice matters.

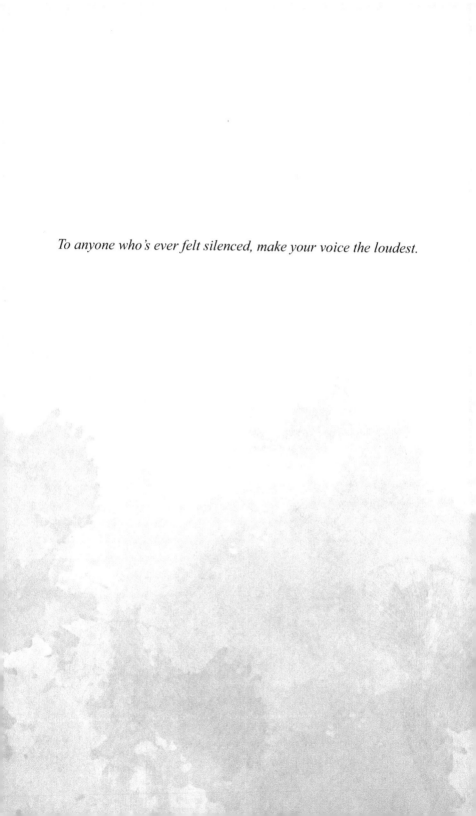

To anyone who's ever felt silenced, make your voice the loudest.

"Lastly, she pictured to herself how this same little sister of hers would, in the after-time, be herself a grown woman;

and how she would keep, through all her riper years, the simple and loving heart of her childhood."

— Lewis Carroll, *Alice's Adventures in Wonderland*

Playlist

Sunflower, Vol. 6 — Harry Styles
Somebody's Problem – Morgan Wallen
Mastermind — Taylor Swift
Fictional — Khloe Rose
Girl in a Coffee Shop — Zach Seabaugh
Feels So Easy — Her
With or Without You – Chris James
Good as Hell – Lizzo
Pony — Ginuwine
boyfriend — Ariana Grande, Social House
Super Freaky Girl — Nicki Minaj
Sunflower — Post Malone, Swae Lee
I Like You (A Happier Song) — Post Malone, Doja Cat
Despacito (Remix) — Luis Fonsi, Daddy Yankee, Justin Bieber
Kiwi — Harry Styles
Mona Lisa, Mona Lisa — FINNEAS
Can I Kiss You? — Dahl
1000 reasons – Caleb Hearn
a little more time — ROLE MODEL
Gettin' You Home — Chris Young
Want You In It — James Barker Band
That's Why — Troy Cartwright
The Way I Love You — yaeow, Neptune112
She Is Love — Parachute

If Heaven Had a Landline — Brian Congdon
I Drive Your Truck — Lee Brice
The Good Ones — Gabby Barrett
Hate to be lame - Lizzy McAlpine, FINNEAS
Wonderland — Taylor Swift
AVO TOAST – Clinton Kane
Work of Art – Benson Boone
wonder if she loves me — JVKE
I Saw Love – Forest Blakk
Fall Into Me – Forest Blakk
Pointless - Lewis Capaldi
Pray For You — Grace Kinstler
xanny — Billie Eilish
Lighthouse (Acoustic Version) — Hearts & Colors
Paper Rings — Taylor Swift

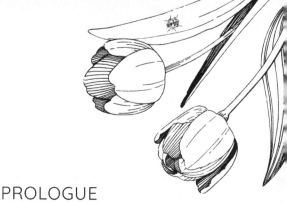

PROLOGUE
SOPHIA

Nine Years Old

"I'm sorry, Sophie Bear. I know you were looking forward to sitting outside," Dad says as I glare at the rain pouring down in sheets.

"You can't control the weather, Papa Bear." I stab the plastic spoon into my ice cream. "It's fine."

It is not fine.

"Well, *anyways*," Sage, my best friend, mumbles with a mouth full of rocky road, "tell your dad about that epic drawing you did of the soccer player for Friday's fall showcase!"

"Oh, is that this week?" Dad asks.

Mom would have remembered.

"Yup," I tell my bowl, mind wandering to *my* favorite picture of a little clay teapot. A few months ago, Chloe, my sister, and her best friend, Leah, were making one in our garage while laughing and singing. Hopefully one day I'll be able to draw their smiling faces too, but for now, that's what I can do. The sketch reminds me of home—*the feeling, not the place.*

My twin siblings are nine years older than me, but they never fail to make me feel included and loved. Especially my older brother, Jake. He thinks we don't notice all the small stuff he does since Mom's been gone, but I do. I notice every single thing down to the burnt pancakes. *They taste better that way anyway.*

"I can't wait." Dad beams, eating a big bite of his chocolate sundae. A loud ring blares throughout the small shop. He sticks his spoon in the bowl before pulling his phone from his pocket and sliding out of the booth.

"How's the mint chocolate chip, Joey?" Sage asks, using the nickname she gave me because of my obsession with koalas. *You make one horrible Australian zookeeper impersonation and never live it down.*

"Everything I dreamed and more." I grin, fighting off her spoon as she tries to steal some.

Dad clears his throat, interrupting our battle for the bite. "We gotta go, girls." He chucks his half-eaten sundae in the trash. "Come on."

"Why?" I ask, eyes glued to the sugary goodness he just wasted. "Can we bring our ice cream?"

"I don't care, let's go." His strange tone has Sage and I sliding quickly out of the booth.

The drive is so quiet I'm afraid to ask where we're going. My ice cream is turning into soup, and I try to focus on the rain pitter-pattering against the truck to calm my nerves. A flash of lightning followed by a rumbling thunder rattles me to my bones, stealing my sense of security. *I hate thunderstorms.* I'm surprised Dad even drove in this weather. He always gets on Jake and Chloe about being careful when it's raining outside.

We turn into a large parking lot, passing a bright sign that reads Longwood Hospital.

"Dad?" I ask, my voice trembling as he parks the truck. "Why are we here? What's going on?"

"Come on, girls," he says, ignoring my questions and hopping out. *Why is he ignoring me?* We follow him through the torrential downpour to the emergency room, ice cream bowls in hand. Dad instructs us to sit in the farthest corner of the room with the promise he'll be right back.

The air conditioning hits my damp skin, sending shivers through my body. My shaking fingers stick to the soggy paper bowl, and I consider looking for a trash can and a bathroom to clean up. *But what if I miss something? Dad said to stay right here.* My eyes fall to the little plastic spoon clinking to the floor.

"I'll throw it away," Sage offers quietly, taking the bowl.

"Thanks."

A wave of nausea hits me at the scent of the room. *It's too clean.* I stare at a hole in the mint-green wall. It's about the size of a fist.

What made someone so mad?

My dad's pleading voice snaps my attention to him. "Please," he begs the doctor. "Please tell me they're going to be okay."

My shoulders shake, and a loud bang has me jump in my seat. Jake runs through the emergency room doors like a soaking wet bat out of hell. His panicked face makes my heart beat faster than it ever has before.

Jake is okay.

Knowing my brother is alive and well calms my anxiety momentarily until I hear the words "Chloe," "Leah," and "accident." Then my stomach drops back to my feet.

Sage must have returned at some point because her arms are tight around me as tears blur my vision. "They're going to be fine, Joey," she whispers.

I struggle to calm my rapid breathing as Jake talks with the doctors. His face is scrunched tight like he's in pain.

What's going on?

Two of my favorite people in the world are just behind those doors, and no one will tell me anything. Dad always thinks I'm too young to join the "grown-up conversations," but I'm almost *ten.* I deserve to know what's going on with my family.

I'm not as oblivious as everyone thinks I am.

I can handle the truth.

The door Jake just slammed through opens again, and Autumn, Sage's mom, comes into the waiting room. My mom should be the one coming through those doors, but here I am, in a hospital on the scariest day of my life, with her nowhere to be seen. *What could be more important than this?*

I roll my eyes, turning my attention to my stuck together fingers, and slowly pull them apart.

Autumn bends down in front of us with open arms. "Hey, girls." I tilt my head. *What in the world is going on?*

She pulls us both in for a tight hug, and I glance up to the sight of Jake collapsing against Dad's chest as his sobs echo off every wall in the room.

His pained cry pierces me like the devil's claws, digging in, dragging me down to a nightmare I never expected to be mine.

1

SOPHIA

Eighteen Years Old

"You know what you're missing?" Sage asks, halting in place on the pathway toward the springs. She grabs my shoulder, spinning me around to unzip my backpack, and Charlie shrugs with an amused grin.

Question: how much bullshit are you willing to endure just to make your friends happy?

Answer: the limit does not exist.

Sage rezips my bag and turns me back around, bringing two empty hands over my head.

"What in the ever-loving hell are you doing?" I ask.

"Putting on your party girl hat." She smiles sweetly. "You've clearly forgotten it was in there."

My shoulders sag as I blow out a heavy breath. "I'm sorry." To avoid ruining the night for everyone, I play along, bringing my hands above my head and repositioning the invisible hat. "My party girl hat is now properly in place." *So is the burning pit in my stomach.*

"That's our girl," Sage says, throwing an arm over my shoulder.

"I didn't siphon the good shit from my parents' liquor cabinet all year, risking eternal grounding, to *not* get shit-faced with my girls on the night of our high school graduation."

"Come on," Charlie chimes in, adding her arm over Sage's. My shoulders are heavy, but I savor the familiar weight of my two best friends holding me close. "Only a few more months till we're at Crystal Bay University, living it up as college freshmen." She cocks a dark brow. "That's something to celebrate."

Change rarely comes easily to me, but moving to CBU is one transition I'm definitely ready for. Maybe I'll finally find some distraction from the swarming thoughts plaguing me at every turn of these familiar back roads.

We arrive at the crowded springs full of fellow high school graduates. The sun dances behind the trees, and although it's cooler than the sweltering graduation earlier, it's a typical late summer afternoon in Florida.

The sunshine state—aka the only place on Earth that's hotter and wetter than the devil's asshole.

We find our way to the drinks table, and Sage adds half a bottle of vodka. Charlie brought four wine coolers, and I set my pathetic contribution of orange juice for mixers on the table. Tucked away in my backpack is a flask of top shelf whiskey I "borrowed" from Dad... but I'm saving that for myself.

It doesn't seem to matter though. There's enough alcohol here to last a month. I'm not sure how a bunch of minors got full bottles of liquor, but *cheers, bitch*.

I spot a handle of Jack Daniels on the table and pour myself a whiskey and ginger ale as Sage and Charlie fill their tumblers with vodka and orange juice.

The girls and I amble along the water's edge, where people are laughing and splashing in the golden sunlight. We set down our things near where the entirety of last year's Longwood High football team is playing beer pong.

My eyes drift around the springs, snagging on *him*. The face of my nightmares—the bane of my existence—my ex-boyfriend Seth Miller. And what is the piece of shit doing? Laughing like he's the happiest person in the world. Like he's just a guy partying with his friends on graduation night. Like the moment permanently imprinted in my mind every time I close my eyes never happened.

How can he act like nothing happened?

Seth drags a hand through his blonde hair, turning around. His eyes connect with mine, and repressed memories surge to the surface. His lips curl upward, and yep, I'm definitely going to be sick.

"Hey," Sage says, snapping my attention back to her sympathetic eyes. "Stop worrying about him. He's not worth your time." Sage doesn't know the true reason for our breakup, but she's my best friend, and if I hate someone, so does she. No questions asked.

"You're right." I lock away my hatred for him so she won't get suspicious of just how deep it runs.

"Of course I am," Sage says.

Charlie's boyfriend, Jonathan, waves to her, blowing a kiss, and she blushes, sipping her drink. They've been dating since freshman year and will no doubt get married and have babies before the rest of us have even finished college. They were the "it" couple at our school—head cheerleader and varsity football quarterback. Totally cliche and totally adorable.

I wrinkle my nose at her. "You guys are so cute."

She grins sheepishly. "Thanks."

"How do you feel about next year?" I ask her timidly, knowing it's a touchy subject.

Charlie lets out a heavy exhale. "I mean, we're going to schools on opposite sides of the state." She looks down at the liquid in her cup before taking a big gulp, doing a little shimmy as it goes down. "So not looking forward to the distance."

"Jonathan will have Seth," Sage says, and I tense at his name. "They can stroke each other's dicks."

I chuckle and shake my head, trying to dispel the visual image. "And you'll have us to keep you plenty busy."

"That *is* true," Charlie says, tipping her glass towards us.

Jonathan walks up, sliding an arm around Charlie's waist and pulling her to him. "Hey, beautiful."

"Hey, babe." Charlie beams, nuzzling into his chest.

"Ladies." He gestures to us with his cup in a cheers motion.

"Jonathan," we coo back.

"Wanna go for a walk?" Jonathan asks Charlie, and she looks to us as if for permission.

"Go." I wave her off.

"Yeah," Sage says, slapping Charlie on the ass. "Get outta here."

"Okay, okay." Charlie laughs, protecting her butt with one hand as she turns away and joins Jonathan.

"Hey, beautiful girls," our friend Benji says, throwing an arm around Sage's shoulders.

"Benji." She smirks up at him. He's a horrible flirt and their relationship is purely platonic, but they both know how to have a good time.

"I've got some party favors if you're interested?" He presents a Ziploc with a few joints.

She turns her eyes back to mine, the wheels in her brain spinning on overdrive.

"Sage." I let out a soft chuckle. "I'm not a wounded dog. I can keep myself busy. Go have fun."

"You wanna come?" Benji asks, dangling the little baggie between his fingers. "I've got plenty."

"I'm good. Think I'll go play a round of pong." I gesture over my shoulder toward the beer pong tournament I have no intention of joining. "You guys have fun."

"Okay, we'll come find you in a bit." Sage squeezes my shoulder, and then they're gone.

The golden hour from the sun is still emitting plenty of light, so I down the rest of my drink, toss the cup in a trash can, and head towards the woods. I glance around, making sure Seth is distracted and doesn't see me leave. I have no interest in talking to him tonight. Especially alone.

He's enthralled in a conversation with one of the other guys on the football team. I make my escape, venturing down the path towards a quiet rock, away from the party. Leah, my bonus sister, has brought me here a few times. It's her favorite place to get away and think. I settle on the cool rock, placing my backpack next to me, and unzip it to pull out my notebook and a pencil. The interior pages are blank, without lines, which is perfect for my particular usage.

Spinning the pencil between my fingers, I fight the urge to draw what always slips to the forefront of my mind. The face I've drawn for years but somehow never tire of looking at. I draw her as a child, a teenager, what she'd have looked like if she grew up and had kids. I've drawn it all and somehow, I never run out of ideas. The current one I'm working on is what she would've looked like at high school graduation. It's a closeup of her face wearing a graduation cap flung to the side.

I sigh at my unhealthy obsession and unscrew the flask, then take a swig of the deliciously potent whiskey. The strong liquid glides down my throat, leaving a familiar burn in its wake.

As I put the finishing touches on my drawing, a rustling in the bushes steals my attention, and my heart stops beating.

Please don't be Seth.

"Who's there?" I shout in attempted bravery. My hands tremble as leaves crunch beneath someone's heavy feet, the sound growing closer by the second. Breathing is a distant memory, and I might pass out if the person doesn't reveal themself soon.

"I come in peace," a male voice says. The unfamiliar husky tone laced with humor relieves my anxieties as a tall figure steps out of the bush, holding his hands up in surrender.

Holy shit. I've died and gone to hot guy heaven.

The spitting image of all my favorite fictional men come to life is standing before me with delicious chocolate brown hair and a panty-soaking, crooked grin. He rubs a hand along his sharp jawline, and adorable dimples pop through as he smirks at me. A tattoo peeks out from his v-neck T-shirt, with more running along his arms. *Am I dreaming?* I dig my fingernails into my palm. *Nope, that definitely hurt.*

"You going to say anything, or are you just gonna keep eye fucking me?" he asks as his gaze rakes over my body, eliciting a shiver.

"I was not *eye fucking* you!" *Liar, liar, panties on fire.* "You caught me by surprise. I thought I was out here alone."

"And I thought my devilish good looks shocked your pretty mouth speechless."

My lips part, and then I smash them shut. "Wow, aren't you *hilarious?*"

"I try." He winks, and I clench my thighs together as his eyes drop to the sketchbook on my lap. *Is it getting hotter out here or is it just me?* "What are you doing sitting here alone instead of at that party?"

"Oh, uh…" I'm definitely not about to tell this stranger the truth. *I'm avoiding my overbearing ex like a coward.* "My friends were momentarily busy, so I thought I'd slip away for a bit of doodling."

"Doodling?"

"Mm-hmm."

"Can I see said doodles?" he asks, taking a few steps closer and extending his hand, presumably for my sketchbook. *Yeah, fat chance.*

"Ha." I fake laugh. "Absolutely not." I snap the sketchbook closed and shove it into my backpack, zipping it shut. If he saw I drew the same face repeatedly, he'd think I was a stalker. Sure, I draw other things too. But most of the time, she's my favorite subject.

When I turn back to face him, his sideways grin has turned into a full toothed smile.

"What?" I ask, unable to keep my lips from curling up.

"Nothin'." He shoves his hands in his pockets. "Just you dramatically hiding the notebook in your bag makes me all the more curious."

"I am *not* dramatic," I scoff, folding my arms across my chest. He raises his dark brows, eyes flicking down at my pushed-up chest before returning to mine.

Oops, I definitely forgot I was wearing a low-cut dress.

"Whatever you say, Sunflower."

I cock my brow. "Sunflower?"

"Yeah, *Sunflower.*" He waves a hand at my torso, and my eyes drop to the little pastel sunflowers dancing across my dress.

"Very creative," I tease, attempting to stop the corners of my lips from turning upwards but failing with flying Technicolor.

"I tend to be quite creative, yes."

"What are *you* doing out here? I can't imagine you're from Longwood. I think I'd remember someone who looks like you." The words escape before I can think better of them. If I could slap my forehead without looking like a damn dork, I would.

He raises a curious eyebrow. "Like *me*?"

"Yeah, someone all tall, dark, and brooding." I bite my lower lip to camouflage a smirk.

"What makes you think I'm brooding?"

"You have this... intense thing about you. Like you're all intelligent and mysterious." The smile breaks through at the thought of one of my favorite brooding men. "It's very Stefan Salvatore."

"Stefan Salva-*who*?" He furrows his brows.

"Never mind." I wave him off. "And besides, you're *also* here talking to me instead of enjoying the festivities, so I don't think *you're* the party boy type."

"You seem to know a lot about me," he quips, obviously amused.

I shrug. "I'm good at figuring people out."

"Oh, is that so? And what else have you figured out about me?" His arm veins bulge as he folds them across his chest.

Fuck, he's sexy.

"Hmm." I tap my finger to my lips. "I think you're a little cocky.

You deflect using humor. You're nosy." I raise my brows at him. "I think you're completely aware of how good-looking you are."

"You think I'm good-looking?" He grins, waggling his eyebrows.

"Let me finish." I hold up a hand. "You're aware of it, but you don't seem to let it go to your head. Otherwise, you'd probably be shirtless by the water, trying to pick up a cheerleader rather than talking to the girl who's avoiding that party like the plague."

"Wow." He nods while rubbing a hand over his mouth. "You figured all that stuff out after a two-minute conversation? Either you're incredibly perceptive or I'm embarrassingly predictable."

"Let's call it a tie." I smirk, enjoying his playfulness. "What I can't figure out... is what you're doing at this party when you so clearly aren't from around here. No one local would wear pure white Nikes to the dirty ass springs." I gesture to his mud-splattered tennis shoes, and he looks down before returning his amused gaze to mine.

"Oh well." He shrugs. "What are shoes for if not to be worn?"

"More witty banter and questions left unanswered." I roll my eyes teasingly.

"Well, I am *not* from around here. As you suspected, Sherlock." He shifts on his heels. "I'm here visiting family and my... uh, brother told me there would probably be a party here tonight if I wanted to get out of the house. So..."

"Oh, is your brother here tonight too?"

"Nah," he responds, shaking his head. "He's older."

"Is it your first time in Longwood?"

"Yeah, I came to meet my... dad," he says with a pained expression. I want to reach out and smooth the wrinkles caused by the frown.

"To *meet* your dad?" I hardly know this guy, but there's this intense desire to learn everything about him.

"My *biological* dad. He wasn't around growing up." A heavy breath escapes him. "A lot of... shit happened earlier this year. So I took the week off to come meet him."

"Weren't you ever curious who he was?"

He looks down at his hands, wringing them together. "I mean... not really. But I made a promise to give Mark a chance so... here I am."

My brows raise upward. "Wow, that must be a lot for you to deal with."

"Yeah," he says sheepishly. "It has been... Sorry, my head's just a jumbled mess, so I guess you're the victim of my inevitable brain dump."

"No apologies needed." My head shakes as I smile reassuringly. "I'm a good listener."

"Yeah?"

"Yep. Certified problem solver," I say, waving a hand at my body.

"Well, how about you tell me why you're out here doodling instead of hanging out with your friends or... *boyfriend?*" He says the last part like a question, and the knife twists painfully in my chest.

"No boyfriend here, single as a Pringle," I mumble. Chloe and Leah said that phrase so many times, but it sounds lame as fuck coming out of my mouth. "And, uh, I'm avoiding someone," I admit.

"Interesting." He narrows his eyes and takes a few long strides toward me. "May I?" he asks, gesturing toward the rock, and I scoot over, allowing him to sit next to me. His shoulder is centimeters away from mine, radiating enough heat to melt titanium. I breathe in through my nose, and the intoxicating scent of his cologne floods my senses, wreaking havoc on my insides.

"Are you wearing Versace?" I ask to fill the silence.

"Were you watching through my bathroom window as I got ready tonight?"

"No... I just happen to like that scent." I don't admit to smelling the men's cologne samples at the mall and assigning them to my favorite book boyfriends. In case anyone is wondering, Nathan Hawkins smells like Giorgio Armani Acqua di Giò.

"Good to know…" He smirks, looking out at the stream. "You come here often?"

A laugh bubbles out of me. "*That's* the best line you could come up with?"

"I'm not hittin' on you," he says cooly, and I fight the disappointment begging to appear on my face. *Why the hell would I be disappointed?* "I meant do you come to this rock a lot, or did you just discover this little hideaway?"

"I come here when I need to clear my head… or escape reality for a bit."

"And is it clear now?"

"Well, this annoying stranger kind of interrupted my self-reflection, so I'll have to get back to you on that." A snarky smile spreads across my face.

"Ha ha." He wrinkles his nose at me, and I struggle not to blush at how cute he looks. "Well, I *have* been told I'm an excellent listener as well, so… you know… if you wanna talk about it?"

He shifts position, and his shoulder bumps mine. Given how he looks, I assumed if he touched me, I'd spontaneously combust or be struck by a bolt of lightning, but the only thing happening is my heart rate accelerating faster than a hummingbird's wings.

"Trust me, you don't want to go down that rabbit hole," I reply. "It's taken my therapist years to unpack the baggage that is Sophia's life."

"How about the condensed version?" he asks, without even a hint of judgment in his voice.

"I'm going to scare you right off this rock," I say, connecting my gaze with his.

"Is that something you'd care about?"

"What?"

"If I left," he asks with a straight face, although there's a slight upward curve of his plump lips.

"Maybe," I say honestly. Although I can't pinpoint why. I don't get attached to people anymore. In fact, I usually push people away so hard they go running for the hills. I especially don't confide in total strangers. My therapist says it's because I have abandonment issues. But what does she know?

"Well, I promise to not go running for the hills," he says as if reading my damn mind. *Who the hell is this guy?* "If you promise you're not a serial killer."

"I am *not* a serial killer."

"I figured." His eyes drop to my feet, then venture slowly back to my face, and damn if it doesn't set me on fire. "What are the chances of there being two of us out here?"

The fire's doused momentarily before I realize he's kidding, of course, and I hit him playfully on the arm. "Hey, don't ruin this spot for me with your Ted Bundy talk."

"Sorry, sorry." He laughs, throwing his hands up, expression softening. "So what's clouding that pretty little head of yours, Sunflower?"

I pick at my nails, contemplating how much I want to share. I guess it couldn't hurt to tell some partial truths to someone I'll never see again. "My older sister, Chloe, died when I was nine." He sucks in a breath, and I shake my head and sigh. Trees rustling in the wind and muffled laughter from partygoers in the distance fill the momentary pause in conversation. "She was in a car accident with her best friend Leah... but Leah survived. They were only eighteen."

"Wow." His eyes are soft as he reaches up, wiping away a tear from my cheek. "I'm so sorry that happened."

"Thanks." His warm, rough palm cradles my face, and I want to lean into it. I force myself to stay stone still instead. "Today was... hard. I kept thinking how Chloe never got to graduate—or go to college—or have any of the firsts I'm about to..." I continue picking off what's left of my nail polish and exhale heavily.

"Keep going," he says gently, rubbing his thumb across my cheek before pulling away.

"I didn't really understand before..."

"What do you mean?"

"I didn't realize the things she missed out on because of her death. I only thought about the things she'd already done. She was in her senior year of high school when she passed and now that I've graduated... I'm about to experience all the things she never had the chance to. I think I feel..." My mind searches for the right word. "Guilty?"

"Sunflower," he says low and gravelly as my stomach swirls at the nickname. "Don't feel guilty for being alive. I didn't know your sister, but I'm sure she'd want you to experience every single thing she couldn't and more."

His piercing blue eyes slice right through me, causing the air in my lungs to dissipate before I regain my composure. "It's been over eight years." I gnaw on my lower lip without breaking eye contact. "I should be over it... I guess I just get emotional sometimes. Maybe it's the whiskey." I huff out a breath, looking away. "This shit must be truth serum. I don't even know you, and I'm verbal diarrhea'ing my entire depressing life story."

After unscrewing the metal top, I take another long swig of the strong liquid, allowing it to burn me from the inside out. I hold out the flask, and he grabs it, taking a swig too.

"Don't ever feel like you need to get over losing someone you love," he says, looking out at the stream before brushing something off his face. "No matter how they left or how long it's been, it's okay it still hurts. Eventually, the pain will go away." I take another pull from the flask, allowing the buzz to sink in as the truth of his words squeezes at my heart. "Damn, a girl that downs whiskey without flinching? That's hard to find."

"Been sneaking sips of Dad's hundred proof since I was fifteen." I down another swig while winking at him, and his dimples deepen.

"Naughty girl." He releases a breathy laugh. "Congratulations, by the way."

"For?"

"Graduating," he says pointedly.

"Oh... Thanks."

"How was the ceremony?"

"Long… hot as fuck… boring." I roll my eyes. "The usual."

"Yeah, sounds about right."

Another sip of the whiskey causes me to lose the last of my filter. "I didn't invite my mom."

He tilts his head. "I feel like there's more to unpack there."

"A few months before Chloe died, my mom abandoned my family, ended up in jail, and never came back home." *If she hadn't left us, maybe Chloe would still be alive.* I shake my head, chest tightening at the unfair thought. "She's been trying extra hard to have a relationship with me, but I just don't know if I can ever forgive her." I take a deep breath. "I didn't invite her because she didn't deserve to be there, sitting in the crowd with all the proud parents, acting like she had anything to do with my accomplishments. Like she deserves to be proud of me. Only my dad can feel that way… He's the one who's always there." I look down at my hands, feeling stupid for blurting so much unrequested information out, but it's been bubbling under the surface since breakfast. "Sorry, that was a lot of background info you didn't ask for."

He reaches out, placing his finger gently under my chin, nudging me to meet his glacier eyes. My breath catches as they bore into mine, the space around us entirely devoid of oxygen. I've landed on another planet where our atmosphere no longer exists. "Stop apologizing for talking about the things that eat at you. It's okay to open up." He drops his hand, and I immediately miss the contact. "It's okay to be vulnerable."

I look down at my feet. "I'm pretty good at being open…" My hesitant eyes wander back to his. "But I'm not very good at being vulnerable."

2

ELIJAH

I have no clue how my day went from "bonding" with my sperm donor to having a therapy session with the most mesmerizing girl I've ever met, but I'm definitely not complaining.

From what she's told me, her life's just as fucked up as mine. Maybe more so. And what do they say? Broken knows broken?

She looked adorable, claiming she already knew everything about me, so I just shut my mouth, smiled, and played along. *Although she wasn't wrong about all of it.*

The sun has set, and it's getting darker by the minute. We probably shouldn't stay out here much longer, but I'm afraid I've imagined this entire encounter and as soon as we leave, I'll never see her again. I'm not sure why that bothers me, but it does.

I'm not the guy who commits.

I'm a fun fuck and a *won't* call you tomorrow.

I'm honest about it, and the girls on campus are perfectly content with any sliver of attention the second-string quarterback throws their way.

Screw you, Noah, for being so damn good my ass is basically glued to the bench.

A tiny ladybug flies in front of me, landing on my knee closest to

Sophia. She immediately reaches out her hand, just barely resting it on my leg, and a breath catches in my throat. The little bug crawls onto her finger, and she brings it in front of her face, smiling. "Did you know ladybugs are considered good luck?"

"Oh, really?"

"Yep." She laughs, the sweet sound surrounding me completely. "Some people even believe if a ladybug lands on you, the number of spots predict how many years of good luck you'll have."

"And how many spots does my ladybug have?"

She examines it, brows pulling together. "I don't know. There's kind of too many to count."

"Guess I'm just a lucky guy." I let out a deep, low laugh, and she grins at me, rolling her eyes.

"Maybe it's just too dark." She frowns as the ladybug flies off her finger.

"Yeah, that's it." I nudge her with my shoulder, and she lets her head fall against me. I take a deep breath, enjoying the fresh air mixed with her floral scent.

"Chloe called me Ladybug," she says quietly. My hands ache to reach out and comfort her, but I keep them firmly in my lap.

"That's sweet."

"Yeah." She exhales heavily, checking the time on her phone. "My friends are probably wondering where I am."

"Oh… yeah," I reply, when I really want to say, *Who cares?*

Her golden hair is splayed across my shoulder, and everything about her makes me want to learn more. I want to see her tomorrow, and I'm pretty sure if I did, I'd want to see her the day after that.

Who the fuck am I?

"Are you coming to the party?" she asks, removing her head and staring up at me with soft green eyes that remind me of early spring.

"I don't think I'm in the party mood after all…"

I choose not to mention I didn't realize it was a bunch of barely graduated high schoolers, which is just not my speed. In fact, I was halfway back to the car when I saw a bombshell blonde walking alone through the woods. *What possessed me to follow her?* I'm not entirely sure, but the Southern gentleman in me claims he wanted to make sure the girl was safe getting wherever she was going. The honest part of me was hoping she'd notice me and I could strike up a conversation. Guess I got my wish.

"Oh… okay." She frowns.

"But I'll walk you," I offer, pleased with her disappointment. "You know… so a Ted Bundy copycat doesn't get you." I wink, and her soft, bubbling laugh rattles all the way to my bones.

"I'd like that." She gathers her things and throws the backpack over her shoulder.

We arrive at the end of the pathway to the springs, and Sophia stops, turning to face me.

"Thanks… for walking me." She fights a smile, placing her warm palm on my arm and giving it a squeeze. "Even if it was only to protect me from a potential serial killer."

A wide grin spreads across my face. "Anytime, Sunflower."

Standing on her tiptoes, she kisses my cheek, letting out a warm breath before pulling away. I fight every urge to close the inches between us and taste her whiskey lips.

"What the fuck, Joey?" a girl with light purple hair shouts, running up to us. *Joey?* "We've been looking for you everywhere." She eyes me up and down like I'm a beefy bean burrito, then returns her attention to Sophia. "Let's go for a dip."

"What?" Sophia shakes her head. "We don't even have suits with us."

"Who cares," the girl says. "Come on!"

She doesn't even wait for Sophia to respond before tugging her toward the water. Sophia glances back over her shoulder with a sad smile, and I ignore the pang in my chest as she's literally dragged away from me.

My cheek burns from the place her lips touched while I walk to the truck.

I think about her the entire drive to Mark's house.

I try *and fail* not to think about her as I relieve some stress in the shower before bed.

What the fuck is happening to me?

"You excited to get back to your summer training camp?" Mark asks as I come in the kitchen.

"Yeah, definitely." I'm returning to Camp Dickson tomorrow to meet the team, and I can't wait to get back to my normal routine.

"When does season start?" He pours a bowl of Frosted Flakes, tops it with milk, and slides it in front of me at the kitchen table.

"Thanks." I take a big bite of the sweet cereal. "It starts in August."

"I'd love to come see you play sometime." He pauses and clears his throat. "If that'd be okay with you."

My eyes lift to meet his. "Really?"

"Yeah, of course." A soft smile plays on his lips. "I'm sure your brother would love to go too."

"There's a parents' weekend in September. I can send you tickets if y'all wanna come?" I offer as my knee bounces nervously.

Mark's smile widens, and the corners of his ice-blue eyes crinkle. "I would love that."

I nod, fighting my own grin. "Cool."

"Hey," he says, and his more serious tone has me turning my attention from the bowl of cereal back to him. "I'm really happy you came to meet me."

"Me too," I admit.

"I know this has been a tough year for you..." He cracks his knuckles in front of him. "But I'll always be here for you when you want me to be."

I rub my knuckles along my jaw. "I appreciate that."

"I know we don't know each other that well yet… but I look forward to changing that. I want you to come home anytime you want." *Home?* "My house is your house, okay?"

I shift uncomfortably in my seat as a strange feeling settles in my chest. "Okay."

My taste buds crave a coffee better than the dirt shit Mark has, so I've come to a place he suggested called The Brew House. A couple in front of me catches my attention as I wait in the long line. They're in their late twenties, and the guy won't stop touching his girlfriend and playing with her red hair.

"I was thinking," she tells him quietly. "Maybe later we can make up for lost time at the ranch?"

"Hmm, only if you promise to ride me like a cowgirl," he replies in a whisper but loud enough it reaches my ears. My amused gaze drops to my shoes as she kisses him like she hasn't seen him in years. One single blink, and I'm sitting back on the rock, craving Sophia's whiskey lips.

A flash of blonde comes into my peripheral, and I snap my head towards it in the same second my hope plummets to the floor.

It's not her.

A weight settles deep inside me. *Why am I so fucking drawn to her?* Maybe it's because I've never had someone, let alone a total stranger, open up to me the way she did. I almost felt brave enough to share my own story.

After retrieving my coffee, I hop back in the truck, pull out my phone and dial the number of the person I always dump my life problems on. His voice comes through the speakers. "Hey, it's Dean. I can't get to the phone right now. Leave me a message… or don't, but I do love me a good voicemail. Have a blessed day!"

The familiar high-pitched tone rings in my ear. "Hey, Dino... Truck's running good, promise I'm takin' care of her." I run my hands around the warm leather steering wheel. "So I gotta tell you, I met this girl last night, and I don't know what it was about her. She was raw and open and real... Thing is, just as I was fixin' to get her number, she was dragged away from me..." I shake my head, reaching for my coffee. "I'm leaving tomorrow, and I probably won't get a second chance to ask for her number. Am I an idiot or what? Okay... don't answer that... but man." I blow out a loud breath. "How can I go on like everything's normal now that I know she exists?"

3

SOPHIA

"I still can't believe Jake comes home for the first time in eight years and gets arrested after three days." I chuckle. "It's almost comical."

Dad's jaw tightens, the corner of his mouth curving upward as he shakes his head. "Don't turn Jake's arrest into a joke."

"It *is* a joke, Dad." I roll my eyes. "He shouldn't have been arrested in the first place."

"Yeah… you're right about that."

My eyes fly to him with amusement at his admission. "So was it really all over a stupid high school thing?" I ask, probing for more information since Leah was cagey as fuck this morning while we waited for Jake to get released. After he was, I insisted she and Jake ride together back to the house. I wanted them to have alone time, but I also wanted to nag Dad for a little more info on the ridiculous events of the morning.

"Honestly?" Dad readjusts his grip on the steering wheel. "I'm not sure what the actual *cause* of it was." I deflate in my seat like a latex balloon at the lack of breaking news. "It doesn't even surprise me Cole arrested your brother… But it's Jake's fault for losing his cool," he says, switching to full-on Dad mode. "Jake let Cole get in his head and reacted in a way you can't ever react around the police."

His eyes flick to mine, leveling me with a look that says *never do what he did*. "Luckily for your brother, Cole was drinking on the job, allowing me to get the charges dropped."

"He was what?" I gawk.

"Yep." His jaw ticks as he focuses on the road. "Chief Danvers was rather cooperative after I shared that piece of information about his son…"

"Why don't you like Cole's dad?" I ask, knowing he'd told Leah as much.

"You're being awfully nosy."

I throw a hand over my chest. "How is it nosy to know my family's enemies?" Dad chuckles. "If *you* hate the Danvers, *I* hate the Danvers. I'm just curious why."

"He's just a liar and a cheat." My lips flatten, unsure what to say. "So how was the celebration at the springs yesterday?"

"It was good…" I certainly didn't meet up with a random stranger in the woods and spill half my life story. And I certainly don't have *any* feelings about not even getting his stupid name. *Why should I?*

"Glad to hear it."

"How was your… date?" I ask with an awkward eyebrow waggle. It's weird knowing he's dating again but considering he and Mom have been divorced for over six years, I guess it was time.

"It was nice," he says with a smile.

"Good." I shift in my seat, looking toward him. "And Dad?"

"Yeah, Bear?"

"I'm happy if you're happy." He blows out a heavy breath. "I mean it."

A wide smile spreads across his face. "Thanks."

We ride in comfortable silence and a few minutes later, my phone vibrates in my lap. I flip it over, and my stomach sinks to the center of the earth.

SETH

> Who the fuck was that guy you were with last
> night?

My veins buzz with anxious energy, the same way they always do when I hear from him. It's becoming less frequent, thankfully, and I can't wait until we're off at college where I don't have to worry about him showing up at my house if I block him.

SETH

> Answer me, Sophia. Who was he?

I roll my eyes, clenching my jaw as I stare out the window at the buildings passing by. I contemplate if I should leave him on read but ultimately decide on a half-truth, hoping it will satisfy his curiosity enough that he'll leave me alone.

ME

> I don't know his name

SETH

> Oh, so you just always go around kissing random
> strangers?

> Tell me who the fuck was talking to my baby girl
> last night.

Anger rolls off my body in waves. I'm so tired of him acting like he still has control over my life.

ME

> We broke up months ago, Seth. I can talk to
> whoever the hell I want to talk to. I'm not and will
> never again be "your girl."

I lock my phone, and it buzzes like crazy in my hand the entire way home.

"That was way too much food," I groan, holding my belly after downing fifteen chicken wings in ten minutes.

"Well, next time slow down, speed racer." Jake chucks a pillow at me from the other side of the couch.

"Says the guy who looked like he was trying to win Nathan's hot dog eating contest," Leah teases, curled into his side with a dopey grin on her face.

"Hey, I hadn't eaten since *yesterday*," Jake counters. "So anyways, I was hoping to take you guys to the mall tomorrow for some last-minute shopping."

My mouth falls open. "You're *willingly* offering to go shopping?"

"Yes." He narrows his eyes at me. "Thought I might buy you two a few things worthy of a Euro trip."

Leah's taking me to Europe for a month as my graduation present.

Cue "London Bridge" by Fergie.

"That's really not necessary," Leah protests half-heartedly.

"Babe, I have more money than I know what to do with, okay? And I'm not here often, so just let me take care of my girls."

"Fine," Leah says, nuzzling her head into his chest as he plants a kiss on her red hair.

"Alright." I roll my eyes in mock annoyance. "If I *must* go help you spend all of your money, then I suppose I can muster up the energy."

"Good." Jake beams with pride as he plays tonight's movie: *Top Gun: Maverick*.

After half an hour, Jake's gaze burns into my face like a laser beam. He opens and closes his mouth, then returns his attention back to the TV.

"It's a little hard for me to enjoy watching *Miles Teller* with a mustache when you won't stop staring at me, Jacob," I grumble, and he and Leah both turn their attention to me.

He pinches the bridge of his nose and exhales heavily before pausing the TV. "Don't get mad, okay?"

"No promises."

"It's just… I noticed Mom wasn't at graduation yesterday…" He purses his lips with a sad smile.

"I mean… not being there for me is kind of her specialty."

"I'm sure she would have come if you'd invited her, Bug." He raises his eyebrows, giving me his signature "I'm disappointed in you" face, which is *almost* worse than Dad's. If he thinks using my nickname will soften the blow, it's not gonna work today.

"She would've gotten an invite if she'd been involved in my life the last ten years, *Jacob*," I snap, sitting up straight. And who does he think he is? He abandoned me just as much as she did. Sure, we might have kept in touch the last eight years, but Jake left me too.

Everybody leaves.

I'm not sure if it's worse to lose someone by death or by choice. That probably sounds insensitive to those grieving… but at least Chloe didn't *choose* to leave me. So even if I miss her, I can't hate her.

But my mom? *Yeah, I definitely hate her.*

"Well, I think if you'd just give her a chance," Jake presses, boring his green eyes into my matching ones, "she'd really like to make up for lost time, Sophia *Elysabeth*." My lip twitches in anger at his reminder I share a name with my mother.

"Since when did you become such a fucking mama's boy?" I spout.

"Soph…"

"Jake." I shake my head. "You just don't get it."

"Why *wouldn't* I get it?" he asks with a flicker of pain in his eyes.

"Mom left and never came back for me."

Neither did you.

"She left me too, Soph," Jake argues.

"Yeah… except you were eighteen and moved out the same year. I had to spend eight more years in our empty house with none of you in it!" I huff and fold my arms over my chest, angry as fuck at him opening up a wound I would rather forget about completely. A wound he contributed to himself by letting his grief pull him away from Longwood, and me, for so long. He frowns, then comes over and sits down next to me, putting his arm around my shoulders to pull me in tight.

"You're right," he admits. "I'm sorry. I shouldn't push you. It took me a long time before I was ready to talk to Mom again… and I guess I just need to respect our timelines may be different. Okay?"

I rest my head against him and release the tension from my shoulders. "Okay…"

"Forgive me?" he asks hopefully.

"I guess so…"

"Rain or shine?"

"Yeah." A weak smile spreads across my face. "Rain or shine."

He pushes himself off the couch and before he can restart the movie, I stand up. "I'm pretty tired from the party last night and worrying about your criminal ass in jail all day." I smirk playfully at Jake, and he narrows his eyes right back. "See you guys tomorrow."

"Night, Ladybug." Leah blows me a kiss, and my lips upturn as I "catch it" and slap it to my cheek.

"Wanna go for a run in the morning?" Jake asks before I reach the stairs.

"Only if you're in the mood to eat dust," I spit back.

"Kinda hard to eat dust when you're the one creating it," he replies.

I dart up the stairs exaggeratedly to show my speed, and their laughter follows me all the way to my room.

My sketchbook and pencils are sitting on my unmade bed. I scoop them up and head to the one place that always makes me feel at peace: Chloe's room.

It's tidy and organized, the complete opposite of when she frequented its walls. The pottery shelf along the far wall contains all of her creations. Every single one, down to the lopsided teacup with a hole in the bottom she made during her first class. In the middle sits the bowl she and Leah made the day they gave me my nickname. I'll never forget my excitement when Leah added *Ladybug* to the bottom in red paint, initiating me into their swarm.

My eyes snag on Chloe's bed, the same white comforter reminding me of all the nights we used to snuggle up as she taught me to read. *Alice's Adventures in Wonderland* was our book of choice, and I always loved the magic of it all. Sometimes I still lie in her bed and read it out loud, like she's right there listening. Closing my eyes, I imagine Chloe in Wonderland, having adventures and searching for the rabbit hole to find her way back to us.

But she isn't in Wonderland, and this small space is all I have left of her.

Sighing, my eyes fall to the ground where I'd sit as she braided my hair for school. On days I was feeling especially down after Mom left, she'd abandon the braid and tickle me until I practically peed myself and begged for mercy. It always helped.

I make my way over to the pink upholstered armchair in the corner that has Chloe's favorite plush pink-and-white striped blanket neatly resting on the arm. Usually I leave it bunched up on the chair, but Leah must have folded it when she came in here yesterday.

Sinking into the cushion, I pull the soft blanket over my lap and glance around. I used to experience debilitating grief every time I passed by Chloe's room—now it's the one place in the world where I still feel a connection to her. The only place she still exists. I miss her like hell, but sitting here surrounded by all her favorite things, I can *almost* convince myself she's not gone.

I can *almost* convince myself I'm just a normal girl, with a normal ass family—not a damaged daddy's girl with raging abandonment issues.

4

ELIJAH

The ear-piercing blow of a whistle sounds through the air, signaling the end of practice. My muscles burn, my body's soaked in sweat, and I feel fucking *incredible*.

"Nice job today, Anderson," our head coach, James Porter, says, hitting me against the shoulder pads. "Keep that up, and you'll definitely be looking at some playing time this year."

"Thanks, Coach," I say, attempting to hide my shit-eating grin.

"Head to your cabins and get cleaned up for dinner," he shouts to the team. "We have a film session tomorrow at nine. If you're late, you'll be running drills until you puke. Understand?"

"Yes, Coach," we all chime in unison.

I grab my helmet off the metal bench and head towards the path to our cabins with the rest of the team.

"Man, your precision was incredible today," Noah, our starting quarterback and one of my best friends, says, saddling up to me.

"Thanks." I try to hold in my smile, attempting humility since I know my gain is his loss.

"Hey, be proud of it." He squeezes my shoulder. "I've got no problem sharing my spotlight with you. There's enough playing time to go around."

Noah's already secured his spot in the draft once he graduates this year—winning a Heisman as a sophomore will do that for you—so his willingness to share the field doesn't surprise me in the slightest.

"Fine." I smirk. "I crushed it today."

"Atta boy." He slaps my butt, and I shove him away.

"You need to catch some ass so you'll stop touching mine." I shake my head as Theo, my best friend and roommate, slides up between us.

"Come on, man. You know my rule," Noah says.

"Wait," Theo says, throwing his arms out and halting us in place. He whips his head to Noah. "The no-pussy-during-season-thing? That's actually *real*?"

"The fuck kind of rule is that?" I cringe, shuddering at the thought. "Is that even possible?"

Theo looks down at his dick. "Don't worry, big guy. We won't be following Cap's lead on that."

"Calm down." Noah waves us off, beginning to walk again. "It's a *less*-booty-during-season rule... Less booty, less bullshit."

"Bro." I shake my head exaggeratedly, holding up a hand. "That is the polar opposite of my mantra."

"Oh yeah?" Noah laughs. "And what mantra would that be?"

"More titties, more touchdowns!" I throw an invisible football, and Theo runs forward, "catching" it.

"See you guys later," Noah says, shaking his head and walking off to his cabin.

"You wanna join for yoga?" Desmond, one of our running backs, asks, catching up to Theo and me.

"No, I'm good," I say, more than ready for a hot shower.

"Nah, man," Theo agrees.

"You sure?" Desmond cocks a brow. "The cheerleaders are *very* flexible and always happy to help stretch me out."

"Okay, fine, I'm calling an audible," Theo says like a desperate quarterback. "I'm in."

I wave a loose hand as they walk off. "See you guys."

Andi, a brunette cheerleader, comes up next to me, placing a hand on my arm. "Glad you're back."

"Thanks."

"Things go good with Mark?"

A heavy breath escapes me. "It was fine. A little weird... but fine."

"Well, I'm proud of you for going even if you were scared as fuck."

"I wasn't *scared*," I scoff, fighting a laugh.

"You pretended to have a stomach bug the day before you left."

"I wasn't pretending." *I was totally pretending.* "Fine... well, I went, didn't I?"

A wide smile spreads across her face. "And like I said, I'm very proud."

"So happy I have the Andi Lyons seal of approval." I throw my arm around her shoulders, and she laughs.

"But seriously, I'm sorry the trip was so weird. Wanna come over later? Get your mind off everything."

It wasn't *all* weird...

Thoughts of a pretty blonde run through my head, a twang of longing flashing through me. "Nah, not today. I'm exhausted."

Sure, that's it.

5

SOPHIA

Leah and I have traveled all over Europe the past month, and it's been the perfect distraction for the parts of my life I'd rather keep buried. I wish we could stay here forever, never returning to the place where the worst moments of my life happened.

I can *almost* understand how Jake and Mom felt all those years. But the difference is, even after adventuring in Wonderland, I know I have to return home and deal with the eventual fallout.

Last week we were on the Amalfi Coast—*un uomo italiano sexy, per favore*—and now we're in Amsterdam visiting Jake for the last stop before returning to Longwood.

We exit the small tattoo shop owned by Jake's friend Luuk, and I'm immediately hit by the warm sunshine. The bustling city surrounds us, with bikes flying by, people rushing around, and a view of the canal across the way sparkling under the sunlight. My eyes fall to the fresh ink on my pinky finger, and I smile at the word "Lovebug" now permanently in black script on my finger, matching Leah's.

Jake's heavy arm falls around my shoulders, pulling me in tight. "Love you, Bug," he says, placing a kiss in my hair, and I nuzzle against him.

"Love you too, Jakey."

Leah comes up, hooking her arm through mine. "See, it didn't hurt too bad, did it?"

"Nope." I let out a satisfied sigh, happy to have something permanent on my skin to remind me of my sister.

"Told you." She quirks a brow. "We don't lie to each other, remember?"

My stomach sinks, and I put on as convincing a face as I can muster. "Yep."

"Where to next?" she asks, thankfully changing the subject off our honesty promise I've been blowing to shit.

"We could go to the Van Gogh museum?" Jake suggests. "You can get a new postcard to start a wall in *our* apartment," he tells Leah.

She rolls her eyes and smirks towards him. "It's not *ours* yet."

"It will be soon." He winks and I giggle, excited they're really doing the damn thing.

Twenty minutes later, we arrive at an open, grassy area where the Van Gogh museum is located. The first things I notice are sunflowers —sunflowers in every goddamn inch of the outdoor space.

"Oh yeah!" Leah exclaims, now holding hands with Jake. "I forgot the *Van Gogh and the Sunflowers* exhibition is this month."

My lips curve upwards at the thousands of beautiful flowers, and my mind wanders to a blue-eyed, brown-haired mystery guy with a smile that stole all the breath from my lungs. Part of me is thankful I didn't learn so much as his name, because the last thing I need right now is to get attached to another person who will end up breaking me.

I know not every guy is like he-who-shall-not-be-named... but I have to protect myself if there is even the tiniest of possibilities. It's just not worth the risk.

I can't help but think something about him was different though. All the things I shared, and there wasn't even a single moment he seemed judgmental.

Maybe he's just a really excellent actor.

Hell, who am I to talk? I'm putting on the performance of a life-time these days.

6

ELIJAH

"Did you snort too much glue as a kid?" Theo asks Noah, who sits across from him. "There's no chance in hell Tampa will beat Pittsburgh this year. No motherfuckin' chance."

Noah leans casually against the booth. "Nah, Pittsburgh blew all their money on a fancy ass coach rather than stacking their team with talented players this year. You'll see."

A typical Friday night: drinking beer with the boys, eating cheap pizza at Lazy Moon, and talking about the one thing we all love more than life itself: football.

My phone buzzes in my pocket, and I pull it out to see "Mom" flashing across the screen. I excuse myself from the table and tap the green button as I make my way outside the loud restaurant.

"Hey, Mama," I answer with a smile tugging at my lips.

"Hey, honey," she says cheerfully. "How's it going? How's practice been?"

"It's actually… It's going really well." I kick my shoe against the ground. "I think I might get a decent amount of playing time this year."

"That's great! I'm so proud of you."

"Yeah, how are you? Are y'all doing okay?"

"Oh, don't worry about us, Eli. We can take care of ourselves."

"I know, Mama." A heavy breath escapes my lips. "I just hate that I'm so far away." While I'm thankful for the distance, in the same breath, my stomach aches because I know how long it would take me to get home if I were really needed. *Six Hours. Six excruciatingly long hours.*

"Hey, we talked about this. You're exactly where you need to be right now. Okay?"

"I know but—"

"No ifs, ands, or buts. We're doing fine here, and you need to focus on school and football. Enjoy being young and spending time with your friends." A stinging feeling settles in my stomach. "You can't be worrying about us all the time. Nama's right next door. She's always here for me if I need something. I'll be fine. Promise not to worry?"

"I can't promise that." I hold my breath, wishing she'd ask me to come home as much as I appreciate her telling me to stay put. "Are you sure?"

"I'm sure, Elijah," she says firmly.

"Okay... well, only if you're *sure*... Love you, Mama."

"Love you too, honey. Call me after your classes start Monday and tell me all about them, okay?"

"Will do." I hang up and head inside, settling back into the booth. I take a sip of my water, hoping it might wash down some of the shame I feel about staying here when I know Mom needs me back home. Even if she won't admit it.

"You in, E?" Theo asks, pulling me out of my head.

"In for what?"

"Tits, tequila, and twerking." He waggles his eyebrows, and my lips curl upwards as I fight a smile at the one person who never fails to suck me into a good time.

"I'll skip the twerking, but tequila and tits?" I shoot finger guns at him, *Rick and Morty* style. "You son of a bitch, I'm in."

We're in the corner of a bayside college bar that smells like stale beer, weed, and sweat. Theo, Noah, Desmond, and a few other guys from the team are standing around, shooting the shit.

Most of the guys are twenty-one, but since I'm not, I ordered a whiskey ginger with the fake Theo got me. I should've chosen any other liquor though because now all I can think about is *her*. I'm in a bar full of beautiful, tipsy girls who've been throwing themselves at us all night, and all I can think of are forest green eyes and a sassy smile.

"Hey, Elijah," Andi says, walking up next to me.

"Hi, Andi." I smirk down at her. *Maybe she's the perfect distraction to get that bewildering blonde out of my head.*

"Hi, *Andi*," the boys all coo.

"Hey, *boys*." Andi flashes them her signature smile and turns back to me. "Let's dance."

"Andi," I groan, my head falling back.

"Come on, you need to have some *fun*." She cocks a brow at me. "Actual *fun*."

"Fine." I huff a breath and force a smile, nudging her towards the dance floor. I'm not a dancer, only if I'm really drunk, but I'll do just about anything if Andi can help me forget Sophia for one damn night. Although she's already tried and failed.

Can someone please explain to me how a total stranger can have you obsessing about them for months? Because I don't get it. All Sophia did was kiss me on the cheek, and you'd think she stole my precious virginity, I'm so damn hooked.

Andi grinds her plump ass against me as we dance squished between fifty other sweaty college kids. Her hips are gyrating to the beat, which is usually the part where I'd get hard, she'd notice, and ask if I want to get out of here—no such luck. Andi turns around and throws her arms around my neck.

"You're so tense today," she says, trailing her fingertips along the side of it.

My eyes wander the room, trying to figure out if I somehow have whiskey dick at the ripe old age of twenty. They snag at the far corner of the bar on a familiar-looking girl with purple hair. My eyes scan frantically to see if… Yep. There she is.

There *she* is.

The golden thread I've been pulling on all summer—each tug leading me toward my complete unraveling.

She's just as breathtaking as I remember. Andi sways to the music, but my body is frozen. Afraid if I blink, Sophia will vanish into thin air. She says something in her friend's ear, and then they both split, the friend heading toward the bathroom hallway and Sophia weaving through the crowded dance floor.

"Be right back," I tell Andi, removing myself abruptly from her grasp.

"Um, okay?" She laughs after me.

I make my way through the bar, almost knocking over an entire group of guys on the way out.

"Hey!" one shouts as I push past him.

"Sorry," I grumble.

I don't see her anywhere, and I'm frantic. *Why am I like this?* I glance at the exit and see a flicker of blonde hair just before the door closes. I rush toward it and throw it open, practically busting it off its hinges.

"Dude," some guy says as I exit the bar.

"Sorry," I mumble again.

Son of a bitch, how many more boots will I have to kiss tonight before I find this damn girl.

I'm spinning in circles, but she's nowhere in sight.

"Fuck," I mumble under my breath as I drag my fingers through my hair. "Shit. Fuck. Son of a bitch. Damnit." I curse at no one. The second chance I had to get her number, and I've motherfuckin' mucked it.

Turning around to head back to the bar, I blow out a breath, feeling defeated. My feet stall at the sight of a curious, amused face staring at me with arms folded over her chest.

A wide smile spreads across my lips as I stand there, breathless, like a fucking lovesick idiot. "Sophia."

"Hi?" she replies with narrowed eyes. "Do I know you?"

My mouth parts open as my brows furrow in shock. I haven't been able to stop thinking about her for months, and she doesn't even recognize me. "Seriously?" Her pondering expression turns playful as the corners of her mouth tug upwards. "Oh, aren't you just fuckin' *hilarious*!"

"Sorry." She giggles. "Thought I'd make you sweat a little first."

"Oh, really?" I raise both brows.

"Yep… Were you looking for me?"

"Maybe." My eyes rake over her, drinking in every delicious drop of the tight black silk dress hugging her gorgeous curves.

"Why?" She forces a smile, her jaw tight. "Looked like you were plenty occupied in there."

My eyebrows rise in surprise. "So you already knew I was here? Why didn't you come say hi?"

She shrugs, maintaining her persona of indifference. "Didn't want to interrupt your lap dance."

"I promise, that's a non-issue."

"Mm-hmm," she hums, unconvinced, eyes full of disdain.

I can't stop the grin from spreading across my face. "Are you jealous?"

"Strangers don't have the right to be jealous, do they?" she asks as the little green monster line dances in her eyes.

"How about we be *friends* instead?" *Friends? What the fuck was that?*

"Friends?" she asks.

"Yeah, you know, two people who hang out, talk, and have each other's phone numbers in case of emergencies… *Friends*."

Who the hell enters the friend zone willingly? Especially with a girl like this.

An idiot, that's who.

"Hmm… It's an interesting prospect." Her face remains passive. "I'll have to think about it."

"Think about it?" Girls usually rip the phone out of my hand to put their number in, and this girl has to… think about it? "What the hell is there to think about?"

She twirls a piece of her golden hair, seemingly unaffected. "I suppose it couldn't hurt to start the semester knowing more than just my friends from home."

"Yeah, maybe being friends with a football player will improve your social standing." *Smooth, you cocky bastard.*

"You're on the *football* team?" Her brows pinch together, and she almost looks… disappointed? Disgusted?

That can't be right.

"Yeah?" I pause, trying to gauge her reaction. "You figured out all that stuff about me the last time we met, but you didn't realize I was a cocky jock?"

"The cocky part I got, the jock thing…" Her eyes rake over me, and my balls tighten at the attention. "I guess I could see that."

"You guess?" I throw a hand over my chest to bandage my wounded ego.

"Yeah, I mean, you need some more weight training." She reaches out and squeezes my bicep, then pulls away. "Fill out a bit more, but I can *almost* see it."

My mouth is hanging open. Is she fucking serious? I weight train every day. I could bench press two of her and barely break a sweat.

Her serious expression turns into a fit of laughter as she folds over, holding her stomach.

"Oh my God," she squeals, pretending to wipe tears off her

cheeks. "You should see your face." Her infectious laugh reverberates around me.

"Well, aren't you just the next Amy Schumer?"

She bows exaggeratedly. "The show starts at eight."

"I'll be there." My eyes linger on hers until she darts them away.

"Guess I was wrong about a few things though."

"And what would those be?"

"I assumed you weren't the party boy type." She frowns, narrowing her eyes at me. "But you seemed to be having a pretty good time."

"Honestly..." I sigh. "I hated every second."

"I doubt that girl forced you on the dance floor."

"I just needed a distraction." I shrug. "Thought she'd be it."

"A distraction from what?"

You. "Practice, school, the usual."

"How'd things go with your dad?" Her playful expression turns soft.

"My dad?"

"What was his name again... Mark?"

I take a deep breath and clear my throat. "Oh, yeah... It went really well."

"I'm happy to hear that." A gentle smile appears on her face. "Alright... *friends*." She sticks out her pinky finger, and I stare at it with furrowed brows.

"Are we pinky promising to be friends? Is that what we're doing?" I chuckle at her adorable schoolyard antics.

"Yep, it's the ultimate promise." She wiggles her cute little finger at me, and I notice a black script tattoo on the inside.

"Fine." I grin like an idiot, reaching out and hooking my pinky with hers. "Friends."

That word's gonna bite me in the ass like a rattlesnake.

"Okay." She opens her palm upwards. "Give me your phone." I pull it out of my back pocket, then hand it to her, and her fingers flash across the screen. "Alright, *friend*, you've got my number… in case of *emergencies*." She winks, handing it back to me.

"Hey, Soph, there you are!" the purple-haired girl says, running up to us.

"Here I am." Sophia opens her arms, palms facing up in front of her.

"You." The girl narrows her eyes and points a finger at me. "You're the guy from the grad night party. *Ohhh*, Sophia wouldn't shut up about you!"

Sophia's eyes go wide, her cheeks turning tomato red, and she gives her friend the sharpest death glare I've ever seen. If looks could kill, that girl would be six feet under.

"What?" the girl says, throwing up her hands. Sophia's eyes return to mine, and I'm unable to wipe the satisfied grin off my face as she rolls her eyes and looks away. "Did you at least get his name this time?" she asks, directing her question at Sophia.

"Yeah." Sophia smirks at me. "It's Cocky Jock."

I glare at her, my eyes narrowing in on her pretty, smartass mouth. "Actually… My *friends* call me Elijah."

"Yeah, or *Elijah*," she responds to her friend.

"Well, hello, *Elijah*, I'm Sage." She extends her hand, and I shake it in response.

"Nice to meet you, Sage. I appreciate your lack of filter."

A teasing smile spreads across her face. "It's my best quality."

"Have you found Charlie?" Sophia asks. *Who the fuck is Charlie?*

"Yeah, and sh—"

"Hey, guys," another girl says, rushing toward us. I recognize her from the cheer team. She eyes me curiously but says nothing. *Looks like Sage is the blunt one.*

"Where the hell have you been, Char?" Sophia snaps at her. *Charlie's a girl. Noted, you jealous idiot.* "We were worried."

"I'm sorry," Charlie says, stifling a yawn. "I'm so exhausted I basically fell asleep at the bar. Sage ordered us an Uber back to your place. Are you ready?"

"Yeah, sure… See ya, Elijah."

"See ya, Sunflower."

She turns to walk away, but I swear I see a tinge of pink hit her cheeks before she does. I bite my lip, watching her until she's hidden in the familiar-looking Uber.

7
SOPHIA

"Holy shit balls, Soph," Sage squeals as the three of us buckle in. The twenty-something driver glances curiously into the rearview mirror but says nothing. "That guy is hot. Like, fuck-me-in-an-alley *hot*."

"Sage," I gasp, risking another glance at the driver, who's fighting a smile.

"What? I'm just being honest. I see why you couldn't shut up about him."

"Yeah, *thanks* for that by the way. Now Elijah's going to think I'm obsessed and have been pining after him since the day we met."

"But... haven't you been?" Charlie counters, nudging me.

"You mention a few small things about someone you met, and suddenly you're obsessed," I say, slamming the back of my head against the seat. "Besides, we agreed, just *friends*. I have no interest in another relationship. This is a relationship-free zone." I use my pointer fingers to draw a hula hoop sized circle around my body.

"If you mean friends who fuck," Sage says, putting up two hands and enacting a double thrust, "I'm all on board."

"Sage!" I hit her against the leg. "There will be no fucking. Just friends-ing."

"No one is *just* friends with a guy who looks like that... And if he's not getting it from you, he can definitely get it from someone else."

A fire burns in my stomach, my lungs constricting as all the oxygen is sucked out of the tiny Uber. "I have no right to care about who he sleeps with," I say ignoring the physical reaction my body had to her words. "Like I said, we're friends. Besides, we barely know each other... And he's just a cocky jock who's trying to fuck and duck." I wrinkle my nose in disgust as the driver snorts, holding in a laugh, and I glare at him. He shifts in the seat, bringing his inked arm up to scratch at the sexy neck tat peeking out from his collar.

"You can't just mark off every guy who knows how to handle some balls," Sage says, pulling my attention back to her, and now I'm the one struggling not to laugh. "Come on, aren't you ready to get over Seth?" My partial amusement vanishes faster than a french fry thrown at a seagull.

I shoot dagger eyes at her. "We agreed never to speak his name again." Flashbacks flicker in front of my eyes that I'd rather pretend are nightmares.

"Soph... I get why you hate him," Charlie says gently. *She's the only one who possibly could.* "But you can also enjoy a sexy friend with benefits so at least that piece of shit isn't the last one who touched you."

"Okay... Can we change the subject?" I groan.

Thinking about Seth always leaves me either enraged or on the edge of an existential crisis. I'm over him—world-record-set-for-pole-vaulting over him—but what he did is embedded permanently in my memory. Moving past it isn't something I know how to do... or if I even should.

"I'm just saying..." Charlie shrugs. "The best way to get over someone is to get *under* someone else."

"Never use one guy to forget another," Sage says uncharacteristically, and Charlie and I both stare at her. "Use two or three."

The Uber driver snorts again. I'm fully convinced he's having the best night of his life listening to my friends shit on me.

"Do you have something you'd like to say, Uber Dude?" I snap at him. Sage cackles next to me, and Charlie covers her mouth.

"I think it's safer if I keep my opinions to myself," he says.

Sage leans forward and squeezes his shoulder. "Good call."

Rolling my eyes, I sigh as he pulls up to the curb, and I'm thanking the universe I can finally escape this episode of carpool *Maury*.

We head to the dorm, and once in the common area of Sage's and my place, I throw myself dramatically onto a bean bag and groan. "Ugh, you guys are so fucking embarrassing!"

"Who, us?" Charlie gasps, clutching her chest, feigning offense while sinking down into the other bean bag.

"That Uber driver now knows more about my current life than Janine."

"I still think it's weird you're on a first name basis with your therapist." Sage walks into her room, tossing a tiny purse on the bed. I've been going to see Janine since Chloe died, and I've only recently stopped since I moved.

"I think it's weird you crumple your toilet paper instead of folding it when you shit, but I still love you," I spit back, and both of them laugh.

"I'm not weird!" Sage calls back. "I'm one of a kind."

Nodding my head, I tease, "That you are."

"Okay," Charlie says, pushing herself off the beanbag. "I'm gonna head back to my dorm."

"You sure you don't wanna sleep here?"

"Yeah, I promised Jonathan I'd call him when I got home, so..." She smirks.

"Ohhh! You guys are totes gonna have phone sex." I waggle my eyebrows.

Charlie rolls her eyes, huffing out a laugh. "See, you need to get laid, babe. It's all you think about."

I place my hands on my hips. "Is not!"

"Is too!" Sage calls from her room.

"Okay, you know what, you bitches are nosy *and* opinionated, so I'm going to excuse myself for the night."

"Night, Soph," Charlie calls, heading out the door.

"Night, Joey!" Sage yells.

I'm finally makeup-free, in my pajamas, and slipping into bed. As I reach for my charger to plug in my phone, it vibrates in my hand.

UNKNOWN NUMBER

UNKNOWN NUMBER

Hi Sunflower, make it home okay?

> ME
>
> Who is this?

UNKNOWN NUMBER

Wow, so many people call you Sunflower you can't even tell who I am? I knew you liked the nickname.

> ME
>
> Hilarious.
>
> Yes, I made it back to my place before the Uber turned into a pumpkin.

UNKNOWN NUMBER

Good.

> ME
>
> Are you still at Salty Pete's working your way through sorority row?

UNKNOWN NUMBER

Hey, Andi's a cheerleader not a sorority girl

Hmm… Andi, is it?

ME

Mhm. Tomato to-mah-to

UNKNOWN NUMBER

Green's a good color on you. Brings out your eyes.

ME

How would you know? Both times we've met it's been pretty dark

UNKNOWN NUMBER

Definitely not too dark for me to notice your eyes are the color of cornfields during crop season

ME

Wow, what a line

UNKNOWN NUMBER

I aim to please

What's your class schedule?

ME

Trying to stalk me? 🔪

UNKNOWN NUMBER

Wow... that was CORNy

I'm just trying to see if we have any classes together

ME

Idk, my classes are probably too advanced for a jock

UNKNOWN NUMBER

Ha ha HILARIOUS, Sunflower.

What's your major?

ME

Fine Arts with a focus in photography and sketching. You?

UNKNOWN NUMBER

Agriculture with a focus in graduating

ME

Boring lol total dumb jock move

I chuckle to myself as I save his contact in my phone.

DUMB JOCK

DUMB JOCK

Ouch. You've wounded me.

ME

Awh, want me to bring over some ice for your bruised ego?

DUMB JOCK

You're so funny. Ha. Ha.

So you have a focus in photography? Call me if you ever need a sex god to pose for you

ME

Wow, your head is bigger than your ass

DUMB JOCK

You checked out my ass?

Sophia likes big butts and she cannot lie

ME

Never said it was big. I said your head was BIGGER

DUMB JOCK

She's hooked and she can't stop staring

ME

I don't wanna get with ya

Or take ya picture

DUMB JOCK

Whatever DJ disses a lot

Send me your schedule, maybe our pre-reqs
overlap

Turns out we have a class together twice a week. How on earth will I concentrate with his stupid, perfect face in the room?

Cosmos, give me strength.

8

ELIJAH

"Are you shitting me?" I mutter to myself, looking down at the tiny phone screen. On the way home from class, I checked the grade from my first world history exam, and I now realize it was a grave mistake. The second I saw D show up in the grade column, my mood went from Martha Stewart-on-4/20 to Martha Stewart-in-prison.

I may have bombed finals last year, but I really thought I was doing better this semester.

This has to be a joke.

Okay, Professor Mintz, you can update with the real results now.

Coach has been killing us at practice—like, running-laps-till-we-vomit killing us—but even though I was exhausted, I still studied every night this week.

What the hell am I going to do?

I already hate this fucking class. To be honest, I probably would've dropped it, but I look forward to seeing a certain ray of sunshine twice a week. Our hardass professor gave us assigned seats like we're kindergarteners, and Sophia's on the opposite side of the room. If I thought Mintz would take a bribe, I'd believe Sophia paid him to make sure we're as far away from one another as logistically possible.

She takes days to reply to my messages, and I'm not about to turn into the guy that double texts. Whenever we see each other in person, she avoids me like Noah avoids Chef Boyardee. It makes no sense to me. I'm not the guy girls avoid, I'm the one they fight over.

Hoping for a pick-me-up, I walk into my favorite coffee shop on campus, Crystal Coffee, and get in the long line. After a few minutes and being only halfway through the line, I pull out my phone, bringing it to my ear.

"Hey, it's Dean. I can't get to the phone right now. Leave me a message... or don't, but I do love me a good voicemail. Have a blessed day!" *Beeeep.*

"Welp..." I shift in place. "I've really stepped in it this time, Dino... Let's just say I won't be winning a Pulitzer in history anytime soon. I have no clue what I'm gonna do this time. I can't risk losing this dang scholarship."

The door to Crystal Coffee opens, and I turn towards it. Sophia steps through looking like a damn vision in denim shorts and a tight black cropped T-shirt tight over her chest that says "Koala-fied to party."

"Gotta call you back, I might've found my saving grace. Love ya." I hang up the phone, move quickly to the back of the line, and lean down to her ear. "Hey, Sunflower."

Without even so much as a flinch, Sophia's head turns to me as an amused smirk forms across her pretty lips. "Hey?"

I step forward to stand directly next to her. "How'd you do on the world history test?"

"Who's asking?" I raise my brows. "Fine." She rolls her eyes and attempts to stifle a smile. "I got a ninety-eight."

"A ninety-eight?!" I balk with my mouth hanging open. "Are you frickin' serious?"

Her lips curve upward. "I'm assuming by your shocked reaction you're one of the disappointments Professor Mintz talked about in his email?"

"Hey," I say, placing a hand on my chest, "I studied *days* for that test."

"You know you have to do more than just have the book in your hands, right? You have to actually open it"—she presses her hands together, then unfolds them in front of her—"and *read* the words on the page."

"Such a smartass." I shake my head, unable to hide my grin as we take a step forward in line. "Okay, I'm buying you a coffee, and then I have a favor to ask."

She raises her eyebrows. "What if you buy me a coffee and I say *no* to the favor?"

"Then I guess we'll have to consider this a date." I wink and she chuckles, unamused, patting my shoulder. "I'm going to pretend you didn't just *laugh* at the possibility of going on a date with me."

"And I'm going to pretend you didn't suggest it."

We reach the front of the line, and I gesture for her to go first. She hesitates but ultimately gives in.

"Can I please get a large black iced coffee?" she tells the barista.

He plucks a plastic cup. "Room for cream and sugar?"

"No, thank you." *Damn, she likes it dirty.*

"Anything else?" the barista asks, and Sophia points a thumb over her shoulder at me.

"Yes sir, can I get a hot medium hazelnut latte with a drizzle of honey and some whip cream, please," I tell him, and Sophia snorts beside me before striding over to the pickup counter. I give him our names, pay, and walk over to join her. "What was that about?"

"What was *what* about?"

I squint my eyes at her. "You laughed when I ordered my drink."

"Yeah." A breathy laugh escapes her. "Because I ordered black coffee like an adult, and you ordered a honey hazelnut latte like a basic bitch."

"Hey!" I put my fists on my hips. "Hazelnut is fucking delicious."

"I bet it is, *Honey* Bee." My lips quirk at the new nickname. "So why'd you bribe me? Need someone to steal your virginity or something?"

I scoff. "As if you really believe I'm a virgin."

Her eyes trail my body with a disapproving gaze that makes my jaw tighten. "I don't know. It doesn't really seem like you'd know what to do with your hands." She pokes my wrist and lets out a mocking laugh.

"Such a mouthy girl." I bite my lower lip. "No, I don't need help in *that* department. Thank you very much. But I do need you to *tutor* me for world history."

"What?"

"Could *you*"—I point at her—"help *me*"—I press a finger to my chest—"study?"

"Elijah. I'm not sure that's such a—"

"Sophia, I'm asking you to study, not fuck in the corner of the library."

Her eyes go wide, cheeks flushing pink, before she controls her expression. "There's a study session every Wednesday at three. Can't you just go to that?"

"No, I have mandatory practice on Wednesdays from two to six." I bring my hands together in a prayer position. "Please, Sophia, I really need to keep my grades up to maintain my scholarship."

"You're here on a *scholarship*?" She gawks.

"Yeah... Don't look so surprised."

"I'm sorry, I just, I guess you're actually good at football then?"

"I mean, I play for a division one school, so yeah, I'm good at football." I laugh, attempting and failing to not sound cocky. "But I won't be playing anymore if I fail my classes, so please, Sophia Summers, *please* will you tutor me?"

She turns her attention toward the counter where our drinks have yet to come out, ignoring me entirely. "Damn, these drinks are taking forever."

"Are you really going to make me beg?"

Sophia looks back at me and folds her arms over her chest.

My eyes rake over her gorgeous body as I consider her silent challenge. I've never begged a girl for anything. Not for sex and definitely not to *study*.

Here goes nothing.

I reach out, taking her hands in mine, and drop down on one knee, ignoring the stares I'm getting from everyone else waiting for their drinks. Sophia's expression turns from amused to shocked. She pulls one hand away, putting it over her mouth.

I flash my biggest dimpled grin at her. "Sophia Sunflower Summers, would you make me the happiest man in the world and tutor me for world history?"

"Elijah... you're making a scene."

"Then end it quickly and say *yes.*"

"I have an iced black coffee for *Sunflower!*" the barista calls out with impeccable timing, and Sophia's eyes fly to him.

"And a honey hazelnut latte for..." He pauses. "*Please?*"

She throws her head back, letting out a bubbling laugh. "I've been set up."

"Come on." I bat my eyelashes up at her while lightly squeezing her hands.

"Fine, you idiot." She giggles. "I'll study with you."

"She said yes!" I jump up off my knees, and the room erupts in hoots and hollers even though they have no clue what they're cheering for. "You will *not* regret this." I cup her face in my hands, grinning down at her.

She rolls her eyes, then fixates them on me in a silent warning. "I better not." The corners of her mouth tug upwards as we grab our drinks and head for the exit. "I do have one stipulation," she says casually before taking a sip of her dirt coffee.

"You already said yes." She looks up at me, and I quickly realize those gripping green eyes could make me do just about anything. "Fine, what is it?"

"You have to feed me after each study session."

"Deal." That's an easy one. If it gives me an excuse to spend more time with Sophia, I'm all for it. "I have a stipulation too."

"Is that so?"

"Yeah." I press my lips together. "You have to promise not to fall in love with me."

She chuckles. "Okay, Mandy Moore."

"Do you promise?" I cock a brow. She reaches out her pinky, and I hook it with mine. "Can we start tomorrow morning?"

"Let me check my *busy* schedule." She pulls out her phone, and it feels like she's taking hours to respond. "Okay, I *guess* I can pencil you in. Meet me in front of the library at nine?"

A rush of excitement floods my veins. "Okay, see you then."

"See you," she says, turning and strutting down the sidewalk.

I watch her sashay away, wondering when the hell I became the kind of guy to make a fool of himself in the middle of a coffee shop for a woman.

Do I need her to tutor me?

Sure.

Did I enjoy the way her face lit up and how her beautiful laughter made my chest swell when I dropped to my knees?

Damn straight.

The lobby of my building is empty as I walk through it to drop my backpack off before heading to practice. Since I'm a collegiate athlete, Theo and I share a two bedroom, one bath suite—more of an apartment than a dorm—that has a small living room and kitchen. I unlock the door and stride inside to see Noah, Theo, and Desmond sitting on the living room couch playing FIFA. Someone pauses the game, and they all whip their heads at me with amused expressions.

"Finally, you're home!" Theo says, jumping up.

"Sorry, *Dad*." I chuckle at his bizarre as fuck greeting. "Did I miss curfew?"

"Did you *propose* to someone today?" Noah asks, with a humorous shocked expression. *I knew this was going to get around.*

"Where'd you hear that?" I ask coyly, throwing my backpack on the floor by my bedroom door.

"That's irrelevant." Noah waves me off. "Did you get a girl knocked up? Is that what this is about? I need to know if I'm going to lose my prodigy to fatherhood." Noah folds his arms over his chest like a disappointed dad.

"What?" I scoff. "No. Jesus, you guys are ridiculous."

"So...?" Desmond presses as they stare at me expectantly. "Why were you on your knees in the middle of Crystal Coffee? Rumor has it you're engaged and getting married next month."

I fold my arms over my chest. "I was asking a girl to tutor me."

"On your knees?" Noah says with raised eyebrows.

"Desperate times." I shrug, and the three of them fold over laughing, unable to control themselves anymore.

"Whatever, assholes." I stride towards my room. "I'm gonna change so we can leave for practice."

"I don't know, Elijah," Theo says between fits of laughter. "I might make you get on your knees and beg me to walk with you." He kneels down and clutches his hands together exaggeratedly. "Please, Theo. Please walk me to practice."

"You guys are the worst."

Those guys are the best.

9
SOPHIA

I've just finished editing the photos for tomorrow's photography class when my phone dings, interrupting my "get shit done" playlist. I pick it up to see my new contact name for Elijah on the screen.

HONEY BEE

> HONEY BEE
> Hey there basic bitch

> ME
> The only basic bitch in this chat is you 🐝

> HONEY BEE
> Getting prepped and ready for our study date tomorrow?

I force myself to count to one hundred before I reply—all part of my "don't get attached" plan.

> ME
> It's not a study date

HONEY BEE

Sorry, our date you're interrupting with studying

One... two... three... *fuck it.*

ME

Elijah. You have to promise to keep things professional or I'm not coming

HONEY BEE

Damn, you're feisty. Fine, I'll keep things above the belt

The lower half of my body is praying he doesn't, and fuck her for not listening to who's in charge.

ME

Promise?

HONEY BEE

Cross my heart

What the hell have you gotten yourself into, Sophia?

I've had two espressos this morning, went for a five-mile run, and now I'm sitting on a bench by the library with my knee bouncing so fast my leg might vibrate right off my body.

Talking to Elijah last night was fun and exhilarating. Something I haven't felt in a long time. But for some reason, I'm constantly busting his balls and pulling away, terrified of what it'll do to me if I get close to another person, just to find out they aren't who I thought they were.

"Hey there, Sunflower," Elijah's velvety voice says, pulling me out of my thoughts.

I glance up to see him wearing CBU football sweatpants and a matching T-shirt that clings to his muscular chest, with his black Nike backpack slung over his broad shoulders. He has a bit of scruff on his jaw, and I'm considering how it'd feel sliding up my thighs while he shows me—*fuck*—*stop it, Sophia.*

Elijah's the epitome of relaxed, and I'm the poster child for anxiety. He's the Blue Caterpillar smoking a hookah, and I'm the Mad fucking Hatter.

"Hey." I stand, readjusting my bag over my shoulder as he approaches.

"Ready for this?"

"Yep," I respond, popping the "p" like a loser.

We walk through the library, and it's impossible to ignore his proximity as his intoxicating cologne surrounds me—the same scent from the night we met. The back of his hand brushes mine. An innocent gesture that has me struggling for air.

"This fine?" Elijah gestures to a quiet spot on the second floor near a window. The table has two seats across from one another.

Good, I need the distance.

"Sure." I shrug, attempting the appearance of indifference. "Fine for me."

I put my bag on the table, and Elijah grabs the back of his chair and drags it over so he's sitting directly next to me.

"So much for the distance," I mumble to myself as I pull out my textbook, a notebook, and a pen.

"No doodling today?" Elijah asks.

"What?"

"You didn't take out your doodle book, and you always have it with you. Even in class I see you scribbling in it during lectures. But somehow you still aced his test."

He noticed?

"Oh, no. Didn't bring it with me today," I reply, shuffling the shit around in my bag so he can't see I'm a big fat fucking liar.

"Still won't let me take a peek, huh?" His knowing eyes tells me he does, in fact, know I'm full of shiitake.

"Why do you want to see so bad?"

"Just curious what's going on in that beautiful head of yours."

I raise my eyebrows at him to say, *Remember the rules?*, but my cheeks betray me and flush with heat at the compliment.

"Elijah, we talked about this. You promised to keep things professional," I say in my most convincing tone.

"Just pointing out facts. No need to go all sexy librarian on me, Sunflower."

"Mm-hmm." I narrow my eyes and attempt to subtly clench my thighs at him calling me sexy, but I'm pretty sure it just looks like I have to go to the bathroom. "Well, are you ready to learn about the pharaohs?" I open my arms, dancing like an ancient Egyptian.

"*Ugh,*" he groans, lips quirking upwards. "Fine."

Two hours and a shitty cup of coffee later, Elijah seems to have gotten a good enough grasp on the subject to break for the day. "Alright, I think we can call it for now."

"Time of death?" Elijah asks.

I check my invisible watch. "Feed Sophia o'clock."

"Oh, thank God. Your stomach finally reminded you it's way past lunchtime?" He flashes a dimple popping smile.

"Maybe." I stifle my own grin as whale noises erupt from my empty belly.

Elijah chuckles and places his wide palm on my stomach. "Aw, it's okay, girl. Daddy's here. I'll feed you now."

"Elijah." I giggle, swatting his hand away. "Don't you ever say that again."

"Sorry, Mommy." He pouts. "So where am I taking you and your belly baby today?"

"I've been taking birth control for years, so no lil' sunflowers in this field." I point at my stomach, and Elijah laughs.

"Okay, well there's a place on campus, Burgers and Brews, that has the best burgers in Crystal Bay."

"Oh, absolutely yes. I pick that."

"Alright, Sunflower. Your belly, your choice."

"Ohhmuhgawd, it's so good," I moan after taking a bite of the most delicious BBQ bacon cheeseburger I've tasted in my entire life—and I've tasted a lot of them. *I'm a bit of a burger-isseur.*

Elijah chews his boring ass cheeseburger, smiling at me, his dimples totally kissable.

"Why the hell are you grinning at me like you just walked into the Playboy Mansion?" Blinking is his only response as his eyes dance with amusement. "Do I have something on my face?" I reach for a napkin and pat my mouth.

"Nope," he says between bites.

"Then why are you looking at me like I have 'loser' written on my face?" I place my pointer finger and thumb in the shape of an "L" on my forehead. *Cue "All Star" by Smash Mouth back track.*

"Would you prefer I sat here scowling?" He attempts to contort his face into a frown, but he's just pouting with the corners of his mouth upturned, the dimples a dead giveaway at his amusement.

"Please, stop." I laugh, almost choking on a french fry. "You're going to pull a face muscle." His false grimace turns immediately back to a toothed smile. "So... are you excited for the game next week?"

"Honestly?" He cracks his knuckles, which I've already come to learn is one of his anxious habits. "I'm kind of nervous."

"The great Elijah Anderson is afraid of a little football game?" He sticks his tongue out at me, and I'm suddenly wondering where else I'd like it to—

"Not scared," he says, interrupting my self-sabotaging thoughts. *"Nervous.* Mark and my brother are coming."

"That's great," I say cheerfully as he cracks another knuckle. "Isn't it?"

"Yes, of course. They've just never seen me play. And I wanna make them proud, you know?"

"You will," I assure him.

"Yeah, if I get off the bench," he grumbles.

My phone buzzes against the table, and I check the caller ID. *Mom.* I roll my eyes, decline the call, and flip it over so I don't have to see the screen anymore.

I gnaw on my lower lip. "What about your mom?"

"What about her?" Elijah asks with curious eyes.

"Is she coming to the game?"

"No, she can't come." He frowns, pushing his burger away. "She has a lot on her plate right now, and I totally understand. I just miss her... you know?"

Not really...

"I'm sorry, Honey Bee." In a moment of weakness, I place my hand on his. He flips his upward, holding mine in his large, rough grasp.

"Thanks." He smiles softly while his finger draws rings of fire in the center of my palm.

Sophia, pull that hand away, are you crazy? We are entering falling off the wagon territory.

A large hand claps Elijah on the shoulder, causing me to jump and yank mine away. "Hey, Anderson."

"Hey," Elijah says, looking up at him.

Are they printing off *GQ* models at the Amazon warehouse or something? Because *woof.*

This is one of the hottest guys I've ever seen.

Aside from...

"Is this the infamous woman who dropped our boy to his knees?" he asks as his soft green eyes scan over my body, sending a welcome shiver down my spine.

"It *is*," Elijah responds proudly.

"I'm Sophia." I offer my hand. "Elijah's *tutor*."

"Oh, trust me. I know exactly who you are." He smirks at Elijah before taking my extended hand. *Weird...* "I'm Noah." I find it hard to contain my flustered expression as I stare at a face that screams *sit on me*. Apparently, I've forgotten how to act around someone attractive.

"Don't get any ideas, Sunflower. He's a *dumb jock* too." Elijah folds his arms over his chest.

Busted.

"I'm not allowed to introduce myself to your friends without you assuming I want to sleep with them?" I ask, mirroring his position. His gaze flicks down momentarily, then slowly climbs back to mine. "Besides—I bet he knows what to do with his hands." My lip quirks upwards, and Elijah's jaw ticks.

"If any dumb jock's hands are going to be on you, they're gonna be mine," he says firmly while pointing at his muscular chest, and a flood of heat rushes south.

"Way to be a cock block," I grumble, unable to suppress the amusement on my face as Elijah stares at me with his jaw clenched.

"Sophia's gonna give you a run for your money, isn't she?" Noah asks Elijah, running a hand through his perfectly tousled brown hair.

"I'm counting on it." Elijah's gaze locks on mine.

"Alright, well, I'll let you guys get back to whatever"—Noah waves a hand between us—"this is. Don't eat too much shit before practice."

"Sir, yes sir." Elijah puts a french fry in his mouth and winks at me.

Noah chuckles and rolls his eyes before walking his perfectly conditioned ass to a table with a few guys who, I now realize, are staring right at us with dopey grins on their faces. Also... all disgustingly gorgeous. I assume they're teammates of Elijah's too. It appears CBU's recruitment criteria demands attractiveness.

Elijah snaps his fingers in front of my face, and I turn my attention from Noah's ass back to him. "You got a little drool there." He reaches across the table and drags the pad of his thumb slowly along my bottom lip. All of the oxygen leaves the restaurant, and the smirk on his face says he feels it too. I clench my thighs together at the contact, but he thankfully removes his finger.

When did the simple touch of a thumb become so fucking sexy?

Probably because it's attached to the walking depiction of Apollo.

"Well, he sure loves giving you shit," I say in an attempt to curb my non-friend-zone thoughts.

"*Almost* as much as someone else I know."

10
ELIJAH

Seventy thousand screaming students and parents alike pack CBU's stadium to the brim. We're three quarters in, and I've ridden the bench the entire forty-five minutes of playing time. Déjà vu from the past few games we've had. As if Noah could get any better, he just beat his personal record and threw a sixty-three-yard touchdown. I'm thankful to be on a winning team with an extraordinary player, but damn, he's a tough act to follow.

We're beating the University of Michigan by fourteen points with ten minutes left on the clock when our offensive line runs back on the field. Noah calls one of our tougher plays, and the guys set up on the line of scrimmage.

"Hike!" I barely hear him yell over the roar of the crowd. Julian, our center, hikes the ball, and it lands in Noah's hands flawlessly. He runs backwards, scanning for an open man. Theo, one of our running backs, flies down the field at record speed without a defender in sight.

"Throw it to Theo!" we all yell from the sidelines, but it's no use, the stadium is too loud.

A defensive man from Michigan sneaks through and heads straight for Noah. *Where the fuck are his guards?*

Noah is tackled to the ground, causing us to lose five yards. *Damn it.*

The clock rolls as Noah and the other player get up. Noah looks at his wrist, rotating it. *That's not a good sign.* Coach Porter calls a timeout, stopping the clock. Noah runs over to Coach on the sidelines, and they both talk intently. Simultaneously, their heads snap in my direction, and a wave of electricity jolts through my body like lightning.

"Anderson!" Coach Porter shouts.

Am I imagining this?

"Elijah!" Noah yells, waving his hand at me. "Get over here!"

I grab my helmet off the bench, then pull it on my head and tighten the strap as I run towards them.

"You remember the play we did in practice yesterday?" Coach Porter asks, fixing his brown eyes on mine. "Little birdy?"

"The one where I don't get tackled and bomb it as far as possible towards the end zone? Yeah, I remember."

"Good, run that." Coach Porter slaps me on the helmet and nudges me toward the field. "Now get out there."

I run towards the guys huddled near the line of scrimmage. We have thirty-five seconds to get the ball hiked.

"Alright, boys," I shout over the stadium crowd as they welcome me into the huddle. "Little birdy is flying the coop. You ready, Theo?"

"Sure am." He holds up both arms, pretending to kiss his biceps with his helmet.

"You too, Des?" I ask.

"Good to go," he says.

"Alright, break." I clap my hands together, and the boys line up thirty yards from the end zone as I get in position behind Julian.

Nine seconds to hike the ball.

I take a deep breath to tune out the rumbling from the screaming fans as I make sure the boys are all ready.

"Hike!" I yell as loud as my lungs will allow.

Julian launches the ball between his legs, and it flies through the air, landing perfectly in my hands.

I backpedal a few steps, taking in every chaotic movement on the field, then zero in on my running backs. Theo and Desmond are both running fast, but Theo's ahead. I cock my arm back and launch the ball towards the right side of the end zone, where Theo is just a few small strides away. It spirals beautifully through the air, and there's nothing I can do now but stand and watch. Theo turns his head just as the ball reaches him and catches it effortlessly in his hands.

"Touchdownnnnn, Stingraysssss!" the announcer shouts through the loudspeaker. The stadium erupts, and I can't hear anything else. My teammates split and run to either Theo or me.

"Damn!" Julian yells. "Atta boy!"

We celebrate the touchdown for a few more seconds as we run off the field so special teams can set up for the extra point.

"Nice job, kid," Coach Porter says when I reach the sidelines.

"Thanks." I beam, unable to wipe the shit-eating grin off my face.

"Dude!" Theo runs up to me, and we jump and bump hips. Our little tradition. "More titties!"

"More touchdowns!" I grab the bar of his helmet and tap our heads together. "Good job, T."

"Good job, E," he says, grinning as he removes his helmet for some air.

Michigan makes another touchdown, but we still hold our own the last eight minutes and score a win.

We finally have our reprieve to the locker room, and I take the world's quickest shower, eager to see Mark and my brother. After exiting the stadium, I find them standing by the Stingray statue where we agreed to meet. I jog up to them with an ear to ear smile I can't seem to wipe off. "Hey, guys."

Mark's face lights up the second he sees me. "Elijah." He laughs and pulls me in for a tight hug. I'm surprised at how comfortable I am with the contact. "Great job, son," he says, and my shoulders tense. *I don't think I'm quite ready for that...*

"Good job, man," my brother says, pulling me away for a hug of his own. "That game was amazing!"

"Thanks."

"You boys want to get something to eat?" Mark asks.

"Always." I rub my stomach exaggeratedly.

"Any recommendations from the big man on campus?" my brother asks, clapping me on the shoulder.

"There's a burger place I go to a lot. That good for y'all?"

Mark throws his arm around my shoulder. "Sounds like a plan."

11
SOPHIA

Today was a blast cheering on the team with Dad, his *girlfriend*, Diane, and Leah. I wish Jake could have been with us, but he's back in Amsterdam for his soccer… "football" season.

The four of us are sitting at Burgers and Brews, waiting for our order, and I've never been more excited for food in my life. I've barely eaten all day and used all my energy screaming at the game.

I didn't know Elijah's jersey number, but when someone ran on the field after our starting quarterback, Noah—the sit-on-my-face guy—got hurt, I could tell it was him instantly. The way he commanded the attention of his team. How they all fell into a rhythm immediately.

Is he still a cocky jock if he has the skills to back it up?

"So how are you liking your classes?" Diane asks, giving me her full attention.

"I really like them… Actually, in my world history class, we had our first test, and basically the entire class failed." I put my hands flat under my chin and smile sweetly. "Except for me. And my photography professor said I have a lot of potential, and she's excited to see how I grow this semester."

"Wow, that's great, Soph," Leah says, giving me a high five—my number one fan.

Elijah walks through the entrance, and the moment his eyes connect with mine, a heart-stopping smile spreads across his face.

"Hey, Soph," he says, striding up next to me at the table. An older man and a guy that looks equally hot but about ten years older are standing behind him.

"Hey." I beam up at him. "Great game today."

"Thanks," he responds with a grin, a bit of pink tinging his cheeks as he places his palm between my shoulder blades. It's a friendly gesture, but the look my dad gives Elijah makes me want to call an ambulance.

Someone get this man a laxative because he looks constipated as fuck.

"Hi, sir." Elijah removes his hand and offers it to Dad. "I'm assuming you're Mr. Summers? I'm Elijah."

Dad looks at Elijah's hand briefly, then returns the gesture. "Call me Will," he replies, with a tight-lipped smile.

"Pleasure to meet you. Oh…" Elijah says, turning towards the two men standing behind him. "This is my, uh—Mark, and my brother, Cole."

Why does that name sound familiar…

"Nice to see you, Will," Mark clips.

What the…?

"Mark," Dad replies, his jaw tight.

"You guys know each other?" Elijah asks, obviously not seeing the enormous elephant in the room.

"Leah." Cole nods in her direction, smiling smugly.

"Cole," she says, with narrowed eyes and a sarcastic smile.

What in the ever-loving hell is happening?

"Alright…" Elijah says, eyes bouncing between our weird as fuck families. "Well, we're gonna go eat now." He points a thumb over his shoulder. "Nice to meet y'all." He waves at my family. "See you Monday, Sunflower."

They walk off and when I turn back to the table, six eyes bore into my soul so hard I flinch.

"Can't believe you guys all know each other." I laugh nervously. "Small world, right?"

"Do you know who that was?" Leah asks with an amused grin.

"Should I?" My eyes bounce between them, connecting with Diane's, and she looks as confused as I am.

"Mark and Cole *Danvers*," she replies, her eyes widening briefly.

No fucking way.

"Cole Danvers?" I mutter to myself as the perplexing puzzle pieces fall into place. "The one who arrested Jake?" I whisper-shout to the table.

"The one and only," Dad says.

"So... Mark is the dickhead chief?"

"Yep," Dad says, blowing out a breath and shaking his head.

"Wow, a lot of stuff makes sense now," I mumble to myself, wishing the ground would open up and swallow me fucking whole at the revelation.

"Is that your boyfriend?" Dad asks with eyes so fiery they could burn a hole right through me.

"No! We're just friends," I assure everyone, and Dad relaxes immediately. "I'm tutoring him."

Of course the one guy I befriend is the son of the only man on the planet my dad hates.

Lucky me.

"Mm-hmm." Leah cocks a brow at me, and I widen my eyes at her.

The waiter thankfully chooses that moment to walk up with our food, placing the dishes in front of us.

An hour later, we stand outside the three-story garage where Dad parked his truck.

"I'll call you tomorrow, okay, Bear?" Dad says, throwing his arm around me.

"Alright, love you, Papa Bear." I give him a hug and kiss on the cheek. "Bye, Diane." I hug her, and she embraces me tightly.

"Bye, sweetie." Diane pats my back.

Leah and I wave as they turn and disappear into the parking garage.

"Wanna get a coffee before I hit the road?" Leah asks.

"Are koalas susceptible to chlamydia?" I ask, and she stares at me blankly as the corner of her mouth twitches upwards. "Yes… yes, they are. And koala chlamydia is a very serious disease."

"Okay, weirdo." She chuckles, rolling her eyes. "Let's go."

"Do you want to go to Starbucks or Crystal Coffee?"

"Whichever one's closer."

We stroll along the sidewalk to the campus Starbucks. "That was awkward earlier, huh? With Elijah and his family…"

"It was fine," she says in her fake polite flight attendant voice.

"Leah." I grab her arm and pull her over to sit on a bench. "Come on, level with me here. That was more awkward than a giraffe on roller skates."

"Fine." She lets out a sigh of defeat. "It was a *bit* awkward."

"I mean, I know Cole arrested Jake, but what does that have to do with Elijah?"

"Absolutely nothing," she says, brushing some hair behind my ear and smiling tenderly. "I know Will was a little weird, but he's just protective. And sometimes people just don't like one another…" Dad's reaction during our conversation in the car comes to mind. "But you're right, Elijah isn't Cole, and he isn't Mark."

"Okay…" I sink further into the bench.

"But Jake probably won't be happy about your new *friend* either…" she says, flattening her lips. I know better than to suggest she doesn't tell him. We all tell each other everything.

No secrets, no lies. That's the only rule between us.

If only they knew the secret I've been keeping.

The thought alone has a trapped lion clawing at my insides, attempting its escape.

I swallow, the animal remaining securely in its cage.

"We're *just* friends," I say, trying to convince the both of us.

"Mm-hmm." A wide, knowing grin spreads across her face. "He's the mystery guy from the springs, isn't he?"

I throw my face into my hands, grumbling against my palms, "Maybe."

"I knew it!" She laughs while poking me with her finger. "Why have you been so against the idea of him? You still missing Seth?"

"God, no." I shift uncomfortably, considering sharing words I never thought I'd willingly repeat out loud.

My gaze wanders down the sidewalk, noticing the temptation himself heading in our direction. *Looks like the universe wants me to leave my demons in the past and focus on the present.*

"Hey, Soph," Elijah says with an oxygen-stealing smile as Leah nudges my shoulder. "Hi, Leah."

"Hey," we chime in unison, standing up.

"I actually have to get going," Leah says, pointing behind her shoulder at nothing.

"No, you don't," I say with wide eyes. "You said you had time for coffee."

"Sor—" She cuts herself off with an exaggerated yawn, throwing a hand over her mouth. "*Ooo*, sorry, the jet lag just hit me."

"Mm-hmm." I squint at her, hoping she gets my telepathic message–*you're full of shit.*

"Love you, Ladybug." She leans in, kisses my cheek, and whispers, "Call me later. Full report." Then she waves at Elijah before turning and walking off to who knows where.

"I can take you to get that coffee," Elijah says with baby blue eyes I couldn't say no to if I tried.

"Only if you promise not to order a basic bitch drink," I say sternly, my mouth quirking on one side, giving me away.

"Sorry, I don't make promises I can't keep."

What's the worst that could happen?

I open my mouth to protest, but his hopeful expression has me caving faster than a shopaholic at the mall on Black Friday. "Fine. I'll allow it."

Elijah straightens his shoulders, looking pleased with himself as we make our way to the coffee shop. "So Leah calls you Ladybug too?"

"Yeah." The corners of my mouth tip up as my thumb rubs against my pinky. "We all had our own bug nicknames. Chloe was Lovebug, Leah was Scaredybug, and I was Ladybug."

A gentle smile spreads across his face. "Adorable."

"That's why I got this tattoo," I say, holding up my right pinky. He takes my hand, looking down at the scripted "Lovebug" tattoo on the inside of my finger. "For Chlo."

"That's really sweet," he says, tracing the ink with his thumb.

"Thanks."

I pull my hand away, and he throws his arm around me. "Now I understand you giving me my own bug nickname."

"What?" I furrow my brows, looking up at him.

"Honey *Bee*?"

An amused laugh escapes my lips as I shake my head. "That is *not* the same."

"You initiated me into your bug gang." He squeezes my shoulder. "I'm honored."

"Fine." I roll my eyes, leaning into his touch. "Welcome to the bug gang, Honey Bee."

"Think you've got Hammurabi's Code handled?" I ask Elijah as textbooks cover every inch of our table at Burgers and Brews.

"If anyone bring an accusation of any crime before the elders," Elijah says, holding a finger in the air and speaking in a fancy British accent, "and does not prove what he has charged, he shall, if it be a capital offense charged, be put to death."

I rearrange my hair to one side, clearing my throat. "Excellent, Mr. Anderson. A-plus."

"Sweet! Can I finally order my burger now?" I told him he couldn't eat until we finished fifty flash cards for tomorrow's quiz, and it was an excellent motivator. He juts out a pouty lip, batting his puppy dog eyes at me. "Please, Ms. Summers?"

I roll my eyes, smirking at his dramatics. "Yes, you may order your burger." I slide over a menu, which he snatches up quicker than a fumbled football.

My phone buzzes against the table, and Jake's face lights up the screen. I've been expecting his call since the fifty shades of awkward family meet and greet.

There's no doubt in my mind Leah told him who my study buddy is.

"Go ahead." Elijah gestures toward my phone, so I answer the call.

"*Hellooo*, J," I say exaggeratedly.

"Hey, Bug… You got a second to talk?"

"Yeah, sure." I glance up at Elijah, who's doing a shit job of pretending he's not paying attention to me. *Be right back,* I mouth at him before sliding quickly out of the booth to make my way out to the sunshine.

A heavy exhale comes through the line, and I feel like I'm about to be chastised by Dad for breaking curfew. "You're friends with a *Danvers*?" As much as he tries to remain calm, the frustration in his voice is obvious. "Seriously?"

"He's not even technically a Danvers," I clarify in an annoyed tone.

"Okay, but he's *technically* Cole Danvers's younger brother," Jake argues, his words laced with venom.

"Okay? And?"

Elijah watches me through the window with furrowed brows. He mouths, *Are you okay?* at me and I nod, forcing a smile with a dorky thumbs-up.

"And? Sophia, I'm your older brother. I'm trying to protect you." His tone turns more sincere, and I take a deep, unsteady breath. An angry Jake I can ignore. A concerned Jake? That's a different story. "Cole is bad news and if his brother is anything like him… then, you know…"

"They barely even know each other… and besides, I'll be friends with whoever I want," I say firmly as my irritation grows. "Please, stop treating me like a child."

I glance in the window and see Elijah's curious eyes locked on me.

"I'm sorry, Soph, I'm really not trying to upset you." He lets out a frustrated breath. "Fuck… this didn't come out right. I just know his family, and I really don't think you should surround yourself with that type of negative influence. Okay?"

"You're entitled to your opinion, Jacob."

"Don't use my name like that. You only call me that when you're mad at me or want to annoy me."

"Your point, *Jacob*?" My lips unconsciously curve upwards. I know it drives him crazy.

"Sophia Elysabeth Summers, don't make me come over there," he says in his best Dad impersonation.

"Stop." I attempt to maintain my composure, but a laugh still bubbles out of me. "I'm still annoyed at you."

"And I still love you, Bug."

I exhale heavily and roll my eyes. "Love you too, Jakey."

"Rain or shine?"

"Yeah… Rain or shine."

I stare up at the blue sky and curse it for the only black cloud being directly over my head.

12

ELIJAH

Professor Mintz has been droning on about the Babylonian Empire for what feels like centuries, and I'm counting down the seconds till class is over.

I keep glancing at Sophia, whose attention is focused solely on our teacher. Not sure why because this lesson has been boring as shit, and she hasn't met my gaze once, which is *not* like her. Typically, she catches me looking, fights a smile, then pretends she can't feel my eyes on her while she squirms in her seat.

It's my favorite part about coming to this class.

"Alright, see you guys Thursday," Professor Mintz announces, and I quickly gather my stuff, throwing my backpack over my shoulder. I turn around to make my way toward Sophia, but she's already gone.

Damn, speedy little thing.

I rush out of the classroom but don't see her anywhere, so I pull out my phone and text her.

SUNFLOWER

ME

You shot outta class like a racehorse today, you good?

SUNFLOWER

Cool as a cucumber 🥒

ME

Any plans later?

I go to the stadium, endure a grueling practice, shower, go home, make dinner, and *still* no response.

What the hell's going on with her?

A full twenty-four hours goes by, and Sophia still hasn't texted me back. I get into bed after another long ass day, then scroll through our chat to see if there's anything I could've done to upset her. Everything seemed fine Monday, although she got a little weird after her brother called, but I'm not sure what that would have to do with me.

After staring at the ceiling for what feels like hours, unable to fall asleep, I decide to text her again.

ME

Thanks to Monday's study session I think I've got tomorrow's quiz in the bag

I guess your use of food as a motivator was pretty effective

Worry gnaws at my chest like a vulture on roadkill. If I knew where her dorm was, I'd show up right now, but I'm afraid it would look a little stalkerish to show up at ten at night for no damn reason.

I do the only other thing I can think of and scroll through my contacts, tapping call.

"Hey, it's Dean. I can't get to the phone right now. Leave me a message... or don't, but I do love me a good voicemail. Have a blessed day!"

"I'm real tired of gettin' your voicemail, Dino." I blow a raspberry between my lips. "It's been a shit week... Starting to think my sunflower's seriously ticked at me... just can't figure out why. If you've got any advice for figuring out a woman, drop it my way... Alright, well, it's pretty late, so guess I'll try to hit the hay. Love ya."

Walking into class the next day, my eyes immediately gravitate to Sophia's empty seat. A tight feeling settles in my chest as I sit down, unpacking my stuff. My eyes are heavy, and even the basic bitch latte I picked up on the way to class isn't cutting it. Professor Mintz hands out the quiz, and I peer over to find Sophia sitting there, not even bothering to glance in my direction.

Unsurprisingly, by the time I hand in my quiz, she's already gone. I pull out my phone in another last-ditch effort to get her to respond.

ME

How'd you feel about the quiz?

A shit practice, one more sleepless night later, and I still haven't heard from her. I am going absolutely mad, and every fiber of my body is cursing myself, wondering how the hell I got so pussy whipped without even getting any. Clenching my phone in my hand, I go for the direct route, hoping she won't avoid me calling her out.

ME

Damn, you're turning me into a guy that quadruple texts, we good Sunflower?

SUNFLOWER

Sorry, been busy

ME

Same, wanna study tonight?

SUNFLOWER

Sorry, can't. Rain check?

ME

Sure

Rain check. What a load of horseshit. Shoving my phone in my pocket, I try to ignore the kettlebell crushing my chest.

She's avoiding me.

But why?

Two more days have passed of me feeling like a lovesick idiot. Even the three-hour-long training session, followed by an hour of film Coach just made us endure on a fucking Sunday, hasn't distracted me.

My body aches as I walk home from the stadium, and I'm starting to think Desmond might be on to something with his whole yoga every day bullshit. A flash of blonde catches my attention on the other side of the street, and I snap my head toward it to see Sophia power walking down the sidewalk.

"Soph," I call out, but she doesn't react. "Sophia!" She continues pretending I don't exist as I run across the street. I stop in front of her, and she glances up with puffy, red-rimmed eyes and flushed cheeks.

"Elijah, I'm busy," she mumbles, her voice cracking.

"What's going on?" I ask, holding her distraught face in my hands. "What's wrong?"

"I really don't have time for this." She steps away, and my hands drop to my sides.

"Please. I hate seeing you like this." My mind spins in confusion as I take in her broken appearance. A mismatched and oversized sweatsuit hangs on her small frame instead of her usual graphic tees and denim shorts. Her hair is disheveled and unbrushed—under eyes dark like she hasn't slept all night. That paired with the puffiness of them has my pulse pounding. "I'm worried about you. You've been ignoring me all week, and now I find you like this. And you... you don't seem okay."

"I'm not *fucking* okay, Elijah." Tears stream down her cheeks, but she quickly wipes them away. "I'm freaking out."

"How can I help?" I ask softly as my stomach churns with worry.

"I don't need your help," she snaps.

"Really, I don't mind—"

"I can figure this out on my own." She shakes her head, and I think back to the first time we met and her admission that being vulnerable isn't a strength of hers. The whiskey loosened her lips, but now she's stone cold sober, locking her feelings up tighter than a bull rider's grip.

"Sophia... It's okay to ask for help sometimes. You don't have to figure out everything on your own. Let me help you."

Her pained eyes connect with mine. "I don't think you can."

"Try me."

She finally lets out a sigh of defeat. "I-I lost—Oh my God, this will probably sound so stupid to you."

"Sophia, I promise whatever it is, if it has you this upset, it can't be stupid." The urge to reach out and hold her is overwhelming. "Can I hug you?" I open my arms and watch as war wages behind her emerald eyes. About what? I have no clue.

She falls flush against me, snaking her arms around my waist. I rub my hand along her back as her rib cage expands and contracts in my embrace.

"Whenever you're ready." My fingers idly comb her golden blonde hair.

"I lost my sketchbook," she mumbles into my chest.

"I'm sorry." I squeeze her gently. "Want me to take you to get a new one?" She hiccups against my chest, and her breathing becomes sporadic. "Soph?"

"You don't understand," she whimpers quietly.

"Explain it to me?" I ask gently, desperate to determine the source of her sadness.

"I... It's just..." Tears trickle down her cheeks.

"Breathe, Soph," I instruct, taking her face between my hands and angling it towards mine. I make an exaggerated breathing motion, and she holds my eye contact, following my lead.

In.

Out.

In.

Out.

"It's not just a doodle journal," she admits between breaths.

"I gathered that when you wouldn't let me peek," I tease while rubbing my thumbs under her eyes to brush away stray tears.

She burrows her face against my chest, and I wrap my arms around her. My chin rests on her head, and I'm enveloped by the scent of coconut and something fruity.

"Well... you know how I told you my sister died?"

"Yes."

"It's my way of... kind of... You're going to think I'm crazy." She shakes her head, and I pull away just enough to look into her beautiful green eyes.

"Sophia, I won't think you're dramatic or crazy or whatever else is going on in that pretty little head of yours. I promise. Just tell me."

"It's how I deal with my grief... I *draw* her." She smiles weakly as the tears start to dry. "I draw her whenever I miss her... which is still a lot. Today I went to draw in it because it's—because she—" Her misty eyes darken with pain before she falls back against me, choking on a sob. "I can't believe I still cry like this after all this time," she says after collecting herself again. "Today it's been nine years..."

Oh.

"I'm so sorry."

"Every year, on the anniversary of her death, I draw her a little older. Imagine how her features would have matured if she was still around. You know?" I drag my fingers through her hair, untangling a lock of it. "Sketching makes me feel like I still know her even though it's been so long... I don't know, it's silly."

"Stop doing that." I rub my hands along her shoulders and up her neck, then angle her face to mine. "It's okay to miss her. It's okay to draw her every damn day if you want to. That's *your* grief process. It's unique, and it's beautiful."

One corner of her mouth pulls up before she returns to her rightful place on my chest.

"I think I feel better now... Thank you."

I have a strong feeling that isn't why she's been avoiding me all week, but this definitely doesn't feel like the right time to ask about it.

"Always," I mumble into her hair. "Seriously. You need me, I'm there. Okay?"

Another sigh as her body melts against mine. "You got it, dude."

"Atta girl." I chuckle, feeling her smile as she holds tighter. "Okay, time to find your sketchbook. Where's the last place you had it?"

"I drew during world history this week, but I already checked there... I'm on my way to my English classroom now."

"I'll help you search."

"Elijah, I appreciate the gesture... but it could be anywhere. This campus is huge, and I have no clue where I left it."

"Go back to your dorm, look through your room, and I'll check your classrooms, okay?"

"I already looked in my room," she says, staring at me as if I'm the village idiot. Then again, I did pinky swear to be *just friends* with her, so maybe I am.

"Just check again, okay?"

She studies my expression. "Why are you helping me?"

"Sophia..." I push a golden lock behind her ear. "You've already brought me to my knees. Do you really need to ask?"

Her lips turn upwards, and the corners by her captivating eyes crinkle. "Okay... thank you."

"I'll text you in a bit." I pull her in for another hug, kissing the top of her head like a reflex, and she squeezes me a little tighter.

"Okay, see you." She pulls out of my grasp, turning to walk away. A few seconds later, my phone buzzes, and when I check it, a picture of her sketchbook fills the screen. *Time to find this bitch.*

BIG STING ENERGY

ME

Hey, I need a favor

THEO SCHROEDER

Got your dick stuck in some poor girl again?

ME

It's not my fault she had a piercing I was unaware of

And we agreed never to speak about that again.

JULIAN LISCERO

YOU said we weren't allowed to talk about it. We politely declined

NOAH CARUSO

We are never NOT talking about that.

THEO SCHROEDER

I've earned my right to talk about it

DESMOND BALL

Yeah, that's definitely staying in rotation

ME

Alright, we'll circle back to that

But I'm gonna have to call immunity necklace on this one

Immunity necklace. The one trump card we have in our group. When you call it, no one can judge whatever ridiculous shit comes out of your mouth next.

NOAH CARUSO

Fine, immunity necklace. What's up?

ME

My friend lost a notebook and I'm helping look for it but her classes are all over campus.

It'll take forever if I do it by myself

THEO SCHROEDER

Are you talking about your hot tutor who inhaled that burger in five seconds flat?

That was sexy as fuck. I've never seen a girl look so hot eating a burger

ME

First of all, I call dibs

THEO SCHROEDER

You can't call dibs. What is this seventh grade?

ME

Well I just did, so keep your dick in your pants. And second, I called immunity necklace, no judging. Those are the rules

DESMOND BALL

Damn dude, you're so far gone lol

JULIAN LISCERO

You are pussy *whip crack*

ME

Fuck off guys, are you helping or not?

DESMOND BALL

Fine, I'll help

THEO SCHROEDER

Okay, okay, me too

JULIAN LISCERO

If I must

NOAH CARUSO

Send it in the team chat too

ME

Thanks

I send the picture of her book in the team chat, and Noah follows it up with the reward that if someone finds it, they can skip keg fees for the rest of the semester. The guys were very enthusiastic, and now football players are all over campus searching for Sophia's sketchbook.

If it wasn't for how devastated she looked earlier, it would almost be comical.

13
SOPHIA

I throw the last pair of shorts out of my now empty dresser drawer. Unless there's a secret compartment I forgot about, the sketchbook isn't fucking here.

Karma is really out for me.

Sage strolls through my door and freezes in place. "Jesus, did you fuck a Tasmanian devil in here or what?" Her eyes widen, taking in the crime scene of my ripped apart room. I even looked through places it would never be, like my underwear drawer, which is why lace scraps and granny panties litter the floor.

"I still haven't found my sketchbook."

"Joey…" Sage approaches and turns me to face her. "Calm down, okay?"

"I can't, today is—"

She takes my face in her hands. "I know. We'll find it."

I pick up my phone and see too many texts from the absolute last person I want to hear from today.

MOM

MOM

Thinking of our Chlo today.

Hope you're doing well in your classes

Call me when you've got some time

A low groan escapes my lips. *When I've got time?*
I do *not* have time for her right now. *Or ever.*
"Elijah's helping me look, but he hasn't called yet," I tell Sage before throwing my body dramatically on the bed in a starfish position. "So I'm sure he hit a dead end... just like me."
"Hmm... interesting," she says, her tone laced with amusement.
I lift my head to peer up at her. "What?"
"On my way back from the dining hall, I saw a few groups of football players running around like they were on a damn scavenger hunt." She giggles.
"Okay... But what does that have to do with me?"
"I'm not entirely sure..." She smirks. "But I overheard one of them saying they needed to find some notebook so they could drink for free, and I didn't really think anything of it at the time... but it's making a lot more sense now."
My mind wanders to one of those guys actually finding my sketchbook.
What if they look inside it?
OH MY GOD.
What if Elijah finds it and looks inside?
I suck in a sharp breath, bolting up so fast I almost fall off the bed. "Fuck, fuck, fuckedy fuck!"
"Sophia, babe?" Sage snaps to get my attention. "You're spiraling again."
"Fuck!" I shout, pulling my knees to my chest. "Sage, I've drawn *him*... multiple times." Since I started tutoring Elijah, I get distracted

when doodling and once I snap back to reality—there he is. All brooding, with sharp jawlines, that crooked grin, and tousled hair. I drag my hands across my face. "He's going to think I'm a stalker."

Even this past week, all the time I spent *not* talking to him, I was drawing his gorgeous face. That's how I've been getting him out of my system. When I wanted to reply, I'd draw him instead. I was already feeling weird after my call with Jake. Then Tuesday morning, I woke up with a bombarding amount of texts from Seth, and it all just reminded me why I don't want to be in a relationship. They're fucking messy.

People get hurt, people hurt you, and some people don't listen no matter how much you beg.

I added distance between me and Elijah because I have no interest in a repeat of that crippling heartache just for some guy.

But over this past week, I've slowly realized Elijah isn't just *some* guy. I've barely slept in days, battling myself over responding to his messages. He's not even my boyfriend, and I've missed him so badly even my fictional boyfriends can't distract me. His gaze was burning into me during world history and at the end, I ran out like a scared little shit.

The last drawing I did was Elijah in class, smiling as he looked at something in the distance.

Fuck.

There goes my persona of indifference.

Sage gives me a knowing smile. "Okay, we'll circle back to that revelation later… But it'll turn up, take my word for it. And if Elijah is one of the good ones, which I think he might be, he won't look inside." I groan again, and she throws her arms around my shoulders. "Am I ever wrong?"

I rest my chin on my knee, turning my face to her. "No."

"And I won't be today either. Now text Loverboy and see if he's made any progress."

"Loverboy? Seriously?" I say with a choked laugh. "We're just *friends.*"

The word is spoiled milk on my tongue.

"Mm-hmm." She purses her lips and mockingly nods at me. "Friends who can't stop eye fucking each other. You know what, I have a better nickname anyway: Honey Dick."

"Sage!" I squeal, throwing the closest object I can find, which, luckily for her, is one of my stuffed koalas. She ducks out of the way, and it flies past her, knocking a water bottle off my dresser. "Never say that again." I grab my phone off my bed, pulling up my text thread with Elijah.

HONEY BEE

ME

Any luck?

HONEY BEE

Maybe, I'll let you know soon

I scoop up the lace scraps from the floor, tossing them back in my underwear drawer. My phone buzzes, and I open it to see a picture of my sketchbook next to Elijah's smiling face.

Damn if those dimples don't do something to my insides.

"Thank sweet baby Jesus!" I shout, texting him back the same phrase.

"What?" Sage asks, whipping her head around from the pile of clothes she's folding on the floor.

I stare at the picture, unable to believe my eyes. "He found it." Relief washes over me, but it's immediately replaced by paralyzing fear. "Do you think he looked?"

"Calm down, Joey. Like I said, I think he respects you more than that."

My phone buzzes again.

HONEY BEE

I'll bring it over now. What's your building and room number?

"He wants to bring it over."

"There's no way he can come here with the place looking like…" She glances around my bomb of a bedroom, and I'm picking up what she's throwing down.

"Okay, I get it. The room's a mess."

"Tell him we'll meet at his place."

"We?" I smirk.

"Yeah, *we*. I need to find out if he has any hot, single football friends."

ME

Can we come to your place?

HONEY BEE

We?

ME

Yeah, me and Sage

HONEY BEE

Oh the purple skittle, I like her

ME

OMG, you did not just call her that

HONEY BEE

Why not? It's cute. Purple skittles are my favorite

An uncomfortable feeling settles in my gut. Am I seriously jealous from the mere mention of him suggesting my best friend is cute? I maybe—definitely—eye fucked Noah at Burgers and Brews, so it's not like I have room to judge.

ME

Just send me your dorm deetz

"Okay. Let's go," I tell Sage.

"Change first, you look like a hobo." She laughs, dragging her eyes over me with a look of disapproval. I glance down at my over-sized orange sweatpants and the faded blue Longwood High hoodie I threw on before sprinting out of my room when I realized my sketch-book was missing. A gasp catches in my throat at the realization Elijah already saw me in this.

"Yeah, good call." I snap and shoot finger guns at her before changing into something less spring-break-hangover.

"312," Sage says, reading the number off the door in front of us. "This is it."

Muffled chatter from deep male voices rumbles on the other side, and I inhale deeply, hoping it brings a hearty dose of serotonin with it. I've been doing my best to set boundaries, but if Elijah sees he's been my muse, I will die on the spot. I will melt into a pile of embar-rassed shit and die.

Cosmos, Jesus, Allah, Buddha, whoever you are, please don't let him open my fucking notebook.

I hold my breath, raise my fist, and knock hard on the door. I'm about to try again when it swings open and the loud chattering drifts into the hallway. Another *GQ* model stands in front of us with a crooked grin. I think he was at Burgers and Brews with Noah the other day.

"Uh, hi," I say, shifting uncomfortably on my heels as he leans a shoulder against the door frame.

"Hi." He smiles at the two of us while running a hand through his short dirty blonde hair.

"Does—uh, Elijah live here?"

He flashes a grin as his bluish-green eyes flick between Sage and me. "Who wants to know?"

"Cut the shit, gorgeous," Sage says, and I stifle a laugh. "Is the honey dick here or not?"

He narrows his eyes at her and bites his lower lip before turning his head. "E!" he shouts, looking behind him. "Your fiancée's here!"

Sage bumps me with her shoulder and waggles her eyebrows.

"His what? I'm not—"

"Hey there, Sunflower." Elijah comes into view, sporting the world's most breathtaking smile.

I flatten my lips to suppress the huge grin on my face from his infectious expression. "Hey."

"Hi, Purple Skittle," Elijah says, turning his attention towards her.

"Honey Dick." She smirks back at him.

"Sage!" I whisper-shout at her, and I didn't think it was possible, but Elijah's smile grows as his eyes flick to mine, full of amusement. He opens the door wider and gestures for us to come inside.

A dozen massive guys crowd the small living room, watching a football game. Elijah clicks the front door shut, and twelve sets of eyes flick in our direction so obviously it's almost comical.

"Guys, this is Sophia and Sage," Elijah says, gesturing toward us. "Girls, this is Theo, my roommate." He points at the smartass who opened the door. "And these… are the guys."

"Hi, guys," Sage says with her flirtiest smile—I would know, I've seen them all.

"Hey." I wave awkwardly.

"*Wowww*, we don't even have names?" Noah says, folding his muscular arms tightly over his chest. "We're all just *the guys*?"

Elijah rolls his eyes, turning his attention to me, and grabs my hand. "Come on." My body is soaked with gasoline, and his single touch ignites me. "I have something for you."

"Are you coming?" I ask Sage.

"I'll be fine here," she replies as Elijah tugs me away, leaving a burn trail towards his bedroom.

Once inside, he shuts the door behind us, presumably to give us some privacy from the Super Bowl party happening in his living room. I glance around, and my eyes snag on my sketchbook sitting atop his perfectly made full-sized bed.

"I can't believe you found it!" I snatch up the sketchbook and flip quickly through the pages, then hug it tight to my chest. A rush of relief floods through me, and I turn to sit on the edge of his bed before my knees buckle from the overwhelming feeling. "Where was it?"

Maybe karma isn't gunning for me after all.

"One of the guys found it in the library lost and found." He grins down at me as his gaze sweeps from my head to my toes.

"So it's true?" I ask once I've recovered from the laser beams.

"What?"

"You sent the football team on a scavenger hunt to find my sketchbook?"

He grins proudly, the mattress dipping as he sits next to me. "I guess you could call it that."

I shield a smile as my fingertips dance over the sketchbook in my lap. "Thank you."

"You're welcome." He turns toward me, our knees brushing in the process, and my tongue gets stuck in my throat as he places his rough, warm hand over mine. "Are you okay now?" he asks sincerely, looking so deeply into my eyes I can *feel* the concern in them. *He was worried about me.*

"Yes." I flip my palm to meet his, giving it a light squeeze. "Thank you again."

"You don't need to thank me." The corner of his mouth curves upward. "You needed me, and I'm glad you let me be there for you."

My eyes drop to our connected hands, and I struggle to breathe as I gather the courage to ask a question that terrifies me. "Did you look inside?"

"Of course not," he answers quickly, and I let out a shaky breath of relief as he looks down at me with those electric blue eyes. "If there's something you want me to see, I'm confident you'll show me yourself." He brushes a strand of hair behind my ear as I resist the urge to lean into his touch. "Is this why you were keeping to yourself last week?"

"I'm really sorry." I shake my head. "There was some... family stuff going on and... I'm sorry." The hurt in his eyes makes me feel guilty for the cold shoulder.

"It's okay." His tone is sincere as he blinks away any previous disappointment. "But next time, I'd appreciate a heads-up when you need some time for yourself." He places his palm on my neck, grazing his thumb against my throat. "I was really worried about you."

My heart swells at the admission. "I'm sorry I made you worry. I promise not to do that again."

"Good... I almost looked for your dorm like a crazy stalker."

I throw my head back, laughing, veins buzzing with nervous energy at the thought. "Damn, quadruple texting. Stalking my dorm. What have I done to you?"

A soft chuckle escapes his lips. "I think you've broken me."

I'm next...

Elijah Anderson will ruin me, and I'm going to thank him for it.

14
ELIJAH

"Bro, you're playing awful today," I tell Julian, who's currently sucking ass at Madden on the PS4.

"Sorry my thumbs aren't as magical as my dick," he grumbles, slamming all the wrong buttons.

"Okay, okay, let's stop before you hurt yourself." I laugh, and we pass the controllers to Noah and Theo. I get up and go to the fridge, pulling out a water bottle.

"Beer me," Julian says, holding out his hands, and I toss him a can.

"So what do you guys want to do tomorrow?" Noah asks as his gaze stays locked on the TV. "Last Saturday off for a while."

"It's going to be hot as shit," Julian points out, as if we aren't all painfully aware of Florida's hellscape climate. "Pool day?"

"Nah." I shake my head. "Think bigger."

"Boats and *hoessss*," Theo calls from his position on the couch.

"Sorry, sailor." Julian chuckles. "My parents are in the Bahamas for a few weeks with it. So no boat."

"Damn it," Theo groans.

"*Beach* day?" Julian suggests, cocking a brow.

"That'll do." I tip my water toward him before taking a sip.

"Alright, well, I don't want it to be a total sausage fest like last time," Theo chimes in. "Let's invite some hot dog buns."

"Dude, you're ridiculous." I release a breathy laugh, shaking my head. "Who'd you have in mind?"

"How about your girl and her cute friend?" Julian says.

"Which girl? Andi or Sophia?" Theo asks like the asshole he is.

"I haven't talked to Andi in a month." I glare at him. "And you know she's never been *my girl*. We're casual." I choose to avoid correcting that Sophia isn't actually mine either. *Yet.* I'd rather the guys think it's true so they won't make a move.

"Mm-hmm," Theo hums sarcastically.

"Okay, back to you," I say, returning my attention to Julian. "Her 'cute' friend?"

"Yeah, Sage, the one with the purple hair." He grins while nodding his head. "She has a smart little mouth I'd like to explore thoroughly."

I let out a low, amused laugh. "How would you know?"

"You can learn a lot about people during a ten-minute Uber ride," he says casually, gaining Theo and Noah's attention.

I point a finger at him. "I knew that car looked familiar! What else did you learn about the girls?"

"Nothing I'm gonna tell you," Julian replies, cracking open the beer and taking a swig.

"Come on. You'll drink my beer but won't tell me what you learned?"

"Nope, sorry," he replies firmly. "Uber driver/rider confidentiality clause."

"That is not a real fucking thing," I deadpan, and he shrugs while smiling smugly. "So why should I invite Sage if you won't tell me shit?"

His lips curl into a knowing grin. "You're gonna invite her so your little sunflower actually comes."

I roll my eyes, knowing he's right, and pull out my phone. "Ugh. Fine."

SUNFLOWER

ME

Hey 🌻, got any plans tomorrow?

SUNFLOWER

Girls day 💅 We're having a Bridgerton marathon
and eating our weight in dill pickle chips

ME

Okay, first of all, gross.

Second of all, why don't you leave your woman
cave and have a beach day?

SUNFLOWER

With you?

ME

Yeah and the guys. It's a bye week so we wanna
get some sun and fun

You can bring the girls

SUNFLOWER

Ohhh, so that's why you really need me. For
recruiting more tits to your sausage fest. 🌭

Maybe it wouldn't be so difficult for you if you
knew how to use your hands

ME

One of these days I'll show you exactly how good
I am with my hands

And tits is always a bonus... but that's not why I'm
inviting you

SUNFLOWER

I'll take your word for it... And fine, we'll come.

Will you pick us up? I hate getting sand in my car

> **ME**
>
> Sure

SUNFLOWER

I have a photoshoot on campus tomorrow but I'm done at 10

> **ME**
>
> I'll pick you up when it's done, just let me know where. Then we'll get Sage & Charlie

SUNFLOWER

Fine Arts building

> **ME**
>
> Okay. Wear green, it brings out your eyes

I pull my attention away from the phone. "Alright, the girls are in."

"Awesome," Julian says, slapping my shoulder. "Thanks."

"Yeah, yeah. You owe me one."

"Take a number," Noah shouts from the couch.

Sophia exits the Fine Arts building clad in her usual uniform of denim shorts and a cropped graphic tee that reads "Yeah Buoy" with a lighthouse on it. The green strings of her bikini top are poking out near her neck, and I smirk, pleased she listened to my request.

"Hey there, Summers," I say, grabbing her attention.

Her head whips to me, and she beams with soft eyes. "You didn't have to walk me. I could've met you at your car."

"Well, I wanted to." I hold out the iced black coffee I picked up for her. "And I thought you'd want this as quickly as possible after all your hard work."

She snatches it and takes a long sip before narrowing her eyes at me. "Is this hazelnut flavor?"

"Yep. Gotta turn you into a basic bitch like the best of us."

"Never," she scoffs before placing her plump lips back around the straw, and now I'm wondering how they'd look wrapped around my cock. "It's good, thanks."

"Wow. Are you admitting defeat?"

She rolls her eyes. "Just take the W, Anderson."

I throw my arm over her shoulder. "Fine, I'll take the W."

We head toward the parking garage, and I'm still surprised Sophia requested I drive after how standoffish she was last week. I'm glad to know she's willingly spending extra time with me. I lead her over to my truck.

"*This* is your ride." Sophia smirks as her eyes scan the length of my black jacked-up F-250.

"Yep." I slap the hood. "Ain't she a beaut?"

"Compensating for something, Honey Bee?" She giggles as I lead her to the passenger door.

"I can show you better than I can tell you." I wink, opening it wide.

"Compensate how you must."

I offer my hand.

"Elijah, I don't need you to help me into the truck. I'm perfectly capable of doing it on my own."

"Humor me, would you?"

Her stubborn eyes analyze my face, and I savor the attention. "Fine," she huffs, grabbing my extended hand, a small smirk spreading across her perfect lips. I steady her, and she steps on the foot bar, hoisting herself into the truck. She looks over at me. "What?"

"Nothing." I press my lips together, the corners curling upwards. "I just never realized how tiny you were until I watched you get into my truck."

"I'm not tiny!" She scoffs. "Maybe your truck is just too damn big."

"It's not an insult. You're the perfect size." I step up on the foot bar, grab the seat belt, and pull it over her, clicking it in place. Her breath hitches when I nudge her arms so she'll unfold them, and my heart rate skyrockets as my pinky accidentally grazes her breast. "See." I clear my throat. "Nice and safe." I jump down and slam the door shut, then make my way to the driver's seat to start our drive towards her dorm.

A few minutes later, we pull up to the curb of Sophia's building, and I spot Sage with a surfboard tucked under her arm.

"Do we need to wait on Charlie?" I ask while Sage puts her board in the truck bed.

"She's gonna meet us there later," Sophia tells me. "One of her cheer friends is coming too, so they're riding together."

"Oh, okay, cool beans."

Sage gets in the truck, and I pull out of the lot onto the main road. "I have a friend I want you to meet," I tell Sage.

"Oh, really?" she replies, her tone laced with curiosity.

"Yep."

"Care to elaborate?"

"Nope. But I think you've met him before." I smile to myself.

"*Ooohh...*" She sings. "Now I'm intrigued."

"What about me?" Sophia asks from the passenger seat.

I take my eyes off the road briefly to narrow them at her, then return them forward. "What *about* you?"

"I'd love to get to know Theo a little better." My jaw ticks as she grins over at me. "Can you make a formal introduction? He's a smoke show."

Shaking my head, I exhale heavily to expel the burning feeling in my veins. "No fuckin' way."

"Why not?" She juts out a pouty lip. "A sunflower needs lots of honey bees, Elijah." She gestures a hand loosely towards her body.

I let out a deep laugh before stopping abruptly. "No."

"What do you mean, *'no?'*" she repeats using air quotes.

"If *my* sunflower wants a honey bee, I'll be the only one sucking up her nectar," I say, picking up my almost empty iced coffee and taking a long, loud, slurping sip. Her pretty lips part open before she snaps them shut. Sage loses it in the back seat, cackling so hard I might need to give her an inhaler. Sophia sits with her arms folded in her seat and while her body language says she's annoyed, the wicked grin on her face tells an entirely different story.

"Well, what about—"

"The *only* one," I cut Sophia off firmly. Sage winks at me in the rearview mirror, which only encourages my teasing as Sophia's cheeks tinge bright pink.

"Mm-hmm," Sophia hums, sinking into her seat. "We'll see about that."

I turn into the beach parking lot, pulling between a few familiar cars. We amble down the path toward the ocean and once my toes sink into the warm sand, I pause for a moment, taking it all in. The salty air, the blazing sun on my skin, and the beautiful girl who I'll win over. *Eventually.* We make our way toward the guys, who've already made their presence known on the beach, and put our stuff down.

"What's up, E?" Theo calls over, a cheerleader already tucked under his arm.

"Just another day in paradise, T." He strides over to us, dragging the poor girl along.

"Hey, Elijah." She turns to the girls with a wide smile. "I'm Stella."

The girls pull her into their orbit, and they chat while setting up their towels.

"She given in to the Anderson charm yet?" Noah asks, handing me a can of Bud Light in one of Theo's custom koozies.

"Soon."

"Yeah, right." Julian chuckles, sticking his surfboard in the sand

and joining our conversation. "You'll be lucky if you ever get to first base."

"Bullshit, I'm a home run kinda guy," I say before taking a long pull of my refreshing beer. "Ready to meet the spicy purple Skittle?" I ask Julian.

"Oh, you know it," he says, rubbing his hands together.

"Sage," I call over to her, and the girls look our way. Sophia's eyes go wide before schooling her expression as she and Sage walk over, whispering to one another along the way. "This is Julian."

"Uber driver. I'd recognize that neck tat anywhere." Sage smirks, holding out her hand.

"Hi." He shakes her hand slowly. "Glad I made an impression."

Her hazel eyes sparkle, and I search for an exit from this conversation I'm clearly no longer a part of. His eyes flick over to her surfboard. "Wanna catch a wave?"

"You any good?" Sage cocks a brow.

"I guess you'll have to find out." They pick up their boards and jog out to the water. Sophia stares after them with an unreadable expression on her face.

"You alright?" I ask, biting my lower lip to suppress a smile.

"Mm-hmm." She watches as Julian and Sage dive into the water with their boards.

"Are you praying there's an Uber driver/rider confidentiality clause?" I ask, repeating Julian's lame excuse for keeping his damn mouth shut.

Her terrified gaze flicks to mine. "Possibly."

"Anything you'd care to share with the class?"

"Nope. Nothing you need to worry your pretty little head about," she says in a sweet Southern accent before booping me on the nose with her pointer finger.

"Mm-hmm." I hum down at her soft pink lips. All it would take is the slight dip of my head to touch mine against them.

"Hey, Elijah!" Desmond calls over with shit timing, per usual.

"Yeah?" I answer, attempting to hide my annoyance.

"Come throw with us. Noah wants to practice a few plays."

"Give me a sec," I tell him and turn my attention back to Sophia. "All work and no play…"

"Makes Elijah a dull boy." She smiles lazily, and the sight alone has me considering ignoring the boys' request and staying right here.

I grip her chin between my fingers. "I can assure you I'm anything but boring, Sunflower." Walking away, I try to shake out the tingling feeling where my fingers touched her skin.

After at least an hour of playing catch with the boys, I'm finally able to sneak away. Sophia's lying on her side, reading a book. I settle in the sand, resting my head on her hip, and look up at her.

Her amused eyes move from the open book down to me. "Can I help you?"

I give her my most dazzling smile. "Whatcha doin'?"

She wiggles her book at me. "Reading."

"Whatcha reading?"

She bats her eyelashes, a coy smile playing on her lips. "Porn."

"Oh, really?" My brows fly to my hairline as I reach up and pluck the book from her manicured fingertips.

"Elijah," she squeals, trying to steal it back as I open to the page she was just on. Sighing in defeat, she falls back on her elbows, and I lay my head on her stomach. My eyes scan the page, and every drop of blood in my body rushes south.

I glide my tongue along her collarbone towards her neck. The soft skin is like silk against my hungry lips. My impatient palm drags slowly up her thigh towards her soaking wet pussy, and my dick throbs in anticipation.

I flick my gaze to hers, excruciatingly aware of how well this bathing suit is *not* hiding my raging hard-on. "You were telling the truth."

"I'm an honest girl."

"You know…" I rest my cheek against her soft skin. "I'm happy to offer my services if you'd like to recreate that chapter."

She lets out a bubbling laugh. "Is that so?"

"Mm-hmm." I hold out the book, and she snatches it from my hand, tossing it on the towel before returning her attention back to me.

"Did you just come over here to interrupt my reading, or do you need something?" She smirks, and I find myself distracted by the way her eyes sparkle in the sun.

"Just a poor, lonely honey bee checking on his sunflower." I bat my eyelashes innocently.

"This sunflower is just fine, Elijah." She flicks her golden hair over her shoulder.

"Have you always liked to read?"

She turns her attention to the water. "Yeah... My sister and I used to read together."

"You read those types of books with your *sister*?" I ask teasingly.

"No, I was definitely too young for the good stuff back then."

I brush my finger lightly against her shoulder, and her eyes lock with mine. "What was your favorite book to read together?"

She waits a few beats before responding, and then her lips curve upwards. "*Alice in Wonderland*."

"Really?" I reach up to cup her neck, rubbing my thumb along the side of her throat. "I love that book."

"Me too." She rests her jaw on my hand and looks out at the ocean. "Did you have any favorites when you were younger?"

"Yeah." I huff out a laugh. "My gramps always read *Charlie and the Chocolate Factory* to me. It was one of his favorites."

"Was?" Sophia asks quietly, and a rock settles in my stomach.

"Yeah... was."

I scoot myself behind her so she's directly between my legs. Her sun-kissed thighs brush against mine, and I suck in a breath. The salt water has tangled her hair, so I bring it all behind her shoulders, brushing through it with my fingers before gathering it together. My fingertips rub against the soft skin of her neck in the process, goosebumps rising in their wake.

"You cold?" I ask, gliding my palm gently along her shoulder.

"Mm-hmm." She hums. "Freezing."

"Sure." I chuckle as I separate her hair into three parts and start twisting the strands in the way I've done so many times before.

"Are you *braiding* my hair?" Sophia asks in a surprised tone as my fingers work quickly.

"Yep. Do you have a hair tie?" She hands me one from her wrist, and I twist it around the bottom of the braid, flinging it over her shoulder.

She picks it up, looking at the end. "My sister used to do that for me…"

I snake my arms around her, and she leans into my embrace. Squeezing tighter, I nuzzle my face into the crook of her neck, the scent of coconut and her sweet sweat flooding my senses.

"Well, I'm happy to do it anytime," I mumble, my lips brushing against her skin. It takes all my control not to press a kiss against her as her pulse pounds against my lips in invitation.

Sophia angles herself to look up at me, remaining in my arms. It's the first time she's ever let me hold her like this, and I never want to stop. "Why are you so good to me?"

"What?" I tilt my head. "What do you mean?"

"I mean, I know we're friends and friends help each other out, but… I don't know. You're just so good to me. Even though we're just friends." *Just friends, my ass.* "And I'm thankful for you." She falls against me, and I wrap my arms around her tiny frame.

"Well, I'm thankful for you too, Sunflower." *So fucking thankful.*

During the darkest days of my life, I found her—*a sweet shot of sunshine illuminating every shadowy corner.*

She scoots back, her ass rubbing directly against my dick, and if I don't change positions, I'm not going to be able to hide how much I want her right now. "Wanna go for a walk?"

"I'd like that." We stand up, brushing the sand off us.

"Hey, good looking!" Charlie says, skipping up and crashing our perfect moment. *Why do all our friends have such shit timing?*

"Hey, Char." Sophia throws an arm around her. "So glad you're *finally* here."

"I know, I know," Charlie says with an apologetic smile. "It took a little longer cause I had to finish baking *these*." She angles the Tupperware she's carrying to show us cupcakes inside.

"Oh, hell yeah," I say, reaching for one, and she slaps my hand away.

"Not yet." Charlie laughs. "I also had to wait on this one." She points a thumb behind her.

"Hey, Elijah," Andi says, smiling wide.

"Hey," I reply as she steps forward, throwing her arms around my neck, and my entire body freezes. We don't see each other a ton, and I haven't had a chance to tell her I'm—hopefully—seeing someone.

"You okay?" She looks up at me, mouth inches from mine. I'm painfully aware of how this must look to Sophia. "You're so tense," Andi says, rubbing her hands along my neck and shoulders.

"Oh, yeah." I untangle her from me, and her brows crease slightly before she schools her expression. "Tough week." I glance around for Sophia, my heart pounding against my chest, and spot her down by the water taking pictures of Sage and Julian as they surf.

Shit.

"Hey there, gorgeous," Theo says, walking up and throwing an arm around Andi's shoulder. "Glad you made it."

"Yeah, I was definitely in need of a beach day." She grins up at him. "Thanks for the invite."

My eyes flick to Theo's, and he winks at me with a mischievous grin. *Shit stirrer.*

Asshole, I mouth to him, and he laughs, dragging her away.

15
SOPHIA

"Finally, some sweet relief!" Charlie says as she, Sage, and I settle under an enormous umbrella the boys set up.

"Yeah, and the view is spectacular," Sage says, practically drooling as she eyes Julian a few yards away. "Remind me to thank Elijah for the introduction to that fine tatted piece of ass." Julian's entire torso and arms are tatted up to his neck, and I've gotta admit, it is pretty damn hot.

"Yeah, sure." I huff out a laugh as my gaze wanders to Elijah, who sits on a cooler a few yards away. He's making casual conversation with the guys, and Andi throws her head back, laughing at every single thing he says, inching closer each time. She's on him like flies on shit. *Bitch, he's not that funny.*

"Earth to Sophia?" Sage says, snapping in front of my face, and I blink rapidly, returning my attention to her.

"Sorry, what?"

"Girl, what's your deal?" She follows my line of sight. "Oh."

"Do you think they've hooked up?" I ask the air.

"Well…" Charlie says, shifting awkwardly on the towel. "I know they did at camp over the summer. But I don't know if they have since."

Did he know she was coming?

Was he just using me for entertainment until she got here?

I shake my head, feeling angry at myself. I know better than to let my guard down and allow people in. They just end up disappointing me. Not that Elijah and I are even anything… Not that I have any right to be jealous when I've pushed him away at every turn. It shouldn't bother me he has a beautiful *cheerleader* flanking his side, but there's a nauseating feeling in my stomach telling me I'm anything but unaffected.

"Are you seriously gonna sit here and let that girl piss all over your man?" Sage asks, obviously over my pity party.

"Excuse me?" I stare at her.

"So what? They've smashed. Big deal. We're in college, Soph. This isn't the 1950s, where everyone finds one boring person to suck and fuck for the rest of their life. Did you really think Elijah hadn't slept around? My God, look at him." I glance over and must agree, he is totally fuckable. "You're into him. Who gives a shit he's stuck his honey dick in another flower?"

"How am I supposed to compete with that?" I ask, looking toward the tall, gorgeous brunette all the boys seem to be enamored by.

"Um, with your banging bod and magic pussy," Sage responds, gesturing towards me.

"Damn, Sage." I smile wide, appreciative for the over-the-top pep talk. "You should be a motivational speaker."

"I'll take it into consideration." She throws an arm around me and kisses the side of my head. "Now go mark your territory."

The three hard seltzers running through my veins determine my next action. "Fine." Buckling my belt bag across my body, I grab my Polaroid camera and strut to the water.

Click. One of the ocean, capturing the mesmerizing way the sun gleams off the water.

Click. Another of our friends, sitting on coolers and under umbrellas.

Gotta make sure I'm not too obvious about my real target...

Slipping the other two photos into my bag, I angle the camera toward Elijah.

He's eating a cupcake, and I frame the image to emphasize his glorious, muscular top half, which includes a tattoo on his chest I'd like to inspect further. His gaze flicks toward me, and a panty-dropping, closed lip grin dances across his face before he takes another bite, leaving a bit of frosting on his upper lip. My mouth curves upward as I think about seeing the adorable result on film.

Before the shutter clicks, a thumb comes on to his face and wipes off the frosting. My eyes flick from the lens towards the person the finger belongs to. *Andi, of course.* She sucks the frosting off her thumb.

Okay, this was obviously a mistake.

My eyes flick back to Elijah, who looks at me with an unreadable expression. A loud clapping sound interrupts our staring contest, and we turn our heads.

"Who's ready for some shirts and skins?" Theo asks, walking up with Stella, who has a football tucked under her arm. The guys all hoop and holler as us girls shake our heads at their excitement. "Let's pick teams and get to it."

I end up on shirts with Noah, Theo, Sage, and Stella. Skins is Elijah, Charlie, Julian, Desmond, and, of course, Andi. *Perfect.*

"Let's get some music going for this showdown!" Charlie yells out, then hooks her phone up to a Bluetooth speaker.

"Good as Hell" by Lizzo starts playing, and we face off on the line of scrimmage, with our team having the ball first. Sage hikes the ball to Noah, and I sprint down the beach; the sand slows me down but I'm still surprisingly faster than most of them. The ball soars through the air, landing directly into my hands. *Fuck yes.* Elijah's quick on my heels, and his arms wrap around me just as I've entered our end zone.

"Ha!" I scream as Elijah picks me up off the ground. I hold the ball into the air, and my team cheers. He lets me down, my body sliding against his in the process, and I shiver.

"Damn. Maybe I should nickname you Forrest Gump."

"Thought you'd be a lot faster... How's it feel coming in last for once?"

He bends down, his lips gliding against my ear, and a breath catches in my lungs. "The only time I come last is when I fuck."

I'm stunned so silent I can't even point out he did, in fact, lose as he turns and jogs back to the line of scrimmage.

Charlie's phone goes off, interrupting the music, and she runs over to it. "Sorry, guys. I've gotta take this. I'll be back."

"Come on, Char!" I shout over to her. "Really?"

"Sorry." She looks back down at her phone. "It's Nash."

Whenever Charlie's little brother calls, she always answers, no exceptions.

"Fine," I grumble, turning my attention back to the other team. "Can you guys still hang a player down?"

"Really, Sunflower?" Elijah taunts. "Don't insult us."

We get in formation. Julian hikes the ball to Elijah, and Andi runs downfield, looking for Elijah's pass. I sprint after her just as the leather ball lands in her hands. I lunge forward to tag Andi and we both end up tumbling to the ground.

"Ouch." She laughs, pushing up out of the sand, and extends her hand down toward me.

"Sorry," I mumble as she hoists me onto my feet.

"It's okay. These guys have a way of turning on our competitive sides, huh?"

I laugh awkwardly. "Yeah."

"Um, Soph," Theo calls over. "You know we're playing *touch* football, babe."

"Yeah, yeah." I wave him off as Elijah sends a glare his way.

The score is tied after another hour of back and forth, with our team now having possession. Sage hikes the ball to Noah as Stella and I sprint toward the end zone. Noah makes eye contact with me and sends the ball soaring my way. I extend my arms, but Andi jumps in front of me and intercepts it, sprinting to their end zone and winning the game.

Elijah's team celebrates with high fives and backslaps while we boo them, giving double thumbs down. It would be hilarious if it weren't for the way Andi jumps on Elijah, wrapping her long legs around him as they celebrate their win. He sets her down, and she spanks his ass, causing my blood to boil.

I walk back toward my towel and yelp when I'm thrown over a large shoulder. "Good game, Sunflower," Elijah says in a husky tone.

"Put me down." I laugh as he spins me around. "You're making me dizzy."

My body slides down his front, and he scoops me cradle style in his arms. "You gave me a run for my money back there." He grins down at me.

"What can I say? I have a pro soccer player for a brother. Hustling is in my genes." His smile widens as the sound of water sloshes beneath his feet. "What are you—" I'm flying through the air and into the cool water of the gulf before I can finish my question. I emerge soaking wet and giggling wildly. "What the fuck was that for?"

"Being a sore loser." He smirks, then grabs my ankle and pulls me toward him.

"Maybe you were a sore winner. I saw you twerking in the end zone." An amused smile spreads across my lips at the image of Elijah dropping it low.

"Mind your manners, Ms. Summers." He rests a hand on his muscular chest. "*I* am a gentleman... Besides, it was a *celebratory* twerk."

"Mm-hmm." He tugs me closer, and my legs wrap around his wet body instinctively. *If we weren't in the ocean I'd probably combust.* His muscles are firm under my touch, and I'm losing the ability to think clearly. "There was a lot of celebratory ass grabbing going on too."

"Oh, really?" He cocks a brow. "And did that bother you?"

"No," I say defensively. "You can have your ass grabbed by every cheerleader at CBU. What can I say about it?"

"You're entitled to say whatever you'd like." His shoulders shake as he chuckles in amusement. "Are you jealous?"

"Excuse me?" I scoff. *Of course, you dumb jock.*

"That you didn't get to join in on the celebratory ass slapping?" His hands inch lower on my waist, and I squirm against him. "I can make it up to you right now if you'd like."

Yes, please. "No, thanks."

Goddammit, Sophia.

"Too bad." He pouts. "Your ass looks totally slappable in this."

I throw my head back, laughing. "What a line. What a line."

"It worked."

"How? You're not touching my ass." *Unfortunately.*

"I wasn't trying to touch your ass. I was trying to hear that pretty laugh of yours." He taps his forehead to mine. "It. Worked."

"Hey!" Sage shouts from the beach, and our heads snap toward her. "We wanna go grab pizza. Y'all in?"

"Yeah!" I reply a little too quickly, and Elijah laughs as Sage walks away. "What?"

"Nothing," Elijah replies. "It's just amazing how someone so small can always be so damn hungry."

"I'm not that small, Elijah. I've gained five pounds since the semester started. This sunflower is truly on her way to the freshman fifteen."

"Five more reasons to wanna smack that ass." He winks.

"God, you're such a flirt." I wiggle out of his grasp and swim toward shore. I glance over my shoulder, and he's in the same place, watching me swim away. "Loser buys dinner!" I shout before sloshing as fast as I can to the beach. He loses by a landslide, and I wonder if he even tried as I watch him sporting a dopey grin, wading out of the ocean. The water beads down his rippled muscle and if I wasn't already soaking wet, I definitely am now.

We all collect our stuff and walk towards the parking lot. Elijah's in front of me, hauling a cooler while talking to Noah, and I find myself entranced with the way his arm muscles flex with each step.

"Hey," Andi says, running up and startling me. "You've got a hell of a tackle." She lets out a light warm laugh. "Any harder and I might have broken a rib."

"Sorry," I say sheepishly. "I have an older brother, and I guess I got a little carried away."

Sure, that's why, Soph.

"No worries." She grins. "So... Charlie texted and said she had to head out."

"Really?" *I wonder why she didn't text us herself.*

"Yeah, she said something about helping Nash."

"Oh, okay."

"So it looks like I'll be riding with you guys." She readjusts the bag on her shoulder. "Maybe we can get Elijah to play carpool karaoke."

"Oh, God." I let out a hearty laugh. "I'd pay money to see that."

"How's five bucks sound?"

"You get Elijah to do carpool karaoke, and I'll give you ten."

She smirks. "Deal."

We get to the parking lot and throw our stuff in Elijah's truck bed. I round the back and see Andi hauling herself into the passenger seat as Sage comes up next to me. "Girl, she even stole your spot," she whispers before going to ride with Julian.

I sigh, then open the back door and slide in.

As promised, Elijah willingly participates in carpool karaoke. All Andi has to do is play "She Thinks My Tractor's Sexy" by Kenny Chesney, and he puts on a full show without hesitation. It's hilarious and adorable, and I can't help but feel disappointed at the fact Andi knew exactly how to trick him into it. I slide ten dollars into her hand when we get out of the car, and she tells me to keep it.

We've just downed our ginormous pizza slices from Lazy Moon, and the boys are demolishing a pitcher of beer. I tried to distance myself from Elijah by sitting on the outside of the booth, but somehow he ended up directly across from me with, of course, Andi flanking his side. Theo's to my left, and I'm choosing to make the best of it by enjoying his company. He's a shameless flirt, and I haven't stopped laughing the last hour.

Currently, he's retelling all of Elijah's most embarrassing sexcapades, and I think Elijah's three seconds away from throwing all Theo's shit out their dorm window.

"And the worst, *by far*, was when Elijah hooked up with a girl who had a surprise piercing." Theo lets out a deep, throaty laugh before taking a sip of his water, and my eyes flick to Andi.

"Hey," she says, putting her hands in the air, "don't look at me. My lady parts are piercing free."

"And your tits?" Theo asks her.

"You told him?" Andi asks, glaring at Elijah. "Seriously?"

Elijah purses his lips without replying, avoiding eye contact with everyone as he sinks lower into his seat in an attempt to disappear.

"Anyway," Theo says, returning to the story, "Elijah was screaming from his room for me to come get him untangled from the poor girl." He throws his head back, laughing, and Elijah's lips quirk upwards as his jaw ticks. "They were stuck, and I had to literally cut his bush free."

"Well, now I know why you've always been so good about manscaping." Andi laughs towards Elijah. "I've never seen a guy with such an excellent grooming regimen for their dick."

"Okay, that's enough," Elijah says, leveling Theo and Andi with a look that would have me folding in on myself but only makes them laugh harder.

"That's hilarious." I giggle, although there's a familiar buzz under my skin.

"It was." Theo nods, and Andi throws her arm around Elijah's shoulder.

"Come on," she says looking up at him. "Be a good sport."

Elijah narrows his eyes down at her and smiles sarcastically.

"Don't encourage him."

"I still don't understand how it happened." Theo shakes his head. "That would never happen to me."

"Oh, really?" I smirk with raised brows.

"Yep. I'm a professional." He waves a hand along his muscular body. "I know exactly *what* to put *where* to make sure she's screaming in *pleasure* not *pain*." He arches his brow at Elijah on the last word.

"I bet you do." I laugh.

"You can never have too much practice." He winks.

Julian takes over the conversation, telling a story about getting caught for public indecency and how Noah had to talk the campus police out of arresting him.

"Lucky for you, or Coach Porter woulda had your ass," Theo says, placing his arm on the booth behind me, seemingly casual, and Elijah's gaze burns into me.

"I'd rather he had *my* ass," Sage says, smirking, and I giggle, shaking my head.

Theo leans down to my ear. I stop breathing as his warm breath hits my neck. "Don't freak out." He lets out a low chuckle, trailing his fingertips on my shoulder, and my mind is swirling. "I know this is driving you crazy watching E with Andi." *Understatement of the fucking century.* "But I also know he's watching me right now, ready to kill me for being so close to you."

My lips part at his words, heart pounding hard against my chest.

"Giggle. Right now." I do as I'm told. "Good girl." My lips quirk upwards at his praise. "Now look over at him." I flick my gaze toward Elijah, whose unreadable eyes are locked on me as Andi chats in his ear. "Look away." I return my gaze forward and catch Sage's curious eyes.

"You're bossy." I smirk, enjoying the game.

"Okay, now do you really wanna have some fun?" My eyes find Elijah again, who's now chugging a beer.

I bite the inside of my cheek. "Sure."

He moves away and gestures for me to stand up. I slide out of the booth, and he follows behind as Elijah's gaze is focused on us.

"I'm gonna take Soph home," Theo announces, and I purse my lips together to contain the laugh threatening to break free.

"No," Elijah says firmly, standing up.

"It's really no problem," Theo replies cooly, his confidence unwavering as Elijah's stone-hard eyes bore into him.

"All her stuff is in my truck," Elijah says, his jaw ticking.

"She can get it from you tomorrow," Theo counters, not missing a beat.

Elijah's hopeful gaze flicks to mine. "Soph."

"Sorry, Honey Bee. Theo stopped drinking at the beach and you just basically shotgunned a beer... so I think I'm more comfortable with him taking me home."

A tightness forms in my chest as Elijah looks down at his empty glass before pushing it away. "Okay." His gaze flicks to Theo. "Be careful."

"Yeah, yeah. Don't worry, I'll keep our girl safe." Theo throws his arm over my shoulder and steers me toward the door.

"You're crazy," I whisper to him.

"I don't even have my car here," he murmurs back, and we both laugh until we're outside on the sidewalk. "E was so jealous he forgot I rode with Noah."

Was Elijah really jealous?

"Uber?" I suggest.

"Yeah, Uber." He chuckles and pulls out his phone.

Two minutes later, the door of Lazy Moon swings open, and a wide smile spreads across my face.

"Somebody request an Uber?" Julian asks as Sage winks at me.

"Sure did." Theo grabs my hand and starts dragging me toward Julian's car. "Hurry before E sees us."

"He's gonna kill you, bro," Julian says, laughing as we all pile in.

A satisfied smirk spreads across Theo's face. "But it's gonna be so worth it."

16

ELIJAH

"See ya," Noah says, walking past the table to exit Lazy Moon.

"Later," Des adds, following closely behind, leaving me and Andi alone.

"You okay, E?" she asks, having now moved to the spot across from me.

I tighten my hands around the water I'm now drinking. "Yeah, I'm fine."

"You sure? I'm stressed just looking at you."

Releasing a deep breath, I sink even further into my seat. I didn't want to argue with Sophia that we could totally take an Uber home if she was more comfortable. Or that I'd only had one beer and wasn't planning to leave for another hour or so anyway.

I should've been the one to take Sophia home tonight. *Did Andi being here ruin everything?*

But I couldn't argue with Sophia in front of all our friends if she really wanted Theo to take her. It's not like we're dating.

"Actually, I think we should talk," I tell Andi, ready to solve problem number one.

"Um, okay. Why does this sound like the start of every break-up speech *ever*?"

"Andi..." I tilt my head with apologetic eyes, and she huffs a laugh.

"We're fuck buddies, bro." She waves a casual hand. "You don't need to give me the 'I'm ready to see other people' speech."

I furrow my brows in disbelief at how chill she is. "Okay?"

"Seriously, we're cool," she says in a completely relaxed Andi way.

"I just thought..." I shift in my seat. "I don't know, that you might be a little more..."

"What?" she asks in amusement. "Heartbroken? You want me to cry and tell you I wanna be more than fuck buddies? *Pick me? Choose me? Love me?*" She laughs, shaking her head. "Sorry, babe. Wrong girl."

I chuckle. "Okay... cool."

"Is this why you were so stressed today?" Andi tilts her head. "I was really worried about you. I thought it might've been because—"

"No," I say quickly, cutting her off. "I'm good. I was just worried I was giving you the wrong idea since we hadn't officially talked yet."

"Oh, okay, good... I do have one question for you though." She clears her throat. "You know, one *ex*-fuck buddy to another."

"Sure." I roll my eyes, taking a sip of water.

"Are you waiting to ask Sophia out until Theo's balls deep or what?"

I choke on my drink and have to pound against my chest to reclaim oxygen. "Why the fuck would you say that?"

"Which part? Because we both know you're into Soph. I mean, you moaned her name the last time we fucked for God's sake."

My face burns with shame as I struggle to come up with a suitable response. "I am *so* sorry about that. I really thought you didn't notice."

"I did, I just didn't give a shit. I was picturing Olivia in my head anyway." The corner of her lip curls upward.

"I'm a little hurt right now," I say.

"You'll get over it." She pats me lightly on the forearm.

"And hold up." I raise my brows. "Olivia?"

She blushes, fighting a smile. "Yeah, I think she wants to start hooking up again."

"So what? You were going to break up with *me*?" I tease.

"Olivia and I aren't quite there yet…" She rubs her hands against the condensation of her waterglass. "But I guess you beat me to the 'we were never exclusive in the first place' talk."

"That's awesome," I say genuinely. "I'm really happy for you."

"Thanks."

My mind wanders back to Sophia and where she is right now. "Do you really think she'd fuck Theo?"

"Honestly?" She laughs, looking at my terrified expression. "No… but I wouldn't blame her if she did."

I glare at her, veins filling with fire at the thought of Sophia with Theo. "Then why did you say that?"

"Because I'm hoping you'll pull your head out of your ass and go get your fucking girl, dude."

I throw my face in my hands and groan.

If only it were that simple.

Every time I think the play is in motion, Sophia calls a timeout and we lose ten yards.

Andi waves before ducking into her building, and I immediately pull out my phone.

SUNFLOWER

ME

Hey Sunflower, you make it home okay?

I sit in the parking lot for five minutes, waiting for a reply, trying to fight myself from driving to her dorm. Just as I'm about to back out of the spot, my phone buzzes.

SUNFLOWER

Nah, I'm still with Theo

ME

Where?

SUNFLOWER

At his place

ME

TF you mean at his place?

You mean MY place?

If you're at my place you better be in MY bed. Alone.

I don't know what came over me to send such a possessive text, but my heart pounds against my ribcage as I pull out of the parking lot.

They better be fucking with me.

At a red light, I unlock my phone and pull up my voicemails. My finger hovers over Dino, then taps to play his most recent one.

"Tag, you're it!" A soft laugh escapes me as I shake my head at the familiar voice filling the cab of the truck. "Bummed I missed ya... Uh, it's about four o'clock... Friday. I'm sure it's probably not a great time for you but just wanted to see how that arm's feeling... And if you're still not feelin' tip top, remember, pain always goes away. And regarding Coach Porter, I know he's young, but he's really been pulling through. And I hate to say I told you so, but... I told you so." Another deep laugh of his fills the cab. "Just wanted to letcha know I'm thinkin' about ya. Call me when you've got some time. Love you, Buck."

"Love you, Dino," I mumble, grateful for the voicemail that helps calm my nerves so I won't act like a goddamn idiot.

When I park near my building, there's still no new message from Sophia. My mind swirls with all the reasons she could not be answering right now.

ME

> Sophia, you're going to give me a fucking heart attack. Please answer me.

The direct route doesn't work, and I'm losing my patience. I opt to take the stairs and by the time I get to the second floor, I've broken into a full-on sprint.

That's it. I've lost my damn mind.

I get to my hallway, and it feels like the distance has grown two football fields from the stairs to my door. I'm equally terrified and eager to get in my place and see what the fuck is going on.

I rush down the hallway, shove the key inside the lock, and throw the door open, accidentally banging it against the wall, stumbling inside. Four heads whip in my direction, all with amused smirks on their faces.

I'm panting, out of breath, and am fully aware I look utterly ridiculous.

"Late night cardio to work off that pizza, Honey Bee?" Sophia says, and my gaze snaps to her. My eyes fall downward to the sight of her wearing nothing but a bikini and her little denim shorts in the company of Julian, Sage, and Theo.

I shut the door behind me and try to regain my composure as I turn to face them. "Yep."

"Mm-hmm," Theo hums sarcastically, and my jaw ticks as I see him shirtless inches from Sophia. *What the fuck is going on?* They're all sitting on the floor of the living room around our coffee table.

"Where's Andi?" Sophia asks, her tone laced with jealousy. *Unless I'm imagining that.*

"At her place." I take slow steps toward them. "What are you guys up to?" I ask hesitantly, knowing I won't like the answer.

"We're playing strip poker." Sophia smiles up at me sweetly. "Want us to deal you in?"

Well, I'm sure as shit not about to let you play against my two horniest friends without me.

"Sure." I kneel between Sophia and Theo, pushing her to the side and situating myself directly between them. Sophia lets out a sweet laugh but says nothing as Julian shuffles the cards.

"You're joining late, so we'll need an article of clothing as payment." Sage smirks while raking her eyes over me.

My gaze flicks to Sophia. "Your choice. What should I lose?"

Sophia's eyes scan from my head to my dick, and a rush of blood heads south as I harden from the attention. "Definitely your shirt."

A smirk spreads across my face as I pull it over my head and toss it behind me.

Theo pulls out a tequila bottle, and we all take a swig straight from it before playing. A few rounds go by, and I'm impressed at how good Sophia is. She hasn't lost any more clothing, which I'm equally thankful for and disappointed about. My veins are warm from the liquor, and I have to admit I'm having a good ass time considering I walked in here ready to kill my *beloved* roommate.

I have two tens in my hand with a third showing on the board. It's only Sophia, Sage, and me left and if I win this hand, they both lose an article of clothing. I still have my board shorts and boxers on so I'm feeling confident. Sage and Sophia are down to just their bikinis and shorts.

Sophia narrows her eyes at me, then lays down her cards. She has a measly pair of sixes, which isn't enough, and I grin. We look at Sage, who lays down two eights, matching another eight on the board for trips.

"That's right, honey dick!" Sage holds up two hands, thrusting the air. "Boom. Let's see you beat that."

"Damn, that's hot." Julian laughs while resting his arm on the couch cushion behind her.

I take a deep inhale, my eyes bouncing between them. Sophia already knows she lost but still looks happy as hell waiting to see if I'm right there with her.

"Would you ladies please stand up?" I instruct, and they both look at me with narrowed eyes. Sage attempts to maintain her confidence, but it falters at my words.

"Why?" Sage asks.

"Humor me?" The corner of my mouth curves upward as I glance at Sophia and wink.

They both huff and stand. I throw my cards face up on the table.

"Drop 'em, ladies," I say, chuckling while reaching up and dragging a finger under the side hem of Sophia's denim shorts. Theo starts "Pony" by Ginuwine on his phone, and the girls play along, slowly unbuttoning their shorts. I can see Sage out of the corner of my eye, but my attention is focused purely on the gorgeous woman in front of me as she does a hilariously adorable strip tease. She lowers back down, sitting on her heels in nothing but a bikini, and I have to forcibly fight myself to not reach out and touch her. I glance at Theo, who's shamelessly checking out Sophia, and I glare at him so hard he must feel it. His amused expression meets my furious one, and he laughs out loud before grabbing the cards to shuffle them up.

"Better hope you ladies get a good hand this time," Theo says, dealing them out. "I mean, I pray to God you don't but... you know." He bites his lower lip, fully amused, and all of my previous enjoyment is gone.

He's screwing with me on purpose. I can tell.

The hand is dealt and after the first three cards are shown, Sage, Julian, and I all fold, leaving Theo and Sophia. My pulse picks up. If she loses this hand, she'll have to drop another piece of clothing, and there is no way in hell I'm letting Theo or Julian see Sophia's tits. *I haven't even fucking seen them yet.* The first time will not be with my two best friends watching while I'm forced to pretend I don't have a damn tent in my shorts.

Sophia is sitting close enough that I *happen* to get a glance at her cards and see she already has a pair. *Thank God.* After the last card comes, there's a pair on the board too. I stretch back to see Theo's cards and although I'm embarrassingly obvious, he chooses to ignore me.

Son of a bitch.

He has four of a kind.

Sophia slaps her cards flat on the table with a victorious smile and eyes Theo. He winks at me, then lays his cards down. I can't explain what comes over me, but before I can blink, my arm has swiped all the cards off the table and onto the floor.

"Oh, too bad…" I try holding in a grin as Sophia stares at me with her mouth open, the corners of it curling upward. "Guess you gotta keep your top on, Sunflower."

"Fuck you, Elijah!" Theo chucks cards at me. "I was about to see them perfect titties."

"Watch it." I glare, and he howls with laughter.

Why does that never work?

"Aww." Sophia pouts at me. "I was ready to go full-on Mardi Gras."

"No beads for you today," I say firmly.

"No?" Sophia reaches behind her and toys with the tiny string holding her bathing suit together. My hand flies to hers, holding it firmly in place on her warm skin.

"Yeah, come on, Elijah," Sage says, folding her arms. "I wanted to see Soph's tits too."

Sophia winks at Sage. "You can see them anytime, baby."

Great, and now I have that beautiful mental picture in my head.

This girl really is going to give me a fucking heart attack.

17
ELIJAH

"Sophia, if I have to hear the word enlightenment one more time, my head is going to explode," I say as calmly as possible, although I'm very serious about the head exploding part. We've studied five hours for next week's midterm, and my brain is mush.

"Fine, I guess you can feed me now."

"Where to today, Sunflower?"

"Seriously, Elijah?" She raises her eyebrows at me, pretending to be annoyed, but the upcurved corners of her mouth tell a different story. "Are you ever going to stop calling me that?"

"I guess I can call you something else." I shove my study materials into my backpack.

"Victory!" She fist pumps, and I chuckle at how damn cute she is.

I stand up and throw my bag over my shoulder. "Ready to go, babe?"

She bites back a smile, narrowing her eyes. "Why did I even think for five seconds you'd be going the other way with that?"

"Guess you don't know me well enough yet, sweetheart."

"I should've left you alone with sunflower," she grumbles, standing and picking up her tote bag.

"You'll learn someday, sweet pea." I throw an arm around her shoulders as we stroll towards the exit.

"Ughhhhhh," she groans dramatically, then leans her head against me.

I know you love this, Sunflower.

We walk into Señor Rita, a small Mexican restaurant off campus that has killer tacos and deadly margaritas. They don't card, which is stupid on their part but brilliant for us.

"So... do you have plans for Halloween?" Sophia asks after we've ordered our food and a bowl-sized margarita has been placed in front of her. I opted for water because I don't want Sophia to have a single reason to get in a vehicle that's not mine today, or ever again.

"We have a home game against Texas A&M in the afternoon but nothing after. Why?"

She takes a long sip of her blue concoction. "Just wondering."

"Care to elaborate?" I probe, gesturing loosely with my hand.

"Okay... well... I don't want you to make a big deal, but it's actually my birthday."

"On Halloween?"

"Yep."

"Interesting." I nod while taking a sip of my water.

"Why?"

"I guess that explains why you're always ghosting me."

"Ha ha. *Sooo* funny. Well, anyway, the girls are making me go out, and I was wondering if you and some of the guys might wanna come? We're bar hopping by the bay."

"Yeah, of course. I'll talk to them." I feel a wide grin break through my cool guy facade, excited she's opening up. "What's your costume?"

"You're going to laugh," she says, cheeks flushing pink.

"Try me."

Her expression stays serious, but her eyes dance with mischief. "A sexy koala."

"A... *sexy* koala?" I repeat with a smirk as she shrugs, eating a tortilla chip dripping with red salsa.

She darts her tongue out, slowly licking a bit of the salsa off her lower lip. *It's fucking pornographic.* "Yeah, you know, a koala but... *sexxxyyy.*" She drags out the last word, wiggling her shoulders in a seductive motion, and my dick twitches in my jeans.

"Is it even possible to make a koala sexy?" Who am I kidding? Sophia could dress as a hot dog, and I'd be happy to lick the ketchup off her buns.

"I knew you'd think it was stupid." She drops her eyes to the table.

"I'm kidding, baby." I put my hand over hers and give it a light squeeze. "You're going to look stunning... as usual. The hottest koala in the zoo."

She hides behind her hand, a grin slipping through. "Thanks."

"I mean it. You'll make all the boy koalas go '*waaaaa.*'"

Her mouth falls open, a wide grin spreading across her face. "Did you just make a *Princess Diaries* reference?"

I shrug. "Perhaps... and I know what my costume is gonna be."

"What's that?"

"Since it's your birthday, I'll just wear gold boxers, tie a bow around my neck, and call it a day."

"So what... you're my gift?" she asks, unamused.

"Guess so."

"Are you returnable?"

"Sorry, baby. No returns, no refunds."

"What kind of return policy is that?" She chuckles with a smile that steals the breath from my damn lungs.

"The good kind, *darlin'.*" I wink, exaggerating the pet name to drive her crazy.

"You have *got* to stop calling me things like that." The crinkles by her eyes tell me her protests are half-hearted.

"You call me honey. What's the difference?"

"I call you Honey *Bee*. It's totally different." She throws her arms out, almost knocking over her margarita.

"You're so cute when you're annoyed, doll face." I chuckle, and she rolls her eyes, letting her arms fall back to her sides before taking a big swig of her margarita.

"I don't have a fake ID, so maybe you can help get me some drinks?" She rests her face on her hands, batting her eyelashes at me, and I bite down so hard on my lower lip I almost taste blood.

"Is that all I'm good for?" I raise my brows. "Feeding you and getting you drunk?"

She narrows her eyes with a crooked smirk. "I didn't say to get me drunk. I said to sneak me some libations, kind sir."

"Yeah, of course. I shall keep your glass mighty full," I reply in an excellent British accent, eliciting a sweet giggle from her.

My phone buzzes on the table so I pick it up, glancing at the screen.

BIG STING ENERGY

NOAH CARUSO

Party at The Baller Pad tonight to celebrate last night's ass kicking

DESMOND BALL

Boobs & Beer in heavy supply

JULIAN LISCERO

And bud

NOAH CARUSO

No bud.

JULIAN LISCERO

Kidding, Cap. No bud.

;)

That ass kicking better lead to some ass licking

ME

Bro lol...

But yeah, obviously I'm in

"You have any plans later?" I ask Sophia, setting the phone on the table. "And if they entail dill pickle chips and your TV, for the love of God, say no. Those are *not* plans."

She narrows her forest eyes at me. "For the record, this week's snack is cool ranch Doritos... But if those are the parameters, I suppose, no, I do *not* have plans."

"Noah and Des are having a party to celebrate last night's win. You and the girls should come."

"I don't know." Sophia leans back in her seat, folding her arms across her chest. "A house full of jocks?"

"A house full of *hot* jocks." I waggle my eyebrows at her.

"Oh, okay, a house full of *cocky* jocks." Sophia grins, and I nudge her foot under the table. She nudges back and somehow our feet end up tangled together. *Footsie instead of fucking—who am I?*

"Just text the cute purple Skittle and the cheerleader. Come on, it'll be *fun*."

"Seriously? Do you have trouble remembering people's names or do you just enjoy horrible nicknames?"

"Sorry, tell the cute purple Skittle, *Sage*, and the cheerleader, *Charlie*, that you guys are going out tonight."

She mutters something to herself just as our waiter arrives with the food. My mouth immediately waters when he places down my beef burrito and Sophia's tacos with salsa verde. She picks up the taco and bites into it as I take a sip of my water.

"Holy fuck balls!" Her tongue falls out of her mouth, and she fans it with her hand. "These tacos are hotter than a jalapeño's coochie."

Water sprays out of my mouth all over the table... and her.

"What the fuck?" She freezes, taking in the feeling of my Sammy Sprinkler.

"What the fuck *me*? What the fuck *you*!" I'm laughing so hard I can barely catch my breath. "A jalapeño's coochie? What the fuck does that even mean?"

"I don't know." She lifts her shoulders as her cheeks tinge pink. "Jalapeños are spicy, and so were the tacos... Made sense in my head."

"I love it." Using both our napkins, I wipe the water off the table.

Two massive margaritas later, Sophia is on cloud fucking nine, giggling so much you'd think we're at a comedy show.

"So, you ladies in for tonight?" I ask, hoping her mood will have changed her answer.

"I don't know..." She taps her pointer finger on her plump lips that are sporting a teasing smile.

"Have you even asked them yet?" I raise my eyebrows, and she looks away, whistling the tune of a song I've never heard. "Give me your phone."

"Excuse me?"

"Pull up your lady chat and hand me your phone." I wiggle my fingers in her direction.

"My *lady chat*?"

"Sophia."

"Fine." She rolls her eyes. "Here."

I take the phone and look down at the group name, almost choking on my tongue.

C.OCK S.UCKIN S.ISTA's

"Is there a problem?" Sophia teases.

"Cock sucking sisters?" I stare at the phone with wide eyes. "What the hell is that?"

"C for Charlie, S for Sophia, S for Sage." She looks at me like I'm an idiot. "Duh."

I stare at her for a moment, trying to decipher when I fell so hard for this ridiculously beautiful and uncontrollably hilarious woman. "Okay..." Sophia turns her attention back to her margarita, and I get to work.

SOPHIA

Hey babes, you in for a party tonight at Noah's house?

SAGE

Abso-fuck me-lutely

CHARLIE

I'll be studying

SOPHIA

Bullshit, you're coming

SAGE

Damn Soph, you tell her

But come on Char, you have GOT to get out

CHARLIE

Fine... okay

Sophia has changed the group name to **SKITTLE BABES**

CHARLIE

Care to explain the name change, Soph?

SAGE

Yeah and does the football party mean you're finally gonna get that gigando honey dick

I snort, covering it up quickly before Sophia notices. I glance up, and she's sipping her drink and swaying to the beat of the mariachi music playing over the loudspeaker. My lips quirk upward at her light and carefree mood. Sophia's phone rings in my hand, and *Mom* flashes on the screen.

"Your mom's calling," I say, attempting to hand her the phone.

The smile falls off her face as she takes another sip of her drink. "Just ignore it."

"Are you su—"

"*Ignoreeee.*" She waves a loose hand. "*Pleaseee.*"

"Okay. Ignoring." After the call stops, I go back to the group chat and text the girls one last message.

SOPHIA

Pick you guys up at 9

"The Skittle babes are in." I hand her phone back.

"I'm sorry... the who?" She looks at me with a puzzled expression.

"You heard me. I need to change before we go to Noah's. Let's go back to my place, and then we'll stop by yours and pick up the girls?"

She stares at me, a battle waging behind her sparkling emerald eyes. Apparently, the devil—or the tequila—won because she says, "Okay."

18
SOPHIA

"Do you mind if I hop in the shower real quick? It won't take long," Elijah asks as we walk into his room.

"Sure, go ahead."

"Make yourself at home."

Sophia Summers, how in the world did you end up in this boy's bedroom?

The bathroom door clicks shut, and I stand in the center of the room with my hands on my hips. Last time I was here, my mind was so focused on getting my sketchbook back I didn't bother paying attention to my surroundings. His MacBook sits on a wooden desk with a well-worn leather Bible next to it— surprising. I've never considered him the religious type. There's a small walk-in closet with an NFL football poster for the Atlanta Bears taped to the door. Makes sense considering he's from Georgia.

A metal hunting bow is mounted on the wall with arrows clipped to it. *Damn, that's sexy.* Every surface is spotless, which is shocking, since most guys our age are serious slobs.

On his small dresser are a few framed photos of him and an older woman—assumedly his mom. I've heard him on the phone with her a few times, and they seem to be really close. *I wonder what that's like.*

A small plant sits on his desk, and the thick leaves appear to be totally healthy. My lips quirk upwards at the thought of Elijah tending to his little snake plant.

My eyes snag on Elijah's bed looking cozy as all hell with a soft black comforter and fluffy pillows. I catapult myself onto it face first and quickly realize it's a mistake. His intoxicating scent surrounds me, and I melt into it—because if you're gonna torture yourself, you might as well commit.

Every new thing I learn about Elijah makes it harder and harder to remember exactly *why* I'm keeping him in the friend zone.

The squeak of the shower knobs and the water shutting off has my mind wandering to the image of liquid dripping down his naked body toward his—

Pull yourself together, you horny sunflower.

Flipping over, I rest my back against his pillows and pull out my phone, immediately regretting it when I see a new notification.

SETH

SETH

Hey, how've you been?

Call me sometime. I miss you.

Why won't he get the freaking hint? How am I supposed to move on from what happened if he won't just leave me the hell alone?

Maybe the universe is telling me I shouldn't move on from it... that I should do something about it.

I tap into his contact information, doing what I should have done months ago, and block his fucking number. I've been nervous it would lead to him showing up here, but I'm finally at the point where I'm willing to risk it for the chance to be rid of him.

If Alice can slay the jabberwock, surely I can handle Seth.

The bathroom door opens, and I glance up, expecting Elijah to be fully dressed. He steps into the room, a black towel wrapped low around his waist as steam pours out from behind him. All negative thoughts relating to my ex vanish quicker than beer at a frat party.

My lips part open, and every coherent thought in my mind dissipates as Elijah runs a hand through his dark, wet, unstyled hair. I have an unrestricted view of the beautiful black and gray deer tattooed dead center on his chest, with two small cardinals perched on the antlers. It's intricate and beautiful, and my God is it sexy.

I hungrily drink in the full view of the tattoos on his arms, including a raven wrapped around his bicep, only shifting my focus when I notice water droplets gliding down his hard-earned abs, along his V, and disappearing under the towel.

My eyes are glued on his gorgeous body, and I try to speak, but words fail me entirely as I gaze at the sexiest fucking man I have *ever* seen.

He grins but doesn't comment on my embarrassing as shit reaction to seeing him in nothing but a towel.

Way to play it cool, you IDIOT.

Elijah walks past me to his closet, and my eyes follow him like the damn Mona Lisa. He turns away, allowing me to unabashedly savor the sight of his ripped shoulders down to the dimples of his back, and fuck if I don't see stars.

I'm more screwed than a rabbit during mating season.

"How much longer do you need, Honey Bee?" I tease to distract myself from the image of a steamy, half-naked Elijah that's been stored away as a core memory.

I'll be adding that to my spank bank, thank you very much.

"That depends." He turns to face me with a playful grin dancing on his lips. "Do you need more time to eye fuck me before I put my clothes on, baby?"

Busted.

My mouth falls open, cheeks flushing with heat. "I am not! Oh my God, you're the worst."

He places a warm hand around my ankle and squeezes lightly. "You love me."

"I like you."

"Well, that's an improvement."

The party is already in full swing when we arrive after picking up the girls. Elijah agreed to remain our designated driver for the rest of the night since I was already three margaritas deep by the time we got to his apartment earlier. I'm blaming my lack of chill regarding seeing him half naked on the tequila.

I wasn't affected like that at the beach, but there was something intimate about being in his bedroom and knowing the only layer covering him was an easily droppable towel.

"Noah lives here with Desmond," Elijah says, holding open the front door for me and the girls. "Theo and I are supposed to move in next year."

"This would be a hell of an upgrade." The modern, open concept house has people scattered all over the living room, dining area, and kitchen. It seems to be the entire football team, along with the complete female population of Crystal Bay.

A game of quarters is in full swing on the kitchen island, a freshman's doing a keg stand in the corner, and people are shaking their asses off on a makeshift dance floor in the living room.

"Hey! Glad you guys could make it." Noah greets each of us with a hug. "There's liquor and a keg in the kitchen. Help yourselves." In the same breath, he's gone, having dragged Elijah along with him.

"Damn, we're in school for two months and already got invited to a party for the fucking football team," Sage says.

"They invited *me*," I clarify teasingly.

"Whatever, potato, potahto. Let's get fucking wasted," she says before darting off to the kitchen.

"I love that little party animal," I say to Charlie.

"Yeah," she agrees as Julian envelops Sage in a hug before handing her a drink. "It's good to see her enjoying life, you know?"

"Totally."

Charlie pulls out her phone, frowns deeply, then immediately shoves it back in her pocket.

"What's wrong, Char?" I ask, throwing an arm around her shoulders. "Don't you know like half the people here?"

"Yeah. It's nothing." She plasters on a fake smile. *Typical Charlie—shoving down her own worries to please the rest of us.*

"Come on, Char Char." I tap my head to hers. "You can tell me anything."

"I don't want to bring down the party mood."

"Nothing is bringing down this fuckin' fiesta. Spill it, babe."

She blows out a raspberry. "It's just—Jonathan and I have barely had time to see each other since school started. With the distance and our practice schedules..." She looks to the floor. "Any free weekend I have I go home to see Nash and Denny, and I just miss him."

"Man, you're right. That sucks big ass balls." *Maybe I should slow down on the tequila.* "Why don't you invite Jonathan for my Halloween Birthday Bar Crawl?" I ask with jazz hands, waggling my eyebrows.

"You wouldn't mind?" Charlie asks timidly.

"Of course not!" I wave her off. "He's yo *man*. Let him keep your fine ass busy the whole night for all I care."

She throws her arm around my shoulder, squeezing tightly. "You're the best, Soph."

"Here you go, hotties," Sage says, appearing back in front of us with two drinks in her hands and Julian flanking her side. She offers me a plastic cup filled with some tequila concoction, and Julian hands one to Charlie. *Guess it's full speed ahead.*

"Here's to getting litty as a titty," Sage shouts, holding her cup in the air, and Julian shakes his head, laughing.

Charlie and I raise our cups. "To getting litty as a titty!"

"Super Freaky Girl" by Nicki Minaj blares over the speakers as Charlie and I spin around the middle of the "dance floor." She sings it word for word, and it's absolutely hilarious. We've had plenty to drink and are having the time of our lives shaking our asses to the rhythm. It feels like old times, and I'm so glad she's feeling better about the Jonathan situation.

The smell of Versace envelops my senses, causing a rush of anticipation as his tall frame towers over my backside.

"Hey," Elijah says, placing his hands loosely on my shoulders. "You girls having fun?"

My ass grazes the front of his jeans as I wiggle to the beat. "What do you think?"

"I'm gonna go get another drink." Charlie winks before leaving us.

Elijah slides his warm palms down my arms, taking one of my hands in his. He spins me around and pulls me close to him. We sway to the rhythm, dancing prom style to "I Like You" by Post Malone and Doja Cat, and the thought makes me laugh.

Elijah leans down, his lips brushing against my ear. "It's nice seeing you let loose, Sunflower." His warm breath causes the hairs on my neck to stand as he pulls away, looking down at me.

"I'm enjoying it too."

"Who knew all it took was a little tequila to get your beautiful self to dance?" He presses his forehead to mine.

"Who knew?"

I get one more song with him before we're interrupted.

"Hey, E," Desmond says, squeezing Elijah on the shoulder. "I need a pool partner. Noah's sucking ass."

"In a bit," Elijah replies, not taking his eyes off me.

"Come on, you can see your lil' sunflower later." He argues. "Please, Soph?" He turns his dazzling smile on me. "Sharing is caring."

My eyes find Elijah's as I force a smile so he can't gauge my disappointment. "It's fine, Honey Bee. I can keep myself *plenty* entertained."

"That's what I'm worried about." He scowls down at me, and it's absolutely adorable—like a pouty chocolate lab.

"You in or what?" Desmond asks, and Elijah releases a frustrated breath.

"Fine," he concedes, turning his attention back to me. "Be a good girl, will you?"

I fight a smile. "Never."

"Sophia." He steps forward, grabbing my chin in his usual way. "Don't make me kick someone's ass tonight," he says lowly, his lips so close to mine I can almost taste them.

"Now why would you do something silly like that?"

Elijah's gaze flicks down to my mouth and crawls slowly back to my eyes. "You know exactly why."

The words sit between us like a ticking bomb. I fight the urge to close the distance, knowing the second our lips touch, my little plan to stay just friends will disintegrate into oblivion.

"Fine... I'll be a very, *very* good girl." I wink and he groans, shooting a death glare at Desmond before returning his full attention to me.

"I'll come find you soon. Okay?"

"Have fun, boys." I give him a flirty wave as he backs away smiling and spins around, heading toward the pool table with Desmond.

I go to the kitchen for another drink and run into Sage.

"Enjoying yourself?" I ask her.

"Oh, fuck yes. I seriously don't think I've laughed this much in forever."

"Good." I boop her on the nose. "I'm glad you're having fun."

"Hey, beautiful babes," Char says, joining us with a wide smile.

"I'm glad *you're* enjoying yourself too."

"Me too."

Julian appears and throws his arm around Sage. "I need a darts partner. Save me from sucking?"

She rakes her eyes over him. "Only if you play to win."

"Always." He grins, grabbing her hand and dragging her away.

They are too fucking cute.

Charlie is texting incessantly on her phone, and there's a worry crease on her forehead.

"I've gotta call Nash, I'll be right back," she says, spinning away without looking up from her phone.

I decide to check how Elijah's pool game is going and weave my way through the crowded house. I'm almost to the table when I see him and Andi standing near each other. He smirks down at her, and my heart drops to my stomach. I spin around just as Theo appears, holding two shot glasses with lime wedges on the brim.

"Another one... really?" I ask, groaning.

"You can handle it." He winks with a mischievous smile that screams trouble. We clink before downing the tequila, and my throat is so used to the liquor at this point it doesn't even burn.

I suck on the lime, face twisting slightly. "Care to continue what we started last week?"

His eyes flick over my shoulder, then back down at me, and he smiles like the Cheshire Cat. "Elijah's right. You really are the perfect woman."

19

ELIJAH

"Where are you hoping to get drafted?" I ask Noah as he lines up his shot.

"*If* I get drafted… anywhere but Florida." He taps the tip against the cue ball, sending one of his striped balls against the wall, missing the pocket. "I'm ready for a change of scenery."

"*When* you get drafted," Desmond corrects.

"Yeah, we all know you're a first-round pick," I agree, lining up the cue ball, angling towards the eight. "You may be shit at pool, but you're damn good at throwing a pigskin."

Noah rolls his eyes, fighting a smirk. "Stop sweet talking me, Anderson."

I slide the pool stick between my fingers and pocket the eight, winning the game.

"Nice!" Desmond says, high-fiving me.

"Alright, who's next?" I ask, holding up the pool stick, ready to get back to Sophia.

A freshman on the team grabs it, and I make my way through the house. My eyes snag on a blonde head bobbing back and forth near the dance floor. Another familiar frame comes into view, and I stop dead in my tracks at the sight of Theo holding Sophia close. Her arms are around his neck as she sways with him to the beat of the music.

My brain knows he's doing this to screw with me, but the adrenaline pumping through me says to break this shit up right now.

I take a calming breath, heading directly toward them. My hand finds the small of Sophia's back, and I lean down to her ear with clenched teeth. "This isn't what I'd call being a good girl."

"Maybe not." She spins around, smiling at me with glossed over eyes, and grinds her ass against Theo. "But I'm having *sooo* much fun," she slurs.

Great, she's wasted.

My eyes flick to Theo, who's wearing an amused grin on his face, and I want to hit it right off him. Sophia turns back around, hooking her hands around his neck. *Really?* I mouth at him with raised brows.

He lets out an amused laugh before gently grabbing Sophia's hands from around his neck.

"Sorry, angel face," he says, tapping his forehead to hers. "I think that's enough fucking with E for tonight." He pulls away, locking eyes with me, then bends down and whispers something in her ear, causing her to roar with laughter.

Well, guess who's getting a horse tranquilizer in his morning coffee?

He leaves us, and I immediately grab Sophia's hand and pull her to me. She huffs and rolls her eyes but doesn't fight me as I hold her close, swaying us to the beat.

"Why are you such a wet blanket?" she asks, eyes filled with irritation. "Really putting a damper on my *fun*."

"You're drunk, Sunflower. And I promise Theo was only after one thing."

"Oh yeah?" She rolls her eyes dramatically. "Maybe I wanted that one thing too."

I narrow my eyes down at her as my veins buzz with jealousy. "*Oh yeah*? And what's that?"

"You know *exactly* what," she says, mocking my earlier comment.

"Spell it out for me."

She attempts a serious face. "Tryna get my jalapeño coochie wet."

I let out a rumbling laugh. "Shit, baby, you *are* drunk."

"You know? Someone to soak up this sunflower's sweet nectar." Sophia gestures to her silhouette. In a moment of weakness, I reach out and place my hands on her hips. She rests her palms on top, dragging mine along her every curve. My eyes flutter shut, savoring the feeling of her body under my touch. "So if Theo's only after one thing... what are you after?"

Opening my eyes, I look down at her and glide my thumb along her jawline. "Just making sure you don't do anything you'll regret tomorrow."

"What makes you think I would regret Theo?" she asks, her eyes dancing with mischief as she silently challenges me.

I take a deep breath, trying to calm the pounding in my chest. "You might not, but I'd regret letting you leave with him again," I admit, staring down at her intently.

"Why? Weren't you enjoying the company of *Andrea*?"

"She prefers Andi."

"Right." She looks away from me. "And it seems like you prefer *Andi* too. You didn't have to interrupt me and Theo."

A dumbbell presses on my chest at the realization I made her unintentionally jealous. *Is that why she danced with him?*

"First of all, there is no 'me and Theo.'" She smirks as I grab her chin and bring her gaze back to mine. "And Andi and I are just friends." I rest my forehead against hers.

"With benefits?" she asks with a tight jaw.

"No benefits." I shake my head, making sure she gets the point. "Not anymore. *Just* friends."

She stares up at me, eyes wandering all over my face before returning to mine. "Good."

"And for the record, I prefer *you* over anyone." I rub my thumb over her bottom lip. "Anyone."

"Good," she repeats breathlessly.

"Now will you shut your cute mouth and dance with me?" I twirl her around, and she stumbles against my chest. Her sweet laughter hits my ears just as the song switches to "Sunflower" by Post Malone. I glance up to see Theo winking at me from near the speaker.

The tranquilizer sabotage might have to wait.

Sophia looks at me with a curious gaze. "Did you pay someone to play this?"

"Lucky coincidence?" I smile down at her.

"You know what, Elijah?" she slurs before resting her head against my chest. "You're my favorite."

"Your favorite what?" I ask, running my fingers through her hair.

"Just my favorite."

"Slow down, damn," Sophia calls from behind me as we finish up our sixth mile in the perfect overcast weather for an afternoon run. Slowing my pace, I come to a complete stop as she jogs up next to me, trying to catch her breath.

"Who came in last now, baby?" I waggle my eyebrows at her.

"It's not fair." She gasps for air. "You were sober last night, and I'm fighting off a raging hangover."

"Next time don't do tequila shots with Theo."

Seeing them dance together snapped something inside me. He's my best friend, and I was ready to poison his morning coffee for grinding with a girl who's not even technically mine. I've never felt that vindictive before. Ever.

That's Theo's area of expertise.

"Shit happens." She shrugs, and I roll my eyes playfully. Sweat drips down her chest, disappearing in the valley of her breasts, and my mind wanders to all the other ways I could make that happen.

"You know, you're trouble sometimes, Sophia Summers."

She giggles. "You have no idea."

The perfect overcast darkens, and small drops fall from the sky. Sophia's head falls back, allowing the cool water to sprinkle over her. We walk down the sidewalk towards our dorms, and Sophia is still trying to catch her breath.

"Damn, girl, I thought you were a runner."

She levels me with a single glare. "Raging. Hangover." The sky splits open, pouring buckets of rain on us. "Great."

"Let's go to my place, it's closer."

"Sure, whatever," she agrees, not picking up the pace.

"Come on, babe. Speed up. You're gonna catch a cold."

"I'm trying." She groans. "And you know, sometimes you sound like a ninety-year-old woman."

I spin around, jogging backwards. "Just a little farther. You've got this."

"Seriously, I can't." Sophia stops completely, holding her hands against her forehead. "It's fine. It'll wash off the sweat." I walk towards her and bend down. "What are you doing?" she yelps as I throw her over my shoulder.

"Getting out of this damn rain before you get sick."

"That's a myth!" she shouts through fits of giggles as I jog towards my building. "People dance in the rain all the time and don't catch colds!"

"Well, I'm not taking any risks," I say breathlessly.

"No risk, no fun!"

By the time we walk into my apartment, we're both sopping wet from head to toe.

"It's colder than a penguin's balls in here," Sophia says as an involuntary shiver overtakes her body.

"Told you you'd get cold." I smirk down at her, and she rolls her eyes.

"That's not the same thing."

"You can borrow some clothes, and I have chicken noodle soup if you need it."

She stands there, scrunching her face at me. "I'll just take the clothes. Thanks."

"Fine, no soup for you," I mutter, retrieving my CBU football T-shirt and matching sweats from my dresser.

"Mind if I use the shower?" she asks as I hand them to her.

"Be my guest. Towels are under the sink."

She goes into my bathroom, and I refrain from making a joke about saving water since I'm just thankful she agreed to come back to my apartment in the first place.

I use Theo's shower, pull on a pair of sweats, and head back to my room just as Sophia is stepping out of the bathroom. My clothes swallow her whole, and it's cute as shit.

She pauses in the doorway, eyes roaming over me from head to toe.

The wind picks up outside, battering rain against the window, and Sophia's amused eyes rip from mine, looking toward it.

"I checked the radar, and it's supposed to be pretty bad till morning. You're welcome to stay here." She looks at the bed, and I can see the wheels turning in her brain. "If it'll make you feel better, we can build a pillow wall," I suggest, unable to stop the teasing grin from spreading across my face.

"That seems unnecessary. I think we can keep our hands to ourselves."

I'll do my damndest...

We get into the full-sized bed, our sides touching.

"Here." I turn on the TV and hand her the remote. "Pick whatever you want."

"*Whatever* I want?" she asks, grinning.

"You heard me."

I made us sandwiches to help fight Sophia's hangover, and we're now four episodes deep into some show called *The Vampire Diaries.* I tried to get her to pick something different, but she said "no takesies backsies"… and here we are.

"So this is the Stefan guy you compared me to?"

"Yep, although now I'm thinking you're more of a Damon," she says matter-of-factly.

"I don't know if I should be offended or not."

"Trust me, Damon has his redeeming qualities." She grins.

"Guess I'll have to take your word for it."

A strike of lightning cracks outside the window, and a loud rumble of thunder follows quickly after. Sophia jumps, grabbing my arm as my bedside lamp flickers and the TV shuts off from the power surge.

"You okay?" I ask as her forehead creases with worry lines.

"Yeah." She looks up at the ceiling, green eyes glistening. "I just hate storms."

I roll on my side to look at her, and she turns toward me, mirroring my position. "I'm sorry." Her hand is resting on my arm, and I take it in mine, interlocking our fingers. With my free hand, I brush a stray hair behind her ear and rub my thumb along her cheek.

"Little sun showers and stuff, I'm fine." She blows out a breath. "Just bigger thunderstorms freak me out… It's how my sister died."

Lightning pops again, causing another round of rumbling thunder. Sophia squeezes her eyes shut, tensing under my touch as her breathing grows sporadic.

"Hey." I tip her chin upwards, and her eyes pop open, connecting with mine. "Breathe, baby."

We inhale and exhale in rhythm, just like her panic attack when losing her sketchbook.

In.

Out.

In.

Out.

Once her breathing steadies, I tug her closer, and she melts into me. There's so much I want to say, to ask, and the longer we lie tangled in my sheets, the closer I get to revealing exactly how desperate I am for her.

"Thank you for this," Sophia mumbles against my chest. She snakes a hand around my waist, rubbing her fingertips along my exposed skin, and goosebumps scatter across my body.

"Of course." I pull away, memorizing every inch of her face.

"What?" She smiles up at me.

"You're breathtaking..." I'm struck down by the thought of her doing this with anyone but me. "I'm so crazy about you," I murmur, unable to keep the words from spilling out. "Every time I think you're feeling it too, you pull back... Why?"

She nuzzles her face into my chest. "I'm just... I'm afraid."

"What are you afraid of?" I pull away slightly, resting my palm against her soft cheek. "Please tell me what's keeping you from finally being mine."

"What if you leave?" Her voice breaks on the last word, cracking my chest wide open.

"Why would I ever leave you?" My eyes scan every feature of her beautiful, pained face.

"Everybody leaves."

She says it so matter-of-factly, it's a sharp sword through my heart. I place my hand on her hip, tugging her closer until we're lying nose to nose.

"I won't." My tone is sure and unwavering.

"You can't promise that."

"Yes, I can. I won't *ever* leave you."

"Elijah—"

"Sophia, you are the most perfect woman I have ever met. You're funny and kind, and where the hell else would I rather be than right here? With you." My heart pounds in my chest, and I pray to God she feels it too.

"There's stuff you don't know about me..." She swallows hard, and my stomach dips. "If you knew..." She shakes her head. "You'd leave."

As if there's anything in my sunshine girl's life that would scare me enough to leave her.

"I wouldn't," I assure her firmly. "I won't judge you, Sophia. Ever." I brush a strand of hair behind her ear. "You don't have to tell me whatever it is right now... but I hope one day you do. And that by then you'll realize I won't leave you because of it."

I know what it's like to have things you're not ready to share with anyone... things you're not ready to admit are real.

"Even if that's true... and you still want me after..." She pauses and blinks a few times. "Maybe it won't be your choice to leave," she says quietly as tears brim her eyes, and another bolt of pain ripples through me at my understanding of her double meaning.

"Sophia." I place my palm against her neck, rubbing my thumb along her throat. "That's not fair."

"But it's true." I want to promise her nothing will ever happen to me. That as long as she's earthside, I'll be here too. But I don't make the rules, and sometimes God has other plans. Even if they make no fucking sense. "You *can't* promise me you'll never leave because it might not be your choice."

"I can promise you I'll never *choose* to leave." *I really hope that's enough.* "But if you still aren't ready to give us a try... I'll wait."

"Elijah." She smiles with a soft laugh. "Wait until when?"

How long would I wait? Days? Weeks? Months? *Years*? I'm so devastatingly gone for this girl, she could leave the country, not speak to me for decades, and my heart would still belong inextricably to her.

She's entirely unraveled me.

"Until you're ready." I shrug, knowing it's the truth.

"What if that's never?" A tight knot forms in my chest at the thought of us never even having a chance to see where this goes.

"Trust me, Sunflower," I say, trying to convince the both of us,

"I'll wear you down, eventually." She rolls her eyes as her lips curl upwards.

"I might break your heart." She looks down at our entangled hands.

"Sophia..." Her eyes flick back to mine. "You're already breaking it every second we're *not* together."

Her breath hitches, mouth parting, and I swipe my thumb over her perfectly plump bottom lip.

"Kiss me, Elijah," Sophia says softly as her lips curve into a seductive smile, sucking the breath straight from my lungs. I roll on top of her, smiling as I replay the three sweetest words she's ever said to me on a loop in my head.

Kiss me, Elijah.

"Didn't we pinky promise to *just* be friends?" I tease as my face hovers mere inches above hers. She licks her lips, and my cock twitches in my sweatpants.

"Seems like *somebody* didn't get the memo." She grins victoriously with raised eyebrows, gesturing towards my Benedict Arnold of a dick.

"I don't want to start kissing you and end up doing something you're not ready for," I say, looking at her seriously. "Because if I kiss you..." I exhale a heavy breath, thinking of all the things I want to do to her. "I might get a little carried away... But you can always call a timeout, okay?"

"Elijah." She lets out a melodic laugh, her breathing getting heavier. "For fuck's sake, would you kiss me already?"

I love how impatient she is for me.

How she went from fighting our connection to begging for me with a single admission.

I lower my head slowly with the full intention of teasing the shit out of her, but the second my lips touch Sophia's, an uncontrollable hunger grows inside. I part her mouth with my tongue, entangling hers with mine, then roll onto my back and pull her with me so she's settled on top, a leg on each side.

"Do you have any idea how bad I want you?" I mumble into her mouth between kisses as I gently brush her hair back.

"Why don't you show me?" she asks breathlessly while ripping the borrowed hoodie over her head and tossing it to the floor. She isn't wearing a bra, and I gasp at how perfect her breasts are. "Prove to me you know how to use those hands."

I bite my lower lip, releasing it slowly. "Yes, ma'am."

20
SOPHIA

The second Elijah told me I was breaking his heart every second we're apart, I lost all control, because mine was shattering to pieces every damn day just the same. Each time his eyes connect with mine, it fuels that insatiable hunger.

I need him.

Touching me.

Inside of me.

Everywhere.

And for the love of God, all at once.

There's a fire burning inside of me, and Elijah Anderson is one-hundred-percent pure kerosene.

My legs straddle him as my center rests flush against his muscular stomach. The sweatpants I'm wearing are getting in the way of reaching that glorious feeling, and I'm dying to grind skin to skin against his firm, rippled abs.

I've gone from hesitant to desperate in seconds.

He can't possibly promise he won't leave me after learning every dark part of me, but I'm choosing to live in the moment and enjoy the man in front of me—or rather, under me.

His stone-hard dick twitches against my ass as he pushes himself up off the bed, wrapping his arms around me while trailing kisses from my cheek, along my jaw, and down to my neck. He exhales a warm breath, and the hairs on my arms stand, my breathing increasingly more unsteady by the second.

With a bent head, he drags his teeth down toward my collarbone, sucking lightly. He's definitely going to leave a pretty bruise, but it feels too euphoric to give a shit.

Elijah flips me onto my back, hovering above me before gliding his tongue to the center of my neck. My eyes flutter closed as he trails kisses downward to the top of my aching breasts. He stops abruptly, and my eyes flick open and downwards to the sight of his sensual, mischievous grin.

"What do you want me to do to you, baby?" he asks, dragging a finger along the hem of my sweatpants.

I would give my left tit if you'd suck the right one right the fuck now.

"Anything you want," I pant impatiently.

"*Anything* I want?" he asks with eyes so filled with lust I'm dripping with desire.

"You heard me."

"Hmm," he hums against my chest, and the vibration rattles to my core. "Tell me, Sophia, are you the kind of girl that makes love or likes to fuck dirty? Should I be Jack Dawson or Christian Grey?"

My clit throbs from his deliciously filthy line of questioning, and I grin at his casual reference to not only *Titanic*, but *Fifty Shades of Grey*. "How about you just be Elijah Anderson for tonight, and we can save the role playing for tomorrow?"

His eyes dance with amusement as he bends his head and sucks my nipple between his teeth, causing a yelp to escape me at the combined pain and pleasure.

He continues nibbling as I glide my hands down his exposed torso to his sweatpants, slipping just below the hem. I drag a finger slowly along the edge of his briefs, pausing in the middle before venturing lower—inch by inch. He rolls his hips, causing his bulging cock to press against my hand, and I wrap my fingers around it.

If I could choose one superpower in this moment, it would be to blink and be buck fucking naked.

There's too much clothing, not enough skin contact, and I am too damn empty. It's embarrassing how impatient I am for him to fill me completely.

Question: what does it take to turn Sophia into a desperate little ho?

Answer: apparently a six-foot-four football player with an eight pack and a filthy mouth.

He tugs both my hands out of his pants, bringing them over my head, and twists them together. One of his large hands holds my wrists in place with a single grasp.

I've never seen Elijah be so dominant, and fuck me sideways, I love it.

I wiggle my arms to test how strong his hold is, but he has me locked in place.

His hungry gaze softens for a brief moment as he stares down at me. I give him a slight nod of approval, and the passion reignites, transforming his eyes into a flick of blue fire.

Elijah leans down, kissing me lightly before slipping his tongue between my lips, enveloping me with his addicting taste. *And just like that, cinnamon's my favorite flavor.*

His hold remains firm on my wrists as he lowers his head to kiss my jaw. He nips the center of my neck before dragging his tongue from my collarbone down between my breasts to the hem of my pants. I can't believe his arm span is wide enough to keep me "hand-cuffed" but if there is actually a heaven, I think this would be it.

"I'm assuming we're going the Christian Grey route," I tease, wiggling my hands under his firm grasp.

"Well, you do seem like you're enjoying it." He grins up at me as his face hovers inches away from my throbbing center.

"I'd be enjoying it more if we had fewer clothes on," I admit.

Elijah's starved gaze burns me from the inside out. He's about to destroy me, and I'm going to enjoy every delicious second of it.

Releasing my hands, he climbs off the bed and stands in front of me like a damn god.

I'm ready to drop to my knees and worship the fuck out of him.

Elijah grabs the hem of his sweatpants, dropping them to his ankles along with his boxers. His dick pops free, standing at attention.

"Hello, soldier" slips out of my mouth, and he lets out a deep chuckle while kicking his pants off, standing before me gloriously naked. My mouth parts open at the sight. He's *fucking* huge. Like, big-as-a-walrus-dick huge.

Okay, that may be a slight exaggeration... but huge nonetheless.

"I don't know if that's gonna fit," I blurt. *Goddammit, Sophia. Are you going to play it cool at all?*

He strokes himself, arm veins on full display, and drool pools in my mouth.

"Don't worry, baby." He grins lazily, gaze wandering from my toes slowly upwards until it finally lands back on my eyes. "I'll take my time stretching your tight little pussy till it's ready for me." My body trembles at the promise as heat radiates between my thighs.

He grabs both my ankles, yanks me to the edge of the bed, and grabs the bottoms of my sweatpants, tugging them off. I'm not wearing any underwear, and he stares down at my naked body with parted lips as his chest heaves.

"Damn perfection," he says breathlessly.

He grips my thighs, dragging me until my "tight little pussy" presses directly against his hard, throbbing cock.

"How bad do you want me, baby?" he asks teasingly, rolling his hips against me.

I'm ninety percent sure if he does that again, I'll come on the spot.

"Elijah," I say breathlessly, trying to maintain my composure, but there's none to maintain. I am so horny I could pass out. "If you're not inside of me in the next ten seconds, I'm putting my clothes back on and walking out of here."

His cock twitches against me as an irresistibly devastating grin forms on his lips. Any of my previous worries about him not fitting have been moved to the "we'll worry about how to walk tomorrow" pile.

"Damn, Sunflower, you're my every fantasy come to life." His searing hands glide down my sides as he chuckles softly, stepping forward to press his delicious dick against my opening. My clit throbs so hard the rhythm itself is about to give me an orgasm. A breath catches in my lungs as he swipes the tip between my lips.

"Five... four... three..." I count down, taunting him.

As if I have a single ounce of willpower to drag myself away from this man.

"Calm down, baby." He chuckles, obviously amused. "I want to enjoy you." His ravenous eyes narrow at me. "I want to taste you." My lips part at the insinuation as he glides his warm, strong palms up my inner thighs and pushes them apart, spreading me wide for him. He finds my clit, rubbing his thumb over the sensitive spot, and my back bucks off the bed as I arch against his hand.

"It's been ten seconds," he says. "Would you like to leave?" I try to play along, but I look like a damn fish opening and closing my mouth, unable to say a single syllable, causing a smug smirk to break out across his face. "That's what I thought."

Elijah drops to his knees. I'm teetering on the brink of nirvana just thinking about him touching my soaking wet lips.

"Look at my pretty pussy," he praises just before dipping his head and tasting my most intimate place. He glides his tongue upwards, flicking it over my throbbing clit.

"*Oh, fuck,*" I moan breathlessly, unable to stay quiet at the pure euphoric pleasure.

"Mmmm," he hums against my aching flesh, the vibration sending ripples of desire throughout my entire body. "Fucking delicious, baby."

He continues swiping his tongue against me, and a breath catches in my lungs as he glides a single thick finger into my opening.

"We've gotta get you nice and stretched for me," he says in a gravelly tone while pumping his finger.

He adds a second finger, continuing the rhythm. It's too much and not enough, and my entire body is a raging inferno—each touch bringing me closer to my inevitable combustion.

"More," I moan greedily.

"What?" he asks, eyes dancing with amusement.

"I. Need. More," I pant out.

My opening burns as it stretches to accommodate the addition of another large finger. I've never felt such delicious pain.

I'm so close to being close.

Elijah bends his touch inside of me, hitting that glorious spot, and a loud, pleasure-induced scream leaves my lips. He slides his fingers out abruptly while rising to his feet, staring down at me with heaving breaths.

"Damn, woman, are you trying to make me come without even touching my cock?"

"Are you trying to give me blue balls, Elijah?" I pant. "What the fuck?"

A devilish smile plays upon his lips as he opens the drawer next to his bedside table and pulls out a condom. The implication sends a wave of anticipation through me. Using his teeth, he rips the packet open and rolls it on his thick cock before positioning himself back in front of me at the edge of the bed. He swipes his dick between me, pressing gently against my opening.

He slides inwards, allowing me time to adjust to his size, then pushes a few centimeters more. He hooks his arms under my legs, gripping the sides of my thighs, continuing to stretch me little by little—I whimper at the euphoric burn. Elijah stares down at me, his hungry gaze flicking to my breasts jiggling with each thrust. A few inches of his thick cock are inside of me, but I'm growing impatient.

"Please," I beg, placing my hands on his and staring into his eyes.

"I don't want to hurt you, baby."

It amazes me how a man so obviously desperate for me can be this infuriatingly patient.

"Elijah," I say in the most convincing tone I can muster. "So help me God, fuck me now or I'll do it myself."

A dark brow rises in surprise before he pulls out of me, and I whimper at the loss. "Needy girl." He chuckles, then uses both hands to flip me onto my stomach. "Get on your knees," he commands, and I happily oblige. He squeezes both cheeks before serving a stinging slap, and I yelp. "Damn, baby. You're so perfect."

I giggle as my pussy tightens, and he tugs me to the edge of the bed.

"Lift your hips, sweetheart." I do as instructed, and he presses his dick against my opening, slipping just barely inside. "Are you sure you're ready?" His fingertips firmly grip my hips—a hot, searing touch branding me for life.

"If I get any more ready, I'll be coming on your cock, Elijah."

"Okay." He chuckles. "If I'm ever hurting you, ju—"

"Yeah, yeah. Trust me, I'll let you know." The last syllable leaves my mouth, and he sinks inside, filling me fully. I moan out in plea-sure—in pain—in pure and utter bliss. He thrusts in steady rhythm before reaching around and placing his hand on my throbbing clit. He rubs his fingers against me, and it's overwhelming in the best way.

"I—Oh my—Oh, Elijah…" I cry out loudly, but I'm too in the clouds to fucking care. Theo isn't home, but it wouldn't surprise me if the whole damn building can hear me moaning Elijah's name.

Let them hear.

"That's right." He chuckles breathlessly. "Tell everyone who this sweet little pussy belongs too."

"*Elijah!*" I scream louder.

I'm not a vocal girl, but something about his dick twitching inside of me and the desperate tone of his voice has me turning the sound up to eleven.

"Good girl," Elijah rasps in my ear, and goosebumps trickle down my spine. "Now I want you to fall apart."

His long, hard dick presses directly against the bullseye, and I close my eyes, ready for the fireworks. He thrusts deeper, and the orgasm rips through me like a tornado, forcing a high-pitched moan to escape my lips. "You take me so well, baby," he praises, and a new kink has been unlocked. "Milk my fucking cock."

As requested, I fall completely apart, my insides convulsing around his perfect dick.

A throaty moan escapes his lips, and I wish I could see what I'm doing to him—watch his face as he comes inside me, knowing I'm the one who made him lose all control.

Next time we do this position, it's going to be in front of a damn mirror.

He thrusts one more time, then stills, removing his hand from my clit, and holds himself above me.

"Sophia," he pants in my ear. "You look like an angel. Fuck like a goddess. I've never been more in love."

I chuckle at his words, my heart racing at his mention of love, but I know it's just a figure of speech. He pulls out of me, and I whimper at the loss as he stands up, then rolls me gently onto my back.

"Don't move," he instructs, disappearing to the bathroom as I try to calm my erratic breathing. Rain ticks against the window and my eyes flick toward it, but instead of debilitating fear, I feel nothing but bliss.

Turns out letting Elijah in was the best form of replacement therapy.

He returns, sans condom, still butt-ass naked, and stands at the foot of the bed, staring down at me appreciatively.

"What?" I ask, laughing as I lie there spread eagle, praying for a round two. My wrecked pussy disagrees, but she's not in charge right now.

"Where have you been all my life?" he asks, climbing on the bed to lie down next to me. He rests his head on his hand and places his warm palm on my hip, skimming it with his fingertips.

"763 Parker Lane."

"Well, screw the guy who didn't plug that into my GPS years ago." His rumbling laugh vibrates throughout my entire body as he tugs me to him for a deep kiss. "Thank you for not breaking my heart today."

"Thank you for not breaking my vagina." I wink.

"Sophia!" He bursts out laughing. "Damn it, I can't with you."

"You love me," I say before I can think better of the words.

"I like you," he replies.

"Well, that's an improvement."

I wake the next morning to sunlight flooding through the window as Elijah's large arm drapes over, holding me flush against his warm body. He pulls me tighter, and something hard presses against my bare butt.

Well, good morning to you too.

"Elijah," I say.

"Hmm," he grumbles into my hair.

"Think you could tell your little friend to stand down?"

I feel him chuckle against me. "Sorry, baby, he's just happy to see you."

"Could he be a little *less* happy? I'm so sore I might never be able to have sex again."

"Hold your horses, darlin'. That's crazy talk." He tugs me closer, resting his head between my shoulder blades while nudging his "friend" against me.

"*Elijah*," I beg.

"Fine, I'll go see if he'll *stand down.*" He begrudgingly rolls out of bed and heads to the bathroom.

As soon as Elijah shuts the door, I hop off the bed and scoop up his huge shirt, tugging it over my head. His intoxicating musky scent surrounds me as I walk over to his desk, looking for a blank notebook or paper and a pencil. I have an image in my mind, and I have to get it down right now.

I want to freeze this moment forever.

"Whatcha doing over there, Sunflower?" Elijah asks, leaning against the bathroom doorway in tight black boxers with arms folded. I struggle to pull my eyes away from the perfectly toned V pointing towards his glorious—

Sophia! Focus.

"Oh…" I frown. "I was hoping to draw, but I don't have my sketchbook."

He twists his mouth to suppress a smile. "I was going to give this to you for your birthday." He strolls over to his desk, my eyes drinking in every flex of his muscles as he does, and rustles through the top drawer. "But I guess a week early won't hurt."

"*Ohhh!*" I clasp my hands together. "Early presents? Yes, please."

"Sit on the bed and close your eyes," he instructs, and I climb on the mattress. "Hold out your hands."

I extend them, wiggling with excitement as he places something weighted in my palms.

"Okay, you can look." The mattress dips as he sits next to me, and I blink my eyes open. My lips part, but no words come out.

In my hands rests a notebook. The cover has a crumpled paper background covered in sunflowers and the words "We're all mad here" embossed in the middle. Tiny lady bugs sit on the petals and leaves, along with a honey bee buzzing near a sunflower.

"Elijah," I say, blinking back tears, unable to find any other words. This man is truly incredible.

"I just… You always draw the things important to you. I thought you might want an extra sketchbook in case you ever lose yours again." He reaches out, wiping away a lone tear of happiness that escaped. "I hope you like it."

"It's perfect…" I say quietly, staring into his heartbreaking baby blues. "*You're* perfect."

"Happy early birthday, Sunflower." He runs his fingers through my hair, then pulls me in for a long, soft kiss.

"Thank you," I mumble against his lips.

"Anything for you." He jumps on the bed in nothing but his boxers and poses with his arm under his head. "Now draw me like one of your French girls."

I giggle and nudge him with my foot before grabbing a pencil and doing exactly what I planned to do in the first place: draw this hot as fuck man half-naked.

It's just after eleven in the morning when I open the door to my room and find Sage leaning against the pillows on my bed with her arms folded. I'm wearing Elijah's huge T-shirt and sweatpants, so there's no way of getting around this.

"Well, well, well," she tsks. "Look who's doing the walk of shame."

An unabashed smile spreads across my face. "I'm not ashamed."

Her eyes grow wide, expression turning amused as she jumps to sit on her heels. "Tell me everything."

"I don't kiss and tell." I smirk, flopping onto the bed, facing her.

"Bullshit. I had to hear about every unsatisfying non-orgasm you had with Seth for months."

"Okay… then I guess I don't *orgasm* and tell."

She places a hand over her heart, sucking in a breath. "Now you *have* to tell me."

I pinch my fingers together, swipe them across my flattened lips, then throw away the invisible key.

"Okay, fine… But can you at least confirm it was Elijah?"

"Nah, I just thought I'd fuck some other guy, then wear a T-shirt home with 'Anderson' across the back," I deadpan, turning around.

"Sophia!" she gasps. "You *fucked* him?"

"Yep," I say proudly.

"Finally! One to ten, how good was his honey dick? Because if he fucks as good as he looks… I don't think I'd ever be able to walk again."

"Sage!" I throw a stuffed koala at her, and we're both bubbling with laughter. "I am *never* going to be able to walk again."

21
ELIJAH

There are thirty seconds left in the fourth quarter, and Texas A&M is beating us fourteen to twenty-one. We're on offense, twenty yards from the end zone, and all we need is one touchdown to tie the game and go into overtime.

Texas's defense is rough.

They slammed Noah so hard last quarter, Coach took him out for the rest of the game. Noah says he doesn't mind sharing the field, but I can tell all the play time he's missing from getting injured is bothering him.

I run onto the field and join the boys, getting into position. We have one play to make this happen. With burning lungs, I shout, "Down, set, hike!"

Julian launches the ball, and it lands flawlessly in my grasp. I scan upfield, finding both Theo and Desmond covered by defenders. The roar of the crowd is so loud I can barely hear myself think. I'm used to it from years of playing, but sometimes it still overwhelms me.

A defensive lineman slams me down so hard we both skid across the ground. The ball pops out of my hands, and I scramble, but it's no use. A player from the other team has already scooped it up. He only gets a few steps before he's tackled, ending the game. Shaking my head, I kick my cleat against the grass, frustrated as shit with myself. We were so damn close. All I needed to do was get that ball to the end zone.

The boys and I shuffle off the field, our heads hanging low.

Guess the team's better off with me riding the bench than calling the shots.

Once we get into the locker room, I sit down and bury my face in my hands.

"Anderson, it's not the end of the world," Noah says, sitting next to me and throwing an arm around my shoulders. "Does it suck? Hell yeah. We were close. We had those guys by the balls. But we'll do better next week."

"I feel like I let everyone down." Standing up, I tug my jersey over my head before chucking it into my locker.

"It's a team game, Elijah. It's not just you against the world." He squeezes my shoulder. "We win as a team, we lose as a team," he yells loudly. "Right boys?"

"Hell yeah," the team yells in unison.

"We'll work our asses off at practice this week, and then we'll kick USC's ass next Saturday. Okay?"

A slow smile spreads across my face. "Yeah, alright."

And this is why he's captain.

"Alright," Noah says, grinning at me. "Go shower. Don't want to be late to see the birthday girl."

We walk into Salty Pete's, the first bar of Sophia's Birthday Bar Crawl—insert jazz hands—and it's filled with drunk college students in ridiculous or slutty costumes. Noah, Desmond, Theo, Julian, and a few other guys from the team are staggering in behind me dressed as different zoo animals.

Girls ogle us hungrily as we pass, which used to give me a rush, but there's only one girl's eyes I care about being on me right now. I've barely seen her since she left my place Monday looking like a damn vision in sweats with my name blazoned across her back. If I thought I was in trouble before... I'm really up the creek now.

Everything about Sophia Summers is perfection.

Her beautiful face, her curvy body, her smartass mouth.

Damn. Perfection.

I've had my fair share of beautiful women in my bed, but she is hands down, no contest, the best I've *ever* had. Fantasies about that night have played in my mind for months, but they were child's play compared to the real deal.

We're out tonight with all our friends, but all I can think about is getting her home.

My eyes land on Sophia, who's standing by the bar chatting animatedly with Sage, a clear plastic cup with blue liquid in her hand.

"Hey there, birthday girl," I say, placing my hand on her side. Her little koala ears almost hit me in the face, and *damn*, we're finding a stock room right the fuck now. She's wearing a tight gray jumpsuit showing off her every curve, gray fuzzy ears, and black paint on her nose. Adorably sexy, just like her.

"Elijah," she squeals, pulling me in for a long, deep kiss, even slipping her tongue in my mouth. She tastes like sweet tequila, but I'm missing the intoxicating hint of whiskey from the night we met.

"Hey there to you too," I mumble against her lips. "I've missed you."

She nuzzles her black painted nose against mine, then kisses me again before admiring my costume. I'm clad in brown combat boots, khaki Chubbies, a dark brown belt, no shirt, and a brown floppy hat.

"*Hello*, sexy Steve Irwin," Sophia exclaims, rubbing her hands all over my stomach. "You are the hottest zookeeper I have *ever* seen."

"I almost dressed as a tree so you could climb me," I tell her with a straight face, and she giggles.

"No. *This* is perfect."

"So I'm guessing you don't want to return me then?"

"Absolutely not." She turns back to the bar and picks up her drink.

"Just so I'm up to date, how many have you had?"

"A few birthday shots at the dorm before we came." She tips her cup toward me. "And this drink Sage somehow got me." She stands on her tiptoes, giving me a peck on the lips. "I was waiting for my man so he could order me a real drink."

Her man.

"Oh, is that so?"

Another kiss. "Mm-hmm." A dopey grin spreads across my face as I savor the welcome PDA, excited she's not keeping us a secret. It's clear by the way I look at Sophia that I'm hers, and I guess this is her way of showing everyone she's mine too.

"Well, I'll gladly order your drinks, but I thought you might want to have something in case you need to order your own sometime." Her brows pull in confusion as I slip the small ID out of my pocket and present it to her.

"You got me a fake?" she shouts, snatching it from me.

"Damn, baby," I shush her looking around with a broad smile on my face. "Be cool."

"Sorry…" She giggles, her eyes squinting as she looks down at it. "Now I know why Sage asked me to take pictures on a white background… She told me it was for her portfolio. Lying bitch." She glares at Sage standing next to us, who wiggles the fake ID I got her as payment between her fingers before winking and blowing Sophia a kiss. Sophia reads the details on her own ID, and her eyes flick to mine. "Sunny Anderson?"

"Yep." I straighten my shoulders. "Thought Sunflower Anderson would sound a little too hippie dippie."

"At *23* Penelope Lane, Georgia." She cocks a brow, probably realizing I made my jersey number her address.

"Mm-hmm."

"I guess it's better than McLovin."

"Now would you like to get a drink, *Mrs. Anderson?*"

"You've been dying to use that line since the moment you got me this, haven't you?"

"Maybe." I shrug. "Just go easy on the tequila. I don't want you to be too drunk later when I give you your other birthday present."

"You got me *another* gift?" she asks with wide, excited eyes.

"Well, not so much I *got* you something as I'm going to *give* you something."

I wink, and she folds her arms over her perfect chest. "Your dick is my gift, isn't it?"

"You seemed extremely excited about my dick the other day," I scoff, and a tinge of pink rushes up her neck to her cheeks.

"Well, you better at least wrap a damn bow around it."

I wink at her as Sage pops up next to us. "Are you gonna drop and suck his cock right here in the bar or can we get this fucking party started?" Sophia's mouth falls open, and she shoots back the cutest death glare I've ever seen. "What?" Sage holds her hands up in defense. "Just saying what the rest of us are thinking."

"Alright, time for tequila shots," Theo says, turning from the bar and handing me and Sophia a glass.

Once we've all got a shot, Theo gestures for me to say something. I glance over at Sophia with a wide smile spread across my face. "To the sexist koala in the zoo. Happy birthday."

"Happy birthday!" Everyone cheers, and we knock back our shots.

We're at the next bar on the itinerary, and I'm discussing our shitty loss with Noah while watching Sophia across the crowded room chatting with her friends. A feeling of relief comes over me, knowing I can finally show her how much I care without all the mind games. Two guys come up behind them, and Charlie practically tackles one before sucking his face like an octopus.

"Who the *fuck* is that?" Noah grumbles next to me.

"Apparently Charlie's boyfriend."

The other guy, who's bigger than a Mack truck, places his hand on Sophia's lower back, then bends down and says something in her ear.

"Who the hell is *that* guy?" I say, mirroring Noah as my jaw clenches.

He doesn't remove his hand, and she doesn't shake him off. She looks up at him, and I can't tell if she wants to kiss him or cry.

"Apparently, you have some competition," Noah quips.

"Bullshit." I make a beeline for the bar and a girl runs into me, spilling her drink all over my exposed stomach. The cool liquid glides down to the hem of my shorts.

"Oh my God, I'm so—" Her gaze falls to my rippled abs, and her mouth drops open.

"It's fine," I say as I continue towards the bar, but Sophia's vanished, and so has the mystery guy.

There's no way she would cheat on me in the first week of dating. Okay, well, we aren't *officially* anything but... We're together.

I mean, I'm not seeing anyone else... *fuck.*

Now I'm regretting not coming right out with the "are we exclusive" talk, which is a talk I have *never* had and never even wanted to have—until Sophia.

Where the fuck did she go?

I make it to the bar, where Charlie is still wrapped around the other mystery guy.

"Hey, Charlie," I say, tapping her shoulder to get her attention.

"Elijah, hey!" she says, with a wide smile plastered on her tipsy face. The guy glances down at my hand on her shoulder, then back to me. "This is Jonathan, my boyfriend."

"Hey, nice to meet you." I remove my hand and offer it to him, which he accepts.

"Hey," he replies, and I return my attention to Charlie.

"Where's Soph?"

"Uh…" She glances awkwardly around the room.

"She's outside with Seth," Jonathan interjects casually, pointing towards the exit.

As if it's the most normal fucking sentence in the entire world.

She's outside with Seth.

Who the fuck is Seth?

"Thanks." I leave them, walking towards the exit. A hand grabs my elbow, and I spin around to find Purple Skittle glaring up at me. "Yes," I say, flustered.

"Don't go out there acting all jealous asshole." She raises her brows in warning.

"Excuse me?"

"I know what you're thinking, but you have *nothing* to worry about," she says with sincere eyes that only make me feel a grain of sand better.

"Who is he?" I ask, unable to help myself.

"Her ex," she says calmly.

"Who came here for her *birthday?* And I'm supposed to… what? Let him beg for her back?" I scoff.

"No. But you *are* supposed to trust she'll turn his ass down without you having to be her honey dick in shining armor."

"Sage," Julian coos, coming up and putting an arm around her shoulders. "Wanna dance?"

"It's about damn time." She looks up to him and smirks before turning her attention back to me. "Just think about what I said. Seth's a total hothead. She needs to know you're different. Also… Sophia doesn't like when people help her. She's a little too independent for her own good, so don't go smothering her already. You'll only push her away."

My brain says she's right, let Sophia handle this herself, but the liquor in my veins encourages something else entirely. I want to take Sage's advice. I want to take it so badly I surprise even myself by walking out to the patio.

My eyes scan the outdoor space, finding Sophia and her ex near the same place I tracked her down a few months ago.

"Please, Sophia, I miss you. I fucked up so bad. I didn't mean to —" he says loud enough I can hear across the deck.

"Oh, you're finally ready to admit you fucked up?" Sophia asks, folding her arms over her chest, and I stride toward them.

"Yes. Please, just… give me a chance." *What the hell is going on?*

"If you really know what you did was wrong, then let's go to the police." He glares at her, and I suck in a breath, freezing in my tracks. "Tell them the truth."

The police?

"No." Seth's voice lowers, turning cold as he towers over her. "We're not doing that. And don't forget you're in this with me, Sophia." His smile turns wicked as Sophia's eyes flicker with uncertainty, and a chill runs down my spine. "We're tied together for life."

For life?

What did you get yourself into, baby?

"So would you just stop pushing me away?" he tells her. "I fucking miss you."

Sage's words run through my head, reminding me not to be a

hothead. I take a deep breath, exhale slowly, then proceed towards them as calmly as possible.

"Hey, Soph," I say, smiling and pretending to not have heard the entire insane conversation that has a million questions running through my mind faster than Usain Bolt. Questions that can wait until a night that's not her birthday.

"Hey." She shifts uncomfortably.

"Do you mind, dude?" the dick says, scowling at me. "We're kind of in the middle of something."

"Sorry, *dude*, but it looked to me like the conversation was over." I glare at him before turning my attention on my wilted sunflower. "Wanna go inside and get a drink, babe?"

The prick looks between Sophia and me before a wide grin spreads across his face.

"This guy?" He laughs.

He fucking laughs.

"Seth, just leave." Sophia's shoulders deflate.

"Gladly." He smirks. "You coming with?"

"Excuse me?" she scoffs.

"Why don't we just get out of here and I can remind you how good *we* were together," he says with a smug grin.

The audacity of this dickwad.

"Yeah, there's *no* damn way that's happening," I say, slowly losing my cool guy facade.

"Honestly, man," Seth snaps, turning his attention to look down at me, "could you just stay out of this?"

I square my shoulders, trying to ignore the fact he's almost double my size. "Considering you're trying to take home *my* girlfriend? No."

A flash of surprise crosses Sophia's face, but she quickly recovers.

"You'll regret this, Soph," Seth threatens, walking toward the door to the bar.

Sophia runs a frustrated hand across her face, then looks up at me with worried eyes.

"Your ex?" I ask.

"That obvious?" she groans. "How much did you hear?"

"Nothing really." A bitter lump forms in my throat. "Want me to kick his ass?"

"*Ughh*," she groans, slamming her face against my chest. "Add another stuffed suitcase of emotional baggage to my pile. You ready to run yet?"

"Baby." I pull away and angle her face up to meet my gaze. "When are you going to get it through your beautiful head I'm not going anywhere?"

Am I curious as hell what she and the asshat were talking about? *Of course.* Does it have me considering even for one moment I don't want her to be mine? *Not a chance in hell.*

"You called me your girlfriend." She tilts her head, and my lips curve upwards.

"I know."

"Did you mean it?"

"Did you want me to?" I counter, and she scrunches her face, trying to shield her emotions, but the smile comes bursting through. "I'm not sleeping with anyone else," I add. She lets out a heavy breath, which I assume is in relief, then grins up at me. I wait for her to say the same, but it doesn't come. "And…?"

"And what?" she asks, pulling her blonde brows together.

"Are you going to sleep with anyone else?"

"Elijah." She laughs in amusement, rubbing her thumb along my jaw. "I've slept with two people in my life. That prick I know you just wanted to beat the shit out of, and you."

"Good." I place my palm against her cheek, looking directly into those gorgeous eyes. "Tonight I'm going to fuck you until that dick's name is permanently erased from your memory. Then we'll make love so good you'll never forget mine."

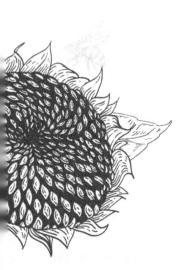

22
SOPHIA

Unmoving.
Not breathing.
Blood.
Blood everywhere.
Why is there so much blood?
Bile rises in my esophagus as I walk closer.
Please move.
You can't be dead.
Please, please, please, no.
No.
Wake up.
Please wake up.
Please wake up.
Please wa—

"I know, but I still think I could've done better," Elijah says to Noah, snapping me out of the nightmarish memory that causes a shiver to run down my spine. Elijah's arm is slung over my shoulder, a whiskey in his other hand as they talk animatedly about today's loss *—again.*

It's been a shit show of a night—Seth's a prick, Jonathan's encouraging it, and Sage and Julian got us thrown out of the last bar because they fucked in the bathroom. I honestly can't wait for the night to be over so I can go home with Elijah and get my second present.

I'm three margaritas deep, but once Seth showed up, any chance I had at a buzz died instantly. If it weren't for the fact all my friends came out to celebrate me, I'd have left immediately after that fight with Seth. I can't believe he had the audacity to show up, and I'm flabbergasted Jonathan brought him without warning me first. I knew blocking Seth's number would result in this shit. He didn't leave, of course, and I asked Elijah to be cordial so Charlie could spend some time with Jonathan.

We're at the last bar for the night, and it's almost two in the morning. Every time I see Seth's face, I have to fight the urge to vomit. I'm unbearably exhausted from carrying around this secret. It eats at me like a lion with its prey—teeth sinking in, ripping apart my flesh—leaving behind nothing but the carcass of who I once was. I've been so distracted with Elijah and school I *almost* forgot about it. The second I saw Seth, the lion of my nightmares returned to haunt me from the shadows of every room I'm in.

"I don't feel that good," Charlie slurs, swaying with a scrunched, queasy face as she leans against Jonathan. "I think I'm gonna go to the bathroom."

"Do you want me to come?" I offer, begging for relief from Seth.

"No, it's right there. I think I'll be okay," she says before disappearing into the women's restroom. I straighten my back to give myself the strength I'm currently lacking.

"She's such a fucking lightweight," Jonathan says to Seth, rolling his eyes.

"Maybe you shouldn't have shoved shots of vodka down her throat like water," Noah snaps, surprising all of us.

Jonathan's jaw goes tight. "Charlie has to learn when she's hit her limit."

Noah stares at him, shakes his head, and walks away.

"Girls, man," Seth says, chuckling and turning his attention to me. "Remember that time you got so shit-faced I had to carry you over my shoulder from the springs to my truck?" He folds over, laughing. "We had to sneak you in through your bedroom window so your dad wouldn't know."

My blood boils at his mention of our shared past, and Elijah's arm tenses around my shoulders.

"You threw up for two days and told your dad you had the flu... and he bought it," Jonathan adds in, laughing harder as my skin crawls with a thousand cockroaches at the unwelcome memory.

"I swear I was gonna pass out trying to lug your heavy ass up the side of the house to your second-story window," Seth snorts.

"You almost passed out carrying *her?*" Elijah scoffs in disbelief. "Damn, you're a bigger pussy than I thought." Seth's face turns beet red as Elijah turns his attention to Jonathan. "And shouldn't you go check on your girlfriend, Jonny boy? Make sure she's okay?"

"Her gag reflex is embarrassing. I'm sure she's having no problem pumping her stomach in there," Jonathan says before downing whatever's left in his cup.

When did he become such a dickwad?

"Wow... I think you two have been spending too much time with each other," I snap at Jonathan. "You're turning into an even bigger prick than him." I shoot dagger eyes at Seth.

"Thanks for the compliment, baby girl." Seth smirks at me before flicking his gaze to Elijah.

"Call her baby all you want," Elijah tells Seth calmly. "We both know whose name she'll be screaming later." A small laugh escapes me, and I immediately regret it after noticing Seth's expression.

It's his "I'm about to whip some ass" face.

In the ten months we were together, he was in seven different fights. He won all of them, thanks to his brawn not his brain, and I have no desire to see how he would fare against half of CBU's offensive line.

I glance down at Seth's clenched fists. He takes a step towards us, but I'm partially in front of Elijah since his arm is still protectively slung around my shoulders.

"I know her better than you *ever* will," Seth tells Elijah so icily I shiver, nauseated by the notion he's probably right. There're things I don't think I'll ever bring myself to tell Elijah. *How can I?*

He'll think I'm a heartless monster.

Then he'll leave.

Just like everyone does.

Elijah laughs and shakes his head. "Then you should know better than anyone how bad you fucked up losing her."

"I'm not worried." Seth smiles lazily. "Eventually you'll figure out who she really is." Seth's gaze finds me, his fiery eyes a warning to keep my mouth shut. "Then you'll be tossing her at my doorstep, begging me to take her pathetic ass."

I can't deal with this bullshit anymore. Seth's attitude gives me whiplash. One minute he's trying to get me back, and the next he's talking about me like I'm the most awful person he's ever met.

I'm so glad he's not a part of my daily life anymore.

I wish he'd cease to exist completely.

"Seth, will you just *leave?*" I plead, looking into his bloodshot eyes. "And it's obvious you don't care how Charlie is," I tell Jonathan. "So maybe you should both just go crawl back into whatever trash can you climbed out of."

"I never said I didn't care about Char," Jonathan says, mock hurt.

"Actions speak louder than words."

Seth laughs and shakes his head. "You know what?" He tilts his head. "Let's play a little game of two truths and a lie right here. Let Elijah get to know his *girlfriend* a little better," he mocks.

"How about we don't and you go fuck yourself?" I smile sweetly.

Seth's lips curve up into a sneer so sinister I physically shudder. "I'd rather fuck you instead."

"I'd prefer not to be fucked by a Tic Tac, thanks," I spit back.

"God, you're such a bitch sometimes."

My hand flies forward, the contents of my cup flying directly in his face.

"What the fuck?" Seth shouts as the blue concoction drips down his chin.

"I suggest you hit the road before the next thing thrown at your face is my fist." Elijah's voice is low and commanding. "And I won't be gentle."

"Come on," Jonathan says, annoyed, tugging Seth away. "She's not worth it."

Seth stares at me with devilish eyes that shake me to my core, and I swallow hard.

"You're right," Seth says, chuckling menacingly to Jonathan. "This used-up whore isn't worth it." Elijah takes a step forward, but I tug him back. "Let's go. Tell Char her salty ass friend made us leave."

They turn around and push their way through the crowd, out of the bar, and hopefully out of my life forever.

"I know I told him to leave," I say to Elijah as we walk into his place an hour later. "But I can't believe he actually did!"

"I don't know what to tell you, babe, he's obviously a dick," Elijah says.

"Who leaves their girlfriend puking on the bar bathroom floor?" I shake my head. "For fuck's sake, Noah had to carry Char to the Uber and bring her home. Shouldn't that be her *boyfriend's* job?" We get into Elijah's room, and he shuts the door, not bothering to lock it since Theo went home with a girl from the bar. "Like, I'm glad Seth left, but Jonathan didn't even make sure Charlie was okay before taking off!" My mouth moves a million miles a minute as we remove our shoes. I don't know if it's from the adrenaline or tequila, but I *cannot* shut the fuck up. I'm worried thoughts will slip out that I'd rather keep to myself.

"Sophia," he says, exasperated, pulling me to him in the middle of the room. "Everything's fine." I wrap my arms around his neck, looking up into his gentle baby blues. "We're home."

I frown, feeling guilty. *I'm so tired of feeling guilty.* "I'm sorry for bringing up my shitty ex."

He shrugs lazily. "I'm gonna make you forget him in a few minutes anyway."

"Oh, is that so?" I quirk a brow, determined to suppress the vicious lion of my past and live in the present.

"Yep." He kisses me and pulls me in for a tight hug. "That is so."

"Well, I'm still sorry."

"For what?" His eyes scan my face.

"Just… for the shit show that is my life. And all the stupid baggage I have." *And all the things I haven't told you but wish I had the strength to.*

"Babe," he says, using both hands to hold my face. "You have *got* to stop apologizing for being you. I want you, all of you, every single damn part. The good, the bad, the baggage, all of it."

But you don't know all of it.

I smile up at him weakly. "You're too good to me."

"You're too good *for* me, Sunflower," he counters, and I allow my lips to curve upwards at his words. "Now can we focus on the good parts of the night?" He kisses my nose, and I mentally decide to do just that. To enjoy my hot as fuck *boyfriend* like I've wanted to since the second he walked in the bar dressed as my Australian wet dream. "Like how damn sexy this outfit is on you."

Elijah eyes me appreciatively, then takes my hand and has me do a little spin. His fingers run along my sides and down to my ass. He rests a large palm on each cheek, then squeezes and pulls me toward him.

"Well, you looked pretty hot yourself there, Ranger Rick." My fingers memorize the feeling of his bare stomach.

"I only have one complaint." Elijah pouts.

"What's that?"

"This is *not* the kind of outfit you wear to screw in a supply closet."

"Elijah." I giggle, hitting his chest. "Can't we leave that M.O. to Sage and Julian?"

"Come on. We should be crazy sometimes too." His lips find my neck, sucking softly before he mumbles against my skin, "Sneak away and fuck while all our friends wonder where we are... Almost getting caught is half the thrill."

"Uh, sorry, Honey Bee." I laugh, clenching my thighs together at the fantasy. "I don't think that's *ever* going to happen."

"Sounds like you could be convinced." He lifts me up, and I wrap my legs around him. "Have you ever had sex in the shower?"

"Nope. Just boring, on the bed, missionary." I roll my eyes. "My past sex life is about as vanilla as they come."

"Well, how about this time we do mind-blowing, in the shower, your back against the wall. And next time we'll find someplace a little crazier." Elijah winks. "We can turn that boring ass vanilla into a hot fudge sundae... with nuts."

I throw my head back, laughing. "Mind-blowing, yes please. In the shower, fuck yes. Somewhere crazy and public? Never in our lives," I say sternly.

"Never is a long time, baby," he replies, pressing his mouth to mine, carrying me backwards into the bathroom. Whiskey envelops my senses as his tongue brands me for life.

He lowers me to the edge of the vanity, his palms still gripping my thighs.

"What's the fastest way to get you out of this contraption?" Elijah's lust-filled eyes analyze my jumpsuit.

"Honestly?" I giggle, remembering how hard it was to put on. "To let me do it."

"Watch you strip for me?" He sits on the already closed toilet seat with an appreciative gaze. "With pleasure."

I slide the thick straps off my shoulders and tug the top down to my hips. I have a black strapless bra keeping Elijah from getting the full show just yet. This jumpsuit is clinging to me like saran wrap, and I'm struggling to pull it down and off. Elijah grabs my arm, tugging me over to him, my chest directly in his face. He angles down to kiss my soft stomach. I run three miles a day and still can't seem to get my own set of abs. *What kinda bullshit is that?*

Using his large hands, he pushes the jumpsuit down my legs, freezing when noticing my iridescent black lace thong.

"You had this on all night?"

I bite my lower lip. "Yes."

"Sorry, baby," he rasps. "Next time we're *definitely* pulling an S & J."

"We are *not* making that a thing."

"It's *already* a thing." He chuckles, rubbing a calloused hand against my hip. "But it needs to be an S & E thing."

I take a step back, his hand dropping from my hip, and maintain eye contact while peeling the rest of the jumpsuit off.

Note to self: koala costume is sexy on but sooo not sexy to take off.

Elijah's amused expression turns starved, his gaze burning into my skin, bringing goosebumps bubbling to the surface.

He stands slowly, staring into my eyes while backing me towards the wall, caging me in. His warm palms glide along my exposed hips as he drops to the floor in front of me, and I will never tire of bringing this man to his knees.

He's level with the black scrap of lace, looking up at me with those "fuck me, baby" eyes.

Elijah grips my hips firmly, planting soft kisses on top of the fabric before exhaling a hot breath. My knees buckle, but his muscular arms hold me up as a soft moan escapes my lips.

He growls in approval, kissing along the hem of my thong before dragging his tongue underneath the fabric. I'm trying to remain patient and not act like the horny fucking teenager I was last time, but the movement has me letting out another quiet whimper.

He stands abruptly, and I frown. "Why did—"

"Take your panties off," he commands, undoing his belt buckle and ripping it off.

My gaze remains on the belt in his hand. "Make me."

He looks down at the thin strap of leather, then back to me, recognition flashing across his face. "Are you sure?" His stare is so intense I stop breathing as a rush of adrenaline rips through my body.

"Yes, Mr. Grey."

23

ELIJAH

Sophia gives me the sexiest "I dare you" look I've ever seen before placing her hands on the wall, awaiting her punishment.

I'm in so much damn trouble.

My chest heaves in anticipation as I stare at the belt in my hand. The idea of hurting her has me second guessing my offer, but if she wants to fulfill a bad girl fantasy, I'll happily oblige.

I fold the belt in half as her body trembles. Stepping closer, I place my free hand against her exposed side, and she stills under my touch.

"You've been a naughty girl, Mrs. Anderson." I hum into her ear. My mind wanders to how naughty she's really been in her past—the secrets she's keeping.

No, not now.

"Well, then why don't you punish me, *Mr.* Anderson?" she rasps out, playing along and bringing my mind back to the delicious present.

I step back, lift my arm, and crack the belt against her exposed ass cheek. The sound ricochets throughout the small room, her breath hitching as she yelps in pleasure.

"A *very* naughty girl." I drop the belt, and it clangs to the floor as I rub my hand over the raised red mark. "Now take. Your. Fucking. Panties. Off," I growl into her ear while squeezing her ass cheek in my hand. She lets out a shaky breath before shifting her fingers to the string of her thong and dropping it to the floor. "Good girl." I hum in approval before sucking her earlobe into my mouth and nibbling on the soft flesh.

I snake a hand around, placing it between her legs, and my fingers drench on contact. We stumble toward the shower, and I release my hold as she steps inside, turning on the water. She faces me, and my eyes wander over her perfect body, following the stream of water gliding between her breasts. My stone-hard dick throbs with the urgency to be inside her.

"I'll be right back," I tell her before walking to my room and grabbing a condom out of my bedside drawer. I return to the bathroom, setting it on the shelf near the shower. Sophia's already washed off the cute koala nose she was sporting all night. She's fresh faced and about to be freshly fucked.

Sophia's eyes follow my every movement as I release the button of my shorts, pull the zipper down, and drop them to the ground. Her smile only grows when I fist my cock, pumping it slowly as I step into the shower, pulling the curtain closed.

Stepping closer, I cage her against the side wall of the shower. The warm water beats down on us as her chest rises and falls.

"You made me a promise earlier."

"What was that, baby?" I ask, pressing myself against her wet, naked body.

"You promised you'd fuck me so good I'd for—"

"I remember," I cut her off, smirking.

"I'm ready to forget." She wraps her arms around my neck, squirming impatiently against me.

I glide the tip of my cock between her soaked pussy, our breaths hitching at the direct contact. She hooks a leg around my waist, tugging me closer, and I grip her thigh tightly to hold her in place.

My hips roll by reflex, grinding against her while I suck lightly on her neck, causing a quiet moan to escape her lips.

I reposition us towards the back of the shower so we're out of the direct stream of water, then grab the condom off the shelf and roll it on.

I grip my cock tightly as I swipe between her again, slightly disappointed at the loss of direct contact. That feeling vanishes the second Sophia breathlessly moans, "Elijah, *please.*"

All plans to tease her fade to the background as my dick guides itself toward her impatient pussy. I press my tip against it, and she curves the corner of her mouth upwards, satisfied she's finally getting her way.

"Take my cock like a good girl, would you?" I tease, and she lets out a soft moan at the promise.

I slide partially inside and consider asking if it hurts, but we're doing *Fifty Shades* tonight, so I keep that shit to myself. My hands wander down to her perfect ass, squeezing it firmly as I lift her up. She wraps both legs around me, and I step forward, slamming her back flush against the wall, knocking a breath from her lungs.

With slow pumps, I stretch her until she relaxes beneath my touch. I pull out partially, leaving just the tip in her warm, pulsating pussy, then slam back inside, filling her completely. She moans loudly in approval, encouraging me to increase my rhythm.

I fuck her.

I fuck her until she screams my name at the top of her lungs.

I fuck her so hard she cries out, begging me for more.

I fuck her until that prick's name is permanently erased from her memory.

The sound of our wet bodies slapping together echoes throughout the small shower as I give her everything I promised.

"I never want to stop fucking you, baby," I say breathlessly, inches from the edge.

"Who does this cock belong to?" she asks, and my lips curve upward at her filthy mouth.

"My sexy Sophia," I say, looking down at her perfect bouncing breasts as I pound her against the wall.

"I told you koalas were sexy," she replies with a breathless, fuck-fueled laugh.

I chuckle while maintaining my pace. "And I told you, you wouldn't mind my return policy."

She slips a hand between us, circling her clit, and moments later she's screaming my name for the second time. She pulsates around my cock, and we tumble together as she milks me fucking dry.

I hold her in my arms, unable to move or set her down until I calm my reckless breathing.

She's smiling at me, and I lean down, planting a sweet, slow kiss upon her lips.

"Incredible," I rasp, too out of breath to mutter another word. Thank God, because I'm one "come fuck me" look away from saying three more…

"Good morning, Sunflower," I tell Sophia as she lies naked under the crumpled sheets.

"Hmm," she hums against the pillow.

"I brought you coffee."

Her head pops up, and she blinks at me with sleepy eyes. "What kind?"

"Dirt black, just how you like it."

She smiles, sitting up and covering herself with the sheet, then reaches out with grabby hands. "At least I'm not basic."

I sit on the bed next to her, and she snatches the coffee and takes a big gulp. Thankfully, she doesn't burn her tongue. *I have detailed plans for it later.* She puckers her lips, and I lean over, kissing her softly.

"Can you stop covering up?" I snatch the sheet, exposing her breasts, and she gasps.

"Hey!" she protests but doesn't bother covering back up as she takes another sip of her drink. I don't hide it as my gaze drops to her perfect chest. Her nipples are hard and staring directly at me, begging for attention. My mind goes blank as I try to remember what I was doing before I came in here. Her stomach grumbles, jogging my memory, and my lips curve upward.

"I'm making your belly baby breakfast," I tell her. "Any special requests?"

She rolls her eyes, then smirks. "You can cook?"

"Does that surprise you?"

"I mean, a little. We always eat out..." Her brows furrow. "You're telling me my man can cook, and I've been eating burgers and ramen this whole time?"

"Don't forget the coochie tacos."

"Please never say that again."

"You said it first," I point out, and she shrugs, taking another sip of her coffee. "Okay, back to breakfast. What sounds good?"

"Options?"

"Eggs, cereal, panca—"

"Pancakes," she says, cutting me off. "Definitely pancakes."

"Okay. If my girl wants pancakes, that's what she'll get."

I head to the kitchen, whip up the pancake batter, then place a few scoops of it onto a hot skillet. A few minutes later, Sophia comes out in nothing but my large blue and white practice jersey.

"Sophia." I groan, looking up at the ceiling to take a calming breath. "There's no way I'll finish making your breakfast with you wearing *that*."

A seductive smirk finds her lips as she pads barefooted to the kitchen counter, hopping onto it. "Well, don't you need to eat too?" She spreads her thighs wide, and fuck me, she's wearing absolutely nothing underneath my jersey. A perfect pink pussy sits there, awaiting my hungry mouth. I abandon the stove, drop to my knees, and glide my palms up her soft skin.

I glance up at her, and the seductive smile on her face has me biting my lower lip so hard I almost draw blood. With slow movements, I push the jersey up so it rests on her hips and drag my fingernails down her thighs. "I can't decide what I want to do to you," I rasp out.

She lets her head fall back, arching her pussy towards me. Her sweet smell draws my mouth toward it like a magnet. I glide my tongue against her clit, and she squirms beneath me.

"More," she begs, and I pull away slightly.

Our eyes connect, and I lick her taste off my lips. "Don't worry, sweetheart. I'll take care of your needy little pussy." I dip back down, flicking my tongue over her most sensitive spot, and slide a single finger into her.

"Elijah," she moans just as the front door swings open. My head snaps up to see Theo standing in the doorway with a relaxed, amused expression. Sophia gasps and clutches my shoulders, her fingernails digging into my skin. Luckily her back is to him and the only thing visible are her exposed thighs. I stand up so he can't catch a glimpse at the places only I'm allowed to see.

"Damn, bro, pussy for breakfast?" He smirks and looks at the stove. "I'm gonna go take a shower. Make me some pancakes when you finish your appetizer." I give him a death glare as he continues to his room. "And Elijah, don't leave a drop of sweet syrup on that plate." He turns around, standing in the door frame, and stares at us. "We don't need another lousy review." He shuts the door, leaving us alone in the kitchen as his muffled laughter echoes through the walls.

Sophia stares at me, her mouth dropped open and a mortified expression on her face that quickly turns to laughter. "Well, that's a boner killer."

My forehead drops to hers, and I rub her hand against the front of my shorts. "Sweetheart, the whole damn team could walk through that door right now, and I'd still be this fucking hard for you."

Reaching over, I turn off the stove, then grip Sophia's hips, pulling her flush against me. She wraps her legs around my waist, and I lift her by the ass, making the way to my bedroom.

"Want to finish your appetizer?" she teases.

"Appetizer?" I lick my lips, stepping through the threshold of my room. "Baby, you're a whole damn meal." I kick the door shut behind me and toss Sophia on the bed to finish my all-you-can-eat buffet.

My muscles ache as I pull on clean clothes after our bitch of a Monday practice. Coach made us run drill after drill in the ninety-five-degree weather as the sun baked down on us, and I'm whipped.

"Anderson!" Coach Porter shouts, and I snap my head in that direction. "My office, now!"

My heart races as I make my way toward it, the guys grinning at me with stupid ass expressions all saying the same thing: you're in trouble. *What the hell could he want from me? I threw a forty-seven-yard touchdown pass during practice today.*

I pop my head in the doorway to see him sitting at his desk. "Yes, Coach?"

"Take a seat." His tone is stern, which only heightens my anxiety. I do as I'm told and sit down in the seat facing him. A heavy sigh escapes him as he folds his hands on top of the desk. *Shit. Maybe I am in trouble.* "Do you know why I called you in here?"

My knee bounces anxiously. "No."

"I spoke with Professor Mintz about the last test you took… How the fuck did you get a fifty-two on a damn world history exam?"

A fifty frickin' two. Are you kidding me?

"Shit." I run my fingers through my hair and sigh heavily. "I swear I've been studying, Coach. I even have a tutor. It's just… He's a hardass. I'm trying, I swear."

"And what about your statistics class? You have a C minus. If you don't pass your finals for both classes, your GPA is going to drop, and I don't need to remind you what that means." He cocks a dark brow, folding his arms over his broad chest.

"No, Coach." My elbows rest on my knees, and I stare at my feet. *How am I gonna get out of it this time?*

"Listen…" His tone turns sincere, bringing my gaze back to his. "I know you've had a tough year. I'm sympathetic, I really am, but you've gotta get your grades up or I'll be forced to bench you."

"Bench me?!"

I want to scream.

I want to throw up.

I want to punch something.

I'm finally getting a decent amount of playing time, and now Coach wants to freaking bench me.

"I have no choice, Elijah. Pass both classes or you're benched for the rest of the season. And hopefully you'll still be with us next year." My eyes burn as tears threaten to develop from frustration.

At my professors.

At all the pain in my life.

Most of all at my damn self.

I exhale heavily, and he continues, "You have to focus the next few weeks and pass your finals. If you need to skip a practice or two, let me know. We'll make it work. Alright?"

"I'll do my best, Coach. I promise."

How the hell am I supposed to focus when Seth and Sophia's conversation has been on repeat in my mind all weekend?

If you really know what you did was wrong, then let's go to the police.

I want to ask her what the fuck's going on, but part of me is scared as hell to learn the truth. Terrified of how simple words could shatter the thin glass of our happy bubble.

Sophia is the brightest light in my life. Most days I push away the darkness, pretending it doesn't exist, and being near her makes that exponentially easier.

What if she's not the sunshine girl I thought she was?

What if she's done something I can't ever forget or forgive?

What if she was right?

What if her truth changes everything?

A flash of golden hair snaps me out of my thoughts as Sophia walks out of her last class of the day.

"Hey, Sunflower," I say, getting her attention.

"Hey!" She beams and runs over to me, planting a rough kiss on my lips. My day instantly goes from pile of shit to pile of daisies. "How was practice?"

"It was fine," I say, my throat tightening.

"What's wrong?"

Just everything I've worked for is about to go up in flames. "Nothing, just a tough practice." The last thing I need is Sophia worrying or thinking I'm an idiot.

"Okay… Wanna get something to eat?"

"Sure." Another fake smile finds its way on my face. "Where does my girl want to go today?"

"Lazy Moon?"

"Yeah, that works."

24
SOPHIA

My taste buds explode as I chew on the delicious pepperoni pizza. *So fucking good.*

"Slow down, baby," Elijah teases, letting out a warm laugh.

"I can't," I mumble between bites. "It's the most delicious thing I've ever tasted. *Mmmmm.*"

"You say that every time we come here."

"And every time I mean it," I say, spotting Desmond walking through the door, and I wave at him.

"Hey, Soph," he says, coming up to our table. "Yo, Anderson, you got *ripped* by Coach today. What did he want?"

Elijah glances at me, then back to Desmond. "It was nothing."

"It didn't seem like nothing," Desmond pushes. "You were in there for a while."

"Drop it, Des," Elijah says firmly, with a clenched jaw.

"Damn, bro. Namaste." Desmond flattens his hands together. "Didn't mean to hit a nerve." Elijah rolls his eyes, attention turning back to his pizza. "See you guys later."

"Bye." I wave, and he walks away. "What was that about?" I ask once Desmond's out of earshot.

"Nothing."

"Come on, Honey Bee." I nudge his foot with mine. "What's going on?"

He looks up at me, frowning. "I failed my world history exam."

My heart sinks as I furrow my brows. "I thought you were doing well in that class now. You have an excellent tutor." I wink at him, and he chuckles weakly.

"Yeah, I know. I don't really get it..." He looks down at his pizza. "I'm kinda failing my statistics class too."

"What?" I ask, my tone full of surprise. "I had no idea you were struggling with another class. Why didn't you tell me?"

"You're just so damn smart..." He smiles at me sadly. "I didn't want you to think I'm just a dumb jock."

"Seriously? That was a complete joke." Shaking my head, I grab his hand, my heart aching behind my sternum. "I promise I don't think that. I'm so sorry. I didn't realize it bothered you."

"It didn't... It's just... my coach pulled me in his office earlier, and they could bench me for the rest of the season if I don't pass our finals." He pulls his hands away from mine and drags both over his face, leaning back in the chair. "I could lose my scholarship... I could lose everything."

"Elijah," I say softly, pulling his attention back to me. "We can figure this out together."

"I just... I didn't think it was going that bad, but I failed another quiz, and I *have* to pass my midterm or my only hope is finals."

"I wish you would have told me sooner." I place my hand on his.

"I know, I'm sorry. I just figured you couldn't help anyway since you're an art major and I didn't want to stress you."

"Well, I might not be able to help, but Charlie's an education major and has helped me with all of my math homework since seventh grade. I bet she'd be happy to tutor you."

"Really?" His face lights up. "That would be awesome."

"But you can't have the same arrangement with her we have."

"You mean how I fuck you before and feed you after?" He bites his lower lip, and I fight a smile.

"Yeah, definitely not that."

"Do you understand it now?" Charlie asks Elijah calmly after repeating the process of sampling and biases for the third time. Somehow she still hasn't gotten annoyed with Elijah, and I owe her big time. She really will make a great teacher.

"I think so..." His facial expression looks more like *what the fuck?*

"Did you read the notes I gave you?" Noah asks, referring to the stuffed binder he gave Elijah from when he took the class a few years back.

"Yes," Elijah groans. "I really appreciate it... but your hand-writing sucks, bro."

Noah throws a hand over his chest. "Hey. My John Hancock is excellent."

"Your John Hancock is horseshit," Elijah taunts, and Noah throws a pen at him.

Charlie's eyes bounce between them, an amused smile on her lips. "Are you boys done yet?"

"Yes, Ms. Benson." Noah smirks, eyes raking over her.

Noted.

"Do you guys want something to drink?" I ask, getting up off the couch.

"Water, please," Charlie replies.

"Tequila... stat," Elijah says, slapping a hand against the coffee table. I raise my eyebrows, and he sinks back in his seat. "Fine, water."

As I'm walking toward Elijah's kitchen, my phone vibrates in my pocket. I tug it out, almost tripping over my own two feet when I see the message.

UNKNOWN NUMBER

UNKNOWN NUMBER

I meant what I said on Halloween. We're in this together.

Shoving the phone back in my pocket, I swallow hard, trying to push his threat from my mind. Noah joins me in the kitchen as I pour the waters. He bends down, looking into the oven at his baked ziti, and I hope like hell it's almost finished because my mouth has been Niagara Falls since he put it in.

"Where'd you learn to cook?" I ask him.

"My mom." He grins proudly. "She taught me how to make her famous *panzerotto fritto* by the time I was ten."

"And it's paid off!" Elijah calls from the couch. "That shit's delicious."

"I went to Italy last summer, and my *nonna* wouldn't let me leave until I perfected making ravioli from scratch."

"Do you speak Italian?" Charlie asks Noah as she scribbles something on her notebook.

"Quando voglio sembrare sexy." *When I want to sound sexy.*

She bites her lips to stifle a smile, and I chuckle, carrying the waters back to the table.

"Something funny?" Noah asks me, sitting back down.

"Solo che ovviamente parli italiano." *Just that of course you speak Italian.*

Elijah flies forward in his seat, staring straight at me. "Hold up now. *You* speak Italian?"

"Quando voglio sembrare sexy." I wink at Noah, and he laughs. "Not a ton, but Leah and I spent a few weeks in Italy this summer, and I had to learn some important phrases."

I place the waters on the coffee table and Elijah pats his lap, so I lower myself onto it. "Say something else." He grins, slipping a finger under the hem of my shirt, rubbing soft circles on my back.

"Like what?"

"Anything. I just want to hear you talk again."

"Okay... hmm..." I flick my eyes to the ceiling, trying to think what I should say. Leah and I did quite a bit of practicing after being hit on by a few slimy Italian guys in Positano. *Ohhh, yes. That's the one.* "Sei solo un ragazzo eccitato che cerca di bagnarsi il cazzo." *You're just a horny guy trying to get his dick wet.*

Noah chokes on his water, and I giggle as Elijah bites his lower lip. "Damn, that was sexy... Another one," he rasps out.

I laugh but happily oblige. "Non mi interessa il tuo micropene." *I have no interest in your micropenis.*

Noah gasps for air, and Elijah smirks between us. "Care to translate?"

"Nope." Noah holds his hands up. "I'm good."

Charlie's cell buzzes on the coffee table for the umpteenth time. It's buzzed every thirty seconds for the past ten minutes. Jonathan's tried FaceTime, calling, and texting—she's ignored each one.

"Are you gonna get that or should I?" Noah reaches for it, and Charlie's eyes go wide as she snatches it off the table.

"It's fine." She clutches it to her chest. "I'll get it."

"You can use my room," Elijah offers.

"Thanks." Charlie smiles faintly, then rushes into his room and shuts the door. Noah rolls his eyes, slumping back in his seat.

"What's with you?" Elijah asks Noah.

"Nothing," Noah clips.

"Come on," Elijah presses, Noah's gaze connecting with his.

"Her boyfriend is a prick," Noah mutters, his face void of any emotion.

"No shit," Elijah says. "He was a total ass on Soph's birthday."

"Yeah..." Noah clears his throat. "The next morning too."

"What do you mean, the next morning?" I ask, gawking.

"It's not what you think." Noah waves me off. "I didn't want to leave Charlotte alone." He shakes his head, and my lips curve upward at his use of her full name. "She was super sick. So I stayed over and slept on the floor. He showed up the next day and..." Noah drags a hand through his dark hair. "I just fucking hate him."

The sound of Charlie yelling through the walls has all our heads snapping in that direction. Noah shoots out of his seat, his entire body tense as he rushes closer to Elijah's door. "Goddammit, Jonathan, I'm so sick of the fighting," Charlie says loud enough we can all hear. "I told you, nothing fucking happened with Noah!" My eyes snap to Noah, whose ear is all but pressed against the bedroom door as Jonathan screams through the phone.

The vein bulging in Noah's forehead tells me it must not have been good, and he's ten seconds away from breaking down the door to throw Charlie's phone at the wall. The entire apartment goes so silent you could hear a pin drop, and I'm assuming one of them hung up. Charlie swings open the door, slamming directly into Noah's chest. He reaches out, steadying her.

"Why do you let him talk to you like that?" Noah asks, exasperated.

"This is none of your business, Noah," Charlie snaps, pushing past him.

"Yes, it is." He spins around, trailing after her. "I'm sick of watching that guy walk all over you."

"I don't need this right now." She rushes to the front door and throws it open. "I'm going for a walk." The door rattles as she slams it behind her.

I hop off Elijah's lap and rush to follow her, but Noah holds a hand up, stopping me.

"I got it," he says before running out of the apartment.

"I didn't even realize they were actually friends." My eyes are glued to the door. "I mean, I totally agree with everything he said... just a bit surprised, that's all." I go to Elijah and sit back in his lap.

He tugs me close against him. "What can I say? Us CBU boys are overprotective of our girls." He kisses me on the head, and I smile. "And you don't know how hard it was for me to talk Noah out of beating that guy's ass when I wanted to join in on the fight." I swallow hard. "I hated hearing how Jonathan and your shit bag ex talked about you."

His shoulders are tense under my touch as I lean my face into his neck, groaning. "Hopefully we never have to see them again."

I knock on Charlie's door before nudging it open. "You okay?"

"I'm fine," she says, exasperated, turning to face the wall while lying on her bed.

"I brought your stuff from Elijah's." I set her backpack down on the floor next to her desk and walk over to her. "Char, come on. Talk to me."

She rolls to face me, and her head rests against the pillow. "I don't want to talk about it."

I lean down and hug her shoulders. "Char, we *have* to talk about this."

She sits up, releasing a frustrated breath. "I don't even know where to start."

"Try the beginning?"

"I just... I don't know what's gotten into him lately." A tear falls down her cheek that she quickly wipes away. "He's... he's always been such a great boyfriend. He was with me through everything. You know how much he helped me with all my family shit in high school. I just... I think playing college ball and all the classes are really stressing him out, and he's taking it out on me."

"Yeah, but that doesn't make it okay, Char." She looks down and starts picking at her pink nail polish. "It doesn't matter what the stress is in his life. He shouldn't talk to you the way he does."

"You sound like Noah," she grumbles.

"Yeah? What's going on between you two?"

"What do you mean?" Her curious gaze connects with mine.

"You and Noah…"

Her eyes go wide. "There is no *me and Noah*."

"I know… just, you know what I mean."

"I love *Jonathan*," she emphasizes.

"I know that, babe." She picks at her nails again, and I take her hands in mine. "I'm just curious. Noah seems to really care about you."

"We're just friends… We see each other around a lot during and after practices."

"And at away games," I point out, waggling my eyebrows.

"Yeah, there too." She grins with narrowed eyes. "But as I said, we're just *friends*. I've got a boyfriend, and Noah has a savior complex."

"I don't blame him with the way Jonathan talks to and about you."

She shakes her head. "You guys just don't know him like I do."

"Come on, Char," I say gently. "Even Noah said Jonathan was being awful to you the morning after Halloween."

Her eyes fall to her lap. "He'd find any reason to paint Jonathan the villain."

"Maybe you should stop making excuses for him and realize he might actually be the goddamn villain, Char."

"Can we talk about something else?" Charlie asks gently, and my mind wanders to the real villain of our story.

I let out a shaky breath. "I don't know what to do about Seth," I admit, and her eyes fly to mine. "On Halloween he kept crossing the line…" A chill runs down my spine. "He just—he gives me fucking whiplash. I don't know what to do anymore. I know he wants that secret kept, but I also know he wants me back. Both things equally terrify me because I'm afraid of the lengths he'll go to make sure he gets his way." Charlie's eyes go wide before she schools her expression. "I'm hoping after Halloween he realizes I've moved on and if anything, he's only worried about our silence. As long as we keep our mouths shut… he *should* leave us alone."

Charlie runs a hand down her face, not speaking for an excruciatingly long amount of time. "I can't believe things have gotten so out of hand," she finally whispers.

"I know." I clear my throat. "Sometimes I wonder if we made the wrong choice." Charlie's eyes connect with mine. "Sometimes I wonder if listening to him was signing our own death sentence."

25
SOPHIA

We stroll through the third floor of the library, finding an empty table in the corner to sit down. Elijah lets out a loud breath as he takes his books out, and I can't help but feel like there's something going on with him today.

He's been hot and cold since Halloween, and I'm wondering if he heard more of Seth's and my conversation than he let on.

I won't dare ask. I'm way too terrified to know the answer.

"Did you get your score back for our history test yet?" I ask, hoping that's the reason for his distance.

"I got an eighty-four." He grins, then flips open his statistics text-book, and the front lands against the table with a loud plop.

"That's awesome." I beam.

"Yeah… but I still have to pass the final." He shifts in his seat. "How'd you do?"

"I got a ninety-two," I say. He looks up and grabs my chin between his fingers, pulling my mouth to his.

"That's amazing, baby. You're so smart." He nuzzles my nose. "Too bad I can't siphon that knowledge through my cock when I'm fucking your brains out."

I throw my head back, laughing. "Yeah... too bad." He lets go of my chin, going back to his work, worry lines still prominent on his forehead. His tense posture is stressing me the fuck out. I want to ask him to open up, but I'm too scared of his answer.

Question: what's the best way to relieve your boyfriend's tension?

Answer: pound it out.

I place my hand on Elijah's knee. "Hey."

His eyes flick to mine, a slow smirk spreading across his face. "Hey."

Standing up, I extend my hand. "Come on."

"We just got here."

"It won't take long."

His eyes flicker a shade darker before he stands up, taking my hand, and follows me through rows and rows of books. When we're in an empty aisle, I pause for a moment, spinning to face him. His hands wrap around my waist, tugging me against him, and his grin is so damn sexy, I'm wet just looking at it.

He steps forward, caging me against a shelf of books, then whispers in my ear, "We're in the fantasy section... Should I show you a whole new world?" I kiss his neck, biting down on the soft flesh, and he groans.

I slip out of his grasp and arch a finger for him to follow me while painting on my most seductive expression. He rubs a hand against the front of his athletic shorts, hungry eyes raking over me as he hurries after. We finally arrive at a dark study room in the back corner, and I push open the door. Elijah follows me inside, reaching towards the light switch, but I grab his wrist, stopping him. His eyes connect with mine as I shut us inside the dark room, with only a faint light shining through the small window on the door.

"What are we doing in here, Sunflower?" he asks, his voice low and gritty.

I tug his arm, pulling him over to the back corner, away from the view of the window, and push him up against the wall. "You seem stressed. Thought I'd help get your mind off things."

He finds my sides, pushing up my T-shirt to place his warm palms on my hip bones. "Didn't you say we'd never have sex somewhere crazy?"

I don't need to see his face to know he's teasing me. "Who said we're having sex?" I play along.

"You can't tell me you brought me to this dark room for a make-out session, babe. I'm five seconds from bending you over the table." A thrill of anticipation runs through my body.

He backs against the wall as my hands find his waistband, toying with the edge. A warm breath hits my lips, and I stand on my tiptoes, grazing my mouth against his while slipping my hand completely under his athletic shorts and briefs. He sucks in a breath as I wrap my hand around his stone-hard cock, stroking him gently.

"Baby, you're driving me crazy," Elijah moans against my mouth. I press my lips to his for a soft, tongueless kiss. He rolls his hips, and a breathless groan spills from his lips.

My patience is dwindling, and I drop to my knees. "What are you —" His question is cut off as I tug down his shorts and boxers, finding his long, hard cock with my lips. "*Soph.*"

I glide my tongue along his shaft, flicking the top before taking the entire thing in my mouth. The tip hits the back of my throat, and I gag slightly before regaining my composure. My fingernails dig into his ass as his hips thrust in rhythm with my sucks. His cock jerks in my mouth, the sweet pre-cum coating my tongue, causing me to groan in approval. "So fucking good, baby," he praises with labored breaths that tell me he's getting close.

I stop abruptly and stand up. Before Elijah can complain, I pull the condom out of my pocket and slide it into his hand. He chuckles, and the sound of the foil packet ripping open echoes in the room. I help roll it onto his dick, stroking him a few times to make sure it's properly in place. He spins me away from him, reaching around my waist to unbutton my jeans, and pushes them down to my knees. His fingertips toy with the string of my thong, twisting one side in his hand before I hear a loud snap.

"Did you just rip my underwear?" I laugh as his hands snake to the other side, and another loud snap sounds throughout the room.

"Yep." He tugs them off, then bends down, shoving them in the front pocket of his shorts.

"Was that totally necessary?"

"No, but it was hot as shit." He squeezes my ass cheeks in both hands, and I yelp in pleasure. "Shhh," he hums into my ear, bringing his fingers between my legs. A gasp escapes my lips when he rubs against my clit. I'm so turned on, a damn sneeze could cause me to explode. He nudges me forward with his hips, bending me over the table in the center of the study room. "Mmmm. That's it, baby."

He trails his fingertips along my spine while nudging me with his hard cock. The pulsating between my thighs is out of control as my panted breathing surrounds us in the quiet room.

"Get on the table," he instructs.

"What?"

"Get on the *fucking* table." I climb up on all fours and glance at the small window, only seeing racks of books. The possibility of getting caught causes my clit to throb. *Guess he was right.* Elijah grabs my hips, gliding his tongue against my ass cheek before nipping it with his teeth.

"Elijah." I giggle.

"Turn over." I spin around, holding myself up with my elbows on the cool surface. He grabs my legs, tugging my ass to the edge of the table. I'm regretting keeping the lights off, wishing I could see how lust filled his eyes are right now. *I fucking love watching him lose control.*

Elijah's head drops between my legs, stubble scratching against my thighs, and I savor the delicious friction. He glides his tongue between my soaking lips before landing on my clit, flicking against the sensitive bud, eliciting a whimper from me. He reaches up, covering my mouth with his hand, but doesn't stop. "Elijah," I moan again, and this time he shoves the side of his hand into my mouth.

"Bite down if you feel the need to scream," he instructs. "Just be *fucking* quiet. If you cry out my name like that one more time, I'm going to come before I'm even inside of you."

I giggle, relishing the effect I have on him. "Who's the needy one now?"

He chuckles while kissing my pelvic bone, then stands up, placing his mouth on mine. I taste myself on his lips, surprised by how much it turns me on. He swipes his tip between me, pressing against my entrance. "Please," I beg.

That's all the encouragement he needs before sliding fully inside, causing a low whimper to escape my mouth. He thrusts in rhythm, and I moan as quietly as possible. Apparently it's still too loud because Elijah grabs the base of my neck, placing my mouth against his shoulder.

My lips part, and I lick along his collarbone, nudging the collar of his shirt to the side. He fucks me harder, and my teeth clamp down on his shoulder. A breathless chuckle releases from Elijah's lips as the release builds inside of me with every thrust. He dips his free hand between us, finding my clit easily, even in the darkness. I sink my teeth into his flesh. I've never been someone who was loud during sex, but Elijah makes me want to scream at the top of my lungs in the middle of the goddamn library.

"That's it. Let your pretty self fall apart." He rubs his thumb over my clit, panting praises, with his hot breath in my ear. My entire body shudders, free falling towards the beautiful oblivion before shattering into a thousand pieces of euphoric bliss. He jerks inside of me, thrusting a few more times before going still. Our heavy breathing fills every inch of the small space as I try to come down from one of the hardest orgasms I've ever had in my life. "Did you see stars, baby?"

I laugh breathlessly, sweat trickling down my spine. "I just rocket blasted through the entire fucking galaxy."

He lets out a low laugh that rumbles around, enveloping me, before pressing a gentle kiss against my lips. Our tongues tangle, and I lose myself, melting into him. He pulls away, running his fingers through my hair. "You continue to surprise me every damn day, baby."

"I aim to please." My fingertips trail down his torso. "Hope you enjoyed it."

"Shit, yeah, I did. Now let's get dressed before someone finds us with our pants around our ankles."

I almost forgot we were in the library study room, I was so wrapped up in him. "God, you make me forget where I even am sometimes."

He chuckles. "Tell me about it."

We settle back at our study table with stupid grins plastered across our faces. Elijah's hair screams "I've just been fucked," and it's so damn sexy. He looks down at his textbook, his cheerful demeanor immediately faltering as he flips through the pages. *Seriously? I screwed him in a study room, and it helped for five measly minutes.*

"Elijah?" I say gently, taking his hand in mine. "You're already stressed again. What's going on?" He glances at me, his shoulders deflating. "Let's just talk about it, and then I can make you forget again after." I wink, and his eyes drop to our hands.

"It's just school."

"You're stressed about school?" I ask, feeling relieved.

"Yeah." He frowns. "Just my classes and stuff, you know?"

"Yeah…" I understand, but his words feel forced. Is that really all it is? *Maybe I'm just paranoid.* "Now I feel kinda bad for dragging you in the study room when you *actually* need to study." My eyes drop to the table before he lifts my chin with a finger.

"Babe, don't you dare be sorry for the hottest sex I've ever had in my life." I smirk as he pulls me towards him for a kiss.

"I said I *kinda* feel bad." I nuzzle his nose. "Not bad enough I wouldn't do it again."

"Good."

"Guess we just have to study more and fuck less." I shrug.

"That is *not* happening." He kisses me softly on the lips, slipping his addicting tongue into my mouth before pulling away. "But more study sessions, sure, we can do that."

26
ELIJAH

I'm doing my typical pregame routine. Stretching. Listening to my playlist. Leaving Dino a voicemail. Thinking about Sophia.

The only problem is, the last part usually calms me, but instead it feels like every inch of my skin is crawling with unknowns.

The more time passes since Halloween, the more my curiosity grows.

When we're together, I still feel like she's the girl I've been falling for this whole time. I just hate that she's hiding something from me. *Something she's also hiding from the police?* I thought she had things she just wasn't ready to share with me *yet.* A defense mechanism I understand all too well. There's so much I want to tell her, but I'm just not ready... *Will I ever be ready?*

Our reality is so much worse. She's actively *hiding* something from me. I've never once judged her—always being entirely open and understanding.

So why won't she share this with me?

This *thing* her ex knows and holds over her head like a bucket of freezing cold water, eager for the chance to ice her out.

Man, I hate that guy.

I don't know what else to do to show her she can trust me. Can she tell I'm hiding something too?

Thankfully, the game distracts me the rest of the afternoon. After scoring an easy victory and taking showers, Julian, Theo, and I walk out of the stadium, heading straight for the girls.

"Hey there, Honey Bee," Sophia says, greeting me with a long, hungry kiss. My lips curve up halfway through. Regardless of my doubts, I still crave to be around her.

"Miss me that much?"

"Just wanted to show the world who the star quarterback belongs to."

"I played for one quarter." I laugh, pecking her again, thankful for the ego boost.

"And you made a touchdown." She waggles her eyebrows at me. "A win is a win."

"Fine, a win is a win." I kiss her again. "But you know…" I rest my forehead against hers. "I'd much rather you stroke my cock than my ego." Her cheeks flush pink, and someone clears their throat.

"Okay, on that note," Theo says, ruffling his hair, "can we head out? I told Stella I'd meet her at Noah's party."

I chuckle. "Sure, let's go." We head to the parking garage outside the athletic student dorm. Julian and Sage ride with Theo, and Sophia rides with me.

"Wanna go for a run in the morning?" I ask, pulling onto the main road.

She groans, throwing her head against the headrest. "Can you just let me have one hangover day where I'm not forced to do phys- ical exercise?"

"All kinds of physical exercise?" I glide a hand up her leg, and she clenches her thighs together, trapping it between them.

"Fine," she says, mock annoyed. "Where you don't make me *run* a half marathon."

I chuckle. "Running is the best way to sweat out a hangover."

"I think I'd rather keep in the sweat *and* the hangover."

"Maybe lay off the tequila tonight and you'll be able to manage our morning training regimen," I suggest, wiggling my fingers between her legs, causing her to laugh as we stop at a red light.

"How about I only drink a *bit* of tequila and we think of more creative ways to *train* in the morning." My truck jolts forward, causing my head to snap hard against my seat. "Shit!" My eyes flick to the rearview mirror to see Theo's Range Rover kissing my back bumper. "Are you okay?" I ask Sophia, looking over, but she doesn't appear to have any visible injuries. "Theo just rear-ended me."

"I think so," she says quietly as I pull the car off the shoulder, pressing the hazards button, with Theo following my lead. I take a deep breath to refrain from killing my best friend—for the fourth time this semester—and hop out of the truck.

27
SOPHIA

The truck door slams shut, and it's like a shotgun to the chest, causing me to flinch.

I sit in the passenger seat, unable to move, unable to speak. No.

No.

No.

No.

Not again.

This can't be happening again.

"Turn it up! I freaking love this song," Charlie demands from the back seat of Seth's truck as we drive through the winding country roads on the way home from the springs.

I reach out to turn the dial, and "Kiwi" by Harry Styles blares through the speakers. We all sing along, and I play an air guitar in perfect rhythm with the music.

Looks like all that Guitar Hero really paid off. Who's laughing now, Leah?

Seth reaches over and squeezes my knee before placing his large hand back on the steering wheel.

We come around a bend in the road and the truck jerks, a vibration rippling through the vehicle, rattling my bones as something skids across the road in front of us.

"Shit!" *Seth shouts, pulling the car off the shoulder.*

"What was that?" *I ask, panicked, rubbing my eyes to focus better on the shape unmoving near the side of the road.* "Did you hit a deer?"

We're in the middle of nowhere. Deer cross here all the time. It's always a risk.

It's gotta be a deer...

"That's—it's not—I don't think it was a deer," *Seth says quietly.*

We fly out of his truck, running toward the unmoving shape, and once my mind registers what it is, bile rises, threatening to escape.

There's a shopping cart with random things spilled out of it next to the body surrounded by blood.

Blood. Blood. There's so much blood. Why is there so much blood?

No.

No.

Please move.

Please.

"Seth..." *I say as we walk closer.* "You hit someone." *I exhale a shaky breath.* "You hit a person!"

I sprint to the body, bending down to check if they're breathing, my hands and knees immediately soaked in blood. An older man with a white, unkempt beard lies before me. His clothes are tattered, well-worn, and now stained red. I try to remember the things my dad told me to do in a situation like this, suddenly grateful to be the daughter of a paramedic.

I reach out, pressing my fingers against his throat to check for a pulse.

"What are you doing?" *Seth yells, ripping me off the ground by my arm.*

"I'm checking if he's alive." I pull out of his grasp, bending back down, and he yanks me up by my shoulders, gripping them tightly.

"No!"

"What?" I glare up at him, trying to wiggle free, but his hold is too tight. *"We have to get him help."*

My eyes connect with Charlie's. Her hand covers her mouth, phone clutched tightly in the other.

"Call the police!" I shout at her before returning my gaze down at the bloodied and almost unrecognizable body.

"No!" Seth shouts at her before turning his attention back to me. *"Sophia,"* he says firmly, his hands squeezing my arms. *"Look at him."*

"I... I am." I shake my head as the sticky blood drips from my fingers. *"He needs help. We can help him. I can help him."*

"Sophia," Seth says again gently. *"He's already dead."* Every muscle in my body shakes at once.

"You don't know that! We have to call the police!" The sky spins as I take gasping breaths.

"Damn it, Soph!" Seth yells, grabbing my waist, dragging me towards the car.

I struggle against his hold, spinning around in his arm, digging my toes in the ground, trying to get back to the body.

"For fuck's sake!" He bends down, tossing me over his shoulder before continuing towards the truck.

"Stop it!" I slam my fists against his back, thrashing my legs, trying to get free, but his hold is too tight. He's too big. Too strong.

"Come on, Charlie. Get in the fucking truck before I make you!" he yells, and she trails quickly behind us. Her eyes briefly connect with mine before she darts them away, looking at the ground.

"Seth! What the hell is wrong with you?!" I wail.

"Do you realize what this could do to me? To you?!" he shouts, ignoring my protests. *"We could go to jail, Soph! We'd lose everything!"*

"We have to—"

"I said no!" He cuts me off, shoving me into the truck. I turn to fight him, body freezing as my eyes snag on his shirt covered in blood.

He glances down at it, then back to me with a murderous expression. "Fuck, Soph! Now we have to figure out how to scrub off this evidence."

Evidence? He slams my door, puts Charlie in the back, and rounds to the driver's side.

"It was an accident," I say quietly as he buckles himself in. "We have to call the police."

I grab my phone out of the cup holder, and Seth's large hand wraps around mine. He tries to tug it from my grasp.

"Stop!" I use all my strength, hoping to keep possession of the phone. "We have to call the police!"

"It's still manslaughter!" Seth snarls coldly, overpowering me and snatching the phone. He shoves hard against my shoulder, forcing me back against my seat.

"We have to call the police," I repeat, staring down at my empty hands as Seth puts the car in drive.

"This would ruin our entire lives," Seth says firmly. "We can't ever talk about this again. This never happened."

"Someone is going to wonder where he is. Wonder why he's missing," Charlie says quietly, speaking for the first time.

"We have to call the police."

"Did you see him? His clothes? The shopping cart?" Seth says, his tone laced with judgment. "He was homeless. No one's gonna miss him or ask questions. They'll assume he was walking drunk and got hit. The police won't even think twice about it."

The voice is Seth's, but the words don't sound like his.

"Seth, you can't be serious," Charlie snaps as Seth puts the car in drive. "He's a person."

"He's a nobody," Seth says, tone void of emotion, pulling off the shoulder. "I'm not letting this bum walking in the road ruin my life."

I stare at my red-soaked hands, shaking uncontrollably.

"We have to call the police," I whisper, staring out the window
as Seth drives past the bloodied body on the shoulder of the road
without a single glance back.

*"We're not calling the goddamn police, Sophia!" Seth shouts at
the top of his lungs, and I flinch.*

*I take one last look at the body we left behind like roadkill before
emptying the entire contents of my stomach on the floorboard.*

"We have to call the police," I say, hardly able to get my voice above
a whisper as I turn over my trembling hands, checking them for
blood.

"Sophia?" A familiar husky voice blurs into my consciousness.

"Blood." My hands shake uncontrollably. "The blood." *What
happened to the blood?*

"Are you okay? Baby?"

My breathing is sporadic. "We have to call the police."

"What?" Warm hands grab mine. "No, everything's fine."

"We have to call the police!" I scream, pleading, sobbing, ripping
my hands away to undo my seat belt, looking for my phone.

"Sophia!" A hand is placed on my knee, and I jerk away.

"We have to call the police!" I shout. *Why won't he understand?*

"Sophia, everything is fine. Theo just hit my bumper, but everyone's fine."

Theo?

"No." I shake my head, tears sliding slowly down my cheeks.
"No. No. No. I won't let you do this again! It's not fine. It's not okay.
This isn't okay." I gasp for air, for oxygen, for relief from the debili-
tating pain. "We have to call the police."

"Sophia, baby, please calm down." The familiar voice cracks as
another hand reaches towards me, and I fold in on myself. "Look at
me... Please."

My entire body trembles, and I force my gaze to his, blinking rapidly. Slowly, brown hair and terrified arctic eyes appear before me.

"Elijah?" I croak out.

"Yeah, baby. It's me…" He tilts his head. "Everyone is fine… Can I show you?"

Is he telling the truth? I nod my head slowly, and he helps me out of the truck, putting his arm around me. He doesn't let go of my hand as he guides me to the back of the truck, showing me the small dent Theo put in his fender.

A car honks, pulling my attention toward it. The surroundings slowly blur into my consciousness. There's no trees or forest or shopping cart with someone's entire possessions spilled on the grass. We're on a street by campus as vehicles rush past us on the busy road. *Right.* We were on the way to Noah's.

"There's no blood," I whisper. "There's no body."

"There's no body," Elijah repeats calmly, patiently, squeezing me tighter but not pushing for more—not asking what I'm talking about, not asking me to explain. "See, everyone is okay."

My face twists into a look of confusion. "Everyone is okay?"

28

ELIJAH

Sophia's body shivers uncontrollably under my hold, tears falling hard, quiet sobs ripping through her as she stares at the road. My mind spins like a tornado with every new word that falls out of her mouth.

There's no blood.

There's no body.

"Sophia?" My heart pounds painfully against my ribcage.

"No one is hurt," she mumbles, continuing to shake. I bend down, scooping her up in my arms. I bring her to the truck, placing her on the passenger seat, then haul myself on the foot bar and buckle her in.

"Baby," I whisper. "Look at me, please."

Her glassy green eyes stare straight ahead, and I take her chin gently between my fingers, tilting her to face me. She blinks a few times, the tears dripping down her cheeks.

"Can you hear me?" I ask, and she nods gently, struggling for air. "Good." I run my fingers through her hair. "Breathe, baby. Just like we practiced."

In.

Out.

In.

Out.

"Good girl," I tell her, and her lips quirk slightly upward, eyes still vacant.

I drag my hands all over her body, scanning for any injuries I might have missed. "I'm not hurt," she says quietly, relieving an atom of my anxiety.

Using my thumb, I wipe a tear off her cheek. "So what's got you so shaken up, baby?"

"I..." She looks down, fiddling with her hands. "I think I was having another panic attack... Car accidents just freak me out a little." *If my sister died in a car accident, I'd definitely be afraid of them too.*

"I'm so sorry that scared you." I snake my arms around, hugging her tightly, and she hiccups into the crook of my neck. "Trust me, it was just a little fender bender that Theo will be paying for... thoroughly."

"I'm sorry." She sniffles. "I must look ridiculous crying over this."

"Hey..." I take her face in my hands. "You're not ridiculous. Tacos fall apart, and everybody loves them." She forces a weak smile that doesn't quite reach her eyes. "Also, I'm really proud of you for being able to recognize you were having a panic attack."

"I'd like to thank eight years of therapy for giving me the knowledge to diagnose my tsunami of emotions."

"You're perfect." I rest my forehead to hers. "How about we ditch the party and head home? We can cuddle and watch that vampire show you love so much."

She laughs weakly. "The great Elijah Anderson is willing to skip a party for little old me. Who knew he had it in him?"

"Sweetheart, I'd skip playing in the damn Super Bowl if you needed me. I'm your man now. Get used to the star treatment."

"You feeling better?" I ask Sophia, dragging my fingertips along her arm as we lie tangled in my bed.

"Yes." She releases a shaky breath against my chest, squeezing me tighter. "Thank you."

"I'm still so sorry about earlier."

"It wasn't your fault."

"Yeah. It was Theo's, and I'm gonna knock him into the middle of next week for upsetting you so bad." *The horse tranquilizer is back on the table.*

"I promise, it's okay," she says weakly. "It just freaked me out. But that's a me thing, not a Theo thing."

I lean down, kissing her softly. "Okay. I'll let Theo live to see another day. But he's on thin ice."

She giggles and shakes her head. "Good. I don't want you to hurt my Theo Bear."

"Do I need to worry about you two?"

A loud laugh escapes her pretty lips. "Babe. Come on, don't be so insecure. You know I only have eyes for one honey bee."

"Yeah." My gaze narrows at her. "And apparently one Theo Bear too." She shrugs, biting her lower lip, and my eyes turn to stone. "I'm gonna pretend you didn't just do that."

"Okay." She giggles, returning her head to my chest. I trail my fingertips along her back as I think about her panic attack today.

While I know she was probably freaking out because of her sister's accident, there's one thing that doesn't add up. Sophia told me she wasn't with her sister when it happened... But today she just kept repeating, "we have to call the police." And she told Seth, "let's go to the police," and I can't help my mind from wondering if those are dots I should be connecting.

"Sophia?" I release a shaky breath.

"Hmm," she hums against my chest.

"You know you can always talk to me, right?" Her body tenses under my touch, and I clear my throat. "I know it was a lot for you today... But you always act like I'm going to run if you open up to me, and I just want you to know I won't." She draws circles on my chest with her finger. "So if you ever want to share those thoughts clouding that sunshine head of yours, I'm here. You don't have to deal with anything alone. You have me now."

"Elijah..." She pulls away, her green eyes telling me everything she won't. She's scared, hurt, afraid—needs someone in her damn corner.

Let me be that for you, I beg silently.

"Kiss me," she whispers, rolling on her side to face me.

I press my lips gently to hers, placing my hand against her hip, and tug her closer. She fits perfectly—like her body was specifically made just for me—our broken pieces mixing together, creating a vibrant, dazzling mosaic. Our tongues tangle, and she clings to me, hungry, desperate. Like this is the last time she'll ever kiss my lips. Her hands are impatient, frantic, like this is the last time she'll ever touch my body. I brush my thumb along her cheek and freeze.

"Sophia?" I pull away to the sight of small tears dripping down her cheeks. "Baby, why are you crying?"

She gnaws on her trembling lower lip, and I kiss the tears away before pulling her tight to my chest. "I want to tell you something."

My entire body stills, the pit in my stomach turning into a black hole sucking every ounce of oxygen from my lungs. I tug the blanket over us and rub my hand along her arm.

"Anything."

"Please, don't leave me," she begs, and my bones ache with sadness at her desperate tone.

"I won't," I assure her, analyzing her worn face. "You wanna know one of my favorite quotes?"

"Is it from *South Park*?" she teases half-heartedly.

"No." I nuzzle her nose, pecking a kiss on it before pulling away. "It's Edgar Allan Poe." Her lips curl upward as she nods, seemingly impressed. "Tell me every terrible thing you ever did, and let me love you anyway."

She nibbles on her bottom lip. "Okay." A shaky breath escapes her lips. "Here we go... Earlier this year, months before I met you, I was still dating Seth."

My brow furrows, but I don't interrupt out of fear she'll stop sharing.

"We were... He was driving me and Charlie home from the springs, and we came around a sharp turn and—" Her breath hitches, tears pouring out of her eyes. I find her hand under the covers, entangling her fingers with mine as she takes deep, calming breaths. "He hit someone." She shakes her head, swallowing hard. "He *killed* someone."

I inhale sharply. "Oh." *That explains the panic attack.* "I'm so sorry you had to witness that."

"No. You don't understand. You don't—" She shakes her head without meeting my gaze. "You don't understand."

"Baby," I say softly, tipping her chin to meet my gaze. "Please, help me understand?"

"We... we didn't call the police. He was lying there... He was bloodied and not moving, and I wanted to help him." Her voice cracks. "God, I wanted to help him. But Seth said it would ruin our lives. And the guy was homeless, so Seth said no one would miss him. And... I wanted to call the police. I wanted to, I swear," she wails desperately, searching my eyes for any reaction, but I'm unable to speak. Unable to process the information fast enough. "Seth wouldn't let me since the guy couldn't be saved. But Seth was wrong. The guy wasn't dead when we left him. My dad... he was the paramedic on the case and..." She drags a hand down her face. "The guy may have lived if we'd just called the fucking police..." Her shaky breath is the only sound filling the small room.

"And then it was too late," she whispers, the pained tone of her voice slicing through my body like a machete. "Seth got rid of all the evidence. All the proof. He burned our clothes, fixed his bumper out of state, and made damn sure Charlie and I wouldn't ever tell anyone. They found the body, but they don't know who did it." Tears pour down her cheeks, the dam bursting now that her truth is free. "I just—I made a mistake. I should've fought harder. I should've called the police. Instead, I left the dying man on the side of the road, alone... I'm a *monster*."

"Sophia..." I whisper, my stomach twisted up in a million painful knots. "You are *not* a monster. You are sunshine and kindness and everything that's good in this world. It was a terrible situation, and you were manipulated. That doesn't make you a monster. That makes you human."

Her gaze connects with mine. "You don't think I'm an awful person?"

"Never. You're the best person I know. One mistake doesn't change that."

"You don't want to leave?" she asks hesitantly, gnawing on her lower lip.

"I already told you, I won't ever leave you. Your secrets are my secrets. Your pain is my pain. You and me against the world, Sunflower."

"I just made a... *mistake*," she says quietly.

"You made a mistake," I repeat.

"I'm not a monster," she whispers.

"No, baby. You're not a monster."

She frowns and blinks away the tears. "I wish I could take it all back... I wish I could go back and tell Seth he's wrong and call someone. Then I could move on from this instead of letting the worst thing I've ever done hang over me like a storm cloud."

"Do you want to do something about it?" *Mark would know what to do.*

"There's nothing I can do." Her shoulders deflate. "At this point, it would just be my word against his."

227

"Didn't you say Charlie was in the car? What about her word?"

Sophia shakes her head. "She'll never testify."

I tap my forehead to hers. "Well, if you ever change your mind, I promise I'll stand beside you the entire way." *We have to find a way to end this shit.*

"Thanks." She smiles weakly and reaches up to touch my face. "You're the only one I've ever told about this. Not even Sage or my family knows."

I place my hand on her neck, leaning in to kiss her softly. "Thank you for trusting me."

It might be time I return the favor.

29
SOPHIA

"Nice shirt," Elijah says, eyes glued to my graphic tee that has a huge corn on it with the words "Thanksgiving is A-MAIZE-ING." "The husk really matches your eyes."

A breathy laugh rumbles out of me. "Thought you'd like it."

"Okay, so I have a new mix to show you on the drive to Longwood," he says, opening the passenger door of my car and helping me inside. His truck is in the shop getting the bumper fixed after the accident last week.

"A new mix? What are you, seventy?" I tease. "Also, I will be DJ'ing for our journey, thank you very much.'

"The *driver* picks the playlist," he says sternly as he gets in the driver's seat.

"But it's *my* car!"

"Doesn't matter." He shakes his head. "Driver gets to DJ, that's the rule."

"Fine… But your taste in music better be awesome. I'm not interested in spending two hours listening to Celine Dion."

"Uh-oh. Is that Sophia Summers's deal breaker? Shitty taste in music?"

"Guess you'll have to find out." I shrug, and he narrows his eyes at me playfully.

Elijah connects to my car's Bluetooth as I buckle myself in. He reaches over, placing his large hand on my leg. Even after our talk last week, he's been completely normal. If anything, he's been *more* affectionate. I haven't for one second felt I made the wrong choice telling him. It's like a tremendous weight has lifted off my shoulders finally having everything out in the open between us.

"Starting route to 763 Parker Lane, Longwood, Florida," Siri says through the speakers after Elijah starts the GPS.

An uncomfortable feeling settles in my stomach. In Crystal Bay, I don't have to drive by the spot the accident happened, causing memories to pierce me like bullets. Being back in Longwood, especially after my panic attack last week, might slice the wounds open with a dull butcher knife. It also increases the risk that Seth could show up...

"You okay, babe?" Elijah asks.

"Yes." I scrunch my nose at him, shoving all negative thoughts into the "remember never" drawer.

"You sure?" He tilts his head. "I promise I'll drive carefully."

I lean over, and he meets me halfway, pressing a soft kiss to my lips. "I'm fine, Honey Bee. I trust you."

"Good." He smiles wide and goes back to sifting through his playlists. I'm just about to ask if we're ever going to leave the parking lot when "Super Freaky Girl" by Nicki Minaj flows through the speakers. He performs the song word for word, shimmying in the driver's seat.

"Why do you know this entire song?" I ask, shouting over the music.

"I've heard it at least a hundred times since I watched you shake your ass to it at Noah's party." He smirks at me and continues today's episode of carpool karaoke. I know he's mine, but it still makes my heart soar into the clouds by how much he notices me. How much he *sees* me.

By the time we've reached the highway, Elijah has moved on to performing "Despacito," surprisingly nailing the Spanish verses, and fuck me is it sexy. His phone rings through the speakers, interrupting my private concert.

"It's Mark, I should answer it." Elijah smiles wide, accepting the call. "Hey."

"Hey, buddy..." Mark says before exhaling heavily.

"What's wrong?" Elijah asks.

"Cole and I have to work today." The disappointment in Mark's voice echoes through the car. "Too many people called out, and we just... we've gotta be at the station."

"Oh..." Elijah drums his fingers against the steering wheel. "I—I'm already on the way."

I reach toward him, running my fingers through his hair.

"I left you some money for pizza at the house. We can get breakfast tomorrow," Mark replies hopefully. "I'm really sorry. I wouldn't do this if it wasn't absolutely necessary."

"Yeah... sure." Elijah's shoulders sag, deflated.

"I was really looking forward to spending our first Thanksgiving together." Mark's tone is sad and sincere. "I mean it."

"Me too," Elijah says quietly.

"I've gotta go. Love you, Eli."

"You too," Elijah responds before the line goes dead and his music starts back up.

"I'm really sorry, baby."

"I just... I didn't even ask to come. He offered since I couldn't visit home and said it'd be our first Thanksgiving. Now, the only first is that I'm spending it alone." He lets his head fall against the seat, keeping his gaze on the road.

"Why don't you come to Thanksgiving at my house?" I offer even though the thought terrifies me.

"Really?" He grins like a golden retriever.

"Yeah, sure... It'll just be my dad and Diane, they won't mind." I squeeze his thigh, then pull out my phone to let Dad know about our extra guest.

PAPA BEAR

ME

I'm on my way home

PAPA BEAR

Great

ME

Can I bring a friend for dinner?

PAPA BEAR

Of course, the more the merrier. Who is it?

I stare down at the phone and swallow hard.

ME

Elijah. Mark and Cole both have to work so he's going to be all alone

I hold my breath for the full five minutes it takes for him to reply.

PAPA BEAR

Okay, Diane and I are volunteering at the shelter. We'll be back in a couple hours. See you then

Drive safe. Love you, Sophie Bear

ME

Love you, Papa Bear

I place my phone on my lap and wring my hands together. "I should tell you something before we get there."

Elijah's curious gaze flicks to mine before returning to the road. "Okay...?"

"My dad might not be thrilled we're dating." I gnaw on my lip. "I told him we were *just* friends."

"You told *me* we were just friends too," Elijah jokes. "Maybe he saw through that bullshit as easily as I did."

"Elijah, be serious."

"We're adults, Sunflower," Elijah says, smiling and entirely unaffected. "I think he'll move on."

"Yeah... well, it's just... There's a reason he doesn't want us to date."

"What?" Elijah's face morphs into a look of confusion, and I exhale a shaky breath.

"You know how our families know each other?"

"Yes?"

"So... the day after I met you actually, Cole arrested my brother for assaulting a police officer."

I glance over to gauge Elijah's reaction as his eyebrows shoot to his hairline in surprise. "Really?"

"Yeah... Cole was taunting Jake because of some shit that happened in high school, and I don't know... Jake just lost it, I guess, and accidentally elbowed Cole, so he arrested him."

"Wow." Elijah readjusts his grip on the steering wheel.

"Yeah." I shift uncomfortably in my seat. "I know it's a crazy coincidence... and Jake said Cole had been drinking that day."

"Yeah..." Elijah frowns. "I think my brother has a bit of a drinking problem. Mark actually suspended him from the force after that incident..."

My head snaps toward him. "So you knew about it already?"

"No, of course not," he reassures me, reaching out and placing a hand on my bouncing thigh. "I mean, I didn't know what the incident was, but I knew he was suspended the week I met you... so the timeline adds up. The night before I left, I overheard Mark telling Cole he'd send him to rehab unless he got his shit together."

"Oh... Did he go?"

"No, but he agreed to AA meetings, which I think has been

helping him. This'll be my first time back, so I don't know if he's sober or not. He was at the game though."

"Okay."

Elijah clears his throat. "That was the same week Cole found out about me."

"What?" I ask, confused at his partial change of subject.

"I mean, trust me, I'm not justifying him, but Cole didn't know I existed before I came. We didn't really give Mark a lot of notice before I showed up... I could tell Cole was shaken up by the whole thing even though he tried to hide it."

"Okay?" His hand still grips my thigh, and I rub a thumb over his knuckles. "I mean... I know it's weird, but why wasn't he happy to have a sibling?"

He exhales heavily. "When my mom got pregnant with me, Mark was still with Cole's mom."

"Oh my God, that's awful." I place my free hand over my open mouth.

"Yeah... so to Cole, I was the illegitimate brother who probably caused his parents' marriage to crumble right before his mom died."

I suck in a breath. "Elijah... I'm sure he doesn't see you that way."

"I know he doesn't now... but maybe that week... maybe that's why he was drinking on the job." He shrugs, frowning. "I'm not excusing it at all. Just, I don't know."

"I'm sorry." I squeeze his hand tighter before placing it back on my lap.

"But what does any of this have to do with us?" he asks, resuming his grip on my thigh.

I sigh loudly before answering. "It's just, my dad and brother both made it pretty clear they aren't fond of the Danvers—"

"I'm not even a Danvers," he scoffs, interrupting me.

"I know..." I shift uncomfortably in my seat, regretting bringing up the topic. "But by blood and all that."

"By blood and all that? What is this? Medieval times?"

I tilt my head at him. "Elijah."

"I've fallen for one girl in my life, and I'm already on her dad's shit list."

"I never said you're on his shit list." He gives me an unamused look. "Fine, you have your work cut out for you."

"Challenge accepted," Elijah says smugly. "I'll gladly put in the time for you, sweetheart. I'm gonna make your family fall in love with me so hard, they'll make you keep me forever."

I laugh, shaking my head. "Shouldn't you focus on making *me* fall in love with you first?" I immediately bite my lip, wishing I could take back the words.

"Don't worry." He squeezes my thigh. "Operation Make Sophia Fall In Love With Me is already a go."

I let out a bubbling laugh. "Oh God, you need to work on your code names."

"Operation Seducing Sophia." He winks, and I grin out the window like a lovesick puppy.

We walk through my red front door, and I'm prepared for a cold, quiet house since Dad's an empty nester now. I'm pleasantly surprised to see pops of color everywhere. The scent of pumpkin pie infiltrates my senses, and my mouth waters. A country station plays low in the background even though there's no one in sight.

In the kitchen, I grab a vase for the fresh flowers Elijah insisted on stopping for—sunflowers, of course.

"You want the grand tour?" I ask after placing the flowers on the center of the island.

"Absolutely." He smiles down at me, my duffle bag slung over his shoulder.

We climb the stairs and start in my room. He throws my bag on the floor by the door and places his hands on his hips, looking around. My bed is pushed up against the far wall, with my collection of stuffed koalas placed neatly against the pillows.

Elijah picks one up, amused eyes sliding to mine. "Now I get the koala thing."

I shrug. "They're cute."

"Just like you." He tosses the stuffed animal at me, and I karate chop it back at him. It hits him in the face, and he laughs, catching it and placing it back with the others. He saunters slowly around my room, pausing by one of my favorite landscape sketches hanging next to my closet. "Soph, this is incredible."

I walk over to join him. "Thanks."

"What inspired you to draw it?"

"My dad took me to North Carolina a few years ago, and I thought the view was so amazing, I wanted to look at it every day."

"It's beautiful." Elijah throws his arm around me, tugging me toward him. "You're ridiculously talented. I'm one lucky son of a bitch."

"My boyfriend's a D1 quarterback, and *you're* the lucky one?"

He spins me to face him, then scoops me up under my ass. "Damn straight."

I wrap my legs around him as he carries me backwards toward my bed. "Elijah." I giggle as we fall onto it, my legs splitting over him in a straddle.

"Shhh, quiet, baby." He reaches up, placing a single finger on my lips while sliding his free hand under his back. Scrunching his nose, he yanks out a tiny koala, then glares at me. "These little shits are starting to cock block."

Reaching over, I swipe every single one off the bed. "Now they're not a problem."

His smile widens as he tugs me down to him. "I love getting to see all the little things that make you, you."

"Oh, really?" I nuzzle his nose. "My collection of marsupials didn't scare you off?"

"No way, girl, you meet all my *koalafications*."

My mouth falls open. "He's hot, has a big dick, *and* uses marsupial puns? I've hit the fucking jackpot."

"Guess that means I'm *koala*-fied to be your boyfriend." His mouth swallows my laugh, slipping his tongue between my lips, and I moan. His hands wander along my hips, landing on my ass, tugging me against his hardening cock. "Is it bad I want to fuck you right now?" His tone is low and gravelly.

A rush of heat heads south, and I ache at my next words. "No, but we can't."

He looks up at the ceiling, groaning. "I know."

"I don't want my dad to meet you for the first time with my legs wrapped around you."

"It would be the second time," Elijah reminds me, nipping at my neck, and I giggle.

"Fine, for the first time as my *boyfriend*." He drops his head in the crook of my neck and groans, rolling begrudgingly off the bed and pulling me to my feet with him.

"Come on." I tug his hand toward the door. "Let me show you around the rest of the house." I lead him down the hall and stop outside the closed door to my favorite room.

"So... this was my sister's room." He reaches out, brushing a strand of hair behind my ear. "It's the one place in the world where I still feel her... I know that sounds crazy."

"Baby, it's not crazy at all," he says in a low, husky tone, looking down at me caringly.

I push the door open, ready to show Elijah my most cherished space. Stepping through the threshold, I'm met by a nuclear bomb knocking the breath from my lungs.

What the fuck?

I take small steps into the room, my mouth slightly parted, heart rate accelerating like a jet engine as I struggle for air.

"Soph?" Elijah says quietly, placing a hand on my shoulder.

Nothing comes out when I try to speak.

"Babe, are you okay?" He hugs me from behind, and I collapse against him.

"I-It's-He just—It's gone," I stutter out, tears blurring my vision. "*She's* gone."

My legs buckle, and I fall to my knees, with Elijah following me to the ground as my heart shatters into a million unfixable pieces. The same position I was in when my dad told me the two worst words I've ever heard in my life: "Chloe's gone." Two words that were simple and unrelated until they were placed side by side.

In a moment of strength, I lift my head, forcing myself to take in my surroundings. The only place in the world where I still felt my sister has been turned into a fucking craft room.

30

ELIJAH

I've just finished pouring waters when the front door opens and voices flood down the hallway. I look up to Will and his girlfriend walking into the kitchen.

"Oh, hey," Will says after noticing me.

I abandon the waters and walk over, extending my hand. "Hi, sir, thanks for having me."

He returns the gesture. "Of course."

"Hello, ma'am," I say to the woman, and she laughs.

"Please, call me Di, sweetie," she says. "Ma'am makes me feel a hundred years old."

"You got it."

"I'll be out back setting up," Di says, giving Will a kiss before walking out to the back yard.

Footsteps barrel down the stairs, and Sophia runs into the kitchen.

"I can't believe you!" Sophia wails, barging toward Will, tears streaming down her face.

"Sophia?" Will says, his tone full of alarm as his eyes bounce between us. "What's wrong?"

"How could you clean out Chloe's room and not even tell me!" she sobs, and Will's mouth parts open.

"Sophia…" He releases a heavy breath. "Chloe's room has been empty for nine years… I thought you would have gotten the things you wanted out of it by now. I donated everything weeks ago."

"How was I supposed to move her pink chair to my room? It weighs a ton!" she shrieks. "I went in there all the time. It was *my* place." Her voice cracks again, and every time I die a little more. "It was *our* place." Her voice is so quiet it's almost lost to the air. I'm frozen in place, unsure if I should stay and support her or give them privacy.

"I'm *so* sorry, Bear, I didn't know." Will places a hand on Sophia's back, and she jerks away from his touch.

"How would you have known?" she spouts through the tears. "You were barely here. You were always working."

"That's not fair." His voice breaks, and the agony in his eyes has my heart aching for him. "I did my best."

"I don't feel her," she whispers. "I don't *feel* her anymore."

"Sophia," he pleads, tugging her to look at him. His eyes are glossy, and I have to wipe my own tears away from the overwhelming emotion flooding this room. "Chloe isn't gone." He places a palm on her cheek, and she leans into it. "She's here." He gestures around the room. "She's everywhere."

Sophia shakes her head, but Will continues, "She's the swarm of lovebugs surrounding us every spring. Your beautiful green eyes. The way you always protect your friends…" His lips curl upwards. "Don't you remember the bunny that passed through the yard, and you said it was Chloe reminding you to believe in as many as six impossible things before breakfast?" Sophia lets out a low, quiet laugh. "You don't feel her in one place anymore because she's everywhere, Bear. She'll never be gone. She'll always be a part of you. Even if you can't see her. Even if you don't feel her. She's there. She's *here*." The words settle in my chest like they were meant for me, and I no longer try to hide the tears streaming down my face.

"I have to believe that Chloe is in a better place…" Will continues, choking back tears. "Waiting patiently for us."

Sophia looks up at him, smiling sadly. "In Wonderland?"

"Yeah." Will lets out a weak laugh. "I suppose Chloe's in Wonderland." She throws her arms around his neck, hugging him tightly. "I really am sorry, Bear," he mumbles into her hair.

"Me too," she says quietly. "I know you work hard for our family… I didn't mean to make it sound like I don't appreciate that."

"It's okay."

"I forgive you," she mumbles, and I can physically see the weight release from Will's shoulders. "Can I ask you a question though?"

"Of course."

"When did you start sewing?" she asks, looking at him with a serious face.

Will huffs out a laugh. "Soph, it's not mine. It's Diane's."

"Why would Diane have a sewing room in our house?"

"Well, we planned to tell you at dinner… But Diane moved in last month."

"Oh," Sophia says, a light switching on in her brain as she looks around the room. "Well, I guess that makes a lot more sense than you having picked up interior design at the age of fifty."

"First of all, young lady," he scoffs, "I am forty-nine. Second, I'm really happy. Diane is incredible. Please try to be okay with it?"

"Dad, I'm happy if you're happy… I just wish you would've told me you were clearing out Chloe's room… I could've helped." She takes his hand in hers. "I'm sure it wasn't easy."

"No…" He releases a heavy breath. "It wasn't. But it was time."

"Hey, Will," Diane calls from the door to the backyard. "Can you help me move some of the patio furniture so I can start setting the table?"

"Sure, be right there," he replies, pulling Sophia in for a tight hug and shooting me a weak smile before leaving the room. Sophia stares at me with devastated eyes, and I wrap my arms around her.

"I'm still upset," she says quietly, burrowing her face in my chest.

"I know."

"Is it normal?" she asks, sighing heavily.

"What, baby?"

"Is it normal she's been gone nine years and I have this reaction to a few stupid trinkets being thrown out?"

"There isn't really a *normal* way to experience grief. Grief isn't linear. You don't just wake up every day a little less sad. Some days are worse than others… Chloe was a big part of you, and losing her room probably felt a bit like losing her all over again."

She looks up at me with glossy eyes. "You always have the best advice for this grief stuff."

I shrug, swallowing hard and feeling like a damn fraud since I can't even follow my own advice.

We sit down at the beautifully set patio table Diane created. Tiny turkeys are scattered around, with orange placemats and silverware wrapped in twine. Everything is very festive, and it all reminds me of home. I'm sure Mom has a tablescape mirroring this one set up on the farm table in our kitchen today.

"This looks delicious," I say, dropping a large scoop of mashed potatoes on my plate.

"Thank you." Diane beams. "I love cooking, so this is one of my favorite holidays."

"Hopefully next year, *all* the kids can come," Will says.

"How many do you have?" I ask her.

"I have two boys, but they're playing hockey for a university in DC," Diane replies sadly. "Wish I could've gotten them to stay closer to home like Sophia did."

"Maybe Jake and Leah can come next year too," Sophia says with a bright smile. The same one she always wears when she talks about them.

"Maybe we can join you right now," Leah says, trailing behind a guy who I assume is the infamous Jake.

"Shut the front door!" Sophia squeals, pushing out of her chair so fast it almost falls over. She runs over, jumping on him like a spider monkey. The rest of us stand to greet them as well. They hug Will and Diane before turning their attention to me.

"Hi, I'm Jake." He extends a hand to me. "Sophia's favorite brother."

"You're my *only* brother," she says, raising her eyebrows.

"Elijah." I reach out, shaking his hand. "Sophia's favorite boyfriend." His eyes flick to Sophia, then back mine before he returns the gesture, squeezing a tad bit tighter than necessary.

"Nice to meet you."

31
SOPHIA

"I can't believe you guys are here," I tell Jake and Leah, stifling a moan as another delicious bite of stuffing fills my mouth.

"We wanted it to be a surprise." Leah places her hand on mine, and I glance down to the sight of an enormous diamond with one beautiful emerald on each side.

"What in the ever-loving poppycock is that?" I grab her hand and look between Jake and Leah, who are grinning like idiots.

"You and Leah were always like sisters. I thought we'd make it official," Jake says casually as he takes a sip of his beer.

"Are you kidding me!" I jump up, my chair flying back and falling on the deck behind me with a loud bang. It's long forgotten as I tackle hug Leah and Jake. Elijah chuckles and retrieves it for me. "When's the date? Where will you get married?" My pulse is pounding. "Oh! Will you have a maid of honor?"

"Sophia." Leah releases a breathy laugh as I sit back down. "Jake proposed *last* week. We haven't picked a date yet, but it definitely won't be too far out." She smirks at Jake, who grabs her hand and kisses it.

"Why?" I ask, looking between them. "Oh my God! Are you pregnant?"

Leah chucks her napkin at me. "No, I'm not pregnant!" She puts her hand over her stomach. "This is a turkey baby."

Jake places his hand over Leah's resting on her stomach, then turns his attention to me. "We'll be sure to keep you updated."

"That's all I ask," I say before shoving another bite of orgasmic stuffing in my mouth.

After dinner, Diane and Dad bring flutes of champagne and we all grab one, standing around the happy couple.

"To the love between us," Jake says, holding up his glass. "May it last forever and for always."

Leah grins over at him. "Forever and for always."

We tip our glasses toward them as they lean in to kiss one another. I turn to Elijah, who clinks my glass with his, staring at me with a dimpled smile. I bring the glass to my lips and take a small sip, allowing the bubbles to dance on my tongue while he downs his in a single gulp.

"Do you always chug your champagne?" Jake asks Elijah sharply.

"Not a huge fan of the taste, so I usually drink it as fast as possible, yeah," Elijah replies, seemingly unaffected, setting the flute on the nearby table.

"Makes sense… What do you usually drink?" Jake asks.

"Beer or whiskey," Elijah replies cooly, and I clench my glass tighter.

"Oh, whiskey." Jake nods his head as the rest of our eyes bounce between him and Elijah. "Just like your big bro."

"Jake," Dad says sternly.

"Wouldn't know…" Elijah clips. "He's never drank around me."

Jake huffs out a laugh, and my veins buzz with annoyance. "I find that hard to believe."

My jaw clenches. "*Jacob*, a word?"

His eyes glide to mine, softening briefly before he blows out a breath, following me into the kitchen.

The back door clicks shut, and I explode. "What the hell is your problem?"

"What do you mean?" Jake asks.

"Why are you grilling Elijah?"

"I'm just trying to get to know him."

"Bullshit," I snap. "You're being a royal asshole."

He spins around, leaning against the counter, and folds his arms over his chest. "All I'm doing is trying to get to know the guy who's dating my baby sister."

"By grilling him like you're a cop and he just stole the last donut?"

Jake releases a breathy laugh. "I'm trying to make sure he's good enough for you."

"Sorry, but that's *my* call, not yours."

"You need to realize what you're getting yourself into... His brother's bad news, Soph."

"Are you suggesting I don't date Elijah because of who he's related to?" I scoff in disbelief. "A bit hypocritical, don't you think? Imagine if Leah didn't want to date you because Mom's a fucking convicted drug addict."

"Mom's done her time, and she's changed. She's not like that anymore," he says defensively.

"Oh, sorry, did I offend the mama's boy?" I bark back.

"Really, Soph? This isn't about me."

"It kinda seems like it is about you, actually."

"I just wish you would have at least talked to me before you decided to start dating him."

"Sorry, but you lost the right to comment on my love life when you abandoned me at ten years old!" I throw my arms out in front of me. "I needed you too, you know? And you just left me here all alone."

"Soph." He tilts his head to the side. "I didn't leave *you*. I left Longwood. It was just... too painful. After Mom and Chloe... and Leah. It was all just too much."

"Well, how do you think I felt?!" I scream at him. "You got to run away, and I had to walk by her fucking bedroom every day for eight years until I left for college. I had to stare at her half-used body wash that was still in the shower for months because I couldn't bear to throw it away. I found tiny fingerprints from clay-covered hands all over our house for years after she died. *Years*, Jake!" I shake my head at the excruciating memory. "I had to blare my music in our empty ass house that used to be full of all the people I loved because the silence was fucking deafening!"

"Sophia, I'm sor—"

"I was here!" My pointer finger stabs painfully into my chest. "I had to handle everything by myself. Our mom was in jail, Chloe died, and you just... left."

"Soph, please," he begs, stepping toward me, and I shift back.

"Leah and Dad are the *only* ones who've *never* left me." I glare at him. "So if *they* want to comment on my love life, I'll be happy to hear it. But. Don't. You. Fucking. Dare try to stroll back in here, playing the part of the overprotective big brother when you barely even know the real me anymore." I don't realize I'm crying until my vision is so blurred I can't see. I know my words hurt him, but they're the truth. My breathing is sporadic as I clutch my hands on the edge of the kitchen island.

The back door opens, and Elijah walks in, eyes full of worry connecting with mine.

"Could you just give us a minute?" Jake says in an annoyed tone.

"Why are you such an asshole?" I don't know why I'm being so damn mean, but I can't help it. I'm seeping with anger, rage, and sadness from today's already exhausting events. "And no, he doesn't need to give us a minute. I want him here."

Jake lets out a shaky breath, wiping a tear off his face. "I'm just trying to look out for you, Bug."

"Well, I'm going to date who I want to date," I tell him, and Elijah squeezes my shoulders.

"I just hope for your sake he's nothing like his brother," Jake says calmly, giving Elijah the once-over.

"Well, if Cole's anything like Elijah, then you must not know him as well as you think you do," I say.

Jake huffs out a sarcastic laugh. "Yeah, that's it."

"I know some shit went down with you and Cole..." Elijah says. "But honest to God, the guy you've described and the one I know sound nothing alike. Maybe he hasn't shown me his true colors yet, I have no clue, but... I really care about Sophia, and I just wish you wouldn't write me off based on a family I met six months ago." Elijah's heart pounds hard against my back.

"If you ever hurt her—"

"I won't," Elijah cuts Jake off, staring at him intently.

"Anyone want some pie?" Leah asks, coming into the kitchen.

32
ELIJAH

"How was work?" I ask.

Mark and Cole came straight to the diner in full uniform, and I have to admit, it's a little intimidating.

"Fine," Mark replies. "What did you end up doing, Eli?"

"Went over to a friend's house."

"Oh, glad you found somewhere to go. Who was it?"

My heart rate quickens. Do they hate the Summers as much as it seems the Summers hate the Danvers?

Lord have mercy. Who are we? The Hatfields and McCoys?

"Sophia's," I reply, taking another bite of my waffle.

Mark rubs his hand over his face. "Of all the girls you could befriend, you had to choose Sophia Summers?"

"Actually… she's my girlfriend," I admit.

Cole lets out a rumbling laugh and shakes his head. "Good luck, little bro."

"You're one to talk," Mark scoffs.

"What's that supposed to mean?" Cole cocks a brow.

"You're the one sniffin' around a *married* bartender."

"We're *friends*, Dad. That doesn't mean I'm sniffing around anything."

"Mm-hmm," Mark hums, taking a bite of his eggs, and my eyes bounce between them.

"She's having a hard time, and yeah, if she calls, I'm gonna answer. Doesn't mean I'm looking to home wreck," Cole says defensively.

"Mm-hmm," Mark repeats, and I roll my lips together, thankful the topic is off me and Sophia.

We continue our meal, and the conversation comes easy. I update them on my football season and school, Cole talks about the cases he's working on, and Mark beams like the proud dad he is.

There's a question that's been swimming in my mind since Sophia shared her secret with me, and I've been trying to think of the best way to breach it.

"So... one of my friends is taking a pre-law class, and they were wondering if I could ask you some questions about a mock trial he's working on." *Hopefully it doesn't sound like a crock of shit.*

"Sure, what's up?" Cole says, taking a sip of his coffee.

"So there was a hit-and-run case. The person died, and there was no evidence." They both stare at me expectantly. "If the lawyer found a witness who would talk, is a confession enough?"

"I had a case like that earlier this year," Cole says, and my stomach sinks. *Abort. Abort. Abort.* "Unfortunately, with only a witness and no evidence, there's not much we can do besides have probable cause to interrogate the suspect. But if there's no proof... there's nothing to bring it to trial. It just turns into a giant game of 'he said, she said.'"

"Oh, damn... okay." I push around the food on my plate. "What should I suggest to him to strengthen his case?"

"Hmm." Cole twists his mouth up. "He could check the street cams in the area to see if there's any video footage."

No street cams in the woods.

"He already tried that, no luck."

"Without video evidence these days, it's really hard to make a conviction," Mark adds in.

"What if he found a second witness?" I ask hopefully. *Maybe we can convince Charlie to come forward too.*

Cole ponders the question. "Honestly, it's still not enough. There needs to be hard evidence, or it's never gonna lead to a conviction. Innocent till proven guilty, remember?"

"Yeah," I smile softly. "I'll let him know, thanks."

"Happy to help." Cole smirks, then reaches over and ruffles my hair.

I laugh, ducking away. "Dude."

"Sorry." He chuckles. "I've been dying to fuck up your perfect hair since you walked in here."

After breakfast with Mark and Cole, I knock on the front door of Sophia's childhood home. She insisted we go downtown today so she can show me all her favorite spots. When she swings it open, a wide smile spreads across my face.

"Well, hey there, Honey Bee." She grins before stepping forward and throwing her arms around me.

"I missed you too, Sunflower." I chuckle, holding her tightly and planting a kiss in her sunshine hair.

She spins around, skipping back inside, and I trail after her.

"You just missed breakfast," Will says from his position washing dishes at the sink.

"That's okay. I just ate."

"Cup of coffee?" Jake asks, pouring some of the dark liquid into a mug. The nutty smell hits my senses, and I can't resist.

"Yeah, that would be great actually."

He grabs a mug out of the cupboard and pours another black coffee, handing it to me.

"Thanks." I'm not about to show them I'm a basic bitch by asking for cream and sugar.

He tips his coffee at me, and I tip mine back. Just as I'm about to bring the mug to my lips, my girl comes over, sets down a jar of honey, and pours a healthy serving of creamer in my cup. I smirk down at her, and she leans her head against my shoulder before putting it back in the fridge.

I take a sip, the sweet liquid hitting my tongue, and my lips curve upward.

"So Soph tells me you've got a game tomorrow?" Jake asks in an appreciated attempt to make conversation.

"Yeah, we play at three. Usually I would've spent Thanksgiving with my mom and grandma, but it's a bit too far since they live in Georgia."

"Oh, really?" He smiles wide. "Our mom lives there too." His reaction surprises me, considering Sophia tenses at any mention of her mom.

"I'm gonna run upstairs and finish getting ready, and then I can show you downtown," Sophia says, leaving the kitchen. I watch, making sure she's really gone before turning my attention back to Jake, Leah, Diane, and Will.

"Okay," I say in a hushed tone, causing all their eyes to flick in my direction. "I have an idea for Sophia, and I think it would make her really happy, but I'm going to need some help... from all of you."

"What's your plan?" Will asks, and then I tell them exactly how we can make our girl feel whole again.

33
SOPHIA

"Alright, we'll see you in the morning before you and Elijah head back to school," Leah tells me as she and Jake leave to meet friends at the bar.

"Okay, sounds good." I give them both a hug.

"Love you, Soph," Jake says, kissing my head, and they leave, shutting the door behind them. Elijah already left, Dad's working overnight, and Diane has gone to bed, so I'm all alone. I'm pouring a glass of water in the kitchen when my phone buzzes.

HONEY BEE

HONEY BEE

Hey baby, miss me yet?

ME

Yes, an hour without my honey bee is an hour too long 🙁

HONEY BEE

You think you got enough books at that books drafts and arts place?

I chuckle down at my phone as I wander to the couch and throw myself against the soft cushions.

> **ME**
>
> It's called Books, Crafts, and Drafts
>
> And you can never have enough books
>
> Also, I was looking for some inspiration...

HONEY BEE

Oh really? Let me know when you decide which fantasy you'd like to reenact

> **ME**
>
> Don't worry, I definitely will
>
> I already ordered you the elf ears

I giggle to myself, knowing what his face must look like when he sees my message.

HONEY BEE

If you wanna fuck an elf, just call me Santa's helper

> **ME**
>
> Oh... have you been a naughty elf Mr. Anderson?

HONEY BEE

The naughtiest. I think you should punish me

> **ME**
>
> I have some ideas...

HONEY BEE

I wanna see your gorgeous face

A loud knock comes from the front door, and my smile grows wide. I toss my phone on the couch, practically running to the front door, where Elijah must be waiting to *see my gorgeous face*. I swing the door open, and a thousand needles prick my skin at once.

"Seth," I whisper, gripping the handle tightly. "What are you doing here?"

He grabs my arm tightly, and I stumble over the threshold as he pulls me onto the porch, the door clicking shut behind me.

I've been dragged into the lion's den.

"Saw your little boyfriend today," Seth says with a sneer as the moonlight casts an eerie shadow on his face.

"Okay?" I square my shoulders, manifesting bravery. "And?"

"You never told me he was the son of the police chief," he spits out, boring his icy eyes into mine.

"Didn't realize you were owed the family lineage of the people I date."

"Don't bullshit me, Sophia!" he shouts, and I flinch. "Your new boyfriend is the chief's fucking kid! You better not have told him about what happened."

"And what if I did?" His eyes turn dark—so dark I fear it's not even Seth I'm staring at—as if he shut his humanity off completely.

He steps toward me, and I stumble back against the door. He places his arms on both sides, caging me in. "Don't toy with me, you stupid cunt."

My eyes widen in surprise at his venomous words. I'm not sure why anything he does surprises me anymore. "Why shouldn't I if you're gonna call me shit like that?"

"Don't!" He lets out a heavy exhale, returning his tone to a normal level. "Fucking. Play. With. Me." His warm breath hits my face, and a wave of nausea floods through me. I consider telling him to be quiet, but I'm wondering if I'm going to need help out of this situation. "Tell me the truth."

I'm sick of lying, so fucking sick of lying to everyone. "I told him... I told Elijah what happened."

"You're full of shit." He glares as the air shifts to a temperature much too cold for Florida in the fall.

My knees wobble, and I straighten them, clenching my fists.

"Every. Single. Fucking. Detail, Seth. I told him exactly how *you* hit that guy and left him blee—"

A hand around my throat cuts off my words. "I told you not to tell anyone." A fierce pain rips through my body as he lifts me up, crushing my windpipe, and I fight to touch the ground.

"Seth," I croak out, trying to claw his hand off my neck. My eyes water as I struggle for air.

"If he tells his dad, I could go to jail!" Seth jerks me forward, slamming my head against the door, his grip increasingly painful. "I'll drag you down with me, you manipulative cunt." My lungs desperately fight for oxygen. Black spots slowly trickle into my vision, knees buckling. "You're the one who turned up the radio so fucking loud I could barely pay attention. This is as much your fault as it is mine."

My eyes flutter shut. He's still yelling, but the words are far away and incomprehensible.

I can't breathe.

I'm going to pass out.

I'm going to *die*.

Seth's going to kill me.

His grip on my neck releases, and I fall to the ground, gasping for air. My eyes blur, but I'm too focused on the lack of oxygen to wipe away the moisture.

"Shit," Seth whispers, dropping to his knees. "I'm so sorry, baby girl." He reaches out, touching my knee, and I scramble away from him. "I di—"

"Stop!" I beg, weak and breathless.

"Please, I didn't mean—"

"I hate you," I whisper hoarsely.

His shoes come into sight as he crouches directly in front of me. "You don't mean that, baby girl."

Of course I do.

Tears stream down my face as I gather the small bit of saliva left in my mouth and look up at him. I spit directly into his face, and his entire body stiffens. "You're gonna regret that."

"What are you gonna do?" I cough, the words coming out low and rough as I struggle for air. "Choke me?"

He huffs a heavy breath. "You deserved it."

"Help!" I shout weakly, and his eyes widen. "Please, someone help," I attempt, but no one could possibly hear me.

He rushes to stand, backing away. "Keep your fucking mouth shut... Or I'll be back for your little bitch boyfriend next."

Seth runs down the steps and into the darkness as I lie there on the porch, coughing. My hand rests gently on my neck as if I can feel a scar from what he did. Once I regain my ability to breathe properly, the tears really fall, a sob escaping my mouth.

I can't believe that happened.

He almost killed me.

Why didn't I stop him when I had the chance? Now there's nothing I can do.

I should have been braver before.

Why wasn't I braver?

An undefinable amount of time passes before I peel myself off the floor and hobble back inside. My legs carry me mindlessly through the house. I grab my phone from the couch and stumble upstairs to the bathroom.

I take a hot shower, trying to scrub off the feeling of his murderous hand around my neck.

When the heat becomes too much, I get out and grab a towel, wrapping it around me. I wipe the condensation off the mirror with my fist. My eyes fall to dark red marks straight across my throat. With a shaky breath, I trail my trembling fingertips along the lines created by Seth's relentless grip.

Please be gone by morning.

If I come forward now, I'm terrified what Seth will do.

He almost killed me just for *telling* someone.

He's threatened me before... But this time... this time he actually followed through.

What would he do if I testified against him?

What if Seth hadn't stopped strangling me?

Will he show up at CBU and threaten me again? Or Elijah?

Do I need to warn Charlie?

Will he show up at my house in Longwood every time I'm home for break?

How can I ever feel safe again?

I totter back to my room in a haze, throwing on one of Elijah's T-shirts before crawling into bed, finally checking my phone in hope of a distraction.

HONEY BEE

HONEY BEE

Babe?

What are you up to? Wanna FaceTime?

It's only 10:30 and you're a self-proclaimed night owl. Everything okay?

As I'm holding the phone, a FaceTime comes in from Elijah. I reject it immediately.

HONEY BEE

Okay, now I know you're awake. You rejected my call in .5 seconds lol

I sigh, rolling onto my stomach, deciding to reply so he doesn't worry.

ME

Sorry, I was showering and reading a book

HONEY BEE

Okay, get that inspo 😌 Was just worried about you

Can we FaceTime? I really miss your face

Tears drip onto the screen as I stare down at it. I press it firmly against the blankets, wiping the moisture away.

ME

You saw me like two hours ago

HONEY BEE

And you said it yourself. That was too long ago.

ME

You'll see me first thing in the morning. 🤍

HONEY BEE

Okay. Sleep tight, babe. 😴

ME

You too, honey bee 🤍

I want to tell him to come over. To hold me till I fall asleep. To wash away all the pain and fear I just endured and never leave my side. But if Elijah finds out what Seth did, he won't let it go.

And if Seth could almost kill a girl he supposedly used to love... what would he do to someone he definitely hates?

34
ELIJAH

Sophia shuts the front door, and my eyes stay glued to her as she strolls toward the car for our drive back to campus. She's looking fine as fuck, wearing denim cut-off shorts and a turtleneck tank top, with her duffle bag flung over her shoulder.

"Hey there, beautiful," I tell her as she opens the back door, throwing her duffle on the seat.

"Hey," she clips, getting in the passenger side, buckling herself in without so much as a glance my way.

"You alright?"

"Yeah." She turns toward me, eyes red and puffy, smiling weakly. *Maybe still sad about Chloe's room?* "Just tired."

"Okay…" I back the car out of the driveway, and onto the main road. My fingers strum against the steering wheel, filing the silence. "Thanks for letting me borrow your car while we were in town."

"No problem."

I shift in my seat, confused as all hell about her mood. She was fine when I left her house yesterday, so I don't understand what happened between then and now to make her pull away.

After half an hour with neither of us speaking on the highway toward campus, I can't take it anymore. "Sunflower?"

"Hmm," she hums, staring out the window.

"Are you sure everything's okay?" She rubs her hands against her thighs, then touches her neck and exhales heavily. "Babe?"

"Seth came to see me last night." I almost run the car off the road. *Metaphorically.*

"What?" I say calmly, sure I misheard her, while a fireball of anger threatens to explode out of me.

"Seth came to see me last night," she repeats, picking at her fingernails.

I'm gonna throw up.

"Why am I just now finding out about this?"

"I didn't want to tell you at all," she admits nervously, gutting me like a hog.

"Wow, that sure makes me feel better." She doesn't speak, and her silence only heightens my anxiety. "What did he want?"

"He, um, he wanted to make sure you don't tell your dad about the accident."

"What?" I snap my gaze to hers before returning it quickly to the road. My stomach sinks, but I'm pretty sure my cover story was believable enough it doesn't count.

"Seth saw you guys somewhere, I guess. And accused me of telling you." She clears her throat again. "I admitted I did, and he, um, just wants to make sure you don't tell your dad."

Could he have overheard?

My hands tremble, and I tighten my grip on the steering wheel. There's a sign for a rest stop a few miles up, and neither of us speaks until I pull in and put the car in park.

"Maybe we *should* tell Mark."

"No," Sophia blurts. "No." She shakes her head violently. "We can't."

"Why not?" I snap. "This guy is harassing you and manipulating you. Why are you protecting him?"

"I'm not protecting him!" she shouts, tears streaming down her face. "I'm protecting myself. And Charlie." She pauses. "And you."

"Me?"

"Yeah, just, I don't want you to have any problems with him either, you know?"

I shake my head. "Sophia, I don't need you to protect me. *I* protect *you*. That's how this works."

"Well, sorry, but I protect *you* too," she says gently.

"Please, babe, we have to get you out of this mess."

"There is no way out!" she shouts, trembling with rage. "We just keep our mouths shut and hope Seth runs away to rot in hell and leaves us the fuck alone." I reach out, wiping away a tear that's fallen down her cheek.

"Baby…" I whisper, and her eyes find mine. "Please don't cry."

Her lip trembles. "I'm sorry I pulled you into this."

I slide my seat back, patting my thigh. "Come here." She removes her seat belt, crawling over the center console and into my lap, resting her head on my chest. "Please *always* pull me into it."

"I don't want you to have to deal with this stuff though. It's not your problem."

"You're my girl. If it's your problem, it's my problem. Remember?"

She drags her fingertips along my bicep. "Just please don't tell Mark, and everything will be fine." My chest tightens, and I consider telling Sophia about my talk with them, but she's in such a fragile state I don't want to cause her more anxiety over nothing. "Everything will be fine," she says, reassuring herself more than me.

I rub my palm along her smooth thigh. "Sweetheart, I'm trying really hard not to be angry with you right now, but all I can think of is the fact he showed up and you didn't call me."

She's quiet for one breath. Two breaths. Three breaths. "I wanted to."

"You should have," I say immediately, resting a palm against her face. "I pray to God there's not a next time, but if there is, you have to swear to call me. I would have been over in a heartbeat." Glancing out the window, I curse myself for not following my gut. "I thought something was wrong, but I didn't want to push you. I can't even imagine how you must have been feeling last night."

She swallows hard and whispers, "I was wishing I was in your arms."

"You could've been."

She plays with the frayed hem of her denim shorts. "Elijah?"

"Yeah?"

"Can I sleep at your place tonight?"

"Of course, baby. You can stay over any time you want. If you wanna take over my whole damn room with your sketchbooks and your Polaroids and those tiny koalas, be my guest."

"I don't need to take up all your space." She smiles at me. "I'm small."

"I want you in my space. Every damn inch of it. I want you in my bed. Your sketches on the walls. I want your golden hair in the shower drain and your running shoes sitting by the door. Your half-full black coffee sitting on the nightstand because we got too distracted for you to finish." I brush a hair behind her ear and kiss her softly. "I want all the little reminders you're in my life. All the little reminders you're mine."

She smiles up at me. "Okay... but if you ever want to send me back to my place, just let me know. I don't want you getting sick of me."

"I'll never be sick of you." I chuckle. "No returns, no refunds, baby. Remember?"

"Are you sure you don't want Sage to come over and stay with you while I'm gone?" I ask Sophia, who's snuggled up in my bed as I get ready to leave for the game.

"No." She shakes her head against the pillow. "Like I said, I'm just exhausted... I barely slept last night."

I brush her hair back before rubbing my thumb against her cheek. Seeing her face broken like this hurts worse than being bucked off a bronco. "I'll be back right after the game, okay?"

"You're not going to Noah's?"

My brows pull together. "Are you seriously asking if I'm gonna go to a party when you're here in my bed?"

A small smile pulls at her lips before she glances up at me. "I guess I know you better than that."

"Damn right you do."

I glance at the time on my phone, and I'm already running late. I'm gonna get shit for it but in this moment, I just don't care. Finding the strength to leave Sophia right now is like pulling Excalibur out of the stone.

"Is there anything you want to talk about before I leave?" I ask timidly.

She presses her lips together, only her face visible from the blankets tucked up to her neck. "Maybe later."

I take a deep, quiet breath. "Okay." Leaning down, I kiss her tenderly. "I'll be back as soon as I can."

"Good luck," she says weakly.

I throw my football duffle over my shoulder and force my legs to exit the apartment, leaving Sophia—and my sanity—locked inside.

Seven torturous hours later, I finally walk back in my building after having scored another victory with the boys. A victory I could barely even enjoy because my mind was swimming with worry about Sophia. I enter the apartment quietly in case Sophia is sleeping and tiptoe to my room. I open the door to the sight of Sophia standing in nothing but a towel, with a hand pressed to her neck. Her eyes go wide, and she smiles awkwardly.

"Oh, hey," she says, before quickly turning away and shielding herself with a wall of wet hair.

I can't help my face from screwing together from her bizarre reaction. "That's all I get?"

"Sorry, give me a sec." She shuffles through the dresser drawer I gave her. Seconds pass, and her hands move frantically. Rushing over, I touch her arm gently, and she freezes.

"Sophia?" I say, and she doesn't move a muscle. My heart pounds as my stomach swirls with worry. "Please look at me?"

She takes a few calming breaths, then turns to face me, her hair falling behind her shoulders. My gaze flicks downwards to a small mark on the side of her neck.

Is that a hickey?

It wouldn't be from me. We haven't slept together since we were at school a few days ago. My lips part open, but I can't form words.

"Elijah?" Sophia croaks, her eyes searching my face. I take a step back and notice the marks go across her entire neck. *That's definitely not a hickey.*

"Sophia," I whisper as every bit of breath in my lungs feels like it was knocked out by a linebacker. "What-what happened to your neck?"

Sophia flinches as I bring up a shaky hand. My thumb drags across the bruise on her throat, furious tears welling in my eyes. She takes so long to respond, I think she's lost the ability to speak entirely.

"Babe?" I say, and her face crumples as she looks away, agonizing seconds of torture passing.

"He choked me."

Every molecule in my body vibrates with a rage so strong I struggle to contain it. "What do you mean he *choked* you?"

"When he came to talk to me last night..." Her voice trails off as she sits on the edge of the bed. I pace the room, dragging my hands through my hair.

"Fuck!" I shout, angry tears dripping from my eyes. I'm so furious I don't know what to do with myself. "Why didn't you call me?!" She winces, causing my body to freeze. I drop to my knees in front of her, taking her hands in mine. "Sophia, I'm so sorry for yelling. My anger's not directed at you in any way."

Her eyes fall to our hands. "I know."

Shaking my head, I stare at her tired eyes, the circles under them darker than before. Her makeup must have washed off in the shower.

"Do you want to tell Mark? We can—"

"No." She cuts me off. "Please, no. I just... I want to move forward. There's no reason I should see him again, and-and-I'll be more careful opening the door."

"We need to take pictures. We need to document this shit. Can w—"

"Please don't push me." Her green, glassy eyes connect with mine. "I just want to stop thinking about it."

"But Soph—"

"You can take pictures later, but please not right now."

I clear my throat, trying to shove down the overwhelming emotions I'm feeling.

Mad at myself for not being there to protect her.

Sad Sophia didn't call me afterwards and dealt with it alone.

Angry—so damn angry I consider hunting Seth down and throwing him in a shallow grave for what he did to Sophia.

"Okay," I agree begrudgingly, taking her hands in mine.

"Please."

"I said okay, baby." She nods slightly, her body shaking. "Let's get you into something warm." I walk over to my closet, grabbing my CBU hoodie and the sweats I know she loves so much. I tug the hoodie over her head, pulling her arms through, and she doesn't make a single sound, only confirming how emotionally exhausted she must be.

I pull her to a standing position, and the hoodie falls to her thighs as I tug off the towel. Grabbing the sweats off the bed, I help her step into them and bring them up to rest on her hips.

"Thank you," she mutters. "I know you prefer taking my clothes off over putting them on." Her lips quirk upwards, and I let out a sigh of relief, thankful her defense mechanism of humor has returned. It's exponentially better than the silence.

"I prefer *any* opportunity to touch your skin."

"Oh yeah?" she says, getting cozy under the blanket as I slide in next to her, pulling her close to me, our faces nose to nose.

"Mm-hmm." I drag my hand under the hoodie and rest it on her hip, kissing her softly. Using my fingers, I brush the damp hair behind her shoulder, my eyes dropping down to the bruises forming against her neck. My mouth pulls to hers like a magnet. As if they have a mind of their own, my lips wander to her jaw. I plant light kisses, trailing toward her ear and all the way down until my mouth is hovering over her neck.

Her warm breath is hard against me, but she doesn't protest. Lowering my mouth, I kiss along the discolored skin, praying each one will cure her of the damage he caused.

But as much as I ache to, I can't siphon her suffering. All I can do is be here for her when the ceiling breaks and everything comes crashing down.

35

SOPHIA

"Wow, finally, bitch," Sage says, jumping off the bean bag as I walk into our dorm room.

"I saw you yesterday."

"Okay?" She waves me off. "But you haven't been *home* in like a week."

"I know... I'm sorry."

Elijah's place has been my safe haven since we got back from Thanksgiving last week, and we've been living in an oblivious state of sweet bliss. I know he's angry—hell, so am I—but I'm glad he's allowing us to move forward so I don't have nightmares forcing me to relive it repeatedly.

I wish I could tell Sage everything. About Seth—the accident—Seth choking me over the accident. But I don't want to drag anyone else into this mess. Seth's made it clear he's willing to do anything to ensure this stays under wraps, so the best thing I can do is keep my damn mouth shut.

"That's okay." She hugs me tightly, following me into my room as I grab a few more things for Elijah's. "Damn, Soph, you could have at least told me you were moving out."

"I'm *not* moving out. It's just been nice staying over there."

"His honey dick really that good?"

"Yes." I nod, laughing. "Yes, it is."

"Damn." She whistles, strutting out of my room. "You go, girl."

My phone buzzes, and I pull it out.

UNKNOWN NUMBER

UNKNOWN NUMBER

I hope for your sake your fuck buddy keeps his mouth shut

My blood runs cold enough to give me hypothermia. I delete the message and shove the phone back in my pocket. Another notification has me holding my breath.

HONEY BEE

HONEY BEE

Just finished taking my stats test. I think I crushed it. Dinner before Noah's party to celebrate?

A sigh of relief escapes my lips.

ME

Sure

HONEY BEE

Okay, we can let belly baby pick the place 🐝

ME

You're never letting that go are you?

HONEY BEE

Nope 😆

I grin down at the phone, feeling incredibly grateful for Elijah. Grateful that with everything, he's stood by my side and helped to be a light in my darkness. I stare in the mirror, plastering on a smile, and decide not to let Seth keep controlling my life or my mood. I get good grades. I have an awesome family. My boyfriend is sweet as honey and hot as shit. Time I move forward and enjoy my life again instead of cowering in the past. That's the only hope I have to move on from this.

I will move on from this.

We arrive at Noah's house for the bowl announcement "party" where we get to find out if CBU will play this year. Elijah buzzes with anxious energy as we walk through the front door. Football players and students fill every inch, wearing ugly Christmas sweaters—the theme of the night since it'll be the last big shindig before winter break.

Elijah's sweater is red with white writing that says "Santa," and mine is white and red with the words "So good Santa came twice" across the chest. I about died from laughter when Elijah surprised me with them.

"Honey Bee," I say, grabbing his scattered attention. His blue eyes land on mine, and my lips pull up into a soft smile. "Relax."

"I'm trying, I swear."

I slip my hand into his and squeeze, tugging his arm so he'll lean down and kiss me. He does eagerly, and only the sound of someone clearing their throat has us pulling away.

Noah stands before us with a stupid smirk on his face. "Can I borrow him for a minute?"

"I suppose." My lips curve into a teasing smile.

Elijah kisses me on the cheek before moving his mouth to my

ear, releasing a warm breath. "I swear to God," he whispers low and commanding as the hair on my arms stands, "if I find you being a naughty girl again, I will take you home, spank your ass, and pound the disobedience out of you."

"*Oh, Theoooo!*" I call out, turning away, and Elijah grabs my chin, forcing my attention to him. His jaw is clenched as a wry smile plays on his lips. "Yeah, yeah... I'll be a *good* girl."

He presses a kiss against my smiling mouth. "Be right back, my naughty little ho."

Laughing, I make my way to the couch, where Charlie and Sage are engaged in a heated debate about if pineapple belongs on pizza.

"It's a *fruit!*" Sage argues.

"I'm gonna have to agree," I say, adding my opinion as Sage scoots over, making room for me to sit between her and Charlie. "Only vegetables belong on pizza."

"*Tomatoes* are a fruit," Charlie counters, raising her dark brows.

"Debatable," Sage and I chime in unison.

"Anyways..." Charlie says, obviously ready to change the topic. "I'm ninety-nine percent sure we're making a bowl game, and you guys *have* to come."

"I'm down," Sage replies easily without a second thought.

"Shouldn't we wait to see where it——"

"Girl." Sage cuts me off. "Wherever it is, it'll be fun as shit to go to an out-of-state game. Charlie *has* to go for cheer. Your boyfriend is QB2, and I'm fucking the center. So Sophia motherfucking Summers, I don't care if they're playing in Alaska, we are going to this goddamn game."

"Dang, Sage." I laugh. "When did you become the team's biggest cheerleader?"

"It's an excuse to see the *world*, Joey," Sage says pointedly. "Come on... please? Let's be spontaneous."

I roll my eyes in mock annoyance. "Fine. We'll go to the stupid game."

An hour later, everyone gathers around the TV, waiting for the bowl game announcement. I'm in Elijah's lap on the couch as he grips my thigh, nails digging into the skin.

I lean back, finding his ear. "I'm not a stress ball, baby."

"Shit, I'm sorry." He releases his grip immediately. "Don't worry… I'll kiss it better later."

I shake my head, laughing as someone hushes us, turning up the TV. The room is silent as the broadcast comes through.

"And in Glendale, Arizona, on December 31st, Andrews University will play Crystal Bay University in the Desert Bowl."

The entire room jumps up, screaming, clapping hands, hugging, and cheering. Elijah and I stay stone still as our eyes lock, my heart falling to the floor before running out the door to be run over by the nearest car.

I swallow hard, then muster out, "You have to play Seth."

He nods his head, jaw clenching. "Yep."

And what should be a celebration of my man getting to play a bowl game turns into me trying to figure out how I'm going to gain the courage to go to the damn thing. There's no way I can back out. Sage would never let me hear the end of it.

Looks like my boyfriend and batshit crazy ex will be battling it out on the turf as my anxious body threatens to blow like a roman candle.

Happy fucking New Year.

36
ELIJAH

"Arizona is way better than playing somewhere cold as tits," Theo says just as Sophia returns with another drink for me. *I've honestly lost count of how many I've downed at this point.*

"Thanks, darlin'," I say with a wide smile, taking it from her hands before chugging the whiskey ginger in one shot.

"Damn, baby," Sophia says, laughing. "Slow down."

"I'm good."

I am the opposite of good.

I am duct-tape-on-a-747-airplane's-wings good.

"Okay…" She eyes me curiously before sliding her gaze to Theo.

"I'll be right back," I tell Sophia, kissing her on the cheek and heading to Noah's bathroom for a bit of privacy before I lose my damn shit.

The whiskey warms my veins, only fueling the anger festering underneath the surface. I shut myself in the bathroom and stare into the mirror, gripping the edge of the vanity. My eyes are bloodshot, muscles tense, wrinkle lines on my forehead. I look about as good as I feel.

Spinning around, I lean against the edge of the marble, dragging a hand over my face.

This bowl game should be a career highlight and instead, I'm torpedoing headfirst into a handle of whiskey. I've been trying to ignore the nagging feeling in the pit of my stomach ever since Sophia told me what Seth did. I wish we could talk about how I'm feeling, but I'm worried it'll trigger her.

The one thing keeping my head above water was hoping I'd never have to see that prick again, knowing if I did, I'd probably beat him to death.

Guess that Sasquatch motherfucker is going down.

Pacing the room, I pull out my phone and instinctively hit the call button to hear the one voice that can stop me from flying off the fucking handle.

"We're sorry. Your call could not be completed as dialed."

I rip the phone from my ear and stare down at it.

That's weird.

Holding my breath, I call again.

"We're sorry. Your call could not be completed as dialed."

"No." I shake my head. "No."

My hands shake, trying again.

"We're sorry. Your call could not be completed as dialed."

A tsunami slams into me. "No." The phone slips through my fingers, thudding to the floor, as my only life raft deflates beneath me.

The anchor that bound me to my old life sinks rapidly, dragging me down with it, miles below the surface. The pressure is too over-whelming—too suffocating—too absolutely heartbreaking.

Tears blur my vision as I drop to my knees, flattening a palm over my pounding heart. This is the type of anguish I've been avoid-ing. Filling my life with distractions always seems a hell of a lot more enticing than falling apart on my friend's bathroom floor in the middle of a damn celebration.

I pull myself up to my feet, and my gaze wanders back to the mirror. If I looked bad before, now I look like I'm having a straight up mental breakdown. *That's because you are having one, you fucking idiot.* I shake my head, trying to expel the negative thoughts.

"Come on," I tell myself. "Now is not the time to break down." Tears continue dripping down my face into the sink. I bring up my hand, slapping my cheek. "Get it together!"

I wipe the tears off angrily and turn on the faucet, splashing my face with cool water before returning my attention to the mirror. "Pain *always* goes away," I say out loud, repeating the words all but embedded into my brain since the day I started playing football. Every tackle. Every sore muscle. Every twisted ankle. Every heartbreak.

Pain. Always. Goes. Away.

Taking calming breaths, I lock the grief back in the tiny box where it needs to stay.

After composing myself, I open the door, stepping into Noah's room. My eyes connect with Theo's.

"Hey." He quickly stands from the bed, a hesitant smile on his face.

"Hey."

"You alright, bro?"

The lie is on the tip of my tongue, but the whiskey replies differently. "No."

"What's up?"

We stand awkwardly in the center of the room, and I pull my eyes away, cracking my knuckles. "Just shit."

"Come on, man. Talk to me." The tenderness in his tone surprises me, and I pace, concentrating on the part of my freak-out he can understand.

"I'm just pissed... We're playing in a bowl game, and *of course* it's against Sophia's shithead ex."

"I mean, yeah, that blows." He waves me off. "But she's totally stuck on your honey dick anyway. So who cares?"

"It's not that." I blow out a frustrated breath. "He's just..." My stomach twists as I think about what he did. I wish I could talk about it with someone, but it's not my secret to tell. "He's just a shitty person, and I don't want him anywhere near Sophia."

"We'll all be there. Trust me, no one is getting near her. Besides, the stadium is massive. He won't even know she's there."

I pause my pacing, looking toward him. "There *will* be tons of people at the game."

"Exactly." He strides over, throwing an arm around my shoulder. "Now don't give that limp dick anymore of your energy and focus on pollinating that sunflower of yours." He winks.

"Yeah, you're right."

"I know. So stop moping in here like a little bitch and get back to that sexy ass girlfriend of yours."

I glare directly into his eyes. "Call her sexy one more time. I *dare* you."

He laughs in my face, dragging me toward the door. *Why the hell does that never work?*

"Come on, let's get a drink," he says, leading me back to the kitchen.

We walk through the archway, halting at the sight of Andi sprawled out on the kitchen island in a skimpy elf outfit and Sophia's face pressed into her bare stomach.

"Holy shit!" Theo howls, beating my chest as Sophia finishes her body shot.

Her eyes connect with mine, a slow, sensual smirk forming. She drags her tongue across her lip, licking some of the excess liquor off.

"Remember the mission," Theo whispers in my ear as Sophia makes her way over to us. "Pollinate the sunflower."

I laugh, shaking my head, and Theo goes to set up a body shot on Andi.

"You were gone forever." Sophia pouts, throwing her arms around my neck. "I missed you."

She kisses me passionately, the taste of tequila on her tongue. "Whoa there." I pull back, smiling down at her. "You good?"

"Pot, kettle."

"Okay, touché."

I wrap my arms around her waist, pulling her close, and she stands on her tiptoes to whisper in my ear. "Remember that thing you said about sneaking away and fucking while all our friends wonder where we are?"

Now that would be a nice distraction.

My dick hardens at the thought. "Mm-hmm."

"Is that what you were doing with Theo?"

"What?!" I burst into laughter.

"Kidding."

But I'd happily do that with you…

I bring my lips to her ear. "In two minutes, walk down the hallway to our right and go through the last door."

We untangle, and I wink before heading to the room I just described. It was originally a third bedroom, but Noah and Des opted to set it up as an in-home gym, or as Des prefers to call it—his yoga studio.

Inside, I take a seat on the weight bench and less than thirty seconds later, Sophia comes in with an amused smile on her face before closing the door and turning the lock.

"What are we doing in here, Honey Bee?" she teases, eyes dropping to my already hardened cock before stepping between my legs.

"I couldn't stand it anymore." Pushing myself off the bench, I stand to my full height, towering over her. "You brought up sneaking away, and the idea of fucking you senseless right now just made me insane." I place my hands under her sweater, grip her hips tightly to lift her in the air, and she wraps her legs around me. Stepping forward, I slam her back against the door, which rattles as a breath expels from her lungs.

"Is your sweet pussy wet for me?" I mumble against her ear, and she squirms beneath me.

"Yes," she pants.

"Good." I drop her, and the second her feet hit the floor, my hands find the button of her shorts, pushing them off. She undoes my jeans, shoving them and my briefs to my ankles. I smirk down at her, trying to determine my next plan of action. My eyes settle on the bench.

"You wanna be in charge tonight?" I ask, and her eyes flicker dark and hungry.

"Absolutely, yes."

I lie back on the weight bench, and Sophia's sweet laugh fills the room.

"What?" I glare at her.

"You're really not gonna take off the sweater?"

Sitting up, my balls rest against the cool leather, and I make a mental note to clean the bench after. I rip the sweater off over my head, and her smile grows wide. "What about yours?"

"Mine stays on." A low chuckle escapes me as she throws a leg over my hips, straddling me.

I grab her waist, lowering her against my stomach, and groan, feeling how slick she is for me. "Mmmm," I hum, bringing my hand between her legs, rubbing my thumb over her clit.

"Do you"—she lets out a soft moan—"have a condom?"

"Baby, I'm always packing."

She laughs to herself. "Okay, Sandra Bullock."

I grab the rubber out of my jeans, and Sophia snatches it, making quick work to roll it on. She positions herself over me, swiping my throbbing cock between her before lowering on to it. A deep, quiet moan escapes as her head falls back.

"That's it, baby," I praise. "Ride me like you fucking own me."

She grins, her green eyes smoldering like a forest fire. "I *do* fucking own you."

"Yeah, you do." She rotates her hips, eliciting a breathless groan from me. "Prove it."

Her grip tightens on my shoulders as she wildly bucks her hips, fucking me absolutely senseless. Every coherent thought is screwed right out of my head. I tighten the grip on her hips while she rides my cock like a damn bull rider. She reaches back, fingernails digging into my thighs, and pumps her hips with hard thrusts.

A loud moan escapes her, and I throw my hand over her mouth as she shatters to pieces before me. Watching her ride through the orgasm—the way her eyes roll into the back of her head, how she palms her own tit, squeezing firmly as she loses all control—has me teetering on the edge. A flash of lightning rips through me, and I explode inside her warm pussy with more force than a sonic boom.

Our panted breathing fills the small room, and a satisfied smile breaks across my face.

"Is that enough proof?" she pants, pressing her hands against my chest, with me softening inside of her.

"I don't know." My breath is unsteady. "I think you might have to show me again later."

We redress, dispose of the condom, clean the bench, and make our way back to the party. The second we reach the kitchen, Theo pops in front of us, holding three shot glasses.

"Bro," I groan, knowing I'm going to regret this tomorrow.

"Come on." His eyes bounce between me and Sophia. "We're gonna have a good ass time *celebrating* tonight. Got it?"

He places a shot of whiskey in my hand, and Sophia takes hers, shooting me a cocked brow saying *maybe he's right.* "Fine."

"Sweet!"

Sage and Julian come up with their own shots.

"Fuck yes!" Sage says, holding hers in the air, and we join her. "To getting litty as a titty!"

"To getting litty as a titty," we all chime in unison, clinking our shots.

I shoot back the liquor, letting the familiar burn coat my throat.

"Let loose for one night in your life, E," Theo tells me before filling my glass back up, forcing me to do exactly that.

"Oh, God," I groan as the brightest light I've ever encountered pierces my vision. "Shut that shit off."

"It's the sun." Andi's voice hits my ears like a bucket of cold water, and my eyes fly open.

I bolt up, finding myself on a lawn chair in Noah's backyard, wearing nothing but my red briefs. *I'm gonna vomit.* Andi's arms are crossed over her chest as she smirks at me.

Shit. Shit. Shit.

Why is she here?

Where's Sophia?

I bring my hand up to rake through my hair, finding a Santa hat atop my head instead. My eyes squint down at it, and there's zero recollection of putting one on. "What the hell happened last night?"

"Somebody did a few too many shots with Theo." Sophia's teasing voice immediately calms my anxieties, and I fall back against the chair, letting out a heavy exhale. If she's here, I couldn't have been that stupid. *Right?*

"How bad was it?" I ask, scared as shit of the answer.

Sophia sits next to me on the edge of the lawn chair, holding out a coffee. I grab it, taking a long sip.

"Depends what you define as 'bad.'" Sophia's use of air quotes makes my stomach churn.

"If it was as bad as I feel, I'm afraid to hear it."

Sophia smirks at Andi before sliding her gaze back to me. "Well… there was a threesome that turned into a twosome because *someone* fell asleep."

My mouth falls open, eyes widening as they bounce between Andi and Sophia. The wheels in my brain spin on overdrive as I try to conjure up the mental picture that's tragically vacant from my memory.

Andi folds over in laughter, holding her stomach. "Don't hurt yourself there, tiger."

"Kidding." Sophia giggles, placing a hand on my stomach. "You only got *half* naked."

My eyes bulge as I shake my head. "What?"

"Someone set up karaoke," Andi chimes in. "You stripped off your sweater and sang Sophia 'Santa Baby.'"

"Well, I'm glad I don't remember *that*."

"Don't worry." Theo joins us, waving his phone at me as the sound of my slurred voice blares from the speaker. "I got it on video."

"Fuck's sake," I groan. "Did everyone stay over here last night?"

"Well, I couldn't exactly carry you home once you passed out on the lawn," Sophia says. "Theo and Noah put you on the chair and... I was pretty sure you'd kill Theo if I went home with him alone so..."

I open one eye, taking in her teasing smile. "You're probably right."

"Yeah, and then Sophia needed someone to keep her company so..." Andi winks at Sophia, and she laughs.

"Now there's an idea," Theo says, and I don't have the energy to flick him off.

"I'm *also* kidding," Andi says with a wide smirk across her face. "Olivia left her phone, so we came to get it."

"You women are going to kill me," I growl, and they both laugh.

"We'll be inside," Andi says, dragging Theo away, leaving me alone with Sophia. She places a hand on my face, smiling down at me.

"You look way too happy for someone whose boyfriend passed out on their friend's lawn."

"It happens." She shrugs, seemingly unaffected. "Are you okay though? As much as I didn't mind the lap dance to the sound of

'Jingle Bell Rock'..." I groan, my face flushing with heat. "You didn't really seem like yourself."

I blow out a frustrated breath. "I'm sorry."

"You don't need to apologize. I'm not upset. I was just worried if everything's okay with you, that's all."

I swallow hard, knowing it's time for her to learn the one part of me I'm too damn afraid to even face myself.

I think I'd rather show her instead.

37

SOPHIA

"I can't do it, babe." Elijah thrusts his phone toward me. "Check for me."

Grades were just released from the statistics test he took last week, and he's a jittery mess. He passed his world history final with flying colors—thank you very much to his excellent tutor—but if he doesn't pass statistics, it doesn't matter anyway. He's pacing the room, dragging his fingers through his hair, making me anxious as all hell.

"Elijah." I grab his arm, pulling him to me. "Just relax. I'll check. Lie down and whatever happens, I'll make sure you have a good night, okay?" I wink.

He smirks and climbs on the bed. I climb on top and straddle him, pressing my center directly against his naked abs. He glides his warm palms along the exposed skin of my hips. "I should find out all my life-altering news this way."

"Okay, here we go." I press a few buttons, open up his test, and read the result before placing the phone gently on the side table. I lean down towards his face as his rapid heartbeat pounds against my hand.

"You're killing me, Sunflower." He grips my hips tighter. "In more ways than one…"

I brush my mouth against his ear and whisper, "You got a ninety-one."

He bolts up, almost throwing me off the bed, and catches me with a steady arm. "Are you shitting me?" The smile on his face is so wide and beautiful it makes my heart melt.

"You did it, Honey Bee." In one motion, he flips me onto my back, expelling the air from my lungs.

"I couldn't have done it without you." He rests his forehead against mine. "My favorite girl."

"Your *favorite*?" I scoff playfully. "How many others are there?"

"Let me think…" He sits up, tapping a finger to his mouth, and I roll my eyes. "There's the smart girl, the artsy girl, the one who loves busting my balls. The silly girl, the mouthy girl, the *noisy* girl." He waggles his eyebrows. "The drive-me fucking-crazy girl. The sexy-even-as-a-koala girl. Oh, and can't forget the spontaneous let's-fuck-in-the-study-room girl." I giggle, running my fingers along his rippled torso.

"And which one of those is *actually* your favorite?"

"Every damn one of them… Because they're all what makes you, you."

My head rests on Elijah's bare chest as it rises and falls in steady rhythm. He has to leave for practice soon, but the sound of his breathing has me so relaxed I'm almost lulled back to sleep.

"Baby?" he rasps.

"Yes?"

"Do you have any plans next week?"

Hooking my leg over his waist, I pull myself closer. "No, but if your offer includes more of this, then I'm one hundred percent on board."

"I mean, this will certainly be part of it but... We have a little more than a week off practice for the holidays, and I'm going to Georgia."

A disappointed breath escapes my lips. "Oh."

"I was hoping you'd come home with me."

Sitting up, I look at his hope-filled face as my heart pounds in my ears. "You wanna bring me home with you?"

This is a massive step for us.

"Yes."

"Are you sure?" I pause. "Are we ready for that?"

"Did you forget I've already met your entire family?" he asks with a bemused expression.

"I guess you're right."

"So?" The breathtaking smile on his face determines my answer.

"Well... I'm gonna have to talk to my dad. He was looking forward to having me home next week for winter break."

Even though I'm more than happy for an excuse to avoid Longwood for as long as possible.

"We can still go to Longwood for Christmas. I promise. And you can spend the entire week there before you fly to Arizona for the bowl game."

"I guess it would be just as easy to leave with Sage from Longwood."

"Exactly. See, it'll all work out perfectly. I also think it could be a nice distraction from everything, you know? I don't really like the idea of you being in Longwood when I'm so far away... At least when I'm at CBU I can be there quickly if you need me."

"Yeah... You've really thought of everything, haven't you?" I narrow my eyes at him as a smirk spreads across my lips.

"Of course. I wanted to be ready for whatever arguments you may have to not spend a week with all this," he says, waving a hand at his naked body.

"Trust me, Honey Bee. There aren't enough excuses in the world to keep me away from..." I drag my hand down his abdomen towards his dick that's already standing at attention. "All this."

He laughs, pulling me on top of him. "Then it's settled. You're coming home with me, and we'll make it back to Longwood in time for Christmas."

"A Very Longwood Christmas." I stare down at this perfect specimen of a man, and I'm overwhelmed he's mine. "How cute."

"What about this one?" I ask Sage, placing the third dress option in front of my silhouette.

"It's cute..." She tilts her head. "But it doesn't scream 'let's fuck.'"

"Sage!" I spin to face her. "I don't want it to scream 'let's fuck.' I want it to scream 'respectable girl who's dating my son' when his mother meets me."

"You do know it's cold there, right? Why don't you wear leggings?"

"I can change when we get there." I shrug, twirling in front of the tiny mirror. "Elijah's extra touchy when he drives, and I love the skin to skin."

"Okay." She lets out an amused laugh. "That I can understand. Julian is handsy as fuck."

"Oh yeah? How's it going with the Uber driver?"

She rolls her eyes as a suspicious smile spreads across her face. "Fine."

"Just *fine*?"

"Yeah, you know? F-I-N-E. Fun-Interesting-Naughty-*Erotic*." She winks.

"Okay, that's a new one... and is it really just fucking?"

"Soph." She tilts her head, brows drawing together. "We're keeping things casual. No strings."

"No strings?! Does he still sleep with other people?"

"How should I know? I don't own his dick."

"What?" I scoff. "And you're okay with that?"

"Why not?" She shrugs. "No feelings, just sex. If either of us wants some fun... or a *release*"—my face twists up at her TMI—"we booty dial."

"So he's your booty boy."

"Yeah." She smirks, nodding. "I guess he is. It's mostly fucking and some occasional borrowed kisses."

"Borrowed kisses? That's cute." I grab some underwear, throwing them into my bag, and she makes an exaggerated gagging sound.

"*That's* the underwear you're bringing?"

"What? It's just for under the comfy clothes. I have a few thongs too."

"Girl." Sage shakes her head. "You're going on a winter vacay your man." She hops off the bed, striding over to my dresser and shuffling through it.

"Sure, help yourself," I say, gesturing to the underwear drawer she's ripping apart.

"Okay, what the fuck is this shit. You only have like three pairs of sexy panties."

"I know..." I groan. "I had more, but Elijah has a fetish about ripping them off." I bite my lip to stifle a smirk.

"Girl." She hits me on the arm. "Are you kidding me? These are the dirty details you're holding out on me? That's hot as shit."

"Yeah... But it's also painful because these little things are *expensive*." I twirl a pair around my pointer finger.

"True." She refocuses on my underwear drawer, rearranging the lame contents. "Ohhh... this is definitely going." She pulls out my little hot pink vibrator and tosses it in my duffle bag.

I snatch it out just as quickly. "Absolutely not!"

"Why?" She juts out her lower lip. "Trust me, it'll add to the O."

"Sage, I am not bringing a vibrator to meet his mother for the first time."

"Come on, stop thinking about it like that. Think of it as 'the first time I fuck my boyfriend in his childhood bedroom.'"

"No!" I laugh, struggling to show my sincerity. "I promise I'll have Elijah try the vibrating O on me when we're back on campus. Okay?"

"Mm-hmm," she sasses. A look of disapproval is evident on her face as I toss the pink bullet back in the drawer, slamming it shut. "Okay, we're going shopping."

"What? Why?"

"Because I'm not letting you go on a winter vacay with your man dressing your lady parts like his grandma."

I groan, knowing she's right. "Sage, sexy lingerie is not a priority item on my skimpy ass budget."

"Consider it an early Christmas present."

"I can't let you spend all your lunch money covering my lady parts."

"Trust me, I won't," she says, throwing an arm around me. "I'm going to spend my money making sure your lady parts are *completely* visible."

A laugh bubbles out of me. "I love you, Sage."

"Love you too, Joey."

38
ELIJAH

I white-knuckle the steering wheel, driving up the desolate country road I haven't been on in months. Every time Mom asks me to come home, an excuse flies off my tongue quicker than a speeding bullet— it's just so damn hard being here when *they* aren't. Being away makes it easier to ignore the emptiness created in their absence.

Muddy boots sitting by the door.

Hazelnut coffee infiltrating my senses at six in the morning.

Music blaring into my room even with all the doors closed.

Tools and grease-stained rags scattered around the house, driving Mom crazy.

Instead, all that's left is a clean, quiet, and unbearable shell of a house.

"Elijah?" Sophia's sweet voice says, pulling me out of my trip down memory lane.

"Yes?" I glance over, and her forehead is full of worry lines.

"You look a little stressed."

Reaching out, I rest my hand on her thigh, squeezing it gently. "I'm fine, Sunflower. Just haven't been home in a while."

More like freaking out about surviving the next few days without another whiskey induced breakdown.

She places her hand on mine, brushing over my knuckles with her thumb. "Well, I'm here for you. And if you ever get too stressed, I know *exactly* how to calm you down."

"You better be careful, baby. I'll pull over this truck right here, right now. That little sundress you're wearing would be pretty easy to take off."

"We're in the middle of nowhere."

"Exactly. Who's going to see us?" She shakes her head in amusement, returning her attention back to her book. "Whatcha reading there?"

She clutches it to her chest, smirking over at me. "Wouldn't you like to know?"

"Actually, I would. Is it another one of those sex books?"

"What?" She throws her head back, laughing. "They're called *romance* books."

"Well, then read me some *romance*." I risk a glance her way, and she licks her lips, contemplating my request. "Read me your favorite part."

"Okay," she says cheerily, flipping through it before settling on a page. "Are you ready?"

"Yep." I rub my fingertips along her bare thigh, and she clears her throat.

"He slides his hand up her thigh towards her aching pussy." My gaze snaps to hers with intrigue apparent all over my face before I forcibly return my attention to the road. My hand inches higher up her leg, and she squirms in her seat. "His fingertips play with her lace thong. 'I'm so fucking wet for you,' Sky says in a breathless tone." My dick twitches in my pants, and she's only three freaking sentences in. Sophia lowers the tone of her voice a few octaves. "'Then let me fuck you, baby. Let me fuck you right here. Right now.'" I chuckle at Sophia's impersonation of the male dialogue.

"Don't laugh." She hits me playfully against the arm. "Or I'll stop."

"Please don't stop," I rasp out, attempting to stay focused on the road as my dick strains painfully against my zipper.

"He dips his fingers into her soaking wet pussy, then brings them to his mouth, sucking off her juices. 'Mmmmm.'" I glance in the rear and side view mirrors. We're the only car on the road—have been for miles…

As quickly as I can without freaking Sophia out, I pull onto the shoulder and turn on the hazards. "What are you doing?" she asks as I hop out of the truck and slam the door, rounding the front to her side. I yank open her door and hoist myself on the foot bar before reaching over and undoing her seat belt. "Elijah?"

"Get out of the truck," I say firmly, tossing her book onto my seat, noticing the title in the process.

"What?"

"Get out of the damn truck, Sunflower."

An amused smile spreads across her pretty little lips. She climbs down, and I've hoisted her into my arms before her second foot touches the ground.

Her legs wrap around me. "What are yo—" I slam her against the back door of the truck, and a breathy laugh escapes her. She bites her lower lip, staring up at me with those forest "fuck me" eyes.

"You drive me insane, you know that, baby?" I whisper in her ear, trailing my fingertips along her shoulder, and goosebumps appear directly beneath them. "You make me a desperate man."

"You asked me to read you my favorite part."

"Mm-hmm." I take her earlobe between my teeth and suck it gently. A sweet little moan escapes her lips that has me repeating the action. "Your book was *Pride and Prejudice*, Sunflower. And it's been a while since I've read it… but I don't remember that part." Her mouth opens before she purses her lips, trying to stifle a smile at me finding out her little secret. "That dirty talk was all you, filthy girl."

Her hungry eyes drink me in. "I thought it would help distract you."

"I am well and truly distracted." I lean down and kiss her neck, holding her against the side of my truck.

"Clearly." She presses her lips to my neck, mumbling against it, "Aren't you worried someone will see us?"

"Let them see." Setting her ass on the passenger seat, I angle her legs so they're dangling out of the cab, giving me the perfect view of her translucent, lacy blue panties. "Did you wear these for me?"

"Well, I didn't buy fifteen dollar underwear for Sage." She widens her legs. "But please don't rip these off. I can't afford to keep replacing them."

"I'll buy you all of Victoria's Secret. Just let me have my fun," I tease, gliding my palms up her thighs, lifting her dress. She glances around, her body trembling with anticipation as I tug her ass to the edge of the seat, resting my hands over the tiny strings holding this scrap of lace onto her hips. I twist one of them between my fingers, then jerk it to the side, and her eyes go wide.

"Elijah, I can't meet your mother without underwear on," she says sternly.

"Fine." I tug her panties down, tossing them to the floorboard, and return my attention back between her legs. "There's my perfect pussy." I dip my head down, and she whimpers, dragging her fingers through my hair. I flick my tongue against her clit, gliding my hand firmly up her thigh towards her soaking wet entrance. "Fucking delicious," I mumble against her before sliding two fingers inside.

"*Elijah,*" she moans, arching against me, pulling my head closer. I pump my fingers in a steady rhythm, angling them upwards to hit her favorite spot. She cries out in pleasure so loudly a flock of birds flies out of the tree line.

"Noisy girl." I chuckle. "Keep it up for me, baby. You're almost there."

She rides my hand, and I don't even come up for air until she's clenching around my fingers and collapsing against the seat.

"Holy shit," she pants.

"Holy is right." Her gaze connects with mine, and I suck her sweetness off my fingers, just like her book described. She bites her lower lip, panting as I grab her panties off the floorboard and twirl them around my finger. "Are you *sure* you have to put these back on?"

"Positive," she says halfheartedly. "But you're welcome to take them off again later."

"Promise?" I rake my eyes over every inch of her body.

"Pinky promise."

We hook pinkies, then I put her feet between the thong strings and pull it back up her legs. Grabbing the seat belt, I buckle her back in.

"You know I can do that myself?"

"And?" I kiss her smiling lips. "Let me take care of you... in *every* way." Winking, I hop down and make my way to the driver's side.

"What about you?" Sophia says as I put the truck in drive and pull back on the road.

"What about *me*?"

"I could feel how hard you were..." she says, and I grip the steering wheel tighter.

"And? That was your reward for being a Pulitzer Prize winner in dirty talk."

"Can my reward be giving you road head?"

A groan escapes my lips as my throbbing cock begs me to say yes. *Down, boy.* "Only if you want me to crash the damn truck."

"Fine... I guess I owe you one." She holds up a single finger on her hand closest to me, and I grab it, bringing it to my mouth and planting a soft kiss on her knuckles.

An hour later, I turn onto a dirt road surrounded by oak trees with the sign Anderson Family Farm.

Although Sophia creates a welcome distraction, I can't help but wonder how she's going to feel after finding out what I've been keeping from her. I should've brought it up sooner, but I never knew how to approach the subject.

How do you talk about something that burns like a hot iron every time you think about it?

"Your family has their own farm?" Sophia asks, her tone laced in surprise.

"Is that really such a shock?" I glance at her amused expression. "I literally major in agriculture, babe."

"I mean, yeah. But I can't see the great Elijah Anderson milking a cow."

"It's not that kind of farm." We get to the property's metal gate, and I hop out, pushing it open. "Can you drive through?" I shout to Sophia.

She does, and I close the gate, locking it behind us. I get in the passenger seat and direct her to keep driving. My eyes wander to her tiny body maneuvering the vehicle, and damn, does she look sexy driving my big ass truck. We exit the tree line to the acres upon acres of farmland.

"Oh my gosh," Sophia says, looking around in amazement, her hands remaining on the steering wheel. "It's beautiful. *This* is where you grew up?"

"Yep." I take in the familiar scenery. "Pretty cool, huh?"

"I just…" She laughs, shaking her head. "I seriously never would have imagined *you* grew up on a farm."

I place a hand over my chest. "What's that supposed to mean?"

"I mean, the first time I met you, you just seemed so *preppy city boy*."

"Well, I guess looks can be deceiving now can't they, Sunflower?"

"Elijah, I packed for Atlanta… You said you lived in Atlanta."

"I said I lived near Atlanta. Would you have really known where I was from if I said I lived in Elora?"

"I guess not…" she grumbles, parking between the two houses on the property. "Who else lives here?"

"That's our house," I say, gesturing to the two-story old Victorian-style house with blue shutters and a wrap-around porch. "And that's my grandma's house." I point at the other house closely resembling ours, but it only has one powder blue painted story with white shutters.

"This is so charming." We hop out of the truck, and in the same moment, the screen door from Nama's house slams shut. *The name I used since I was a toddler and couldn't pronounce grandma.*

"Well, if it isn't the most handsome man on the entire planet," Nama coos.

I look up to see her bright, smiling face. "Hi, Nama."

"That's all I get?" She places her hands on her hips. "Six months without my little Elijah, and all I get is a 'Hi, Nama?'" Sophia follows behind me as I stride towards Nama and envelop her in a hug. I plant a firm kiss on her cheek, and Nama's smile widens as she glances over my shoulder.

"This is my girlfriend, Sophia."

Sophia readjusts the bag on her shoulder, then extends her small hand outwards. "Hi, it's so nice to meet you."

Nama grabs it, tugging her in for a tight embrace. "None of that formal crap. In this family, we hug." Sophia's shoulders momentarily tense before she relaxes and melts into her. "Now let me look at you." Nama pulls away, taking Sophia's hand and spinning her around. "Oh sugar. Aren't you just the prettiest little thing I've ever seen?" She shakes her head. "How in the world did my Elijah capture you?" Sophia covers her mouth as blush creeps up her cheeks.

"Nama." I raise my eyebrows at her. "Please don't scare her away in the first five minutes."

"Oh, honey. She seems like she can handle more than five minutes with our crazy lot."

"Yeah, *honey*. I'm a big girl. I think I can handle your family." Sophia folds her arms over her chest.

Nama laughs, smirking at me. "I like her."

"What should I call you?" Sophia asks.

"Grandma Mia." Nama narrows her eyes, putting a finger to her ear before pointing toward Sophia's bag. "Your bag is buzzing, dear."

Sophia's eyes grow wide as saucers. "Oh, um... It must be the alarm I set on my phone to check in with my dad." I roll my lips together to stop from laughing and blowing her cover, considering her phone is securely in my pocket.

"Oh, that's sweet of you. I'm sure he's worried sick, missin' you."

"Okay, well, why don't we get your phone out and then we'll go see Mom," I offer, placing my arm around Sophia.

"I'll see you two later tonight for dinner," Nama says, smiling wide. "We're going to Ricky's Ribs. Be ready by seven o'clock."

"On the dot," I reply, and she laughs, heading back to her house. As soon as the door shuts, Sophia throws her large duffel to the ground and crouches down, furiously searching through it.

"Whatcha got there?" I ask, unable to hide the amusement in my tone.

"I'm going to *kill* her," Sophia mutters to herself, shuffling the contents around, getting increasingly more panicked. "Yes!" She yanks her hand out, holding a little pink vibrator above her head. "Shit!" Clutching it to her chest, she rushes to turn it off before shoving it back in her bag.

"You brought a *vibrator*?" I ask, and she glares at me. "What? These hands aren't enough for you anymore, baby?" I wiggle my fingers, tickling her. "I thought we've established that I'm an expert with my hands—and tongue—and dick."

"No, I mean, yes, you are." She laughs nervously. "Sage suggested I bring it, and I guess she didn't take no for an answer."

"Well, remind me to thank Purple Skittle for ensuring we have the proper tools for our little vacation."

"Mm-hmm." She stands up and I pull her to me, pressing a soft kiss to her mouth.

"You ready to meet my mom?"

"Ready to meet the woman who blessed the earth with all this?" She rubs her hands up and down my stomach. "Hell yes."

"That's my girl." I lean down for another peck kiss and lead her to my house, grabbing our other bags on the way.

"I really wish you would have told me we were going to a farm," Sophia groans, eyeing the suitcase I'm lugging toward the house.

"Why?"

"Um… You'll see when I get dressed later for dinner… I don't really have casual farm town clothes with me."

"You'll look beautiful, babe."

"Mm-hmm," she grumbles.

We walk in the front door of the house, and Hazel, our sweet Australian shepherd, comes sprinting toward us. I bend down to meet her, and she jumps on me, planting slobbery kisses all over my face. "Nice to see you too, girl," I say, laughing as I scratch behind her ears.

Standing back up, I wipe the slobber off my face with my T-shirt, and Hazel begins her inspection of our new house guest. Sophia holds her hand steady as Hazel sniffs it, then nudges Sophia's hand with her nose.

"Who's a good girl?" Sophia says down to Hazel, rubbing her head.

"You are," I say lowly, squeezing her ass.

We leave our bags by the door and head towards the kitchen, where the sound of "Jingle Bell Rock" is blaring out of the speakers.

"Should I grab a chair so you can continue my lap dance?" Sophia teases, with a devilish grin.

"Hush your mouth."

We step in the kitchen just as Mom pulls out a fresh batch of cookies from the oven. An ear to ear smile spreads across her face as she abandons the baking sheet on the counter and runs over to us.

"About time!" She throws her arms around me, hugging tightly and taking my face in her hands. "There is no way on God's green earth you're going another six months without setting foot in this house. I will not allow it. It was too darn long."

"Hi, Mama." I chuckle as she kisses my cheek. "Nice to see you too."

"And you must be the sweet Sophia I've heard so much about," Mom says.

"You told her about me?" Sophia asks me quietly, her cheeks tinging pink.

"Of course I did." I smile proudly.

"You know, Ms. Sophia, this is the first time he's brought home a girlfriend. Ever."

"Ever?" Sophia's eyes bulge.

"Yep, so you must be *very* special." She pulls Sophia in for a tight hug. "I'm Jenna."

"Grandma Mia wasn't kidding." Sophia's amused expression meets mine. "You're a touchy-feely crew, huh?"

"We sure are." Mom nods. "And if you saw her, then you must already know about dinner plans."

"Seven o'clock sharp," I reply.

"That's my boy." She ruffles my hair. "Alright, well, your room is all set up, and then you can take Sophia to meet Penelope."

"Penelope?" Sophia asks, smiling curiously.

"Yep." I glance out the kitchen window towards the pasture before returning my attention to Sophia. "My *other* favorite girl." She narrows her eyes at me and follows me up the stairs to my bedroom. I close the door behind us, setting our bags in the corner of the room.

"Your mom doesn't care if I sleep in here?"

"Nope." My eyes wander the familiar space, an equal sense of longing and regret settling in my stomach. "I'm sure she's just happy I brought you willingly and didn't sneak you in through my window."

"You've done that?!" Sophia freezes in place, gawking at me. "That sounds kinda hot... Maybe later I can—"

"Absolutely not." I cut her off and laugh.

"Why?"

"You could get hurt." I rest a hand on her face, brushing her soft cheek with my thumb.

"Okay?" She folds her arms over her chest, purposefully pushing up her breasts because she knows it drives me crazy. "You didn't care about the other girls getting hurt when they snuck through your window."

I run both hands through her hair and stare down at her intently. "I didn't love any of them."

"What?" she says so quietly, it's almost a whisper.

"I didn't *love* any of them." Her lips part open, the corners of her mouth curving upwards. "You don't have to say it back. But it's the truth, and I won't apologize for saying it." My heart pounds as I take a calming breath. "I can't go another day without telling you how much I love you, Sunflower. So don't make me, okay?"

Sophia nods, wrapping her arms tightly around my middle, and burrows her smiling face into my chest.

"I love you, Sophia Elysabeth Summers," I repeat, thankful I can finally speak the words freely.

"Mm-hmm," she hums against me, and the sweet vibration is all I need to know she feels it too.

39

SOPHIA

I love you.

Those three loaded words grip my neck like firm hands crushing my windpipe. I pace the small floor of Elijah's bathroom, trying to escape the gravitational pull from the black hole of panic.

I love you.

But he can't love me... Love is messy, sticky, dangerous —*deadly*.

Seth's betrayal may have torn me apart like a turbulent tornado... but if Elijah breaks his return policy? What's left of me would be chucked into a wood chipper, ground up until I'm nothing but dust.

Sweat trickles down my spine as the temperature of the room increases, the walls closing in around me. I focus on a single blue tile in Elijah's shower, struggling for air, with a hand pressed against my chest, heart pounding wildly against it.

I love you.

Does him loving me mean anything at all? I never could have imagined Seth would do what he did... Is it possible I don't know Elijah either?

A rock settles in my stomach as I shake my head.

Of course I know him.

Elijah's always honest with me. He safeguards my secrets, ensuring I never felt guilty for having them. He shares *everything* about himself. I know him completely. He would never do the things Seth's done. Regardless of the circumstance.

Gripping the cool marble countertop, I stare at the mirror and wonder what the fuck is wrong with me.

"You ready, baby?" I jump in place, hearing Elijah's voice directly outside the door.

My panicked reflection disgusts me as I take another deep breath. Elijah is *not* Seth. His love is not the same. "Be right there."

After a few more calming breaths, I pull on leggings and a warm flannel Elijah gave me before exiting the bathroom.

His eyes scan me appreciatively as a wide smile spreads across his face. "Well, hello, cowgirl." I force a laugh before he pulls me toward him for a toe-curling kiss, erasing any remnants of my spiral in the bathroom. *Time to enjoy the present and worry about the future later.* "Damn, you look sexy in my shirt."

I bite my lower lip. "If you're a good boy, maybe I'll let you take it off me later."

"Oh, really?"

"Mm-hmm."

"What if I don't wanna be a good boy?" He pouts, gliding his hands under the shirt's hem, tugging me closer to him, and I let out a breathless laugh.

"Then you might have to fuck me with the shirt *on*."

"Damn it, Sophia. I have every intention of showing you around the farm but if you keep talking like that, we're gonna end up stuck in this room the entire trip."

The corners of my lips curve upwards, and I'm enjoying the lightness I feel again. A familiar emotion surrounds me that I'm not quite ready to acknowledge.

We leave the house and walk towards a pasture, where a gorgeous brown and white horse is trotting around.

"Meet Penelope," Elijah says, gesturing towards her as we stop at a white wooden fence.

"She's gorgeous."

Elijah places two fingers between his lips, whistling loudly, and calls her name. She gallops over to us, and Elijah extends his arm, hugging her neck.

"Hey, girl," he says gently, running a hand along her mane. "How've you been?"

If I thought he was sexy as a football playing jock, *woof*. I'm about to let Cowboy Elijah fuck me in this pasture. *Yeehaw, baby.*

"You want to pet her?"

I clasp my hands together, buzzing with excitement. "Can I?"

"Since she's not familiar with you yet, just pet her here on the neck." I pat Penelope's coarse hair, and she neighs, causing me to jump slightly.

"It's okay," Elijah says, placing a hand on my back and petting her with the other. "That means she likes it."

I continue petting Penelope while breathing in the crisp country air. The earthy scent reminds me of the vacation to the mountains in North Carolina.

"She was my dad's," Elijah says quietly, with a wistful look in his eyes.

My head snaps toward him. "What? Mark's?"

"No... My actual dad. Technically, he was my stepdad, but he never once made me feel that way... He raised me from birth."

Blinking my eyes, I struggle to process the words. "You never mentioned him before."

"I know."

My hand falls from Penelope as I turn to face him. "Why not?"

"He died in April."

His admission hits me with the force of an atomic bomb. All his words about love and loss finally make sense. He wasn't just giving advice, he was speaking from experience.

"Elijah..." I tilt my head, rubbing a hand along his arm. "I'm sure he loved you very much."

"He did... Mark might not have been around, but Dino made sure I never felt like I was missing a father figure in my life. He's the one who got me into archery and taught me to play football."

Stepping forward, I hug him tightly. "How did he..."

"He had prostate cancer." A humorless laugh escapes his lips. "It wasn't even bad. He was stage two when they found it." His face twists in pain. "But... I don't know. The treatments didn't work, and neither did surgery. His last chance was a clinical trial from a big pharmaceutical company." Elijah wipes a tear off his face. "But the miracle cure ended up being a lethal injection, and the company knew it."

"Elijah," I whisper, placing my palm against his face. "That's awful."

"Yep... We're suing them, but nothing's gonna come of it. They're a billion-dollar company with the best lawyers on retainer." He clears his throat. "And it won't bring my dad back." Silence hangs in the air between us. "I just want to move on."

"I get that." I place my palm on Elijah's face, and he frowns down at me. His phone goes off, and he pulls it out, stopping an alarm.

"I wanna show you something before we get ready for dinner," he tells me, grabbing my hand and leading me back towards the house. The sun is setting, casting the farm in a beautiful golden glow. Elijah stops in the middle of the field with the houses and a large barn in the distance.

"What are we—"

"Just wait." He cuts me off, throwing an arm over my shoulder, tugging me into his side. "Merry Christmas, Sunflower."

"What?" I laugh. "There's still a few days till—" The words evaporate off my tongue at the sight of thousands of tiny, colorful lights flickering on around us. "Oh my God."

He rests his head on mine. "This is one of the best parts about coming here for Christmas."

Every fence, house, barn is covered in lights. I must have been so distracted by Penelope, I didn't notice them along the wooden posts. "It's beautiful."

"My dad and I used to set it up together." He pauses. "I guess Mom and Nama weren't ready for the tradition to end either, so they had the ranch hands set 'em up before taking off for the holiday."

For the first time, I notice the sadness swimming in his ocean eyes. How the hell did I miss it before? Either I'm entirely self-absorbed or Elijah's better at hiding things than I realized.

"Right this way, please." A waitress dressed in a tied-up flannel shirt, daisy dukes, and cowboy boots leads us through the country-themed restaurant.

"I am *severely* overdressed," I whisper-shout in Elijah's ear.

"Stop worrying, you're beautiful." He kisses the side of my head, dragging his palm down the back of my silk, long-sleeved cocktail dress. "Prettier than a glob of butter melting on a stack of pancakes."

"Good lord, did you exchange your hard drive for the country version when we got here?" I smirk at him as he pulls out my chair. "Thank you."

"My pleasure, *darlin'*." He winks, and my cheeks flush. He continues around the table, pulling out the seats for Jenna and Grandma Mia. It's adorable watching him be such a Southern gentleman.

Elijah sits down, and I can't help but smile seeing him clad in tight Levi's over cowboy boots and a black button-up shirt with the sleeves rolled up. I could get used to the rodeo look.

He smiles, narrowing his eyes at me. "What?"

"Nothing... I was just wondering if you keep a complete bull riding wardrobe here?"

"Ha ha." He scrunches his nose at me. "Trust me. I'd stand out more here if I dressed like I do on campus, babe."

"Um." I wave at my body. "You mean like how I do right now?!"

"Mm-hmm." He leans over, kissing me on the cheek, and I roll my eyes, turning my attention to the menu.

"Howdy, y'all," a waitress says, appearing at our table, and her grin widens when she sees Elijah. "Well, hey there, handsome. I didn't know you were in town."

"Just for a few days."

"I'd love to catch up while you're here," she says.

Um, excuse me, bitch, I'm right here.

"Sorry, Brit." Elijah places his arm around the back of my chair. "I'm here with my girl."

Her smile falters for half a second before she collects herself. "Alright, well, y'all ready to order?"

We amble out of the restaurant with full bellies. Elijah and his mother may look very different, with her having dirty blonde hair and hazel eyes, but they share so many small mannerisms I've lost count. She's incredibly generous, and Grandma Mia is just hilarious. Elijah's arm is slung over my shoulders, keeping me warm, and I'm enjoying being snuggled into his side.

"Dad's truck running good?" Jenna asks, and I glance up at Elijah in surprise.

"Yeah." He tightens his grip on me. "Running great."

Great, I made fun of his dad's truck.

I am the biggest asshole on the planet.

The asshole of all assholes.

A guy around our age dressed in tight joggers and a hoodie hops out of the jacked-up truck parked across from ours, and Elijah's entire arm goes tense.

"Elijah," Jenna says in a sharp tone. "Don't."

I glance up at his dark, cold eyes. "Elijah?" He removes his arm, rushing towards the guy. "Elijah!" He grabs the guy by the collar, throwing him to the ground, and I stop dead in my tracks.

"Dude, stop," the guy shouts before getting back to his feet. Elijah throws him against the truck with a loud bang. "I tried to help!"

"Bullshit!" Elijah cocks his hand back and swings, hitting the guy square in the jaw. He stumbles backward, holding his face, eyes going wide. Elijah grabs him by the collar and swings again, hitting him in the nose.

Blood drips down his chin and onto Elijah's arm that's still clutching his shirt. My heart pounds chaotically in my chest as I watch Elijah lose his shit.

"You deserved that and more." Elijah pushes him away.

"For what it's worth, I'm just glad your sister's okay," the guy says, seemingly genuine.

His sister?

What. The. Actual. Fuck?

"No thanks to you, asshole." Elijah turns around, eyes flicking to mine as an angry tear escapes. He quickly swipes it away and trudges to the driver's side door of his truck.

I follow after him, sliding in the backseat, unsure what to make of all the information I've learned today. I'm grateful he finally shared about his dad with me, but I can't shove away the disappointment it took him so long to open up. Now I find out he has a sister too? Where is she? Why is Elijah so mad at this guy? What the hell is going on?

Why am I just now finding out about the things that have been torturing him on a daily basis? I thought he'd always been honest with me...

Clearly, I don't know him as well as I thought.

40

ELIJAH

Shit. Shit. Shit. Shit.

I told myself I wouldn't lose my cool, and what did I do? Exploded like a damn volcano. The truck is silent on the way home. No one speaks, not even Nama, and she always has something to say. I glance at Sophia in the rear view, but she's staring out the window at nothing in the darkness.

Baby, please just look at me.

The truck's headlights shine against the house as I pull up in front of it. No one moves a muscle when I kill the engine. "Alright, let's get on with it then."

"Jenna said I'm not allowed to say anything," Nama says before opening the door and exiting the truck.

"When has that ever stopped you?" I point out, following her lead, slamming my door shut.

Sophia hops out the back, looking confused as hell courtesy of my Hulk Hogan impersonation in the parking lot. Everything she's learned about me today, my damn freak-out, it wouldn't surprise me if she runs all the way home.

Nama rounds the truck and grins at me. "True."

"Mama," my mom says to her in a stern tone.

"What?" Nama counters. "Is it so bad to tell him he handled that way better than I would have? Hell, if Dean were here, he'd have shot him."

"Dean was a man of faith. He would have done no such thing," Mom snaps.

"Dean was a man who *loved* his daughter," Nama presses, jaw ticking. "He would have done much, *much* worse."

Dean was... Dean was... Dean was...

Anger bubbles inside me with how casually they speak about him in the past tense. I shove it down as my blurred eyes connect with Sophia's. Hers swim with confusion, and I hate that I'm the cause of it.

"This is not the message we should be giving, Elijah," Mom says.

"What?" Nama scoffs. "Like I always say, better to ask for forgiveness than permission."

Mom folds her arms over her chest. "Now what would Father Nolan say about that?"

Nama mirrors Mom's position with a smug smile. "He'd say repentance exists for a reason."

"You tire me, Mama," she huffs, turning her attention to me.

"I tried to keep my cool, I really did." My muscles tense as I think about the situation. "He was just there, and I... I thought about Abbs and everything, and I just—" My head pounds hard as a snare drum. "I snapped."

Mom reaches up, rubbing my shoulder. "It's fine, honey. I'm not mad at you."

My gaze flicks from the ground to her. "Really?"

"Of course not." She tilts her head at me. "He deserved way more than that for what he did to Abigail. I just don't like seeing my sweet boy go all Mike Tyson."

I laugh weakly. "Mama."

"It's fine." She pulls me in for a hug. "Let's all go inside and get some ice for that hand, okay, honey?"

"Well, I'm gonna go to my house where I can speak freely without reprimand." Nama scowls at Mom.

I pull her in for a hug and whisper in her ear, "We all know you're going home to drink Gramps's whiskey and watch *The Bachelor.*"

She chuckles, kissing the side of my head. "Don't tell all my secrets, honey."

I turn to Sophia, placing my arms around her tense shoulders, and guide her to the house. *Have I shattered our glass bubble?*

Sophia and I walk into my bedroom, bag of frozen peas in hand, and I shut the door behind us. She still hasn't spoken a word, and my stomach twists in knots.

"Babe?" I say gently, taking her chin between my fingers and tipping it upwards. "Please say something."

She lets out an exasperated sigh. "I don't even know where to begin, Elijah."

"Anything is better than the silent treatment you're giving me right now."

"No." She shakes her head. "Like, I seriously *don't* even know where to start."

I exhale heavily and pull her to my chest. She rests her head against me, snaking her arms around my middle. "I'm really sorry if I scared you earlier."

"What?" She yanks backwards to look at me with furrowed brows. "I'm not afraid."

"Oh." I breathe out a heavy sigh of relief. "I just... I thought it might've scared you because I snapped, and I don't want you to think I'm anything like Seth, and I—"

"Babe." She cuts me off with narrowed eyes and a sweet smile. "You're nothing like Seth. I'm not mad at you about the fight. I'm just... confused."

A sour feeling settles in my stomach. "I know."

"First I found out about your dad... and now... You have a *sister*, Elijah." She tilts her head to the side with pain-filled eyes. "How did I not know you have a sister? Why did you never tell me about her? Where is she? Why don't you ever talk about her?" She steps out of my grasp and paces the room.

"Because... it's just... a lot." I sit down on the bed, placing the frozen peas wrapped in a kitchen towel against my bruised knuckles. Sophia unzips her boots and throws them on top of her suitcase. She pads over and kneels down in front of me, placing her hand on mine.

"You can tell me anything. Remember?" she says gently with eyes so full of hurt, I struggle to breathe. "I'm a good listener."

"I know. It's not that, it's just... it was easier not to talk about her or my dad."

"Would it be okay if we talked about it now?"

I nod, setting the frozen bag on the ground and pulling Sophia up into my lap. She wraps her arms around my neck, a soft expression on her face. "My sister, Abigail. She..." I pinch the bridge of my nose to warn off the headache that comes every time I think about her. "She's in rehab." Sophia's eyes widen. "In the parking lot... That was Brayden, her boyfriend... Well, ex now." *Hopefully.* "They'd known each other for a while. Always getting into shit together. Once Dad died... she just lost it. Started taking pills—pills I'm pretty sure she got from Brayden. And one night they were at a party, and she took too many." I swallow the lump in my throat that always appears when I think about that day. "She overdosed in the middle of the woods... and he just fucking left her there." Sophia gasps beside me. "Thankfully someone found her and by some damn miracle, she lived."

"That must have been so hard for you..."

I shiver, recalling one of the worst phone calls I've ever gotten in my life. "It was... She'd been weird last year, I don't know why. But after Dad died, she totally spiraled. I was so wrapped up in my own shit I didn't notice until it was too late. And then it was just easier to pretend she didn't exist." My heart restricts as the bitter words leave my mouth.

"You don't mean that," Soph says quietly.

"You're right... It's just, she was in rehab, she was safe. And it was easier to pretend... to only worry about my own shit. You know?"

"I get it," she says with a gentle smile, and a relieved breath leaves my lungs.

"Really?"

"Yeah, I mean I tried to ignore the shit that happened with Seth too." My entire body goes rigid at the mention of his name. "I just hate that you didn't tell me... about Abigail or your dad. There was this massive cloud hanging over your head, and I had no fucking clue. I should've known if something this major was bothering you." She squeezes my hand. "I mean, honestly, it explains why you're struggling so much with school."

"I know. I'm so sorry." Her back is tense, and I rub my hand along it. "Seriously."

"It's okay... Just, please don't keep me in the dark anymore. I've told you all my secrets. I thought you weren't keeping any either." Guilt settles in my stomach.

"I want us to be totally open with each other too." I take a calming breath. "So there's one more thing I should tell you..." The fear in her eyes has me cursing myself for not sharing sooner. "I talked to Mark and Cole about the hit and run." She sucks in a breath, jumping off my lap.

"You did *what?*" she shrieks, a fire igniting behind her eyes as she brings a hand over her mouth.

I stand quickly, reaching out for her. "It's really not what it sounds like."

"Elijah!" she whisper-shouts. "Are you kidding me?" She drags a hand across her mouth. "No." She shakes her head. "Oh my God." She hyperventilates, and it sets off my own panic. "No."

"Babe." I grab her arm gently, tugging her to me, and her glossy green eyes find mine.

"I should've never told you." She swallows hard as a tear trickles down her cheek. "Seth was right."

"What?" I physically recoil, desperate to rein in this out-of-control conversation. "Sophia, I told them I had a friend doing a project for a pre-law class."

She freezes, face morphing into complete confusion. "What?"

"I told them I had a friend in a pre-law class and that *he* was working on a hit-and-run case."

Her eyes wander all over my face before connecting back with mine. "Did they buy it?"

"I mean, they had no reason not to."

"What did they say?" she asks timidly.

"That without evidence… it's almost impossible to make a conviction."

She frowns and rolls her eyes. "Well, we pretty much knew that."

"Yeah." I tuck a strand of hair behind her ear. "I'm sorry, baby. I was just trying to help you find a way out of this mess. I hate that he has this hold over you."

She releases a heavy breath and looks deep into my eyes. "I appreciate you trying to protect me. I'm sorry I freaked out… I just assumed you told them everything."

I tilt my head with a soft smile. "Come on, Sunflower. Give me a little more credit than that. I would've never said anything if I thought for one second they'd figure out I was talking about you. You really think I'm gonna throw the love of my life under the bus?"

A blush creeps up her cheeks. "I guess not…"

"Good." I kiss her delicately. "I'm so sorry about everything. Really. I don't want any secrets between us. I want you to know you can trust me." Her cheeks glisten with tears, and I wipe at them with the pad of my thumb. "I won't ever keep anything from you again, okay?"

She nods weakly. "Okay."

"I pinky swear." I stick out my pinky, and she smirks, hooking it with hers.

"Pinky promise." She kisses me. "The only kinds of secrets you're allowed to keep are the kind I unwrap with a bow."

"Oh, really?" I run my palms down her arms, taking her hands in mine. "What makes you think I have any of those?"

"Well, it *is* our first Christmas next week." She raises her eyebrows, seemingly more playful as I kiss her knuckles.

"Is it?" I tilt my head. "Well, shit, I better call Santa and tell him how naughty you've been this year." I lean in, nuzzling her nose. "I love you, Sunflower."

She melts against me. "I like you, Honey Bee."

I swallow hard, hoping my secrets didn't push her farther away from saying those three beautiful words too.

"Well, that's an improvement."

Blinking my eyes open, a slow smile spreads across my face as I take in the familiar surroundings in the warm morning light. I roll over to face Sophia, and my stomach drops as I find nothing but empty sheets. *Did she leave?*

I bolt out of bed, eyes darting around the room. Her bag is still sloppily in the corner. *Okay, that's a good sign.* Taking quick steps to my window, I immediately spot her running along the fence line with Hazel. "Thank you, Jesus," I mutter to myself, shoulders dropping, and a heavy breath releases from my lungs.

She pauses and pulls out her phone, snapping a picture.

A few minutes later, she trudges in my room, sweaty, with her face flushed red.

"Good run?"

She clears her throat. "Yeah." I sit on the edge of the bed, patting my thigh, and she scrunches her nose. "I'm stinkier than your locker room at CBU."

"I've literally had my face in your pussy. I can deal with a little post-run sweat." Her lips quirk downwards into a look of disgust. "Just come here..." I pat my leg again. "Please?"

"Fine." She sits on my thigh, throwing an arm around my neck. I hover my mouth over hers, her warm breath hitting my skin, before kissing her soft and slow. "What was that for?" she mumbles, smiling against my lips.

"I missed you this morning."

"Sorry." She looks down at her hands. "Just needed to clear my head."

"I was worried."

Her curious eyes find mine. "Why?"

"I thought you might have left." I gnaw on my lower lip. "That you might still be upset about everything."

"Elijah... I would never leave without telling you."

Fear crushes my chest. "I would prefer it if you didn't leave at all."

"I won't," she assures me, but her tone is unconvincing as I grip her warm thigh. "I just needed a little me time, that's all."

"Please, talk to me."

She glances down at my hand before chipping at her cherry red nail polish. "I'm just sad."

I drag my fingers through her hair and tilt her face toward mine. "Why, baby?"

Her green eyes are glossy, and it rips my heart right out. "I just feel like you don't trust me."

"Of course I trust you," I say softly.

"You... you told me you love me, but you couldn't tell me all the things affecting you most on the *inside*." She presses her finger lightly against the center of my bare chest. "I don't just want to know

314

the you from campus—the football playing, funny jock that lights up every room. I want to know the you from *here*—Elijah Anderson, son, *brother*. The man with actual feelings—happy, sad, angry, whatever. I want you to share *everything* with me."

I nod my head, angry as hell at myself for not opening up sooner.

"Fuck!" she groans up at the ceiling. "I feel awful. I'm making this all about me when you're obviously going through so much."

"It's okay... You're allowed to feel how you feel. And I *want* you to tell me how you feel." I place my forehead on hers. "Please... please, tell me how you feel."

"You want to know how I feel?" she asks, her voice breaking. "I feel like I've been dating this amazing guy for almost two months. And he's better than I could have ever imagined. And he knows me, and he cares for me and makes me feel seen. He accepts all the dark parts of my past and makes the shadows hanging over me completely disappear." She pauses, shifting in my lap as her hand trembles on my chest. "But I also feel like I don't even know him *at all*."

Pain zaps through my entire body. I'm connected to an electric chair, and her words flicked on the power.

"Of course you know me." A lone tear escapes her eye, and I wipe it away. "Of course you do, baby. Please don't say that." I rub my fist against my chest to ease the ache, but it does nothing to relieve the torment and regret swirling inside me.

"I just..." She exhales heavily and looks away. "I always thought you were a hundred percent honest with me. It was something I loved most about you..." Her eyes reconnect with mine. "Even at the springs the first time we met, I thought the connection we had as *strangers* was unreal because of all the stuff we shared."

"It was," I assure her. "It *is*."

"And then I opened up to you about one of the worst things in my life. And you've been so supportive... But now I find out there's this huge part of *you* that you kept hidden away from the world... away from *me*. And that makes me sad." Her lips turn downwards at the last sentence as the tears continue to fall. "I'm afraid there's more I don't know. That I'll always be out of the loop."

"Soph, I—"

"Please let me finish," she says gently. "I never thought I would find someone who could love all the parts of me. The darkness, the light, and the shadows in between. Someone who didn't make me feel like I had truckloads of baggage they were accepting but hopped in the driver's seat to share the load." She smiles at me sincerely. "You've done that for me... Every ounce of baggage I have, you lift willingly and eagerly, and you never let me feel damaged or broken for more than the moment it takes the words to leave my mouth."

I rub my thumb along her jawline. "And?"

She shakes her head, and the pain in her eyes makes me sick. "And I know I probably sound like a hypocrite because I hid things from you too..." She swallows hard. "Yesterday you told me you *loved* me..."

"Sophia," I whisper, terrified of her next words.

"I know you want me to say it back." She frowns, and I hold my breath to calm my nerves. "Elijah, I... I'm *afraid* to love you. I'm so terrified to love you because I'm absolutely heartbreakingly petrified to lose you. Or worse, to find out you're not who I thought you were." She swallows hard, and I've lost the ability to speak. "You say you love me, but I—Elijah, I've heard those words before."

I tighten my grip on her body, wishing I could erase every negative thought racing through her mind.

"Someone once promised they loved me." My veins ignite. I'm furious she could possibly compare me to Seth. Furious with myself for giving her the chance. "But he lied." She touches my face gently, and I lean into it. "How do I know you're not lying? How do I know you're not keeping anything else from me?"

"I would never lie about this," I plead, reaching up and placing my palm over hers.

"I think Seth might have loved me before. But when it came down to it, he hurt me for his own selfish reasons." Her hands tremble. "The things he did... If someone can do those things to someone they loved... does the word even mean anything at all?"

A heavy weight settles in my stomach as she looks at me with wet green eyes—two glistening, stained glass windows straight to her shattered, untrusting soul.

"Sophia... please don't compare me to him. I would rather break both my arms and never play football again than cause you even a flicker of pain."

"I don't think that's necessary." I slide her off my lap to the mattress and kneel in front of her, taking her hands in mine.

"I was telling the truth last night when I promised you no more secrets. I won't do anything behind your back. I won't keep anything from you. If you ask me something, I'll answer you fully and honestly." She looks down, and I place my hands on her face. "You know me, baby. You fucking *know* me. You know me more than I've ever let anyone know me, and I'm so sorry I waited to tell you the painful parts of me. I'm so damn sorry. But I mean every word I've said. And the thing I've said that I mean more than anything else..." I brush my knuckles against her cheek. "I *love* you."

My hands rub along her soft skin. "And not the simple 'I love that girl and I'm never letting her go' type of way... I love you to the point my heart shatters at the thought of you doubting me for one millisecond." I take her palm, pressing it flat against my pounding heart. "I'm so devastatingly in love with you, I have to remind myself to breathe every time you smile, and my hands crave your skin like a bad habit I never want to break. I love you unconditionally. I love you *desperately.* I love you more than I've ever loved anything or anyone, and I never want to give you a single reason to not believe that."

She swallows hard, and I take her hands in mine.

"Sophia, I love you so much that the thought of you hurting or someone laying a finger on you makes me insane. I'd do anything to protect you... *anything.*" My voice shakes. "I love you, Sunflower, and I will spend every single damn day of my life proving I do... Please give me the chance."

She kisses me softly, then rests her forehead against mine. "Okay."

I wish she would say those words back. I understand I have to be patient. She has a heavy past, and I haven't exactly made it easy for her... but fuck, I just want to hear her sweet voice say she loves me too.

41
SOPHIA

"I wanna show you something before breakfast," Elijah tells me, tugging a tight long-sleeve shirt over his head.

"Okay…" My curiosity increases when he grabs the bow off his bedroom wall. It's similar to the one at CBU, a dark green metal with arrows clipped to it, but a little bigger. "Hello, Robin Hood." I chuckle, and he winks at me as we leave his room.

A few minutes later, Elijah slides the door open to a huge red barn on the property. "Here we are."

I smile, taking in the extremely country open space. "God, this place is like the set of a Hallmark movie. Will the town be showing up later for a jubilee?"

He shakes his head, grinning, and strolls further into the barn. "I have to admit, I've had my fair share of parties here."

Elijah turns on an overhead light, illuminating it entirely, allowing visibility of loads of hay bales spread around the room. On the far wall, my eyes snag on two round targets that must be for archery practice. "Are you about to turn me into Katniss Everdeen?"

"Let's see if you can hit the target before you go applying to be the Mockingjay," he teases, and I stick my tongue out at him, happy to be feeling lighter after our conversation earlier.

He may have kept his pain to himself, but with how passionately he professed his love for me, it's hard to feel he was dishonest about that.

With Seth, there wasn't some huge declaration of love moment. I think it was just the natural evolution of our relationship. We'd been together a few months, slept together a couple times, and after one of them, he just blurted out the words.

And when you're seventeen and someone tells you they love you...

When Elijah shared his feelings with me this morning, I could practically *feel* the difference—the sincerity in his tone, the assurance in his touch. It's difficult to imagine Elijah's love could ever taint to poison the way Seth's did. Then again, I never would've expected Seth to lay a finger on me, let alone choke the air from my lungs. So what the fuck do I know?

"Come here." Elijah waves me over to a spot directly in front of one target about twenty or thirty feet away.

"Is this place just for archery practice?" I ask, now understanding why the space is so empty.

Elijah shrugs. "It used to be for other stuff too... but with Dad gone, I've cleared it out for this, and I guess Mom isn't using it for anything else." He unclips an arrow. "Step back a little." He positions it on the bow, aiming toward the target. My eyes never stray as his shoulders rise and fall. The arrow releases, zipping through the air and hitting the bullseye.

"Elijah!" I squeal with laughter. "That was amazing."

"Thanks." He turns around with a sheepish grin. "It's been a while."

"Wow. So modest, Mr. Anderson."

He lowers the bow to his side, stepping closer before bringing his hand around the back of my neck, pulling me towards him. "I love it when you're mouthy." He presses a soft kiss against my lips.

"And I love it when your mouth's on me," I mumble against lips.

"I will gladly make that happen anytime."

I take a deep breath, shoving down my remaining insecurities and choosing to enjoy the time we're here. "Later... Now I need you to teach me how to be the Mockingjay."

He laughs, shaking his head. "Sure, sweetheart. Anything for you." I switch places with Elijah, positioning myself in front of the target, and he passes me the bow. My hand drops slightly, surprised at its weight, before repositioning it. "Okay, so hold on to the center of the frame, just barely letting your fingers touch." I slide my hand upward, finding the proper grip. "Good girl."

I glance over my shoulder. "If you keep saying things like that, I'll end up with my hand wrapped around your cock instead of this bow."

His mouth parts slightly before he bites his lower lip. "Is that supposed to sound like punishment? Because that's suddenly a very appealing option I hadn't considered."

I smirk, turning my attention back to the bow. "Okay, moving on."

"Align your thumb with this bottom edge here." He points to a spot on the bow, and I place my hand there. "Okay..." His chest presses against my back as he angles me properly, placing his hand over mine on the bow. He brings a wide arm around me, placing another arrow on the string. "Hold on to it." He guides my hand, pulling the arrow backwards. I lean against him, enjoying the heat radiating off his frame in the cool space. "Breathe in, and then when you breathe out, let go of the arrow."

"Okay." I inhale. Then on the exhale, I release. The arrow travels through the air, hitting the edge of the target. "I did it!" I jump up and down, holding the bow in one hand, and spin to face Elijah. He ducks out of the way just before I knock him with it. "Oh, sorry!"

He laughs and kisses me. "That's okay, and you sure did, Sunflower. Wanna try on your own?"

"Yes, please!" I feel like Alice getting ready to solve another riddle.

Forty-five minutes, a hundred arrows, and two near-death experiences later, I finally make contact with the stupid fucking target again. "Okay, you made that look way easier than it actually is."

He takes the bow and aims an arrow toward the target. "It took me a long time to learn, trust me." Looking into my eyes, he releases the arrow, and it hits the bullseye dead in the center as a smug smile appears on his face.

"Show off," I grumble before stepping closer and kissing him. We make our way out of the barn and back toward the house. "Your dad taught you, right?"

"Yeah." A wistful smile crosses his face.

"He must've been an excellent teacher."

"The best. We used to go hunting all the time. I learned how to score my first buck with a bow by the time I was twelve." He laughs. "Dad and Gramps were so shocked I actually hit it. They just stood there with their mouths open."

"Is that why you got the tattoo on your chest?"

"Yeah." He smiles, rubbing over it with his fist. "Dad called me buck cause of all the time we spent hunting together... So I got that and two cardinals, for him and Gramps."

"That's beautiful." I put my arms around his waist, and he holds me close, planting a kiss on top of my head. "Why'd you pick up archery?"

"Like arrows in the hand of a warrior are the children of one's youth. Blessed is the man who fills his quiver with them," Elijah recites, and I look at him in confusion. "It's from the Bible. My dad always told me he was incredibly blessed to have me in his life. I wanted to be blessed too." A soft laugh escapes him. "With arrows in my hands like a warrior."

"I love that," I say as we reach the house, heading to the kitchen.

"Hey, kiddos," Jenna says from her position at the stove.

"Hi, Jenna." Hazel rubs her head against my leg, and I lean down, scratching between her ears. "Thanks for the sunrise run, girl," I tell her quietly.

"Morning," Elijah says, throwing an arm around Jenna's shoulder, kissing the top of her head. It's strange but somewhat comforting seeing Elijah's relationship with his mom. For the first time in a while, my chest aches with longing for my own mother.

"I made your favorite." Jenna smiles up at him.

"Venison and eggs?" he asks with an ear to ear grin.

"Not unless you went out and shot a buck this morning..." she says pointedly. "Your *other* favorite." She passes Elijah and me each a plate of French toast. My mouth waters at the sight.

"*Mmmm*, thanks, Mom." Elijah smiles and kisses her on the cheek.

"This looks scrumptious."

Elijah hands me his plate, and I bring them to the kitchen table. A minute later, he comes over with two steaming cups of coffee, and the scent of hazelnut hits my nose.

"Now I understand your basic bitch drink," I tease, and he smirks, setting down our mugs.

"It was my dad's favorite."

"And now I feel like shit for making fun of you."

"It's fine," he assures me, walking back toward the kitchen. "I don't mind."

He opens a cabinet, and my eyes widen, seeing it filled top to bottom with jars of honey.

"Someone rob Winnie the Pooh?" I ask.

"My sister had a beekeeping phase," Elijah replies, joining me at the table. "We haven't had to buy honey in years."

"Well, I much preferred that to her BMX racing phase," Jenna says, and she and Elijah share a laugh.

Grandma Mia enters the room, eyeing our food. "You shouldn't feed a college athlete all that garbage," she chastises Jenna, grabbing a plate and piling it high with French toast before taking a seat next to me.

"Garbage?" Jenna scoffs. "Well, that sure isn't stopping you from eating to your heart's content." My lips curve upward as I enjoy their playful banter. I didn't really have a lot of family around growing up, but I can imagine how full Elijah's heart must have felt being here.

"Hey. I lost the need to keep my girlish figure when I married your dad. And now that he's in heaven, I know his love for me grows as my curves do... And he likes me better this way," she says matter-of-factly before extending a hand out towards Jenna and the other toward me.

I stare down at it.

Does she need the salt?

Jenna grabs Grandma Mia's hand and slides her other one into Elijah's. *Are we praying?* Elijah wiggles his fingers at me, and I slide my hands into theirs, pretending I know what the fuck we're doing, my foot tapping nervously beneath the table.

"Dear God," Jenna begins, and they all close their eyes. "Thank you for this morning, for bringing our baby and Sophia to us safely. Thank you for the angels that are watching over everyone at this table." I glance around, and Elijah cracks open an eye, peering at me. I snap mine shut, heat flushing my face. "Please be with Abigail, Lord. We wish she could be here, but we know your plan and timing is best." Elijah rubs his thumb over my knuckles, relieving a morsel of my anxieties. "Bless this food and let it nourish our bodies. In your son Jesus's name, we pray, amen."

"Amen," Elijah and Grandma Mia say.

"Amen," I rush out awkwardly and a bit too loud as we release hands.

Elijah reaches over, squeezing my knee. He winks while chewing on his food, somehow still looking like sex on a stick.

"So how did you two meet?" Jenna asks, waving her fork between me and Elijah.

"He stalked me and scared the bejesus out of me," I say with a serious face, causing Jenna and Grandma Mia to burst out laughing.

"That is hardly the story." Elijah narrows his eyes at me.

"Fine." I roll my eyes dramatically. "Elijah crashed our graduation party in Longwood and chatted me up in the woods. I thought he was a serial killer."

"Why do you think I brought you to my abandoned farm in the middle of nowhere?" Elijah grins, and I let out a bubbling laugh. "But if you *must* know…" He turns his attention back to Jenna and Grandma Mia. "I saw her walking through the woods and was just… I was mesmerized by how beautiful she is." My cheeks flush with heat as my eyes drop to my French toast. "I knew I had to talk to her, so I followed her, and… I guess that was a *little* stalkerish."

"Try Joe from *You*." I point my fork at him. "But please continue."

"It took about ten minutes of her smart mouth to know I was a goner… And I guess it all worked out, huh?"

I smirk as he reaches over, gently squeezing my thigh. "I guess it did."

"But I was an idiot and didn't get her number before her friend dragged her away."

"Couldn't you have just looked her up on Facestagram?" Grandma Mia asks.

"It's Instagram, Nama," Elijah corrects. "And I couldn't find her there. But thankfully, we ran back into each other a few months later. And the rest is history."

"Well, wasn't that a blessing?" Jenna beams, flicking her eyes between Elijah and me.

I feel slightly strange about her acting like our reconnection was some gift from God. It's been a long time since I've believed there was a higher power out there controlling all of this… I mostly just believe the universe creates the life for us it chooses, and that's that. No greater being pulling our strings like puppets. If there were, why would he have caused such turmoil in my life? Why would he have taken Chloe so young? What did she do to deserve that?

"So, sweetie," Jenna asks, pulling me out of my thoughts, "Elijah mentioned you're Will Summers's daughter?"

"Yes, ma'am."

Her face lights up. "You know him and I went to Longwood High together?"

I never considered Jenna may have known my family too...

"Small world," I laugh nervously. *Please don't have more family drama I'm unaware of.*

"Who's your mom?"

Oh, you know... the washed-up drug addict who abandoned me before my sister died and never came back.

"Lysa."

"Are you kiddin' me?" Jenna laughs, and her joy makes me nauseous. "She was always so sweet. I don't think there was a person in Longwood who didn't love Lysa and her delicious lemon cupcakes. I'd love to get her number before you leave. It'd be nice to reconnect."

That sounds nothing like the Mom I remember...

I force a tight smile. "Sure."

"So what are you kids up to today?" Grandma Mia asks, thankfully changing the subject like the real MVP. I smile at her gratefully, and she winks.

"I think spending some time with Penelope," Elijah responds. "It's been a while since I've ridden her."

"Oh, that would be so nice." Jenna claps her hands together. "I try to ride her daily, but with you and Abbs gone... and Dad... she just doesn't get time outside the pastures as much."

Elijah readjusts Penelope's saddle on his shoulder as we exit the barn. He's wearing tight Wranglers that make his ass look fantastic, and a black cowboy hat is situated on his head. I'm practically salivating at the mouth. *I wonder if I can convince him to bring some of this wardrobe back to school.*

"I'm gonna teach you how to go full cowgirl," he tells me with a wink as we make our way to Penelope's pasture.

"I'll be keeping both feet on the ground, thank you very much." I exaggeratedly stomp in place while holding the camera around my neck so it doesn't swing like a pendulum. "My health insurance is *not* good enough to get bucked off a horse."

"You know I'd never put you in a dangerous situation where you could get hurt."

"I know… but I would like to maintain the ability to walk."

Elijah slides his free hand in the back pocket of my jeans. "I can think of more creative ways to assist in your *inability* to walk." He squeezes hard, and I yelp, jumping away.

"Oh, is that so, Mr. Anderson?" I say, using my best sexy librarian voice that always gives Elijah a hard-on.

"Yes, it is, *Mrs*. Anderson."

A bubbling laugh escapes my lips. "Excuse me? So you buy me one fake ID and it's official, huh?"

"Did you already forget our wedding in Vegas last weekend?" he teases. "Aren't husbands supposed to be the forgetful ones?"

A high-pitched laugh escapes my lips. "I lo—"

"You lo—?"

"I love you…r sense of humor." I smirk at him.

"And I love *you*," he replies, kissing me.

We get to the wooden fence, and Elijah whistles for Penelope.

"I'll just sit here," I tell him, gesturing to the wood.

"You sure?"

"Yeah, I'll take some pictures of you and Penelope. It's a good vantage point."

Penelope trots over, and he saddles up. He hooks his boot in one stirrup, hauling himself up and straddling her.

I can't stop my mouth from breaking into a wide grin at this sexy as fuck version of him. I grab the camera from around my neck and snap a few quick pictures while he looks out towards the field.

"I can practically hear my dad telling me 'I told you so,'" he says wistfully, and I hold my camera against my chest. "Damn, I miss his voice." He pats Penelope's mane. "Holler if you need me," he tells me before galloping off like a young Clint Eastwood.

I situate myself on the fence, tilting my head back to enjoy the sun. While the air is cool, the sunshine warms me from the inside out. The smell of the fresh country air surrounds me, and I wish I could bottle it up and bring it home.

My phone vibrates in my jacket pocket, and I pull it out, expecting another text from Sage, who's been sending me daily updates of her trip to Montana. *Mom* flashes across the screen, and my stomach sinks.

Damn, I miss his voice.

Elijah's words ring through my head, and I find myself wondering how I would feel if I never even had the chance to hear her voice again.

My shaky finger hovers over the red button by reflex. I take a deep breath and tap green instead before bringing the phone to my ear. "Hey, Mom."

42

ELIJAH

"Motherfucker," I mutter, scraping my way up the side of my house toward the second floor. Hard to believe I actually made girls climb up this death trap into my room. *I'm such a piece of shit.*

I hoist myself onto the porch roof and crawl over to the window leading to my bedroom. After dinner, I told Sophia to go to my room because I needed to help Nama with something—total bullshit, by the way.

I take a pause below the window to catch my breath, grinning at myself for how excited I know this will make Sophia. She may not be ready to tell me she loves me, but she knows how to show it, and I'm eager to return the favor. Standing from my crouched position, I spot Sophia in bed, lying on her stomach, smiling down at her camera. She's wearing a sexy black nightgown that's so short, the bottom of her perfect ass is on display, and my black cowboy hat sits atop her blonde head.

Seems I wasn't the only one hoping for a wild ride tonight.

A rush of excitement floods my veins as my dick strains painfully against my zipper. I bring my knuckle to the glass, tapping three times, and Sophia's cowgirl head whips in my direction. A second loud knock has her bolting off the bed and striding over to the window like a damn supermodel. She cups her hands against the glass, looking directly into my amused face. The soft smile turns to an ear to ear grin as she pops open the window locks and opens it a single inch.

"Who is it?" she sing-songs sweetly.

"It's the pussy monster," I whisper, and she bursts out laughing. I'm pretty sure she even snorts before collecting herself and returning to the window.

"How will the pussy monster be paying for entrance into my lair?" she asks, unable to keep a straight face.

"How about you let me in before I fall off the roof, and we can negotiate payment?"

She twists her mouth, contemplating my request, but her concern must overpower her desire to screw with me because she sticks her little fingers under the window and slides it fully open. I squeeze my large body through, cursing myself for not considering how tiny the frame is. Sophia giggles when I finally tumble inside and land on the floor with a thud.

"Oh, shut it." I stand up, wiping my hands on my pants before taking off my shoes and socks. A knock comes on the bedroom door, and we both freeze, staring at it.

"Ya'll okay in there?" Mom's voice is muffled through the door.

"Yeah, we're fine," I say just before Sophia throws herself on my bed in a fit of giggles.

"Okay, see you kiddos in the morning. Goodnight."

"Night," Sophia and I chime in unison.

I stroll over to the bed and climb on top of her, tapping the tip of my cowboy hat.

"You know the rule, right, Sunflower?" I ask in an exaggerated Southern accent.

"What rule would that be, Honey Bee?"

"Wear the hat, ride the cowboy." I smirk down at her, straddling her half-naked body with a leg on each side.

"Wow, Elijah, didn't know you were into Elsie Silver books."

"I don't know what you're talking about, but that *is* the rule."

She grins, biting her lower lip. "Well, if that's the rule."

Sitting up, I press my hard dick against her, and she fumbles with my shirt, undoing each button slowly. Her gaze lingers after each new sliver of skin is exposed.

"I'm happy to tell you the name of the book," she says as her eyes scan over me hungrily. "In case you were curious about the fantasy you're bringing to life right now."

"Guess I'll have to take your cute ass to the bookstore tomorrow so you can read it to me on the way home." The last button pops open, and Sophia presses her hands to my exposed abdomen.

"Mmmm," she hums. "I can't believe this washboard is all mine."

"What?"

"You know?" She drags a finger along my stomach. "Washboard abs?"

I shrug the rest of the shirt off my shoulders, tossing it to the ground.

"Allllll mineeee," she says again possessively. I pluck the hat off her head and place it onto mine while I contemplate all the things I want to do to my cowgirl tonight. "Stop looking at me like that!"

"Like what?" I ask innocently, drinking in every inch of her gorgeous body.

"Like I'm a T-bone steak," she says with a serious expression that's now decided my first course of action.

Crawling off the bed, I grab her ankles and drag her so quickly to the edge of the mattress, she yelps with laughter. I fling the hat across the room and lean over her, bringing my mouth to her ear as my fingers play with the silk of her nightgown.

"We're not alone in this house, so I'm going to need you to be quiet tonight. Do you think you can do that, noisy girl?"

"I'm not an animal, Elijah. I think I can maintain my composure for one evening."

"Mm-hmm, that's not how it seemed when I fucked you in the

library," I counter with a smirk, thinking about the bite mark that almost left a welcome scar.

Her playful eyes turn serious. "I don't want you to fuck me tonight, Elijah. You made me a promise on my birthday. I want you to keep it." Every molecule of air in the room shifts as that promise echoes in my mind.

Then we'll make love so good you'll never forget mine.

I slide down her body and drop to my knees between her legs, inhaling deeply. Her sweet scent pulls me toward her like a hunter to its prey. My palms slide up her thighs, and I use my pointer finger to toy with the edge of her lace underwear.

"Do you even know what you do to me? I'm *starved* for you," I rasp out, panting as I try to remind myself she wants to make love tonight.

She doesn't want dirty role playing, Elijah.

She just wants me.

Raw, unfiltered, and *desperately* in love.

I run my hands along her hips and in one quick motion, rip the side of her panties like paper.

"Elijah!" she chastises as I rip the other side before tossing it to the ground. "Are you fucking kidding me?"

A low chuckle escapes my lips. "We can buy you new panties after the bookstore."

"Fine," she huffs with a smirk. "But you have to let me get at least *two* books for my troubles."

"I'll buy you the entire damn bookstore if you'll let me do this for the rest of our lives."

Grabbing her foot, I kiss each of her toes, place a soft kiss on her ankle, and place it back on the bed. I slowly make my way up her body, planting kisses as I drag my stubbled chin against her thighs, the way I know drives her crazy.

I glance upwards, and she's grinning toward the ceiling with her eyes closed—relaxed and perfectly content. I finally feel like things are back to normal between us. I dip down, swiping my tongue against the sweet spot between her legs.

A groan escapes my throat. "Fuck, baby."

"What?" she asks breathlessly.

"I wanna make love to you tonight, but the taste of you turns me animalistic."

"Really, Elijah?" She drags her fingers through my hair. "*Animalistic?*"

I nibble the spot between her pussy and thigh, and she shrieks.

"*Shhh,*" I hum against her soft skin. "Quiet, baby."

"Then don't nibble me like a *squirrel.*"

I pause, lifting my head, and her amused gaze catches mine. "You really want me to stop?"

She narrows her eyes, sucking her lower lip between her teeth, but doesn't say another word. I continue until she trembles beneath me.

"Elijah," she whimpers breathlessly.

I suck on her clit while slowly sliding two fingers into her dripping wet opening. A sweet moan escapes her lips as I arch my fingers towards the spot that always has her screaming my name. "Should I grab your pink toy?"

She laughs breathlessly. "No need. Eat your heart out, baby."

I increase the pace, and she yanks a pillow from behind her, throwing it over her face. Muffled moans have my dick begging to join the party, but I don't stop until she clenches firmly around my fingers and those beautiful cries stop completely. She flings the pillow across the room, gasping for air as I slide my fingers out of her, sucking off the proof of my victory.

"Are you enjoying yourself, sweetheart?" I ask, trailing kisses up her body.

"Did my moaning into a pillow not seem like I was enjoying myself enough?"

"That was only the preview."

"Shouldn't I return the favor first?" she asks between panted breaths. *Oh, hell yes.*

"No," I say firmly as my dick yells at me. "This is the night where I make sure you won't ever forget my name. Remember?"

"As if I ever could," she says seriously.

"I know." Smiling, I brush a stray hair behind her ear. "Because I'm going to give you another orgasm."

"Elijah Anderson. The king of sweet talk."

"Only for you, Sunflower." I nuzzle her nose, then hop off the bed and undo my belt, ripping it off. She smirks at it, and my blood buzzes at the shared memory. "Not tonight." She mock pouts as I drop it to the floor. I unbutton my jeans and kick them off, climbing back on the bed.

"Those too," Sophia commands, freezing me in place halfway over her, her gaze glued to my royal blue briefs.

"Excuse me?"

She reaches out, running her finger between the hem and my skin. "These. Too."

"Ma'am, yes, ma'am," I tease, standing up and dropping them to the floor. I place my hands on my hips and turn my head to the side, pretending to be a statue.

"Don't move," Sophia instructs, jumping off the bed.

"What? Do you want to draw me in all my dick glory?" I laugh, watching as she scoops up her camera. "Oh, no freaking way."

"Come on." She sticks out her lower lip, attempting to pout, but her cute smile peeks through.

"You really want to take dick pics?"

"I am not taking *dick pics*," she scoffs. "This is *art*." She gestures toward me. "*You* are art."

"Fine." I huff, secretly savoring how her eyes appraise me like a million-dollar statue. I put my hands on my hips and straighten my back, and then the clicking of her camera fills the room.

"Get on the bed." She points towards the rumpled covers, and I dive headfirst into them. Sophia laughs, squeezing my ass cheek, before delivering a stinging slap.

"Ow!" I whip around to face her beaming, gorgeous face. "We are making *love* tonight, Sophia."

"We don't have to make love like virgins, *Elijah*." I throw my grinning face back in the pillow I'm holding. "Roll over."

"You're bossy tonight." I do as I'm told, putting my hands behind my head as she fluffs the surrounding covers, strategically covering my dick.

"Fuck yes." She nods her head like an artistic director before snapping away.

"I better get some compensation if this ends up on OnlyFans."

"Sorry, all funds will go towards replacing my torn thongs." She laughs, taking a few more pictures before setting her camera down on the table.

"Whoa, whoa, whoa." I sit quickly and snatch her camera. "If I'm art, then you're the entire damn Louvre, baby. You're the one who should be captured."

"Elijah," she groans. "I look awful. I don't even have makeup on."

"Are you kidding me? You are *breathtaking*. As you are. Right now." I put a palm on her cheek, rubbing the pad of my thumb under her eye. "You are the prettiest damn thing I've ever seen. Your eyes remind me of Christmas trees, and that smile fucking makes my heart explode. I'm the luckiest guy in every damn room. Whether there's a stadium full of people or we're completely alone. Because I have *you*."

43

SOPHIA

"I'll look ridiculous, Elijah," I protest, standing buck naked in the center of his room.

"No," he argues, hands on his hips. "You look *delicious*."

I groan, and he grabs my arm, gently tugging me toward a floor length mirror near his closet. "What are you doing?"

He places his warm hands on my shoulders and spins me toward the mirror. "I want you to look at yourself."

My eyes wander the mirror, taking in our reflection. His glorious, toned, naked frame is behind me as I stand awkwardly. I tilt my head, attention turning to my exposed body, eyes snagging on the tummy pouch I can't get rid of, and I suck in by reflex.

"Stop that."

"What?"

"Looking for things you wish you could change."

"Easy for you to say, Mr. Perfect," I grumble.

"Everyone has things they want to change about themselves."

"Oh yeah? And what the hell would you want to change?"

He sticks out a foot, wiggling his toes. "I wish my feet were smaller."

"What?" I scoff. "There's nothing wrong with your feet."

"And there's nothing wrong with your stomach."

"Touché… And you know what they say about men with big feet." I wink, and he rolls his eyes, then his expression softens.

"I just wish you could see yourself through my eyes." He kisses me on the head. "Repeat after me, okay?"

"What?" I laugh, turning to look at him, but he nudges my gaze back to the mirror.

"Repeat. After. Me."

I exhale a shaky breath. "Okay."

"I am perfect exactly the way I am."

"Yeah, you are." I grin, waggling my eyebrows.

"Sophia. I said *repeat*."

"Fine."

He squeezes my shoulders. "I am perfect *exactly* the way I am."

My gaze drags from my toes back to my eyes. "I am perfect exactly the way I am."

He snakes an arm around my body and rests the side of his face against mine. "I have a beautiful body and an even more beautiful mind."

My lips curve upwards as he grips my stomach. "I have a beautiful body and an even more beautiful mind."

"Now tell me something you love about yourself."

"Now tell me so—"

"Sophia." He cuts me off, and I smirk.

"Fine…" I mutter, taking in my reflection. "I like my eyes."

He brings his hands up, resting them on my biceps. "What else?"

"I like my smile."

Taking my hand, he spins me to face him. "I love your smile too." He grins. "Now. Get. In. The. Damn. Bed."

I copy him by diving face down into the pillows. He grabs a handful of my ass, groaning, and covers it slightly like I did with his delicious dick. To be honest, yeah, it makes the picture of him more appropriate, but also, if I stared at his completely naked body a second longer, I would've hopped right on it. The camera clicks a few times, and Elijah sets me in a few different scandalous positions.

"Okay, I think I've taken enough spank bank material," he says.

"Elijah." I gasp, spinning to face him as he sets the camera on the nightstand. "You can't call it that."

"Sorry." He rolls his eyes, obviously amused. "We have taken enough *art*."

His warm hands trail along my naked body, and I lie on my stomach, melting into the mattress.

"You spoil me." I sigh, smiling softly.

"Because I love you," he says, and my heart pounds in my chest. *I love you. I love you. I love you.* Why can't I just say it back?

Something is seriously fucked up in my head.

The most amazing man in the entire world is treating me like a goddamn goddess, and I can't even allow myself to face those terrifying feelings.

I believe he's finally shared everything with me, and I know he's not anything like Seth, but I can't bring myself to say it back.

Elijah straddles me, trailing his fingertips along my back.

"I love that," Elijah whispers in a husky tone.

"What?"

"How when I do this—" A fingertip drags light as a feather from the base of my neck down my spine, causing goosebumps to ripple across my entire back. "That happens."

"Or when I do this—" He bends down and sucks my earlobe in his mouth while grinding his hard dick into my back, and I whimper in excitement. "You make that noise."

"You seem to know me well," I croak out.

"I know everything about you, sweetheart."

"Trust me, there's always more to learn."

He tugs at my hip, rolling me onto my back, and I stare up at him. "I may not know everything about you, but I know who you are as a person. I know you're sweet, considerate, and creative. You're hilarious and quirky and brilliant. And every single day with you is replacing every bad one I've ever had, and soon all my memories will be sunshine because of you."

I love you. I love you. I love you.

"Thank you," I whisper. *Thank you? What the fuck was that, Sophia?*

"I love you too." Elijah smiles and bends down, pressing his warm lips to mine.

He really does know everything about me. Apparently, he's a mind reader now too.

"There's one last thing I want to show you before we hit the road," Elijah says as we pass Penelope's pasture. He has one arm around my back and is being very secretive about the contents of a large Anderson Family Farm cotton tote bag slung over his other shoulder.

"Pretty sure I only said I wanted to fuck you in a pasture in my head."

"And now I'm considering changing my destination."

"You will do no such thing."

"Fine…" He groans. "But I would like to revisit that."

"Deal."

A few minutes later, we stop at the edge of a lush green field. He pulls me to him, and I wrap my arms around his waist, inhaling his intoxicating scent.

Elijah lowers his mouth to mine, enveloping me in the most toe-curling kiss I've ever experienced. My knees buckle as he slides his tongue into my mouth, holding me close. One more soft kiss and he pulls away, bending back down to the bag. He takes out two sunflowers, handing me one and keeping the other for himself.

"What are these for?" I smile down at it.

"Well, yours is because it's beautiful and I want you to have it.

My little sunflower." He grabs my chin and kisses me on the nose. "And mine is for a game."

Well, my curiosity's officially been piqued.

"A game?"

"Mm-hmm," he hums before plucking a petal off the flower. "She loves me." He grins at me pointedly, and I shake my head as he plucks another petal. "She loves me not." His eyes flick to mine. "She loves me." *She's trying to.* "She loves me not." He juts out his lower lip. "She loves me." He smiles, then continues until there are only three petals left. "She loves me not," he says, plucking one of the last three petals and tossing it to the ground. He stares at the remaining two and frowns, having done the math in his head.

"What now?"

Ripping the last two petals off at once, he shouts, "She loves me!" He grins like the lovable idiot he is, throws the plucked flower to the ground, and scoops me up in his arms, spinning me around.

"You can't do that! It's against the rules." I laugh wildly, shaking my head, trying to wiggle out of his hold.

"I make the rules." He sets me back down and pulls me close. "My sunflower, my rules."

"Is that so?" I throw my arms around his neck.

"Mm-hmm." He gives me a quick peck kiss. "And you know what that means?"

"What?"

"She loves me." He smiles, pulling me in for another stomach dropping kiss.

Of course she does. *So why am I too damn scared to say it?*

We're quiet for a few moments as he holds me close, and I listen to his pounding heartbeat. "Do you know why I call you Sunflower?" he asks.

"Because I had sunflowers on my dress the night we met."

"I mean, it started out that way, sure…" He bends down and reaches into the bag, pulling out an old picture and holding it up in front of us.

"Sunflowers," I whisper, staring at the picture of an older man and a younger Elijah standing in front of a field with thousands of sunflowers.

"Sunflowers," he repeats, turning his attention to me after putting the picture back in the bag. "I used to tend this field with my dad... and damn, is it beautiful." He looks out at the field wistfully, and my hold on him tightens. "When my mom got pregnant with Abbs, she and Dad decided they wanted us to grow up surrounded by nature and started looking for land. When they visited here, the sunflowers were in full bloom."

A soft chuckle escapes him. "Dad always said that something about those sunflowers felt like home... and that's when he knew this was the place." He turns toward me, taking my face in his hands. "I might've started calling you Sunflower as a joke. But I think it was more of a sign." He looks up at the sky. "I think it was my dad's way of saying he sent you for me." Tears brim his eyes, and I wipe them away with my thumb. "The more time we spent together, the more you reminded me of home. Of the happiness I watched my parents have. Of being so in love with someone you know for *sure* you'll never let them go. That you'll do anything for them." My heart swells in my chest, pounding hard against my rib cage. "I call you Sunflower because you're home... You're *my* home."

"Home," I whisper as a tear drops down my face. "The *feeling*, not the place..."

He wipes away the tear, kissing me tenderly. "The feeling *and* the place, Sunflower."

I smile wide, staring into his gentle eyes. "You know how my sister always called me Ladybug?" He nods slightly. "When we were at the springs, and one landed on you... I think that might have been Chloe's way of saying you were for me too." A weak laugh escapes my lips. "Hell, if she could've, I know she would've thrown up neon signs with arrows over your head, but I don't think the universe allows that type of obviousness. So a single ladybug it was."

"With an unlimited amount of luck." He places his forehead on mine, and I nuzzle his nose. "Can you imagine? Our angels have been pushing us together since the day we met, and you kept pushing me away. They must've been very frustrated with you." I look out at the empty sunflower field that has so many memories for the man standing next to me, and my lips fall to a frown.

"What's wrong?" Elijah asks.

"Why don't you ever talk about him?" He glances toward the field, his lower lip beginning to quiver. "Elijah?"

"If I don't talk about it... I can pretend it's not real." His glossy eyes connect with mine, and he squeezes them shut, tears sliding down his cheeks.

"Elijah..." I whisper, and his head drops to my shoulder. I rub my hand along his back as he breaks down in my arms, and my own tears fall. We sink to our knees in the dirt, and I take his face in mine. "Baby?"

He lifts his head, glistening ocean eyes boring into mine. "I'm sorry."

"What? Stop it. You're allowed to express how you feel. I want you to."

"I just miss him so damn much," he croaks out. "I keep waiting for it to stop hurting. I keep thinking if I just move forward, and I don't think about him, or I don't talk about him, maybe one day I'll stop missing him." He sniffles again and I wipe away more tears, but it's no use. He's finally allowed the dam to break.

Placing my palm on his cheek, I bring his tear-stained face to mine. "I understand... But that's not how it works, baby." He turns away, but I force his gaze back to mine. "You *love* him. He's your *dad.*" My voice breaks on the last word. "Ignoring his death won't help ease the ache you're feeling here." I flatten my palm on his pounding heart.

"Then what does?" he says in a pained whisper. "I can't... I can't just keep having this debilitating pain every time I think about him. Pain's always supposed to go away. Why isn't it going away?"

"Pain doesn't go away all at once. It dulls until it no longer controls you."

His eyes flick up to the sky as he takes a deep breath. "Fuck."

"This probably sounds like shit advice, but the only thing that really helps is time... well, that and therapy." I smile faintly. "And the more you think about him, think about all the good things in your life that are *because* of him, your brain will get used to remembering he's gone. And someday, you'll be able to laugh at the memories. There will always be that dull ache in your chest from missing him, but it won't consume you. It'll no longer control you."

He brings both hands to his face, brushing away the tears, then leans back. I settle next to him, and he puts an arm over my leg, tugging me against him. "I love you, Sophia. Dad would've loved you too." He reaches into the bag, pulling out my sketchbook and a pencil, and hands it to me. "Draw me something?"

I smile up at him. "Gladly."

After a Christmas Eve brunch with Jenna and Grandma Mia, we're finally heading to Longwood. Settling in the passenger seat, I connect my phone to the Bluetooth as Elijah hauls himself up on the driver's side foot bar.

He pauses, looking out at the farm with a wistful smile, and slaps his palm against the hood. "Tag, you're it."

Gorgeous farmland spans for miles as we drive towards the main highway. Even in the winter, it's breathtaking.

I love when we drive like this. Windows down, Chris Young on the radio, and Elijah's hand placed possessively on my thigh. If anyone asked me his love language, it is definitely, no contest, physical touch. He always has to be touching me.

A hand on the lower back when we walk through a crowd.

Holding my foot when I'm lying on the other end of the couch.

His warm grip around my waist when we stand in line for coffee.

And I fucking love it.

"You looking forward to seeing Mark?" I ask, turning the topic to our next destination.

"Yeah." He smiles. "I am… How are you feeling about being in Longwood?"

"I'm excited to see everyone, even though it'll be weird not being able to go into Chloe's room…" Elijah turns his hand upwards, and I tangle my fingers with his. *Not to mention the fact I'm hoping Seth won't show up.*

"Did you tell your dad you talked to Lysa?"

"Yeah."

"And?"

"He was happy I'm giving our relationship another chance."

"So am I." He squeezes my hand again. "What is it you're always telling me? Life's short; don't waste a second of it."

"Yeah… Jake always says it."

"Well, he seems like a smart guy. Even if he's kind of dickish sometimes."

I scoff and laugh. "What?"

"Sorry." He chuckles. "I know he's just looking out for you, babe. Hell, if we have a daughter, I wouldn't let her date a guy like me either."

If "we" have a daughter?

Calm down, Soph. It's just a figure of speech.

"Don't spiral, sweetheart," Elijah says, reading my mind like always. "I just meant if we ever get to that point, our daughter could do a lot better than a guy like me."

"You just don't even know how amazing you are, do you?"

"I guess not." He smiles and squeezes my hand.

"Well, you are. And *if* we had a hypothetical daughter, she would be lucky to date a man like you."

Elijah straightens his shoulders, and a huge grin spreads across his face. "You mean that?"

"Of course I do," I reply as my phone buzzes on my lap.

PAPA BEAR

PAPA BEAR

How far out are you guys?

ME

We've gotta make a stop, so about six more hours

PAPA BEAR

Okay, drive safe, love you Sophie Bear

ME

Love you, Papa Bear

PAPA BEAR

And tell Elijah he's welcome for dinner

ME

Okay, I will 😊

"My dad invited you to Christmas Eve dinner at our place."

"Do I get to sleep over?" he asks with a huge smile and raised eyebrows.

I laugh in disbelief. "Of course not."

"Oh, come on, don't you wanna be my little ho ho ho?"

I slap him on the shoulder. "Elijah."

"Come on. You've been such a *good girl* this year. Don't you wanna be naughty for me tonight to get in the Christmas spirit?"

"You're ridiculous."

"I could just sneak in your window like we did at my house." He slides his hand up my leg, causing all the heat to rush south.

"You will do no such thing!" I squeal with wide eyes, slapping his hand away. "My dad would *kill* you."

"The bigger the risk, the greater the reward." He winks with a casual shrug. My heart races at the thought as his hand settles back on my thigh. "Besides, we have to finish what we started last night since you fell asleep after our photo shoot."

"Hey, modeling is exhausting. It takes a lot of effort to look this good all the time." Elijah's fingers inch upwards.

"Yeah, I'm definitely sliding in your chimney tonight."

"Oh my God, stop!" I throw my hand over his, pausing his exploration. "You are so *not* funny."

"My sack will be empty when I'm finished with you." He grips my leg tighter.

"Elijah!" I laugh, hitting him playfully against the arm.

"Fine…" He pouts. "Guess I'll just have to touch my *elf*."

44
ELIJAH

"Go look, and I'll be right back," I tell Sophia as we get to the bookstore in the closest mall on the way to Longwood.

"You're not coming with?" She pouts.

"I know you'll take a while, so just get a head start. I have a little last minute Christmas shopping to do. Okay?"

"Fine… since it's for the presents." She kisses me quickly and skips inside, making a beeline for the romance section.

Twenty minutes and two hundred dollars later, I've successfully acquired Sophia's last Christmas present. I return to the bookstore and find her staring at two books intently with a crease on her forehead.

"What's wrong?" I place my hand on her shoulder, and she looks up at me with a huff.

"I can't decide." She frowns at the small stack of books in her hands. "Too many good options."

I kiss her on the cheek, leaving her to scan over the romance section for some recommendations I found after a bit of research. The Miles High Club series by author T L Swan had high reviews, and I've found all four books side by side. I stack them in one arm and keep browsing.

"What are you doing? Ooh, what's in that bag?" Sophia asks, staring at the large pink striped bag in my hand, but I ignore her, having spotted the other top seller: *Icebreaker* by Hannah Grace.

"I did some research, and these books are supposed to have equally good plot and sex."

Sophia's mouth falls open. "You did *research*?"

"Yes." I glare at her, using my pointer finger to close her mouth. "Don't want you to be bored when you read me all these."

She throws her head back, laughing. "Are you serious?"

"Deadly." I hold up the cute, animated cover with an ice skater and hockey player on it. "Are you sure this one's sexy? It looks so cutesy."

"Oh, yes. That one is *extremely* spicy. But I've already read it." She holds up the okay sign with a dopey smile on her face. "Top tier book boyfriend material."

And now I'm jealous of a fictional man...

"Okay? And now you get to read it to *me* so I can learn how to be a 'top tier' *real* boyfriend." I juggle the books in my arms. "Come on, let's go."

"Wait!" she calls out as I turn away. "I haven't decided yet."

I spin to face her as she holds her own pile of books in her arms. "I told you yesterday, you can buy the whole damn bookstore. Now let's get out of here." I grab the books from her hands, adding them to my pile, and she follows me through the store with a satisfied smile on her face.

We get back in the truck, and I put Sophia's books in the back, but not before pulling out *Icebreaker* and setting it on the center console so she can start that one first.

"Here," I say, handing her the large pink bag. "I don't want to give you this present in front of your family."

She purses her lips and grins up at me. "Elijah, you're spoiling me."

"And? I'm happy to do it."

"I just feel bad. I only got you something small."

"So? You're my gift. Just tie a bow around your tits, and we can call it even." I smirk and she leans over the center console to kiss me.

She settles back in her seat and sifts through the bag, pulling out the first scrap of lace and twirling it around her finger. "Really?"

"What?" I smile innocently. "It looked easy to rip off."

She shakes her head and releases a breathy laugh. "You are so ridiculous. You saw how expensive this shit is, and you're still considering ripping them off?"

"Hey." I slide my palm under her shirt and towards the hem of her leggings. "If the opportunity arises, I guess we'll just consider it an expensive bad habit."

She rolls her eyes, obviously amused as I toy with the string of her thong, and she swats me away.

"Alright, you can give me a fashion show later. Let's get back on the road so we can make it for dinner."

"Wait," Sophia says, leaning back over the center console and brushing her hand against my face. "Thank you."

"You're welcome. Merry Christmas, baby." She kisses me, slipping her tongue inside my mouth, eliciting a deep groan. "Sophia, I just spent half an hour in a lingerie store where all I could do was imagine you in every piece of see-through clothing they had. You have to give me a break or I'll end up fucking you in the back seat."

She gives me another peck before pulling away and snatching the book off the center console. "Fine. I'll start your first book."

"Good." The smile doesn't leave my face as her sweet voice serenades me all the way to Longwood.

45
SOPHIA

"There's our two little elves," Dad says the second we walk through the front door, cinnamon and vanilla hitting my senses immediately.

"It smells like Santa's workshop in here," I say as my mouth salivates.

"Diane made cookies."

"I'm still working off the ten pounds I gained the last time I was here," Elijah teases.

"They just came out of the oven, so help yourselves," Diane tells us, smiling as we come into the kitchen. "Hey, Sophia." She pulls me in for a tight hug, and I melt into her. She has flour in her hair and smells like Christmas morning.

"Hi, Di."

Elijah and Dad are whispering about something, but I choose not to get in the middle of their bonding.

"Why don't you go put your stuff in your room before we eat dinner," Dad suggests.

"Okay, sounds good."

Elijah picks up my bag and follows me up the stairs. We pass Chloe's door and I pause, frowning at the craft room.

"Come on, babe," Elijah says softly, ushering me along. We

continue to my room, and I push open the door, freezing in the frame.

"What—" I whisper as my skin prickles. "What is this?" Elijah places his hands on my shoulders, nudging me closer to the redecorated corner of my room.

Chloe's pink upholstered chair is angled in the corner, with a pink-and-white striped blanket folded neatly on the arm. There's a side table with a familiar porcelain bowl on top. Slowly, I make my way over and pick up the bowl, flipping it over. On the bottom are the words "Lovebug–Scaredybug–Ladybug" painted on.

A ragged breath releases as my eyes blur. I rub at them before taking in the rest of the new space. A painting hangs on the wall of a girl holding a child, reading *Alice in Wonderland*. It's a perfect depiction of Chloe and me when I was younger, and Leah's signature is small in the corner.

Happiness—sadness—nostalgia—grief—every emotion slams into me at once, forcing tears to spill out of my eyes as they memorize the space.

Elijah squeezes my shoulders and kisses me on the side of my head before placing my sketch pad and pencils on the side table. "I'll give you a few minutes, okay? Come downstairs when you're ready."

"Mm-hmm."

He leaves the room, footsteps echoing down the wooden staircase.

I can't believe Dad did this.

I bend down, inspecting the feet of the pink chair. A large scratch runs the length of the left front leg. *Yep, this is it.*

Spinning around, I fall back, sinking into the cushion, and throw the blanket over me. A heavy breath escapes my lungs as I pick up my sketchbook.

I'm home.

46
ELIJAH

"If you add any more frosting, you'll need a spoon," Diane says, laughing as I attempt, and fail, to frost a candy cane shaped sugar cookie.

I point the pastry bag with red frosting towards her. "I never promised to be a decorating expert."

"Don't worry. You'll get the hang of it. It only took Will three dozen cookies to figure it out."

Will narrows his eyes at her and strides over to kiss her. "I'm a paramedic, not a surgeon, babe."

Footsteps creak on the staircase, and Sophia comes into the kitchen. Her face is red and blotchy, but she's smiling. I wanted to stay in her room and hold her, but I knew she needed a bit of time to herself. She goes over to her dad and Diane, pulling them both in for a hug. "Thanks, guys."

My heart swells as I see how relieved she is to have her special place back.

"You're welcome," Will says, smiling and planting a kiss on her head. "But you should thank Elijah." He nods in my direction. "It was his idea."

Sophia glances over at me with furrowed brows. "Really?" I just smile, thankful my girl is happy to be home. She comes over and throws her arms around me, nuzzling her face into my chest. "I can't believe you did this for me."

"I'd do anything for you."

"Knock, knock," we hear as the front door opens and shuts.

"Hello," Jake says, stepping into the room with Leah, wearing a big smile that doesn't falter for a second when he notices me. We all greet them, and Jake comes over to pull me in for a hug. The gesture surprises me, but I lean into it.

"Thanks for taking care of my baby sister," he whispers in my ear.

"Always." I smile as he pulls away, patting me on the shoulder.

He grips it harder than necessary, grinning as he stares in my eyes. "But I'll still kill you if you ever hurt her."

"Noted."

I would rather die.

"Thanks for welcoming me… again," I say to Will as we set the table for Christmas breakfast. I got to spend the morning with Mark and Cole, and now I'm placing Christmas tree shaped paper napkins on the plates around the kitchen table. Very domestic if I do say so myself.

"Of course. We're happy you could join," Will replies, slapping me on the shoulder.

After we're done setting the table, Sophia hands me a coffee mug that says "Get Lit" with Christmas lights around it.

"Hazelnut coffee with honey and *extra* whipped cream." She winks and kisses me on the cheek. I sit down at the kitchen island, chuckling to myself as I drink my basic bitch coffee while Leah and Diane make breakfast.

Will snatches the Santa hat off the counter. "Alright, kiddos, let's go see what Santa brought."

We gather around the living room as Will shuffles the presents under the tree. He digs one out, handing it to Diane with a big smile on his face. "Okay, we can do this one first."

She unwraps new spools for her sewing machine and kisses Will like he bought her a Gucci purse. "Thanks, Willy."

Sophia scrunches her face at me and mouths, *Willy?*

I stifle a laugh and squeeze her knee.

As they open their gifts, big and small, I can feel all the love in the room. "Okay…" Will reads the label. "This one is for Elijah."

My lips break into a wide smile. "For me?"

Sophia sits on her heels, watching me open the small box. I unwrap it, taking off the lid to see a keychain sitting in the box, and take it out to examine it. A tiny bowl and spoon dangle, and there's a thin metal plate reading "Cereal Killer." I shake my head, chuckling at the reminder of our first meeting, and smile at Sophia. "I love it. Thank you."

"You're welcome." She leans over and plants a firm kiss on my lips.

Will clears his throat. "Okay, that's enough of that." The upturned corners of his mouth tell me it's half-hearted. "Here's another one for… Sunflower?"

"Really, Honey Bee?" Sophia narrows her eyes at me before returning her attention to Will. "That's for me." She fights a smile, holding out grabby hands for the large box. She sets it on her lap and rips it open, pulling it carefully from the box. A gasp escapes her lips as she stares down at the gift I custom made for her myself… well, with Mom and Leah's help.

"Elijah," she says quietly, staring down at the golden frame with a pressed sunflower between two pieces of glass. Behind the sunflower is a copied page from our world history textbook. The first page we studied together at the beginning of the year. Her finger traces the tiny painted honey bees on the glass around the sunflower —Leah's doing. "Are you kidding me?" Her grateful eyes find mine. "Thank you."

"You're welcome. Merry Christmas, Sunflower."

47

SOPHIA

"Hey there, Ladybug," Leah says, strolling into my room as I sit on Chloe's chair, sketching in the corner of my room. "Elijah head out already?"

"Hey, Scaredybug." I close my sketchbook and set it on the side table as she throws herself onto my bed. "Yeah, he went to see Mark and Cole."

"Perfect. So now I can finally ask… How was your trip to meet his mom?" She waggles her eyebrows.

"It was… good."

"Good? That's all I get."

"It was *good*," I repeat with raised brows.

"Why do I feel like there're some lines I'm supposed to read between?"

"How do you always do that?"

She smirks. "Do what?"

"Know there's something I'm not saying even when I didn't know there was something I wasn't saying."

"It's my special skill." She winks.

"It was good. It was really good." I smile faintly. "But it was also a really emotionally draining trip."

"Why?"

"Well, first of all... Elijah told me he loves me."

"Oh my gosh, Soph!" she shrieks, sitting straight up with a wide smile.

"Yeah..." Heat flushes my cheeks. "I didn't say it back yet."

"What? Why not?"

I exhale loudly. "I honestly can't pinpoint it."

"You know you can talk to me, Soph."

A heavy rock sinks in my stomach. "I feel horrible for even saying this out loud because I'm making it all about me and it's so not but... I don't know, it's just how I feel..." Leah tilts her head, waiting for me to continue. "While we were there, I found out Elijah has a dad and a sister I didn't know about. I wouldn't say he hid it, per se... He just never talked about them or told me."

"And it hurt your feelings that he didn't share it with you?"

"Damn." I laugh weakly. "You're as good as Janine."

"You're not the only one who went to therapy, Soph. And also, I do know you pretty damn well."

"True... But the thing is, his dad died in April."

Leah's eyes go wide. "And the sister?"

"She's alive."

Leah exhales a whoosh of relief. "Thank God."

"Yeah... It's just, Elijah's been struggling a bit at school, and I guess he's just had all this pain inside I never knew about. And I hate that he didn't trust me enough to be there for him."

"Soph." She looks at me with sympathetic eyes. "I totally understand where you're coming from. I do. But just to play devil's advocate here... People do unexplainable things when they're grieving." Her gaze falls to her hands, and she picks at her fingernails before returning her eyes to mine. "Some people like to share all their feelings, and some people bottle them up, shove them down, and just try to move forward. That doesn't mean he cares about you any less or doesn't trust you. It just hurt him too much to speak the words out loud."

As I contemplate her words, guilt settles into my stomach for blaming him.

"I know... I feel stupid for feeling this way. But I can't help wondering if he's keeping other things from me."

"Come here." Leah pats the spot on my bed next to her, and I pad over, plopping down on the mattress. "He brought you to his family home. He must have known you would find out about his dad and sister while you were there. Don't you think?"

My brows furrow as I process what she's saying. "I guess so."

"Have you considered maybe he was ready to share that part of himself with you but didn't know how else to do it?" Leah takes my hands in hers. "I know it felt like he was hiding something big from you, but you know how hard it hurts to lose someone you love. Elijah also had to open himself up the same way you are. I think him bringing you home was his way of sharing that with you without just *telling* you about it."

"He wanted to show me," I say quietly, feeling shitty about how I reacted to him sharing the most painful parts of himself.

"Just think about it, okay? Think about what's really holding you back from opening yourself up completely."

I lean my head on her shoulder and stare at the pressed sunflower Elijah gave me for Christmas.

"I'm afraid to confess to him, to both of us, what I feel. When I tell Elijah I love him, I'll be admitting to him and the universe that it'll fucking wreck me if I lose him," I reveal quietly, and she hugs me close.

"It's scary falling in love... but it's also beautiful. And once you jump all in for someone, there's really no going back."

"No return policy." I release a breathy laugh, thinking of Elijah.

"Yeah, I guess you're right." She leans her head against mine. "No return policy."

"Thank you." I place my hand on Leah's knee and give it a light squeeze.

"Anytime. So... I heard you talked to Lysa."

An exasperated sigh leaves me. "Yep."

"How was it? Talking to her?"

"Honestly?" I scrunch my face. "It was kinda nice."

"I'm so glad to hear you say that. She was so happy you answered."

"Yeah." I smile down at my hands. "I guess it couldn't hurt to give her a chance, huh?"

"No, I don't think so."

"I think I should call her today."

"I bet she'd love that." Leah rolls off the bed and walks to the door before turning to face me. "Love you, Ladybug."

I smile as she turns and leaves the room. "Love you more, Scaredybug."

After picking up my phone, I scroll for the number I haven't purposefully dialed in years, if ever. It rings so long I think she may not pick up, and just as I'm about to end the call, her familiar voice fills the other end of the line. "Soph?"

"Hi, Mom," I say in as happy a tone I can muster.

"I'm so glad you called. You doing okay?"

"Yeah. Um... I just wanted to call and say Merry Christmas, Mama Bear."

She exhales heavily, and I can hear the smile in her voice. "Merry Christmas, Sophie Bear."

I'm lying on my bed, watching *Miracle on 34th Street* when my phone screen lights up the darkness.

HONEY BEE

HONEY BEE

Ho ho ho, can I come down your chimney?

ME

Hilarious Mr. Claus

How was the rest of your day?

HONEY BEE

Good, but it'll be better soon

ME

Oh yeah? Why's that?

HONEY BEE

Are you in your room alone?

ME

Yes...

Seconds later a knock on my window has my eyes widening as I pause the movie. I shoot out of bed, run over, and open it to Elijah's smiling face.

"What are you doing here?" I ask as he climbs through my window wearing a Santa hat.

"Seeing my girl," he whispers. "The thought of sleeping alone again sounded awful. Being apart last night was bad enough."

"Uh-oh," I tease, pulling off his Santa hat and tossing it on my dresser. "We've got a stage five clinger."

"Ha ha, hilarious." He pulls me into his arms and kisses me firmly.

"But you know," I mumble against his mouth, "you could've used the front door."

"Yeah, but then your dad would know I'm here and probably not be thrilled."

"My dad's at the airport. Diane's going to see her kids, and Jake and Leah are going to some ski resort in North Carolina." I smirk, waggling my eyebrows. "He won't be back for a few hours."

Elijah throws his head back, groaning, and I laugh. "So I climbed the side of your house for no reason?"

"Just consider it a warm-up for the physical activity I'm about to reward you with."

"Mm-hmm." Elijah turns to close the window.

"Leave it open. It's nice out for once."

"*Oh*," Elijah teases. "An excuse to share body heat? Gladly."

I lock the bedroom door just in case Dad checks in when he comes home, then walk to my bed and crawl under the covers. Elijah bites his lower lip before kicking off his shoes and slowly pulling his shirt off, allowing me to savor the sight of his muscular body. He stands there clad in CBU sweatpants and a smile only a man in love has on. *That's my smile.*

I flip back the blanket, and he slides in next to me, pulling me into his arms. I rest my head against his warm chest and melt into the sound of his rapid heartbeat.

"I missed you today," I admit.

"Oh, really?" he mumbles into my hair.

"Yes."

"I was only gone a few hours."

"I know... But it was a few hours too long." He pulls away, and I turn so we're facing one another. "I wanted to apologize."

His brows furrow. "What for?"

"You took me home, shared all the parts of your life that are hard for you to talk about... and I made it all about me." I swallow hard. "I didn't consider the fact you might have taken me home so you *could* share all those parts of you with me."

He brushes a hair behind my ear before placing his warm palm on my face. "You have no reason to apologize. Yes, I was happy I finally got to share all those things with you. But I do think I should've told you sooner... and for that, *I'm* sorry."

"How about we call it even?"

He leans down, pressing a gentle kiss to my lips. "Deal."

"I have one more thing to apologize for though," I mumble against his lips.

"What's that?"

I take a deep breath, choosing not to let the lion of my nightmares keep me from opening myself to him.

"I'm sorry I didn't tell you I love you back." He pulls further away and stares down at me with an unreadable expression. "Elijah…" I place my hand on the side of his face, and he leans into it. "I love you *back*."

He smiles wide. "I told you so, Sunflower."

"You love saying that, don't you?"

"Yeah." He chuckles and pulls me on top of him. "I really do."

I roll my eyes before turning serious again. "I love you, Elijah."

He rubs his thumb along my jaw. "I love you too." His hands wander down to my waist, nudging my T-shirt upward. "Let me show you just how much." His warm, rough palms glide along my skin before he lifts the shirt up and over my head, tossing it to the floor. He flips me onto my back, then leans down toward my breast and sucks my nipple into his mouth. I arch my back as he nibbles on it and takes the other one in his grasp.

"Elijah," I moan as he places his muscular thigh between my legs, and I grind against it.

"Damn, baby," he grumbles against my skin. "Do that again."

I repeat the motion, and he dips a hand down, cupping my throbbing center. He brings both hands to my waist, pushing my sleep shorts and panties off in one motion. I want to joke about him not ripping my thong tonight, but I'm too turned on to utter a single syllable.

"I love you," he says in a low, gravelly tone just before kissing my stomach. "I love you." He kisses each of my hip bones. "I love you." He trails kisses from my toes to my collarbone, sucking lightly on the sensitive skin. "I love you." He hovers over my face, then leans down and kisses me delicately on the lips.

"And I love you, Honey Bee."

He places a palm on the side of my neck, rubbing his thumb along my throat. *Seth's hand wraps around my windpipe, making it difficult to breathe.* I shake my head, pushing away the unwelcome memory.

Elijah yanks his hand away. "Shit, I'm so sorry. Are you okay?"

"Yes." I swallow hard, nodding softly.

"I'm sorry, I didn't think—"

"I'm good. Let's focus on the now. Okay?" I reach out, rubbing a finger along his dark, scruffy jaw. "Just you and me."

"Really, I'm sorry. I di—"

"You. And. Me."

"Okay." He releases a shaky breath, eyes scanning my body, and a lazy smile appears on his face. "You're naked."

"I know." I bite my lower lip. "Your turn."

He stands up and drops his sweats and briefs, but not before fishing a foil packet out of his pocket and tossing it on the nightstand. He climbs back on top of me and bends down, pressing another gentle kiss on my lips. His tongue slips into my mouth, entangling with mine, and I groan at the familiar taste.

"I want you," I rasp out.

"You have me, baby." He nibbles at my neck. "Mind, body, heart, soul, every single piece of it is yours."

"No." I shake my head. "I want *you*." I squeeze his ass. "Inside of me." He lets out a low chuckle. "Now."

He snatches the foil packet off the table, making quick work to roll it on. Once it's secure, he dips his hand between my legs and glides his thumb against my clit.

"Just making sure your pussy's wet for me, sweetheart." He positions himself against my entrance, and I whimper when he slides inside.

"I love you," I moan out as he pushes deeper inside of me.

"And I'll never tire of hearing it." He thrusts in a slow, steady rhythm. Entirely different from any of our times before. It's not hungry or urgent or lustful. It's slow and gentle, and I can tell he's savoring every single second the same way I am. He pushes deeper, keeping his relaxed pace, and I whimper when he hits that delicious spot. "That's it, baby. Let me show you how much I love you. Show you how our bodies speak to one another perfectly and how my name will be the only one ever falling from those sweet lips." The room fills with his loud breaths mixed with my soft whimpers—a melody I could listen to forever. I dip my hand between us, putting pressure on my clit, and he swats it away. "No."

"What?" I protest until he replaces my hand with his own.

"When we're together, I get to make you come." An excited laugh catches in my throat as his thumb increases pace against my clit. "When I'm here, you tell me how you want it and where. And I'll make sure you come on my face or my cock. Always *your* choice."

He either recognizes my impatience or gains some of his own because he increases his pace, thrusting while circling my clit.

"Elijah," I moan loudly, knowing exactly how crazy it drives him. We tumble together, and I clench around his hard cock, draining every drop out of him until he's collapsed next to me, panting into the crook of my neck.

"Damn." His chest rises and falls as he throws his heavy arm over my stomach.

I giggle breathlessly. "Damn."

"Fucking is overrated. I want to do that for the rest of our lives."

"Aw, no more study room sex?"

His eyes gleam with mischief. "Okay... I take it back. We can totally do both. But I definitely prefer making love with you over fucking any day."

"Elijah Anderson, when did you become such a sappy fuck?"

He laughs, running a hand through my hair. "Apparently after I fell in love with you."

We drift off to sleep entangled in one another, and I have the most peaceful dreams I've had in weeks.

A hand rubbing along my bare hip pulls me back to consciousness, and I smile in the darkness.

He tugs me closer to his warm body, kissing my neck, then trails kisses down my side before nudging me onto my back. *God, I love him.* I can't see much in the darkness, so I close my eyes and rest my head against the pillow, savoring his exploration. His gentle fingertips glide over my skin, and I enjoy every touch.

He moves his hands up my thighs, then rubs a finger over my clit. I moan quietly as he dips his head, trembling when he flicks his tongue against me. He pulls away, slipping a finger inside of me.

"Fuck, baby, I forgot how good you taste."

Every cell in my body turns to ice at the realization of whose voice fills my ears. No. No. This is a nightmare. I'm asleep.

"God, I missed you," Seth says, and my body snaps back to reality. I pull my leg back before kicking him in the face, causing him to fly backwards and off the bed. "Ow!"

"What the hell are you doing?" I say with a shaky voice, scrambling off the bed and wrapping the blanket around me. I fumble in the darkness, finally turning on my bedside lamp to see Seth standing with blood dripping down his face.

"You know you were enjoying it." He snickers, and my blood runs cold. I frantically search the floor for clothes, feeling exposed, too exposed. Elijah's T-shirt is crumpled on the ground, and I snatch it up, throwing it over my head.

"Get the fuck out of my room," I say firmly, attempting to exude the confidence I don't feel.

Is my dad back?

Where's Elijah?

"Don't be like that, baby girl," he says, stepping towards me as I grab shorts out of my drawer, trying to tug them on before he reaches me—the simple task made difficult by my hands shaking uncontrollably. "I saw you left the window open for me. Don't pretend you weren't praying I'd sneak in."

My eyes flick toward the now closed window, heart pounding in my ears.

"Have you lost your mind?!" I continue trying to put space between us. "You almost killed me last time I saw you, and now you just... just..." I stutter, eyes glued to the bed, where I'm still trying to process what just happened. "You're insane."

"I didn't mean to hurt you before. Please. My anger got the better of me, baby girl. It won't happen again." He steps toward me, and I stumble against the nightstand, knocking over a glass of water. "I'm trying to make it up to you."

"Get away from me!" My body shakes uncontrollably as his firm hand wraps around my arm, squeezing to the point of pain. "Elijah!"

48
ELIJAH

I'm washing my face in the bathroom down the hall from Sophia's room. My heart soars at the memory of her finally telling me she loves me. *Damn, I'm a lucky man.* My phone buzzes on the vanity, and I pick it up.

Who the hell would text me this late?

THEO

THEO

Wish you were here bro

(1) Video Attached

Rolling my eyes, I chuckle, playing a video of Theo doing shots on a long wooden ski with a few half-naked girls. Looks like he spent another holiday getting fucked up instead of with family.

A muffled voice reaches my ears, and I open the bathroom door slowly. *Is Will home?* The hallway is dark, and Sophia's door is still shut, but light is streaming from the bottom of it. "Elijah!" Her loud, panicked tone has me sprinting towards her room.

"Haven't you realized it by now?" a familiar male voice says as I'm steps away, and my body erupts in flames. "You're mine."

I throw open the door, and my eyes widen, veins filling with rage at the sight of Seth trapping Sophia's arms against the wall. Their heads snap to me, Sophia's eyes filled with terror. Seth's face drips with blood, looking like a deranged animal. *I'm going to kill him.* I snatch Seth by the shoulder, and slam my fist directly into his nose.

He stumbles backward, holding his face. "Fuck!" He lunges toward me, and I stop him with a blow to his mouth. Blood pours, and he spits it out. *What the hell is he doing in here?* Seth grabs my neck, throwing me against Sophia's dresser, causing it to slam against the wall. A picture frame falls to the ground and shatters with the rest of my resolve.

I dig my feet into the ground, using all my strength to shove his heavy body off me. "Don't ever touch her again!" I grab the collar of Seth's shirt. "I swear to God, if you ever come near Sophia again, I'll kill you, you pathetic piece of shit." He brings his leg between us, kneeing me hard in the stomach.

I stumble back, folding over from the blow. "*I'll* decide when I'm done with her!" He throws a right hook at my eye.

I grab his shoulder, pulling him towards me before placing both hands firmly around his neck, squeezing tightly. He slaps at my wrists as his face turns red.

Stop, Elijah.

No, I can't stop.

He deserves this.

He needs to feel exactly how Sophia felt.

To experience what it's like fearing for your fucking life.

"Enough!" a loud male voice shouts, snapping my head toward the door. My entire body turns to ice, unease rolling through me like a chilled, dark wave. Will stands there, an unreadable expression on his face, with a shotgun pointed directly at us. I release Seth and step backward, holding my hands up before glancing at Sophia. She stands in the corner, arms folded over herself, with a void gaze. I want to run and pull her to me, but I'm too afraid her dad might shoot me. Will readjusts his aim directly at Seth, who's coughing, and I exhale a breath of relief.

"Seth," Will says calmly as the sound of him cocking the gun echoes off every inch of the room. "Get the *hell* out of my house."

Will steps back from the door frame, without lowering the gun. Seth stumbles out, still gasping for air, eyes glued on Will, before turning toward the stairs and running down them. Will follows him and as soon as they're out of my line of sight, I spin around to Sophia, who's on the floor holding herself, staring at the wall. I rush over to her and bend down.

"Baby, are you okay?" She blinks without so much as a glance in my direction. I run my fingers over her skin, searching frantically for any markings and thankfully, finding none. "Soph?" I turn her eyes to meet mine, and they're completely vacant. Sliding my arms around her back and legs, I scoop her up. She clings to me as I carry her over to the bed, laying her down gently. I bring the cover over her and drop to my knees next to the bed while rubbing her head.

God, how did we get here?

One minute she was telling me she loves me and sleeping peacefully in my arms, the next I was seconds from justifiably murdering her ex. This has all gotten out of hand. Something has to change.

"We have to tell your dad what's going on."

Her eyes go wide. "I—" She shakes her head. "I can't."

I place my hand on her cheek. "Sweetheart, he needs to know…" I exhale a heavy breath. "He needs to know *everything*. It's the only way we can protect you."

Her green, glassy eyes bore into mine, and she blinks a few times. "I know." Her tone is low, empty, and far away. "Can you do it?"

"Don't you think this is something you should do, baby?"

She looks away, and her lower lip quivers. "Please."

The desperation in her tone is gut-wrenching, and I know there's no way I can deny her. "Okay, I'll be right back."

She nods weakly and rolls away from me, curling into a ball. I pull the blanket over her shoulders and plant a soft kiss on her head. Sophia's wearing my shirt, so I have to go down shirtless, which isn't ideal to talk to her dad, but it's the only choice I have.

I take faltering steps into the kitchen, eyes snagging on the shotgun resting on the counter pointed straight towards me. Will folds his arms over his chest, letting out a heavy exhale. "I want to be mad at you for being in my daughter's room half naked without my knowledge... but I'm glad you were here." I nod. "You wanna tell me what the hell just happened?"

I fill Will in on everything, from the accident to Seth visiting Sophia at Thanksgiving.

"And there's something else you should see..." I tell him, pulling up the photos we took of Sophia's neck.

Will takes my phone and stares down at it. He places a hand over his mouth as he swipes through them, and a tear drips down his face. His glossy, furious eyes connect with mine. "You should have told me about this sooner. We could have protected her. Tonight shouldn't have happened."

A mountain of guilt the size of Mt. Kilimanjaro settles in my stomach. "I know... She's been staying with me on campus, so I thought she was safe. She asked me not to tell anyone, and I didn't want to betray her trust."

"And how well did that work out?" His jaw clenches, and my eyes burn.

"You're right... I should have come to you." I blink back angry tears. "I'm sorry."

"I don't want your apology," he snaps. "I want you to care more about my daughter's safety than you do about having her in your bed."

Anger brews at his insinuation, and I shove it down. "Sir, I *love* your daughter."

"If I ever find out you gambled her safety again..." His eyes flick down to the shotgun and back to mine, and a shiver runs down my spine.

"I won't." I swallow hard. "Her safety is, and always has been, my number one concern... But what can we do? How can we protect her? He won't leave her alone."

"Well, there's not much we can do about the accident or the..." He clears his throat and takes a deep breath, physically repressing his anger. "The choking. But we can get a restraining order against him so he can't come near Sophia again."

"Really? Do you think it would stick?" I ask hopefully.

"Yeah, it's enough. Him harassing her, along with breaking and entering, and the... photos you showed me of her neck. It'll stick. And now you and I are a witness to that abuse." He tilts his head and narrows his eyes. "If you're willing to be a witness?"

"Hell yeah." I nod. "Anything you need."

"You wanna call Mark or should I?" he asks, and all I can think about is that I can't stand to be apart from Sophia a moment longer.

"I think it would be more effective coming from you, but you can tell him to call me if he needs anything."

"Alright, and listen, I can't say I blame you for wringing that kid's neck... but you can't let him get to you like that again." My body relaxes as I watch his anger towards me subside. "We'll find other ways to protect Sophia that don't risk either of us going to jail for murder."

"Yes, sir."

"Now go be with Sophia. I know you're itching to check on her."

"Thank you, sir," I reply before turning around toward the stairs, taking them two at a time, rushing back to her room. I nudge open the door, and the wrecked space makes my stomach tighten. Broken glass, furniture shifted around, blood stains on the floor, and a crumpled-up Sophia sleeping not-so-peacefully in Chloe's chair in the corner. I crouch down, picking up the larger glass shards. *Sophia doesn't need to wake up to this reminder tomorrow.* After I make sure there's no sign a fight ever happened and double check the locks on the windows and door, I scoop her up gently from the chair and place her on the bed.

After turning off the lights, I slide slowly under the covers beside her. She shoots up straight, gasping for air, and stares at me.

"Hey," I say gently, putting my arm around her, and she flinches. "It's me." I sit up, flicking on the light from the nightstand. "It's me, baby." Her wide eyes soften, and she swallows.

"Sorry." She glances down, fisting the blanket. "You scared me."

I struggle to breathe from the devastation of seeing her this way. "I'm so sorry, baby." I run my fingers through her hair, and she tenses under my touch as a stray tear makes its way out of my eye. *Come on, man, get it together.* Sophia's eyes connect with mine, and she reaches up, swiping the drop away.

"You're crying," she says, blinking with glossy eyes. The vacancy in her gaze earlier terrified me. I'm so grateful she's speaking again.

"Sorry." My lips tug downward as I place my hand on her shoulder, pulling her down to the bed so we're facing one another. "I just hate seeing you like this. I wish I could take away every ounce of pain and fear you have and carry it myself."

She tilts her head, a weak smile spreading across her lips. "I would never want you to do that."

"But I would without hesitation." I place my palm on her hip and dip under her T-shirt, craving the warmth of her skin. She freezes at my touch, and I see it in her eyes, the moment it hits her—the moment she fully takes in whatever the hell happened in here tonight —the moment she cracks in two. Sophia's entire body trembles beneath my touch as tears flood her face. My own lip quivers, and I fight back the suffocating emotions flooding my veins at the sight of the only girl I've ever loved breaking down in my arms. I hold her close, allowing her to stifle her sobs in my shoulders until she finally drifts off to sleep.

Holding her tight, I stare at the wall until the sun comes up, plotting all the ways I could murder Seth and get away with it.

49
SOPHIA

Elijah holds open the door of the police station, and I trudge outside after having filed a domestic restraining order against Seth. *I really hope it works.* This temporary injunction will only last fifteen days, and then I'll have to go before a judge to make it permanent. Seth will be at the hearing, and the thought alone makes me want to vomit.

I haven't told Elijah about what happened before the lights turned on. I'm too ashamed.

I should have known it wasn't Elijah. Right?

It may have been dark, but shouldn't I know the touch of the man I love? Why didn't I know it wasn't Elijah immediately?

Elijah held me as we fell asleep last night after the chaos and when his hands touched my skin, all I felt was overwhelming guilt.

"I'm supposed to work today, but I can call out," Dad says as we get close to his and Elijah's trucks.

"No." I shake my head. "It's okay."

"Are you sure?"

"Yes, I'm sure. Honestly. I kinda just wanna go home and watch a movie with Elijah if that's okay."

"Okay." He pulls me in for a tight hug. "Call me if you guys need anything?"

"Of course, sir," Elijah says, shaking his hand.

Dad returns his attention to me. "You don't need to talk to me about what happened last night… But you do need to talk to someone. I made you an appointment with Janine for tomorrow."

I nod, knowing it's long overdue.

Elijah leads me to the passenger side of his truck and buckles me in. He gets in the driver's seat and looks over at me. "I was so worried about you last night."

My eyes fall to my lap. "It was really overwhelming."

He places a hand on my knee, and I flinch, causing him to stiffen. "What's that about?"

"Nothing." I swallow hard. "Just… nothing."

"Sophia," Elijah says softly. "What happened before I showed up?"

I shake my head and look at him. "Nothing, he just was begging for me back and I told him no." I don't want to lie anymore, but I really think Elijah might kill Seth like he promised if he knew the truth. *I can't have more blood on my hands.*

"He didn't hurt you?" His concerned eyes bore into mine.

"No," I lie, swallowing down the bitter word.

A sigh of relief leaves his lips. "Thank God."

I turn my attention out the window as he shifts gears and backs out of the parking space.

Fuck, baby, I forgot how good you taste.

A hot tear rolls down my cheek, and I quickly brush it away.

God, I missed you.

I clasp my hands together to keep them from shaking uncontrollably.

You know you were enjoying it.

The memory pounds into my mind relentlessly, and I fight the urge to throw up the entire way home.

"So, how have things been at school?" Janine asks from her position on the seat across from me. I'm sprawled out on the small couch in her office like I used to do during our sessions.

"Fine," I clip.

"And how have you adjusted to having taken a pause on your therapy?" she asks, holding a pen between her fingers.

"Super," I say sarcastically, and she cracks a smile.

"Would you like to share what brought you here today?"

I sit up and wring my hands together. "Not really."

She nods slightly, her dark ponytail bobbing. "That's okay."

"But I think I should…" I add.

"I'm really happy to hear you say that."

I start off slowly by telling her about my relationship with Elijah and the hurt from him hiding his family. Then I share everything about Seth, from him choking me on the front porch to assaulting me in my bedroom—leaving out any accident-related details—and by the time I'm done, I'm a sobbing mess.

"I just…" I hiccup, blowing my nose into a tissue. "I should have realized it wasn't Elijah."

Janine tilts her head. "You can't blame yourself for being sexually assaulted." Her blunt usage of the words sends a shiver down my spine. But she's right, that's exactly what he did to me. "You had no reason to believe it wasn't Elijah beside you."

Staring at the wooden floor, I think about her words. "Seth sexually assaulted me," I say for the first time out loud, the truth causing my hands to shake.

"Have you considered pressing charges?" Janine asks calmly, and I frown.

"I've filed a restraining order… but I can't file charges for that without proof." Like Elijah said regarding the accident, without proof, there's little chance of a conviction.

"With or without proof, you can still go to the police. Your voice matters, Sophia." I nod slightly. "Have you told Elijah about the sexual assault?"

I gnaw on my lower lip. "No."

"And why do you think that is?"

"I'm ashamed." My body shivers at the memories of Seth's hands on my body. *I'm also afraid of what Elijah might do. He already almost killed Seth for choking me. What would he do if he found out how far Seth really went?*

"Earlier you expressed honesty was an important part of a relationship for you," she points out, and my stomach sinks. "For all your relationships. Do you think keeping these secrets, both from Elijah along with your family, is part of the reason for your recent anxiety attacks?"

"I guess they could be..." Before the accident, I was a person who was always painfully honest. Since then everything has snowballed, turning me into a big fat fucking liar being crushed by the avalanche of my secrets.

"Do you think it's possible you sharing this with Elijah could help release some of the anxiety in your life?"

I think about her question and how the sting of guilt sits in my chest every time I think about keeping this from him. "Yes."

She nods slowly. "It would be healthy for you to have him as a support system as you process the events of that night."

"Yeah... I think you're right."

My mind swirls, thinking about the past week and what the future will look like. Next week CBU and AU play each other in Arizona, and there's no way I can tell Elijah before. He'll never be able to concentrate if he plays, and this could be a career altering opportunity for him.

I make a terrifying decision—I'll tell him about everything.

No more secrets.

But only after he gets back from the game I won't be attending.

"Our time is up, but I want you to take this and give it a read over. It also lists a few support groups if you'd like to take part in one while you're in town."

She hands me a pamphlet, and I glance down at it. There's a statistic on the front that reads, "One in five women have been a victim of sexual violence."

My chest tightens as tears sting my eyes.

I never thought I'd be saying, "Me too."

"What the hell do you mean you're not coming to Arizona?" Sage asks as she and Charlie sit in my room. "Did Janine suggest that?"

"No, it was my decision," I admit hesitantly. "I just... can't."

Sage came over so Charlie and I could fill her in about the accident, and I told them about Seth's two surprise visits, omitting the part where he violated me entirely. I'm not quite ready to share that... especially not before I tell Elijah. In true Sage fashion, she never guilted us for not telling her, and went into straight "fuck Seth" mode.

"Come on, Soph." Sage throws her arm around my shoulder. "There will be, like, eighty thousand people at the game. You won't even be within eyeshot of Seth. As far as he knows, you aren't even there."

I sigh heavily. "I'm just exhausted from it all. I wish we would've talked to the police when the accident happened. It's gotten so out of control."

"You have a restraining order now," Charlie says, rubbing my back. "He can't even come near you, and if he even tried, I know about fifty guys who would break his neck before he had the chance to step foot in your direction."

"We've already bought the tickets and paid for the hotel." Sage smirks, trying to lighten the mood in her usual way. "Let's have a fun time with our friends. Don't let that asshat keep ruining your life."

I'm so sick of him having control over me.

Wringing my hands together, I release a breath. Sage squeezes my shoulder, and I smirk as I glance between her and Charlie. *Why can I never say no to these bitches?* "Fine."

"Yay!" They both cheer, throwing their arms around me.

"Okay." Sage claps her hands together. "I promise to be your personal bodyguard." She clenches her fists and stands in a sumo wrestler pose.

"Wow, you'll really intimidate him."

"Hey!" She throws a hand over her chest. "I may look sweet, but I'm *all* bite."

"Like a little chihuahua," I tease, ruffling her lavender hair, and she jerks away, fake nipping at me.

Maybe everything will be okay.

50

ELIJAH

"Where's your head, Anderson?" Coach Porter shouts at me from the sidelines as I throw another shit pass on the practice field. "Get it together."

"Sorry, Coach," I grumble.

Where's my head? Probably considering all the ways I could make a man disappear and get away with it.

Sophia had a therapy session this morning and is now spending time with her friends, which I hope will help her feel better. But I can't ignore the buzzing in my bones, drawing me to Longwood—to her.

It feels wrong to be at CBU without her after what happened. I know she's a strong woman, but everyone has a breaking point, and I think Sophia just reached hers.

I shake my head, trying to clear the negative thoughts to get through today's practice. The game against Andrews University—aka Seth's school—is in less than a week and if I want any chance of play time, I have to focus on the field.

The boys get in position at the line of scrimmage, and I set up behind Julian. He hikes me the ball, and I scan the field for an open man. In the corner of my eye, I notice Theo pulling forward and launch the ball in his direction. It lands flawlessly in his hands, and he gets another fifteen yards before being tackled.

"Thank you!" Coach Porter shouts, waving his clipboard in the air. "That's what I want!"

My lips curve slightly upward, and I try, and fail, not to think about Sophia the rest of practice. I'm able to improve my performance but by the time we're done, my veins are on fire. Sophia is two hours away, and the thought of going even another minute without seeing her today sounds like absolute torture.

After a hot shower and an agonizing twenty minute long "pep talk" from my coach, I get in my truck to head toward my girl.

It's dusk by the time I reach Longwood and pull into Sophia's driveway. My anxious hands turn off the engine just as Will strolls out of the house, headed to his truck beside mine.

After a calming breath, I hop out. "Hey."

"Hey," Will says, with a tight-lipped smile. "Can't say I'm surprised you're here."

I shift uncomfortably on my heels. "She doing okay?"

He lets out a heavy exhale. "I really don't know. I'm heading to work. I was going to call out but since Sophia got the restraining order… She said she didn't mind."

Clearly a lie.

"Is it okay if I go inside?"

Will huffs out a laugh. "So now you're *asking* for permission?"

My lips curve upward, and I shrug. "Seemed like the right thing to do."

He lets out another heavy exhale. "I can't say I'm thrilled at the idea of my daughter having a boy in her room… but I appreciate how much you care for her." He tilts his head. "I'll be back in the morning. Think you can watch out for her till then?"

"Yes, sir… I think I can handle it."

"Thanks." He sticks out his hand, and I shake it firmly. We make our way to the front door, and he unlocks it, letting me inside. "See you in the morning," he says. "Make sure the house is locked up tight."

"Of course, sir," I reply before shutting the door and locking it behind me.

As I climb the stairs to Sophia's room, I take deep breaths to calm my anxious nerves. Then I knock softly.

"Come in," Sophia bellows.

I push the door open, and she turns around from her closet, lips curving upward when she sees me. She tosses a jacket onto an open suitcase and runs over, catapulting herself into my arms.

I chuckle, holding her frame close to me. "Nice to see you too, baby."

"What are you doing here?"

"Missed you." I walk us toward her bed and lower myself onto the edge. Her legs and arms are wrapped around me, and she hugs tighter.

"I missed you too," she says, her voice cracking on the last word.

Pulling away, I take in her worn face and know I made the right decision to come. Even if I have to leave at seven in the morning to make it back for tomorrow's practice. "How was your day?"

I scoot back on the bed, and we lean against pillows, facing one another. "It was…" She blows out a heavy breath. "A lot."

Reaching out, I tuck a hair behind her ear before resting my hand on her face. "Did the session with Janine go okay?"

"Yeah…" She smiles weakly. "I think it helped."

"I'm glad to hear that."

"It was also really overwhelming." She frowns, and I notice the dark circles under her eyes.

"Anything you want to talk about?"

She nibbles on her lower lip and shakes her head. "Not yet."

"Okay... well, I'm here when you're ready."

"Thank you."

"Don't thank me." I take her hand in mine and press soft kisses on her knuckles. "I'll always be here for you."

"Thank—" I raise my eyebrows. "I love you."

"I love you too, Sunflower." Leaning forward, I kiss her gently. "You seem tired. You should get some rest."

"But you just got here." She juts her lower lip out, looking pouty and adorable.

"I know, and now you can sleep peacefully."

"It *would* be nice to sleep for more than an hour at a time."

My eyes wander toward her bookshelf, scanning it, hoping to find—yep, there it is. I roll off the bed and before Sophia can protest, I've already grabbed the book and slid back under the covers.

"Come here, baby." I position myself against the pillows and gesture for Sophia to join me. Her mouth curves upwards when she sees what's in my hands, and she crawls under the blanket, curling herself into my side. She rests her head on my chest, and I brush her hair down.

"I haven't read this in forever."

"Do you want to read it yourself?"

She shakes her head against me. "No, you read it. Please."

With my arms around her, I bring the book in front of us, flipping to the first page.

"Alice was beginning to get very tired of sitting by her sister on the bank and of having nothing to do. Once or twice she had peeped into the book her sister was reading, but it had no pictures or conversations in it—"

Sophia interrupts me, finishing the sentence in a high-pitched and happy tone. "'And what is the use of a book,' thought Alice, 'without pictures or conversations?'"

I chuckle and continue reading *Alice's Adventures in Wonderland*, with Sophia occasionally taking over to perform her favorite parts.

"You still with me, Sunflower?" I ask halfway through the book. She doesn't respond, her eyes closed and body completely relaxed in my arms. I place the book on the nightstand and reposition us so we're lying down.

Kissing her temple, I mumble quietly against her skin, "And what is the point of life at all without the person you love?"

I'm sitting on a bus full of overly anxious football players on the way to the stadium in Glendale, Arizona. We've been practicing our asses off the last few days making sure we're prepared for the beatdown we're about to give Seth's team in the bowl game tonight. My teeth grind, body tensing at the thought of seeing him.

You've gotta keep your cool, man.

Seth isn't messing up our lives any more than he already has.

He's definitely going to screw with me today, and I'm already mentally preparing myself. Sophia will be cheering me on from the sidelines, and I don't want any reason for her to feel anxious or afraid. I know it wasn't easy to come to Arizona with the possibility of seeing Seth, but the girls insisted, and I can't say I'm upset to know she'll be in my arms after this game is over.

Staring down at my phone, I frown at the reality that the one person I'd call to relieve my anxieties is… gone.

It's the first game I'm not going to be able to call my dad and leave him a voicemail. I know it shouldn't bother me, and it was already ridiculous I did it so long… but I guess leaving those messages was my last lifeline. I finally get why Sophia was so devastated when Chloe's room was gone.

Sometimes there are things we have, or things we do, that still connect us to the ones we've lost. Having that final connection taken away… it's that last big "fuck you."

"What time do the girls get in?" Theo asks, popping up from the seat behind me.

"They should land anytime now."

I check my text thread with Sophia.

SUNFLOWER

SUNFLOWER

Just landed

ME

Good, I didn't like being in different time zones last night

Didn't like? More like barely slept a damn wink.

SUNFLOWER

How are you feeling?

ME

Nervous but excited

You doing okay?

SUNFLOWER

Yes, I'm fine

And you guys got this

You've been practicing your asses off

ME

I know

SUNFLOWER

Hey, Honey Bee?

ME

Yes, Sunflower?

SUNFLOWER

I love you 🤍

ME

I love you most. 🤍

SUNFLOWER

We're headed to the hotel, I'll be cheering for you
from the fifty yard line.

ME

Did you remember the jersey I gave you?

SUNFLOWER

I thought I'd wear Theo's to mix things up

ME

Are you hoping for punishment tonight?

Don't make me pull a Nate Hawkins

SUNFLOWER

Is that supposed to scare me cuz I'm a little
turned on right now

ME

Sophia.

SUNFLOWER

Don't worry. 🥺 I'll have your last name on my
back, number 23 on my chest and face

You can leave your mark on my ass later tonight

ME

Don't make promises you can't keep

SUNFLOWER

I intend on keeping it

My feet feel lighter because I know Sophia's in good spirits
today. I've been so worried about her. The vacancy in her eyes after
the fight with Seth had me terrified I'd never see the light in them
again, but she woke up the next morning *almost* acting like nothing

385

happened. She's a bit off every now and then, but mostly she's been okay, and I'm savoring it. I'm surprised she made a joke about sleeping together though because that's one area she's been distant.

ME

We're almost there, I have to leave my phone in my bag so I can focus today. I'll see you after the game.

Be careful, have fun with the purple Skittle. I love you, Sunflower.

SUNFLOWER

Love you too. Good luck, Honey Bee.

"Bro." I flinch to the sound of Theo from directly over my shoulder. "When did you turn into such a simp?"

"First of all, don't ever read my shit again," I snap at him.

"Aw, come on." He pouts, placing a hand over his chest. "At least now I'll know why Sophia won't be wearing the jersey I gave her."

"I know you're fucking with me but for some reason I'm still angry."

Theo laughs harder. "Like I said, bro, *pussy whipped.*"

"You know what, dick face, I can't wait till you fall in love with some poor girl. I bet you'll be more whipped than the rest of us."

He scrunches his face in disgust, as if it's the most absurd thing he's ever heard. "I'll take all the pussy I can get, but I'll never be controlled by one."

"Wanna bet on it?"

"Bet on it?" He smirks, rubbing his hands together. "What are the stakes?"

"I bet you'll be pussy whipped before we graduate college, and if you are, you have to send me flowers once a month until she breaks your heart."

"What?" Theo scoffs. "Why flowers?"

I shrug. "Sophia loves them. This way she'll enjoy my inevitable win too."

Theo stares at me with an open mouth. "Pussy. Whipped."

"Deal or no deal?" I cock a brow.

"Deal."

Theo settles back in his seat, and I take one last glance at my phone to see another notification.

MARK

MARK

Good luck today, buddy. Not that you need it. So proud of you.

> ME
>
> Thanks

MARK

Cole and I are at Roy's with some of the guys and we're really looking forward to watching you kick ass 🏈

> ME
>
> Awesome

MARK

You doing okay?

A frustrated breath escapes me, guilt settling in my stomach for even considering sharing my game day anxieties with him. It's like I'm replacing my dad, and that thought alone makes me not want to reply at all...

My mind wanders to the last promise I made Dad before he passed.

"Come here," Dad says, holding out his hand as he lies in the hospital bed. I slide mine in his cold palm, and he squeezes it weakly. The strongest man I know, withering to nothing before my damn eyes.

"There's gonna be a day here soon… when I can't be the one to catch you when you fall."

"Don't talk like that. You're gonna get better."

"No," Dad croaks, tears brimming his eyes. "I'm not. I've made peace with that. And I need you to as well."

"No, Dad, I—"

"Please, just listen to me, son…" He interrupts my pleas. "I know Mark's made his mistakes. But I also know that he deserves to know you."

"Come on, I—"

"I want you to meet him after I pass."

"Why? I don't need another dad. You're my dad." Tears blur my vision.

"I know that." He swallows hard. "I'm just asking you to meet him. Give him a chance. I don't want you to be alone."

"I'm not alone," I snap. "I have Mama and Abbs and Nama. I'm fine. Why do I need him?"

"Elijah," he says breathlessly, his hazel eyes boring into mine. "When you grow up, you're gonna realize that even your parents aren't perfect. Mama and I have made our mistakes too… Please, let me go meet the Lord knowing that my boy's family is growing, not dwindling. You deserve to be surrounded by people that love you. And I know he'll love you. So I'm begging you, just give him a chance. Can you do that for me, Buck?"

"Yes," I manage out between sobs. "I can do that for you, Dino."

We're almost at the stadium, and time's running out as I contemplate which answer to send. The *everything's good* lie or the *I might just kill that motherfucker when I get my hands on him* truth.

I settle for the middle ground.

ME

Just praying I can keep my temper in check.

MARK

You will. Keep a level head and show that idiot
you're the bigger man. We'll handle him legally.
Love you

ME

Love you too.

*You deserve to be surrounded by people that love you. And I
know he'll love you.*

"Alright, boys," Noah shouts as we're all huddled on the side of the
field before the start of the game. "We're going to go out there and
kick AU's ass. One, because we're the better team. And two, because
they're a bunch of asshole licking pricks." The guys chuckle, and
Noah winks at me. "Let's make sure we have a reason to celebrate
ringing in the new year tonight!"

The huddle erupts in shouts and howls.

"Stingrays on three!" Noah shouts over the noise. "One,
two—"

"Stingrays!"

The game's flying by, and we're already past halftime. The third
quarter just started and as Noah said, these guys are pricks. I don't
know if Jonathan or Seth said something, but they're not giving us an
inch of space. Every chance he can, Seth sneaks through and tackles
Noah.

My blood boils at the sight of him. Strutting around the field like
everything is fucking normal.

What I'd give to see that guy behind bars. The restraining order
was served a few days ago, and I pray to God he adheres to it. *If he
doesn't... I might be the one who ends up locked up.*

If it's not Seth sacking Noah, it's the other defensive linemen. Each time Noah gets up a little slower.

"You've got to be fuckin' kidding me!" Coach Porter shouts at the referee, pulling at his dark brown hair. "That was intentional."

The ref ignores his protest. The ball is overturned, and defense runs back on the field.

"Shit, man, are you okay?" I ask Noah as he limps over to the sideline, pulling off his helmet.

"That fucker is hurting me on purpose," Noah snaps. "Seth tried to twist my arm on the way down last tackle. And you don't want to know the shit he's whispering in my ear."

"Caruso! Anderson!" Coach Porter shouts. Noah and I jog over, and he glances between us. "Noah, you're sitting out a few plays."

"Come on, I—"

Coach puts up a hand, silencing him. "We're up by two touchdowns, and I don't know what you did to piss those boys off, but it's obvious they're out for blood. So you're sitting a few plays out," he repeats firmly. What *we* did to piss *them* off? If the guys knew what Seth did to Sophia, he would already be in a motherfucking body bag.

"Yes, Coach," Noah grumbles.

"Anderson, can you keep up the momentum?" he asks, turning his attention to me.

"Yes, Coach," I reply, mirroring Noah.

Ten minutes of game time passes, and both teams have scored another touchdown, bringing the score to twenty-eight to fourteen. I ignore Seth entirely as we get into position for another play, afraid it'll screw with my concentration.

Glancing up at Julian, I yell, "Seventeen–thirty-two–twelve—hike!" He launches the ball, and I catch it easily, shuffling backwards while looking downfield. A large frame appears in the corner of my eye just before I'm slammed to the ground.

Ouch.

"Tell your little bitch to keep her mouth shut unless she wants a repeat," Seth snarls before pushing himself off me. "She'll know what I mean." The sinister look in his eyes has me gritting my teeth together so hard my jaw aches.

I slam a fist against the ground, pushing myself up as my blood boils. "Keep *your* fucking mouth shut." *He wouldn't be so damn stupid.*

His eyes flash with anger as he takes a step toward me. One of his teammates grabs him by the shoulders, dragging him away. *Lucky son of a bitch.*

We get back on the line of scrimmage, and my breathing is unsteady. Both from the adrenaline and the absolute fucking fury. Sweat drips down my forehead, and grass stains cover every inch of my uniform.

Come on, Anderson.

Show him you're the bigger man.

"Red. Forty–ten–twenty-two—hike!"

The ball lands in my hands, and I turn my attention downfield, spotting Desmond wide open. I cock my arm back and send the ball spiraling through the air. Desmond catches it just as Seth appears next to me.

He doesn't touch me but comes close enough I can hear him over the crowd. "Man, I'd forgotten how good Sophia's pussy tasted." My head snaps in his direction, every muscle going rigid. "I hope she enjoyed the walk down memory lane as much as I did."

Red flashes in my eyes and a murderous expression flickers across Seth's face as he backs away.

"Come on, E," Julian says, shoving me back toward the line of scrimmage. "Don't let him get in your head."

Seth's words surround me like an endless echo I can't escape.

I'd forgotten how good Sophia's pussy tasted.

I'd forgotten how good Sophia's pussy tasted.

I'd forgotten how good Sophia's pussy tasted.

Mindlessly, I get back in position.

What the hell is he talking about?

"Hike!" I yell by reflex.

He hopes she enjoyed it?

I think about Sophia's reaction after the fight with Seth as I shuffle backward, scanning for an open man.

Memories of her flinching at my touch ricochet in my mind. Sophia was completely naked when I left her in bed and fully dressed when I found them. My eyes scan frantically for an open man, but I struggle to focus.

What the hell happened before I showed up?

51
SOPHIA

Elijah cocks his arm back, throwing the ball downfield, and it lands perfectly in Theo's hands. Sage squeals next to me, and my gaze flicks back to Elijah just as Seth slams into his side. Their padded bodies bounce across the grass, and I throw a hand over my mouth.

Seth pushes himself off Elijah, who remains on the ground. Seconds pass, and a breath catches in my lungs.

Why isn't he moving?

The entire stadium goes silent as the refs run over to him. My heart pounds hard against my ribcage.

"What's happening?" I whisper, and Sage says nothing.

No.

No, no, no, no, no.

"Come on, Honey Bee. Get up," I mutter to myself. Seconds feel like hours, and my hands shake against my side. "Elijah!" I shuffle down the row. *I knew Seth would do something like this. I fucking knew it.*

"Sophia, wait!" Sage shouts, grabbing my shoulder, but I throw her hand off me. I finally make it to the stairs as the medic team rushes toward Elijah, and I sprint down to the barrier of the field.

"That's my boyfriend, please let me through," I say in a firm tone to the security guard.

"Sorry, but I can't," he says. "It's policy."

"Fuck your policy!" I yell at him, losing my shit completely. "Let me through right now!"

He stares down at me, unmoving from his position. Turning my back, I take a few small steps, then spin around, bolting past him.

"Hey, stop!" he shouts after me. I run a few short strides, and then two powerful arms grab me from behind.

"Put me down!" I kick my legs wildly. "Put me down!"

I look insane, but I don't fucking care.

I have to see him.

I need to see him.

I can't do this again.

This can't happen again.

Why isn't he moving?

"I'm sorry," Noah says gently after filling me in on what the doctor told Coach Porter. "That's all we know."

"So what?" I snap, pacing the hospital waiting room. "He's unconscious and none of us can see him because we don't share his blood?"

I glance around at the burly guys all sitting in the chairs around me. Usually you can't get them to shut up, but the room is quieter than our campus library.

"It's protocol, Soph," Charlie says gently. "He's over eighteen. So besides the coach, only his family can get information or visit him."

"This is ridiculous. Elijah's mom can't get a flight for two days because of the holiday. He shouldn't be alone." I collapse into a chair, and Sage settles next to me. "I can't do this again."

Memories of Chloe's accident flood to the forefront of my mind. Everything from the past few months with Seth… It's just all too much. Tears blur my vision, and I try to push them down, but it's no use.

"Everything's gonna be fine, Joey," Sage says, rubbing my back as Charlie places her hand on my leg from the other side.

"He's going to be okay," Charlie says assuredly.

"You don't know that," I snap at her, my voice cracking.

A large hand rests loosely on my knee as I hear a familiar husky voice say, "Hey, angel face." My eyes pop open to the sight of Theo glancing around the room, and then he drops his voice to a low whisper. "Think you might wanna be Sunny Anderson for a few hours?"

Hope blooms in my chest as my heart rate accelerates. "Are you suggesting what I think you are?"

His blue-green eyes bore into mine. "They'll only allow family to visit him in ICU. As far as I can tell, you have an ID suggesting you are." He smiles and winks before striding away. Sage nudges my back, and I stand up, pulling my fake out of the back of my phone case.

Deep breaths calm me, and I head to the front desk as Elijah's teammates smile at me in encouragement.

"Excuse me," I say squeakily to a nurse typing away on her computer.

Her fingers pause, and she glances up at me, expression blank. "Yes?"

"Can I please speak to the doctor on Elijah Anderson's case?"

"May I ask your relation to the patient?" she asks in a monotone voice, returning to type something on her computer.

"I'm his wife."

Her eyes snap to mine. "Can I please see some ID?" I slide my fake across the small counter, and she picks it up, examining it. I risk a glance at Coach Porter, who cocks a brow at me but doesn't blow my cover. "Young love, huh? Let me go see what I can do."

She leaves the room, and I turn around to all eyes on me as slaphappy grins spread across their faces. *Holy shit. Did that actually work?* I give a subtle thumbs up, and the boys all cheer and high five.

"*Shhh,*" I say, gesturing downward with my hands.

Coach Porter turns toward the boys with folded arms, leveling them with a single look.

"Sorry, Mrs. Anderson," Theo coos, and hearing that does something funny to my insides. The thrill of it *almost* distracts me enough to forget the entire reason we're here in the first place.

The seconds tick by slower than sand in an hourglass as I wait for the doctor to come through the doors.

"Mrs. Anderson?" someone calls out, and Sage kicks me when I don't respond.

"Here," I say, jumping up and taking faltering steps toward him.

He introduces himself as Dr. Lowken and ushers me into the hallway, away from prying eyes. "Elijah has suffered a moderate head injury."

A full ten seconds pass as I formulate a response. "Has he woken up yet?"

"Briefly. But we have him sedated to allow his body time to rest while the concussion subsides, while also ensuring he doesn't accidentally hurt himself by waking up."

This can't be happening again. "How…" Letters stick to my tongue as I try to blend them together to create a cohesive sentence. I straighten my shoulders for a sense of composure when on the inside it feels like my bones are jelly. "How long till he wakes up?"

"Typically, we keep patients under for twenty-four to forty-eight hours. The outlook for your husband is promising." *My husband.* "His brain activity seems to be fully functioning but at this point, it's mostly a waiting game."

"So he'll be okay?"

"The outlook is *very* promising." His words mildly relieve my anxieties, but he doesn't confirm anything for sure. I've watched enough *Grey's Anatomy* to know doctors can't make promises... and patients who should easily recover can die.

"When can I see him?"

"We're running a couple of tests, but you should be able to see him in the next few hours."

"Okay, thank you," I say weakly.

"If you have any further questions, please don't hesitate to ask." He shakes my hand before leaving me in the hallway. My back slams against the wall, tears streaming down my face. I sink to the floor like a crumpled piece of paper, staring at the ugly pastel wallpaper across from me as my mind spirals straight into the black hole of worst-case scenarios.

I'm not sure how much time has passed when a large frame sits next to me. An arm slides around my shoulders, pulling me in, and I press my head to their chest.

"He's gonna be okay, Soph," Theo's warm voice says.

"How can you be sure?" I croak out as tears spill from my eyes.

"Because Elijah's a tough motherfucker." He releases a breathy laugh. "Even if he doesn't let anyone see the stuff he's dealing with. He's gotten through the last year. He's strong enough to get through this too."

I furrow my brows up at him. "You knew about Elijah's family?"

"E's my best friend. We live together. He never talked about it with me, but yeah, I knew about his dad."

"I should call Elijah's mom. Let her know I'm gonna get to see him."

Coach Porter's been giving her updates too, but I think it makes her feel better hearing from people who are close to Elijah.

"Do you want me to do it?" Theo offers. I think about how hard it was to keep my composure last time I talked to Jenna.

"Would you?" I ask weakly. *I don't think I can hear her pained voice on the other side of the phone again.*

"Of course," he says, helping me off the floor.

I tell him everything the doctor told me and give him Jenna's number, and he excuses himself to go make the call.

My eyes flutter shut, and I take deep, calming breaths. When I open them again, the room spins around me as Seth's eyes connect with mine. His lips curve up into a devious smile, and I step backward. The air expels from my lungs when I slam against the wall.

"You're not allowed to be here," I say calmly as my insides rattle with fear—rage—pure and utter fucking hatred.

He steps closer, narrowing his dark, dangerous eyes at me, and I stop breathing. "I told you not to fuck with me, Sophia."

My back is flat against the wall as he reaches me. I want to scream. I want to run, but I'm frozen still. "You're not allowed to be within a hundred feet of me."

"Come on, don't be like that." A shiver runs down my spine as he towers over me. "You saw what I'm capable of. Next time I'll make sure he doesn't wake up."

Every cell in my body vibrates with disgust for a man I used to love. Somehow I think that just adds gasoline to the furious fire.

"Why are you doing this?" I ask weakly, a single tear streaming down my face as my resolve starts to break.

Don't let him see you fall apart.

Don't let him see the power he has over you.

"Isn't it obvious?" He laughs mockingly, reaching up, and I flinch as he wipes away the tear. "I'm protecting you, baby girl." My lips twitch at the familiar nickname I've come to loathe. He places his hand on my face, and I slap him away. "Now is that any way to thank me?" he snaps, caging me flush against the wall. His warm body presses into mine, and I have to physically hold my mouth shut to stop the sob threatening to rip out of me.

"Get the fuck away from her!" Theo's voice booms down the hallway, and a shaky breath escapes my lips.

Seth's head whips in Theo's direction. "You really wanna stick up for this cunt?" Once again, Seth's words give me whiplash. Saying he's protecting me one minute and calling me a cunt the next.

Theo grabs Seth by the neck and throws him against the other wall. "Call her a cunt one more time and see if you don't end up in the fucking morgue."

Seth pushes him off, and Theo stumbles backwards just as the door to the waiting room opens and Charlie, along with half of the CBU football team, pours out. Seth's eyes bounce between them all, and I can tell the moment his tiny brain realizes he's outnumbered.

"This isn't over, baby girl," Seth promises. *Why can't it just be over?*

Theo throws his arm around my shoulder, pulling me against him. "Breathe, angel face."

On my first inhale, a loud sob erupts from my mouth, and I slap my hand over it. My vision blurs as Theo pulls me through the hallways to God knows where. A door opens and closes, and then Theo nudges me to sit down. I wipe chaotically at my face, glancing around at the small, empty room with a few tables and chairs.

"Sophia," Theo commands with a serious tone I've never heard from him before. "Breathe."

Seconds turn to minutes as I force my pounding heart to settle and my breathing returns to a normal pace. Theo never once pushes me or shows any signs of frustration.

"Shit," I say, exasperated once I can finally breathe. "I'm supposed to be strong for him, and I'm a pathetic mess who can't even go five minutes without crying."

"Sophia, no one blames you for being upset. E's..." He pauses. "You know... And then your ex... and I know it's a lot for you. It's okay to not be okay."

"No." I shake my head. "I can do this. I can handle this. I can be there for him."

Mint chocolate chip ice cream sticks to my fingers as I shift in the uncomfortable chair of the waiting room. When will people stop treating me like a baby? I wanna know what's happening too.

"Elijah is going to be fine," Theo says, pulling me out of the unwelcome memory.

My head snaps toward him. "Is he?"

A flicker of doubt flashes in Theo's eyes before he schools his expression. "Yes."

"You're a shit liar." I roll my eyes, and he releases a breathy laugh. My phone rings, and I pull it out to see *Dad* flashing across the screen. "I have to answer. He's already called ten times."

"Do you want me to leave?"

I stare down at the phone and shake my head. "No."

The little red button is begging for the touch of my thumb, but I tap green instead and bring the phone to my ear.

"Hey, Dad," I say weakly.

"Sophia?" His voice comes through so loudly I have to pull the phone away. "I've been calling you for hours!"

I swallow hard. "I know. I'm sorry."

"I saw the game on TV," he says, and I'm teetering on the edge of a skyscraper. "Is Elijah okay?"

I'm shoved off the building, hurtling toward the ground at record speed. "No." Theo places his arm loosely over my back, squeezing my shoulder. It's just enough to keep me from making impact.

"I, well, I saw—I saw it was Seth who took him out…"

"He showed up here," I admit, the words slipping from my mouth.

The line is quiet for a moment. So quiet I think he hung up. "He *what?*"

"He showed up here," I mumble. "At the hospital. And he-he…"

Fuck. Tears blur my vision again.

"Are you alone, Bear?" I glance at Theo and shake my head. "Bear?"

"No, I'm with a friend."

"Can I talk to them?"

I glance again at Theo, who pulls his brows together, the expression only deepening when I hold out the phone. He takes it without hesitation, placing it on his ear.

"Yes," Theo says. "Of course, sir." His arm tenses over my shoulders. "Yes, I understand." He clears his throat and shakes his head. "No, of course not. I'd never let that happen." More words from my dad I can't hear. "You too, sir."

Theo gives me back the phone, and I promise my dad I'll call every few hours to check in.

"What'd he say to you?" I ask Theo on our way back to the waiting room.

He lets out a low chuckle. "Basically just if anything happens to you while you're out here, he'll hunt me down, chop my balls off, and feed them to me."

My eyes go wide as saucers. "What?!"

His lips curl upwards, and he shrugs. "I may have paraphrased slightly... but that was the gist of it."

A few hours later, I'm sitting on an uncomfortable chair in the waiting room and my phone buzzes. I flip it over to see a notification from Charlie.

CHARLIE

CHARLIE

I should've sent this to you sooner. I'm sorry it took me so long.

(1) Video Attached

52
SOPHIA

"It's been two days. He should've woken up by now," I tell Noah, who's sitting across from me on one of the uncomfortable chairs a nurse brought in yesterday. Elijah's no longer in the ICU so they've allowed the boys to come in too. Theo and Julian sit on the floor with their heads against the wall. Sage and Charlie wanted to stay, but I insisted they head back to Florida when the rest of the team left. I haven't been able to even think about the video Charlie sent me. I can't think about any of that until Elijah wakes up.

"Today," Noah says quietly. "He'll wake up today."

"I hope so…" I squeeze Elijah's limp, cold hand before placing it back under the warm blanket. "Jenna should be here tonight."

"Good." Noah clears his throat. "Our flight's scheduled for this afternoon… but if you need us to stay longer, we'll push it again."

"No…" I shake my head. "I'll be fine until Elijah's mom gets here."

"Only if you're sure," Noah says.

"I am… I'm gonna go for a walk." Theo stands as I pull myself away from Elijah's bedside. "Alone," I say, and he sinks back to the floor. "I appreciate you guys looking out for me. But I think I can handle a stroll around the hospital."

Seth already left with his team, so I'm no longer checking over my shoulder at every turn.

"Fine," Theo grumbles. "Bring me back something from the vending machine, would you?"

I wander the halls, unsure what I'm even searching for until I stumble upon it. There's a small sign on the door: Glendale Hospital Chapel.

A shaky breath leaves my lips as I push through the door. The room is empty aside from a few chairs and a cross in front of a false stained glass window. There's a pew at the very front, and I make my way toward it, kneeling on the soft cushion.

"Hey, God," I say out loud awkwardly. "It's me... Sophia." I shift uncomfortably on my knees. "Sophia Summers... I don't know if you can even hear me... or if you even exist. Sorry, that was kinda rude of me to suggest you're not real when I'm talking to you. Anyway... I know Elijah believes in you, so if you could listen for his sake, I'd appreciate it." The sound of me cracking my fingers echoes through the room. "I, um, I need to pray for Elijah. Elijah Anderson. He's not doing so great, and if you could send an angel or someone to help him out, that would be really, really appreciated." The awkwardness fades as my eyes blur with tears. "I know I've messed up... a lot... but please, God. Please just let him be okay." I take a deep breath. "I can't lose him." A sob rips through me, ricocheting off the walls and piercing my ears. "Please." I wipe the tears from my eyes. "Um... Amen." I push myself off the pew and leave the small chapel.

Theo's Doritos bag swings from my fingers as I reenter Elijah's room. "Any change?"

"Nope," Theo mumbles, a hoodie thrown over his eyes as he's sprawled uncomfortably between two chairs. Julian and Noah are gone, probably to the cafeteria.

Elijah lays unmoving, the same as the past two days, looking peaceful—calm. The doctors perform tests on him every few hours to check his responsiveness, and so far the results have been good.

Hopefully they can wean him off the medication today. I notice the ketchup stain on my sleeve from yesterday's lunch.

"I think I'm gonna go to the hotel and shower," I say, suddenly feeling about as gross as I look in two-day-old clothes.

Theo pulls his hoodie off and rolls his head to look at me. "The guys will be back in a few. I'll come with you."

"You don't ha—"

"Sophia," Theo says sharply, standing up. "Please stop fighting me every time I try to protect you."

I chuck the Doritos bag at him. "Okay, damn, no need to go all King Triton on me."

He smirks. "Listen, I know you can handle yourself. But if something happened to you, your dad would kill me while Elijah digs the ditch."

I roll my eyes as Julian and Noah stride back into the room.

"We're gonna head out and clean up," Theo tells them. "Let us know if anything changes?"

"I'll come with," Julian replies. "I reek like a stale locker room."

"Alright, I'll stay here," Noah says. "Can you grab my charger? My phone's almost dead."

"Yeah, sure," Julian replies.

We head back to the hotel, and I almost fall asleep in the Uber. My body feels heavy as we trudge to the rooms. Once I get inside Elijah's and Noah's room, I take a steaming hot shower, trying to ignore the shit storm that is my life right now. I stumble out of the bathroom, towel wrapped around me, and collapse on the bed.

A loud bang rips me from a deep sleep. Muffled sounds blur into my ears, along with another loud knock.

"Sophia!"

Groaning, I force my eyes open and roll out of bed. The towel falls off me, and I snatch it up, resecuring it and hurrying to the door.

I open it, peeking my head out to a very worried and impatient Theo. "I've been calling you for an hour. Are you okay?"

"I fell asleep," I say groggily, and his expression softens.

"I figured. But let's go, okay? Noah texted they were stopping the sedation a few hours ago."

"Did he wake up?" I ask hopefully.

"Not yet." Theo frowns.

I rush to dress, and we make it to the hospital half an hour later.

God, I miss his voice.

Theo pushes open the door to Elijah's room.

"Do you think he—" The words fall off my tongue at the sight of Elijah propped up and talking with Noah. I run over to him, and his tired smile widens.

"Hey, Sunflower," he says weakly, reaching for me, and I slide my hand in his.

"Oh, thank God." I lean over him. "Thank you, God. Thank you." My shoulders tremble, and Elijah places his hand weakly on my back.

"You scared the shit out of us, man," Julian tells Elijah.

"Yeah." Theo clears his throat. "Thought I was gonna have to find another roommate."

Elijah laughs weakly. "Love you guys too."

"Let's give them some privacy," Noah says, and the guys funnel out, the door clicking shut.

Elijah looks at me. "Have I told you today that I love you?" Those three words open the flood gates, and I fall against his chest, sobbing.

"Babe," he says gently, rubbing my back. "Why are you crying? It's okay. I'm okay. I promise."

"Why am I crying?!" I bolt up, glaring at him. "Are you kidding me? I saw your body bounce across the damn football field, Elijah. It was fucking terrifying. I have half a mind to make you quit football altogether." The corner of his mouth curves upwards.

"I'm fine, babe. I swear." He rubs his knuckles along my face before taking both my hands and placing them on his chest. It rises and falls beneath them as his heart pounds against my palms. "You feel that? It's beating. I'm here. I'm not going anywhere."

"I can't lose someone I love again," I whisper as the tears continue to stream down my face. "I can't lose *you.*"

"You won't," he assures me with a soft smile. "I'm right here, baby. I told you I'd never leave you."

"The idea of losing you fucking petrifies me. So yes. I am crying. And no, you better never let that happen again. Because I love you so much, I can't even breathe, Elijah."

He pulls me in for a soft kiss. "The doctor said I'm going to be fine. I just have to rest for a few weeks." An amused smirk forms on his lips. "He said he'd be back to talk to my *wife* later."

"They would only let family see you." I smile with flattened lips. "So I used my fake."

"You didn't think to tell them you're my sister?"

"Feels weird to say you're the sister of someone you're fucking."

A low chuckle escapes him. "I guess it would be pretty weird if they walked in on us doing this." He slowly pulls me toward him for a gentle kiss. "I love you, Sunflower."

"I love you too, Honey Bee."

53

ELIJAH

My body aches.

My mouth tastes like shit.

And my head throbs to the rhythm of "xanny" by Billie Eilish.

I want to take a damn shower, and even more than I care about all those things, I want to wring Seth's neck and watch the life drain from his eyes for everything he's put us through.

Theo, Noah, and Julian just left for the airport, and Sophia's head is resting on the mattress at my side. She exhales a shaky breath as I play with her hair.

"I really missed you," she whispers.

"I'm right here, sweetheart." She looks up at me. Something's swimming in those gorgeous green eyes, I just can't decipher exactly what it is. "You okay?"

She nibbles on her lower lip. "I need to show you something."

Her serious tone causes my stomach to sink. "Okay…" I scoot over in the bed, giving her space to sit next to me with our backs propped against the raised mattress. She glances at me, and I rest my forehead against hers. "You can tell me anything, remember?"

She nods, and we turn to her phone as she presses play on a video.

"Kiwi" by Harry Styles plays low. The camera angle shows the front seat of a car with a driver and a blonde passenger. Squinting at the phone, I realize it's Seth and Sophia. She does something silly, and he reaches over, touching her leg.

"Why are you showing me this?" I ask, wishing I could erase the visual permanently from my memory.

"Just watch," she whispers.

A flicker of something appears in front of the windshield before a loud bang explodes from the speaker.

"Sophia…"

Yelling starts, and doors slam. I'm assuming they're getting out of the car. The angle now makes it impossible to see anything of use —flashes of green and blue—but the voices are clear.

"Is this what I think it is?" I say almost at a whisper.

Sophia doesn't reply, but her sniffles next to me, along with the next few minutes of dialogue, give me hope that just maybe, this could be our ticket to finally end this nightmare with Seth.

"Where did you get this?" I ask as my hands shake.

"Charlie sent it to me."

"She had it this entire time?" *Are you shitting me?* "This whole thing could have ended months ago?"

"Elijah…" Sophia tilts her head at me. "I can't be mad at Charlie for being afraid. Even if I had this myself, I don't know if I would've had the courage to use it until a few weeks ago."

"Is that what you want to do?" I ask hesitantly—hopefully.

She nods slowly, and I can breathe for the first time in weeks. "I didn't want to do anything until I showed it to you. But I'm ready to turn it over."

I reach up, brushing tears off her cheeks. "I'm so proud of you for being brave."

She swallows hard. "I'm not brave… I'm balls out terrified."

"No, you're balls of steel." She laughs. "We'll see Mark together, okay?"

"Okay." She nods, and I pull her to me, kissing her lips gently.

"Knock knock," a familiar sweet voice says as my door opens. A wide smile breaks across my face at the sight of my mom standing in the doorway. Sophia gets off the bed, rushing over, and Mom pulls her in a tight hug.

A head pops around the corner, and my eyes widen as my sister comes barreling toward me, flying past Sophia.

She throws herself on me and I wince in pain, putting an arm around her. "Missed you too, Abbs."

Laying her head on my chest, she hugs tighter. "Eli, you scared the hell outta me."

"Just giving you a taste of your own medicine." I smile, taking Sophia's hand as she returns to my bedside.

Abbs looks up at her. "This must be the girlfriend Mama was telling me all about," she says, standing and pulling Sophia into a hug.

"I hope so." Sophia blushes with an awkward laugh.

"I still can't believe it." Abbs's gaze flicks between us. "Jesus, I really was gone a long time."

"Abigail, don't use the Lord's name in vain," Mom chastises.

"Sorry, Mama." Abbs smiles sweetly.

"So how's it feel to be back on the outside?" I ask Abbs.

"I wasn't in prison." She narrows her eyes at me. "But yeah, feels nice."

"I missed you."

She rolls her eyes. "Missed you too, Eli."

"Well, you'll be able to spend plenty of time together next year at CBU," Mom says. *What kinda bomb is that?*

"Excuse me?" I laugh in disbelief, eyes bouncing between them.

"Yep, Abbs got her acceptance letter in the mail last month, but I was waiting till we figured out all the details to tell you."

"You mean you were waiting to make sure they wouldn't retract my acceptance when they found out where I'd spent the first half of my senior year?"

Mom frowns at her. "That too…"

My fingertips trail along Sophia's arms as we lie facing one another in my bed. It's been over a month since we left Arizona, and I'm finally feeling like myself. Sophia had her first deposition today for Seth's case, and she's barely spoken a word.

"How do you feel?" I ask, pausing my touch on her hip.

"I don't know... relieved? Anxious?" She pauses. "Afraid?"

Her eyes flicker with painful uncertainty, and my frown deepens. "Why are you afraid?"

"What if he doesn't get convicted?" Her hands tremble, and I take them in mine, placing them between us. "What if he comes back?"

"Sophia." I kiss her knuckles. "I would die before I ever let him do anything to you."

She tilts her head and smiles faintly. "That's a bit dramatic, don't you think?"

"No. I'm dead serious. This thing with Seth isn't a game, and he's obviously not mentally stable. I promise to protect you regardless of the outcome of the trial."

She shakes her head. "You can't always be around..."

"Your dad put in an alarm system, so you're safe in Longwood. And you already know my place is yours. If Seth tries anything... I will put an arrow directly between his eyes."

"You're so violent when you're possessive," she teases.

"I'm only violent when *absolutely* necessary. You know that."

"I know."

"Trust me, I'm ready to move forward from this as much as you are." I sigh, unsure how to bring up what's been bugging me since the game. I've tried to forget about Seth's words, but I was cleared for *all* physical activity two weeks ago, and Sophia and I have yet to be intimate. His words paired with her avoidance of the subject are really starting to concern me. "Baby, I need to ask you something…" She places a hand on my hip, tracing circles on my skin. "Seth said something at the game before I got hurt." I swallow hard, praying he was full of shit. "He said he… tasted you."

Her hand stills on my side as her mouth parts open. She doesn't speak for an excruciatingly long time.

"Sophia?" I say gently as my heart stops beating. "Why did he say that?"

Her eyes fall, a tear sliding down her face, and I tip her gaze back to mine. "I didn't cheat on you." *She seriously thinks that's where my head is at?*

"What?" I drag a hand through her hair. "I know that. Of course I know that, baby. Please, tell me what happened. What did he do to you?"

I tug her closer, and she cries into my chest. *What could he have possibly done to elicit this reaction?*

"We don't have to talk about it yet if you're not ready," I tell her, even though my entire body aches to know what the hell is going on. She's been seeing a therapist a few times a week, even found a new one on campus with help from Janine, but maybe she still needs time to process everything.

I know I do.

That's exactly the reason I started therapy too.

"No, I'm ready. It's just… I'm so sorry," she whimpers. "I should have realized it wasn't you. I should've known… I should have known it wasn't you."

Pulling away, I nudge her gaze to meet mine. "Please, explain." My heart pounds against my rib cage. "Baby, I need you to explain because I pray to God what I'm thinking is worse than what he actually did."

She takes deep breaths, composing herself, and I feel like I'm miles under the ocean as the pressure completely crushes me. "The night… the night when you came back and Seth had me against the wall…"

"Yeah?" I say, encouraging her to keep going.

She gnaws on her lower lip, avoiding my eyes. "When I woke up that night, you were in bed. You were touching me with your fingertips and kissing my body. It was so dark I couldn't see, so I just enjoyed it. Enjoyed *you*." She swallows hard, and my skin prickles at her confession because I know she's wrong. I did none of those things. "You went between my legs and… started…" I throw a hand over my mouth to hide my disgust. *He wasn't lying.* Acid rises in my throat, and I'm trying not to show my fury out of fear she won't continue.

"He finally spoke," she croaks out. "And I realized it was him immediately. I kicked him in the face, and he flew off my bed." Her entire body trembles, and I hold her tight. "That's when the chaos started. And I turned on the light and found clothes because I felt exposed." She lets out a shaky breath. "So exposed—and Seth wasn't taking no for an answer. He said he wanted me back, and it was so confusing and disgusting." Her entire body trembles, and I hold her tighter. "I really thought it was you."

"I don't blame you, baby. I would never blame you."

"I should have known," she says with pleading eyes. "I should have *known* it wasn't you. I've been so worried you would be angry with me for not knowing."

"Sophia." I rub my thumb along her jaw. "The only person I'm angry with is Seth. If he weren't already in jail, I'd fucking kill him with my bare hands right now."

I still haven't totally thrown out the possibility.

"You're not mad at me?" she whispers, and my chest tightens at the knowledge she's been carrying around this burden.

"Of course not. Sophia, I love you. And I'm so sorry that happened to you, and I'm so angry I wasn't there to stop it. I'm so incredibly sorry."

"It's not your fault," she says weakly.

"I shouldn't have come through your window," I mutter to myself. "Then he never would have gotten in." *I want to throw a fist at the wall for this partially being my fault.* "Is there anything else you want to tell me? I want us to have a clean slate so we can move forward—together."

"No." She shakes her head. "That's everything."

"I just..." My breathing is rapid, and I attempt to steady it. "I wish you would have told me before so you didn't have to deal with this alone."

"I wanted to tell you... but since you were playing Seth, I didn't want you to be distracted. I knew it was an important game for you." She clears her throat. "And then you got hurt..."

"Sunflower, I appreciate you trying to think about my game, but if you think for even one moment I would prefer you keep me in the dark so I can focus on the field, I haven't done my job of proving to you just how much you mean to me. *You* are the only thing I care about. If you have something on your mind, please, baby, please, don't keep it from me. Okay?" She nods slowly. "I love you."

"I love you too."

I rub my hands up her thighs, careful not to venture up too high. "I'm so sorry for what he did to you." She frowns, flicking her eyes away, and I tip her chin so she meets my gaze again. "I don't want you to feel any pressure for us to be physical."

Her brows furrow. "You don't want to be physical?"

"What?" I scoff. "Baby, of course I do. But everything is at your pace."

"We haven't had sex in over a month," she says as if I haven't been counting the days.

"Okay? And I'll wait as long as it takes for you to be ready. I don't want to do anything you're not comfortable with."

"Elijah, as of right now, *he's* the last person to touch me there." She shivers, and a look of disgust crosses her face. "I need that to change."

"Are you sure you're ready?" I ask hesitantly.

"Please… Please show me you still love me."

"Nothing could ever make me stop loving you, sweetheart." I tilt my head, cupping her face in my hands.

"I was afraid you wouldn't want me anymore," she says, low and desperate. "That you'd be disgusted by me."

My lips part, devastated by her unfounded fears. "Sunflower, nothing in our lives could ever make me stop wanting you. Never be afraid of that. You can always be honest with me. God, I love you." Dragging my hands down to her shoulders, I squeeze them lightly. "I love you so much, baby." My hands fall to her soft waist, gliding underneath the fabric. "I always crave you, and that will never ever change. Do you hear me? Never."

"I hear you."

Gripping her hips tightly, I look deep into her eyes. "If you ever want to stop, just say so."

"Okay," she says nervously as her pretty lips tug upwards. I pull the shirt over her head and toss it to the ground. On my knees, her perfect exposed breasts are directly at my eye level.

"Fuck, baby. You're so damn perfect." I lean in, sucking her nipple between my teeth, and she moans. "I missed you." My hands wander down to her waistband, and I'm desperate for her, but I'm worried it could be a trigger. "Is this okay for you?" I ask timidly.

"Yes," she says breathlessly. "Please, keep going."

I gently tug down her shorts and panties, leaving her fully naked in front of me. "I'm so in love with every perfect part of you." My hands wander her body hungrily, admiring every inch of her soft skin. I trail kisses on the insides of her thighs as my stubble scratches against her. She grabs a fistful of my hair and pulls me upwards, angling my face directly over her clit. I flick my tongue over her most sensitive spot.

She falls flat on the bed, and I tug her ass to the edge. Leaning down, I glide my tongue across her clit again, sucking up every drop of my sunflower's sweet nectar.

My torment continues until she's moaning and squirming beneath me.

"God, I love you," I hum against her.

"You know what I love?" she says teasingly.

"What's that?"

"When your hard cock is inside me and you fuck me into another galaxy." My eyes snap to hers, and she's biting her lower lip, looking happy, carefree, amused.

"Mmm, there's my needy girl." I climb on top of her. "Is that what you want me to do to you, hmm? Fuck you into another galaxy?"

She bites her lower lip and nods. I grind against her, and she lets out a breathless laugh. "Please."

"You're so polite tonight."

"You want me to be less polite? Stand up." I climb off her quickly. "Strip naked." I shed every piece of clothing as she licks her lips. "Good boy."

Releasing a breathy laugh, I await further instruction. Her eyes scan my body. The feeling of her gaze imprints on my skin.

"Stroke yourself."

"Seriously?" I chuckle as my hand has a mind of its own and wanders toward my dick.

"You heard me." She smirks, dipping a hand between her legs, and I groan as I fist my cock. Once I'm achingly hard, she says, "Now it's your turn to be less polite."

Releasing the grip on myself, I glide my hands up her legs. "Spread those perfect legs and take my dick like a *good girl*, would you?" She arches her back, presenting me with her perfect tits, and angles her pussy toward my hungry cock.

"Wow, Mr. Anderson. You've been learning a lot from all those books, huh?"

"Maybe I should fuck your sassy mouth instead." Stepping forward, I swipe between her, and a beautiful moan falls out of her mouth. "Hold on, I have to get a condom."

I step back, and her legs fly around me, heels digging into my ass as she holds me against her. "I'm on the pill."

"What?" I say, making sure I understand where she's going with this.

"I'm on the pill. I want you inside of me," she says quietly. "I don't want anything between us."

Without a moment of hesitation, I glide my tip to her entrance and thrust inside. I grip her hips, and she moans as I fulfill my promise to fuck her into another galaxy. It doesn't take long until the feeling of her bare pussy has me close to the edge. I force myself to maintain my composure, allowing her to ride out her orgasm before me. "You gonna come on my cock today, baby?"

"Yes," she moans, and I dip my fingers down between us, rubbing her clit. Beautiful sounds escape her lips as the orgasm rips through her body, and I finally allow myself to finish. A lazy smile spreads across her face as I hold myself above her. "I love you, Honey Bee."

I chuckle and stare down at this beautiful creature who has become the entire reason for my existence. "I love you too, Sunflower."

54
SOPHIA

Two Months Later

I shift against the hard wooden seat, swallowing nails as I clutch Elijah's hand for dear life. His fingers must be turning blue, but he hasn't complained yet as he talks quietly with my dad on the other side of me.

In the front of the courtroom, my eyes snag on the back of Seth's blonde head. He's dressed in a suit and seems way too put together for someone who's about to go to prison for a long time. *Hopefully.* In a few minutes, the judge will return, giving the verdict for his case.

Charlie and I both testified last week and thanks to the video, there wasn't much of a defense. Seth pleaded guilty, and his lawyer has only been negotiating regarding his sentence. His family is filthy rich, but I pray to whoever's listening this isn't a case where they use money to make the problem go away. Seth's mom won't stop glaring at me, and the fire in her eyes tells me they'll probably do whatever it takes to save him from this.

"How could you do this to my Seth?" she asked me in the

hallway last week, and it took all my strength to ignore her and walk away.

If only she knew what a piece of shit her precious Seth really is.

She should be happy we didn't add attempted murder, aggravated assault, and sexual assault to his list of charges.

Elijah leans down to my ear. "You okay, darlin'?"

"Mm-hmm," I hum, squeezing his hand tighter.

"You sure?" he asks, glancing at our joined hands, and I loosen my grip.

"Sorry."

"Don't apologize," Elijah says, lifting my hand and placing a soft kiss on my knuckles. "I'm right here."

I lean my head against his shoulder, releasing a heavy sigh. He's been by my side through all of this—preparation with the lawyers, the days of trials, and the late-night freak-outs. He's not just my rock, he's my goddamn mountain, and I'm so overwhelmingly thankful for him.

Janine was right. Telling Elijah the truth about everything really helped my healing process. I'm still not entirely past what happened, but I'm slowly moving forward, and a lot of that is thanks to Elijah's patience and support—letting me set the pace with things both physically and emotionally.

He leans down, kissing me softly on the lips, and I allow myself to forget the rest of the room. One selfish moment to pretend it's just us. I immediately feel calmer, lips curling upwards as I pull away, resting my head back on his shoulder. I'm so ready for this to be our normal again. Stolen kisses and sweet words between the two of us without all the chaos and darkness.

"All rise. This court is now in session," the clerk bellows, and we follow his orders. I glance at the back row toward Charlie, Noah, Sage, and Julian, who are sitting together near the door. Charlie almost didn't come, but it looks like she wanted to see Seth get what he deserves as much as I did. She gives me a weak smile, and I turn back around.

The door near the front opens, and Judge Hammond comes out and takes her place at the front. "You may be seated," she says to the courtroom, and we sit while Seth and his defense team, along with the prosecuting lawyer, remain standing. Seth shifts on his heels as I clutch both Dad's and Elijah's hands. Theo squeezes my shoulder from his spot behind me. I won't be able to inhale another ounce of oxygen until he's sentenced.

"Seth Miller, you have been found guilty of vehicular manslaughter in the second degree." Although I shouldn't feel guilty, a small part of me does. I know what happened was an accident, but it was the absolute turmoil following that led us to this moment. "I sentence you to ten years in Cross City Correctional facility with the possibility of early parole." I straighten my shoulders and flick my gaze to Seth, who hangs his head as he grips the back of the chair in front of him.

They take Seth out of the room in what feels like slow motion. I struggle to remove my eyes from him, and he turns his head, gaze connecting with mine. Anger rolls off him in waves, feeding the lion of my nightmares.

I swallow hard, trying to collect myself as the court adjourns, and we leave the courthouse. The sunshine warms my skin as Elijah's arm hangs loosely over my shoulders.

I let out a heavy sigh of relief. "It's over."

"Yeah." He nods. "It's over. You're safe now."

"I'm safe now," I repeat.

Dad places his hand gently on my shoulder, tugging me away from Elijah and into his arms. I hold on to him tightly. "I'm so proud of you, Bear. That took courage," he tells me, pulling away.

"Thanks, Dad," I grumble, ready to just move forward from all of this.

"You gonna be okay?"

"Yes, Dad," I assure him. "I'm fine."

"Good." He smiles sadly. "Call me anytime, okay?"

"Okay." I hug him again before he leaves to go home. "You want a ride back to campus?" I ask Charlie since she doesn't have a car anymore and rode here with us.

"No, thanks." She smiles tenderly. "I'm gonna ride with everyone else."

Elijah follows me to the passenger side and opens the door, helping me inside. I smirk at him as he hauls himself onto the foot bar and buckles the seat belt for me.

"How many times do I have to tell you I can do this myself?" I say to him.

"And how many times do I have to tell my girl I'm gonna take care of her before she gets the memo?"

"Elijah, it's not your job to take care of me."

"You're right... It's my purpose." He cups the back of my neck and pulls me in for a deep, tongueless kiss.

"What's that for?" I mumble against his lips.

"Just because I love you."

"Thank you for being there for me today... And through everything."

He tilts his head, staring at me with his beautiful arctic eyes. "Of course, baby. Where the hell else would I be?"

"I don't know. I guess there's still some small part of me worried you'll think this is all too much. That *I'm* too much."

"Sophia." He shakes his head with a breathtaking smile. "What did I tell you about my return policy?"

"No returns."

"And no refunds, Sunflower."

EPILOGUE
ELIJAH

Six Months Later

The technicolor lights in the casino shine against Sophia's face as she sips her martini. Everyone else has split to do their own thing for the night, and I've been savoring the time alone with her. It's true what everyone says: Vegas is Disney World for adults.

"Do you wanna go to bed or play a little longer?" she asks me.

My gaze turns back to the slot machine. Twenty-three dollars is left from the fifty I put in. "I guess I'll do a few more spins, and then we can get out of here?"

She places her hand on my leg, giving me her most seductive grin. "Yes. Please."

Leaning in, I kiss her softly and press the button for my next spin. We watch for a few minutes as the amount dwindles. After I press the button again, the icons spin and one by one, diamonds line up next to each other.

"Holy shit," Sophia whispers. The machine blares, and my eyes bounce all over the screen as I try to figure out what in the living hell is going on.

Winner: $8,932

"Holy shit!" We jump up, and I pull her to my side. "Looks like that unlimited amount of luck still hasn't left me."

She looks up at me. "Guess not."

Sophia and I walk down the Vegas strip on the way back to our hotel. "So how are you going to spend your winnings, Mr. Anderson?" she asks, my arm loosely over her shoulders.

"Hmm…" I smile down at the best part of my life. "How about on making you Mrs. Anderson?"

A high-pitched laugh escapes her, and she slaps my chest. "Oh, come on, be serious. You're a big winner!"

"The only way I'll win tonight is if I get to call you my wife before we go to sleep." I stop on the sidewalk, pulling her over to the side.

"Don't you think it'd be a little rude to get married on someone else's wedding trip?"

"This is just between you and me."

"Elijah."

"Sophia." I drop to my knee.

"Elijah!" She throws a hand over her mouth and tugs on my hand, but I remain in place. "What are you doing?"

"I have been in love with you since the first time you brought me to my knees in Crystal Coffee."

"We've only been dating a year," Sophia whispers.

"And I'll love you for a hundred more, Sunflower."

"Elijah…"

"You are the absolute love of my fucking life. I literally wouldn't be the person I am without you by my side. You were a lighthouse when I was adrift, calling me back to shore. I promise to continue cherishing you and protecting you for the rest of our lives. You're it for me, and baby... I hope I'm it for you too. So please make me the luckiest son of a bitch alive and be my wife? And not just on a stupid fake ID." My heart pounds against my chest as I struggle to find the right words. "I want *our* last name across your back at every game. I want your stupid little koalas cock blocking us on the bed. I wanna make love to you every time the rain pours, reminding me of the day you finally became mine." Tears stream down her face, and I blink back my own tears. "Please marry me, Sunflower?"

"Tonight?" she asks timidly as her hand shakes in mine.

"Yes."

"In Vegas?"

I huff out a laugh. "Yes." My knee is sore from digging into the sidewalk, but I simply don't give a shit.

"My dad's gonna kill you for not asking him first."

"Sophia... Of course I asked him."

"What?" She balks. "When?"

"Over the summer. I told him things tend to fly out of my mouth around you, and I just wanted to make sure I had his blessing before I inevitably asked you to marry me." I smile, remembering the conversation. *It was the second time I thought he was gonna kill me with a shotgun... but so worth it.*

"Oh..." Sophia says, her smile widening. "And what did he say?"

"That you'd be the luckiest woman alive to marry me."

She throws her head back, laughing, and hits my shoulder. "That's true..."

"He also said as long as you're happy... he's happy. Baby..." I release a shaky breath, squeezing her hand lightly. "You gotta answer me cause I'm freaking out here."

Her expression softens. "I'll absolutely marry you."

My lips part open. "Really?"

"Yes."

"Seriously?"

"Yes!"

Tears well in my eyes as I jump off the ground, scooping her into my arms. "She said yes!"

"If you would've told me a year ago my wedding would be officiated by an Elvis impersonator, I'd say you were smoking something," Sophia says as her hand rests on my bicep while I lie in the leather chair.

"If you would've told me I'd marry the girl who told me I don't know how to use my hands, I would've said damn, I showed her."

She laughs, and I wince as the needle pricks my skin again. "You okay there, Honey Bee?"

"I'm fine." I glance up at her pretty face to distract myself from the needle adding a sunflower behind the buck antlers on my chest. It's intricate and beautiful, just like my wife. "Is this sore?" I ask, brushing Sophia's hair to the side to see the small honey bee that was just tattooed behind her ear.

"It's okay… this one hurts more." She scrunches her nose, bringing up her hand, and I smile wide looking at the tiny *E* etched onto her ring finger. "Are we crazy for this?"

"Not at all…" I brush the pad of my thumb against her cheek. "You're my wife now. You deserve a permanent place on my skin. And after the wedding hoopla dies down and we tell everyone, I'm putting a real ring on your pretty finger."

"I'm perfectly fine with the tattooed ring," Sophia says, biting back a smile as she rubs circles on my bare shoulder. "And what happens in Vegas…"

"Is definitely not staying in Vegas, Mrs. Anderson."

Also by Hailey Dickert

Merry Mischief List is the second installment in Hailey Dickert's Crystal Bay University Series. While the main characters in this story are initially introduced in the first novel, *Return Policy*, *Merry Mischief List* can be read as a standalone.

Sometimes it pays to be naughty...

This cheerleader's been dreaming of a white Christmas—but thanks to wild weather and grounded planes, I'm stuck doing my holiday to-do list (of the sugar and spice variety) without a snowflake in sight.

After an airport run-in with my team's football coach, there's hope I may not have to do it alone. Coach Buzzkill, aka James Porter, definitely needs a break from his routine, and my little scavenger hunt could do the trick—if he'll let it.

But his boundaries have me worried I won't check off the naughtier items... until his best friend shows up, ready to join the merry mischief.

Santa baby.

The Sister Between Us

Dickert's debut novel that started it all.

This second-chance sports romance tells the story of Jake and Leah.

One night is all it takes to change everything.

Leah

He was my best friend's brother. My neighbor. The one person I was never supposed to fall for, until lines got blurred—stolen kisses and lies told to the people we loved most.

Jake

When the secrets we'd been keeping came out, broken hearts weren't the only casualties. Though I've spent years chasing my dreams of being a professional soccer player, I've never forgotten the one who got away.

A chance encounter brings me back face to face with the only person I've ever loved.

Can we repair what's been broken?

Has time healed the scars that run deeper than the surface?

Will the sister between us bring us back together or push us apart yet again?

Acknowledgments

The amount of people to thank only seems to grow as my writing journey continues.

As always, I'd first like to thank my husband for supporting our family and allowing me to chase my dreams. I love you exponentially and quite literally couldn't do this without your encouragement.

Thank you to my parents for proving exactly how much hard work and dedication can pay off. I'm so proud of you both.

Thank you to Alli Morgan, who's my number one girl during this process. When you and I work together... magic. I love you and your beautiful mind. (Also, thank you to Mike for letting me steal her on the daily.)

Thank you to my beta readers, who have assisted in improving this novel to the very version you have in your hands today. Without you, this book simply would not be the same. Thank you Alex B., Anna A., Ashleigh D., Brittany S., Carolyn H., Chiara W., Diane G., Emma S., Grace E., Gracie S., Heather H., Julia L., Katie W., Kasandra T., Melissa P., Alexis C., Aadya D., Rachel L., Rhianne B., Tayler M., Katie F., Bronach M., Emily N., Emily P., and Amanda W.

Thank you to my final betas and bookish friends. Because of you all, I have the motivation to keep going every day: Chiara, Dany, Addey, Jenn, Mel, Kas, Lexi, Rhianne, Em, Katie, Anna, Mikaela, Danyelle, Maeve, Mads, Rhi, Lucile, and Gracie. I'm so grateful for our friendships.

Thank you to my incredible editor.

Thank you to Sandra, from Maldo Designs, for the incredible non-discreet cover and tattoo work.

Thank you to Meg Jones, author of *Invisible String*, for the brilliant idea of the 'Dick-tionary'.

Lastly, I would like to thank you, the reader, for taking a chance and reading Sophia and Elijah's story. I hope you enjoyed it!

Dicktionary

For those of you who'd like to find (or avoid) the smut quickly, it can be found in the following chapters:

- Nineteen
- Twenty
- Twenty-Three
- Twenty-Five
- Thirty-Six
- Thirty-Eight
- Forty-Two
- Forty-Seven
- Fifty-Three

Spread those pages.

Content Warnings

Please be aware, ***Return Policy*** contains topics that could be difficult for some readers. These include but are not limited to drug addiction, underage alcohol consumption, vulgar language, death of a sibling, death of a parent, grief, depression, consensual sexually explicit content, physical violence, graphic depictions of death, vehicular manslaughter, mention of cancer, sexual assault, and domestic violence from an ex-partner.

Should you be having a mental health crisis, please reach out to 9-8-8, The National Suicide and Crisis Lifeline. Your mental health is important. Your life is important.

Should you need to speak to someone regarding sexual assault, please reach out to 800-656-HOPE (4673), The National Sexual Assault Hotline. Your voice matters.

About the Author

Hailey (Bruhn) Dickert is a contemporary romance author born in a small coastal Florida town who grew up writing songs in her bedroom. She previously maintained a personal blog documenting her journey of moving abroad to her adopted hometown in Germany.

Dickert's debut novel, *The Sister Between Us*, was released April 2023, immediately hitting the Amazon Top 100. *Return Policy*, her second novel, release June 23, 2023, also immediately hitting the Amazon Top 100.

When she's not writing at her kitchen table or in her favorite local brewery, Sailfish Brewing Company, Dickert spends most of her time reading, making memories with her husband and young son, and traveling. An admitted sports fanatic, she feeds her addiction to football by watching the Miami Dolphins and Minnesota Vikings games on Sunday afternoons.

Keep in touch with Hailey Dickert via the web:

Website: haileydickert.com

Facebook: https://www.facebook.com/haileydickert/

Instagram: https://www.instagram.com/haileydickertauthor/

TikTok: https://tiktok.com/@haileydickertauthor/